DIAMOND DUO

Texas Fortunes

Book No. 1

DIAMOND DUO

Marcia Gruver

BARBOUR
PUBLISHING

Cover Design: The DesignWorks Group, Inc.

Published by Barbour Publishing, Inc., P.O. Box 719, Uhrichsville, OH 44683, www.barbourbooks.com

Our mission is to publish and distribute inspirational products offering exceptional value and biblical encouragement to the masses.

 Member of the
Evangelical Christian
Publishers Association

Printed in the United States of America.

DEDICATION

To Lee, my gift from God.
You taught me the impossible is "no step for a stepper."

To Diana Dinky-Do, my mother and biggest fan.

To my children, grandchildren, and Rae Rea.
See, you really can do all things through Christ.

ACKNOWLEDGMENTS

My thanks to Janice Thompson—without you there'd be no book. To ACFW Crit3—you're brilliant. You make me look good. To Seared Hearts—my beloved cheering section. To Fred McKenzie, historian and owner of Bayou Books in Jefferson, Texas, for your tireless love of anything Jefferson. To Karl Frederickson, manager of Excelsior House Hotel, for going out of your way to help. And to Era E. Johnson of the Marion Central Appraisal District in Jefferson, Texas, for your kind assistance.

CHAPTER 1

Jefferson, Texas
Friday, January 19, 1877

With the tip of a satin shoe, the graceful turn of an ankle, the woman poured herself like cream from the northbound train out of Marshall and let the tomcats lap her up. In the beginning, an upraised parasol blocked her visage, but no lingering look at her features could erase the impression already established by her pleasing carriage, lavish blue gown, and slender fingers covered in diamonds.

Bertha Biddie waited with stilted breath for the moment when the umbrella might tip and give up its secret. All about her, most of Jefferson had come to a halt, as if the whole town waited with her.

Without warning, the woman lowered and closed the sunshade.

Enchanted, Bertha followed the graceful lines of her form to her striking and memorable face. At first sight of her, Bertha thought she was the devil's daughter. She bore no obvious mark of evil. Just smoldering eyes and a knowing glance that said life held mysteries young Bertha had yet to glimpse.

Her hair sparkled like sun rays dancing on Big Cypress Creek. Her lashes were as black as the bottom of a hole, and her lids seemed smudged with coal. Delicate features perched below a dark halo of hair, and a pink flush lit her fair cheeks. Her expression teemed with mischief, and her full ruby lips curled up at the corners as if recalling a bawdy yarn. She turned slightly, evidently aware of the gathering horde for the first time. With a tilt of her chin and barely perceptible sway, she cast a wide net over the men in the crowd and dragged them to shore.

Bertha watched them respond to her and realized Mama had been less than forthcoming about the real and true nature of things. Forgetting themselves and the women at their sides, they gaped with open mouths, some in spite of jealous claws that gripped their arms. Even the ladies stared, the looks on their faces ranging from admiration to envy.

The reaction of the men only slightly altered when the lady's escort stepped out of the Texas & Pacific passenger car behind her. Though his clothes were just as spiffy and he carried himself well, the man who accompanied that gilded bird lacked her allure, bore none of her charm. Yet despite her confident display of tail feathers, the bluebird at his side clearly deferred to him as though he'd found a way to clip her wings.

With great care, the porter handed down the couple's baggage, the matched set a rare sight in those parts, then held out his hand. Her companion tipped the man, gathered the bags, and walked away from the platform without offering a single word in the bluebird's direction. She cast a quick glance after him but stood her ground, her demeanor unruffled in the face of his rebuke.

As was the custom, the Commercial Hotel, Haywood House, and Brooks House, three reputable hotels in town, each had transport standing by to haul incoming passengers from the station. Dr. J. H. Turner, landlord of Brooks House, waited on hand in the conveyance he called an omnibus.

The woman's friend secured passage with Dr. Turner and helped him load their belongings and then turned and crooked a finger in her direction. She pretended not to notice.

"Bessie!" he barked. "For pity's sake."

She lifted her head, reopened the parasol, and strolled his way without saying a word—giving in but taking all the time she pleased to do so. He handed her up into the carriage, climbed in beside her, and settled back to rest a possessive arm around her shoulders.

Dr. Turner eased onto Alley Street and trundled away from the station, breaking the spell cast over the denizens of Jefferson. In slow motion they awoke from their stupor and returned to their lives.

Bertha released the breath she'd held and gripped her best friend's arm. "What was she, Magda? I've never seen anything like her."

When Magda shook her head, her curls danced the fandango. "Me neither. And we never will again. Not around here, anyway."

Bertha leaned past Magda trying to catch another glimpse. "She's no earthbound creature, that's for sure. But devil or angel? I couldn't tell."

Magda laughed. "She's human, all right, just not ordinary folk." She pressed her finger to her lips. "Could be one of those actresses from a New York burletta."

Bertha gasped. "From the Broadway stage? You really think so?"

"She's certainly stylish enough."

Bertha squinted down Alley Street at the back of the tall carriage. "That man called her Bessie. She doesn't look like a Bessie to me."

"Further proof that beneath all her fluff, she's a vessel of clay like the rest of us."

"How so?"

"Who ever heard of an angel named Bessie?"

Grinning, Bertha leaned and tweaked Magda's nose. "Oh, go on with you."

Of all the souls wandering the earth—in Jefferson, Texas, at least—Bertha Maye Biddie's heart had knit with Magdalena Hayes's from the start. They were a year apart, Magda being the older, but age wasn't the only difference between them. Magda easily reached the top shelves in the kitchen, where Bertha required a stool. And while big-boned Magda took up one and a half spaces on a church pew, Bertha barely filled the remaining half. Magda's russet mop coiled as tightly as tumbleweed. Bertha's black hair fell to her waist in silken waves and gave her fits trying to keep it pinned up. Nothing fazed self-possessed Magda. Bertha greeted life with her heart.

Magda nudged Bertha with her elbow. "Earthbound or not, I can tell you one thing about her. . . ."

"What's that?"

The look in Magda's big brown eyes said whatever the one thing was, it was bound to be naughty. She leaned in to whisper. "She knows a thing or two about the fellas."

Bertha raised her brows. "You can tell that just by looking at her, can you?"

"Not looking at her, smart britches. I can tell by the way she looks at them." She fussed with her curls, her eyes pious slants. "No decent woman goes eye to eye with strange men in the street, and you know it."

"I guess some decent woman told you that?"

"Bertha Maye Biddie! Don't get fresh with me."

Bertha tucked in her chin and busied herself straightening her gloves. "Maybe she's fed up with their scandalous fawning. Ever think of that?"

"Any hound will track his supper."

The words made Bertha mad enough to spit, but she didn't know why. "A pie set out on a windowsill may be a fine display of good cooking, but not necessarily an invitation."

Magda narrowed her eyes. "What on earth are you talking about?" Before Bertha could answer, she stiffened and settled back for a pout. "Why are you siding up with that woman anyway? You don't even know her."

The truth was, Bertha's head still reeled from the first sight of Bessie. The way men reacted to her flooded Bertha's young heart with hope and provided an opportunity, if the beautiful stranger would cooperate, to fix a private matter that sorely needed fixing.

Bertha knew a few things by instinct, like how to toss her long hair or tilt her chin just so. Enough to mop the grin off Thaddeus Bloom's handsome face and light a fire in those dark eyes. But she was done with turning to mush in his presence and watching him revel in it. If Bertha could learn a few of the bluebird's tricks, she'd have that rascal wagging his tail. Then the shoe would be laced to the proper foot, and Thad could wear it up her front stoop when he came to ask for her hand.

One thing was certain. Whatever Bessie knew, Bertha needed to know it.

She tugged on Magda's arm. "Come on."

"Come on where?"

Already a wagon-length ahead, Bertha called back over her shoulder. "To the hotel. We're going to find her."

"What? Why?"

"Save your questions for later. Now hurry!"

Bertha dashed to the steps at the end of the boardwalk and scurried into the lane.

"You planning to run clear to Vale Street?" Magda huffed, rushing to catch up. "Slow down. It ain't ladylike."

"Oh, pooh. Neither am I. Look, there's Mose. He'll take us."

Just ahead, Moses Pharr's rig, piled high with knobby cypress, turned onto Alley Street headed the opposite way. The rickety wagon, pulled by one broken-down horse, bore such a burden of wood it looked set to pop like a bloated tick. When Bertha whistled, the boy's drowsy head jerked up. He turned around and saw her, and a grin lit his freckled face.

"Bertha!" Magda hustled up beside her. "If your pa gets word of you whistling in town, he'll take a strap to your legs."

"Papa doesn't own a strap. Come on, Mose is waiting."

She ran up even with the wagon and saw that the mountain of wood had blocked her view of Mose's sister sitting beside him on the seat. They both grinned down at her, Rhodie's long red hair the only visible difference between the two.

"Hey, Rhodie."

"Hey, Bert. Where you going?"

"To Brooks House. I was hoping to hitch a ride."

Mose leaned over, still grinning. "We always got room for you, Bertha. Hop on."

Magda closed the distance between them and came to stand beside Bertha, breathing hard. When Bertha pulled herself onto the seat beside Rhodie, Magda started to follow. Mose raised his hand to stop her.

"Hold up there." He looked over at Bertha. "Her, too?"

Bertha nodded.

Mose cut his eyes back at the wood and then shrugged. "Guess one more can't hurt. But she'll have to sit atop that stump. Ain't no more room on the seat."

Magda adjusted her shawl around her shoulders and sniffed. "I refuse to straddle a cypress stump all the way to Vale."

"Suit yourself," Bertha said. "But it's a long walk. Let's go, Mose."

Mose lifted the reins and clucked at the horse. Magda grabbed the wooden handgrip and pulled herself onto the wagon just as it started to move. Arranging her skirts about her, she perched on the tall stump like Miss Muffet. "Well, what are you waiting for?" she asked. "Let's go."

Laughing, they rolled through Jefferson listing and creaking, ignoring the stares and whispers. When the rig pulled up across from Brooks House, even the spectacle they made couldn't compete with Bessie and her traveling companion.

The couple stood on the street beside their luggage, the carriage nowhere in sight. They seemed at the end of a heated discussion, given his mottled face and her missing smile.

When Bertha noticed the same sick-cow expression on the faces of the gathered men and the same threatened look on the women's, she became more determined than ever to learn Bessie's secret.

The man with Bessie growled one more angry word then hefted their bags and set off up the path. Not until Bessie followed him and disappeared through the shadowy door did the town resume its pace.

Mose gulped and found his voice. "She looked as soft as a goose-hair pillow. Who is she?"

Bertha scooted to the edge of her seat and climbed down. She dusted her hands and smoothed her skirt. "I don't know, but I intend to find out."

"Roll up your tongue, Moses Pharr," Magda said from the back, "and get me off this stump."

Mose hopped to the ground and hurried around to help Magda.

Rhodie, twirling her copper braid, grinned down at Bertha. "What are you going to do, Bert?"

Magda answered for her. "She's going to get us into trouble, that's what."

Bertha took her by the hand. "Stop flapping your jaws and come on."

They waved good-bye to Mose and Rhodie then hurried across the street, dodging horses, wagons, and men—though their town wasn't nearly as crowded as it had once been.

Jefferson, Queen City of the Cypress, lost its former glory in 1873, when the United States Corps of Engineers blew the natural dam to kingdom come, rerouting the water from Big Cypress Bayou down the Red River to Shreveport. Once a thriving port alive with steamboat traffic, when the water level fell, activity in Jefferson dwindled. To that very day, in fits of Irish temper, Bertha's papa cursed the politicians who were responsible.

But through it all, Jefferson had lost none of its charm. Brooks House was a prime example of the best the town had to offer, so it seemed only right that someone like Bessie might wind up staying there.

Bertha and Magda positioned themselves outside the hotel and hunkered down to wait—the former on a mission, the latter under duress. It didn't take long for the girls to learn a good bit about the captivating woman and her cohort. Talk swirled out the door of the hotel soon after the couple sashayed to the front desk to register under the name of A. Monroe and wife, out of Cincinnati, Ohio.

The gentleman, if he could be counted as such, addressed the woman as Annie or Bessie, when he didn't call her something worse. The two quarreled openly, scratching and spitting like cats, and didn't care who might be listening. By the time the story drifted outside, the locals had dubbed her Diamond Bessie due to her jewel-encrusted hands, and it seemed the name would stick.

Bertha shaded her eyes with her hands and pressed her face close to the window. "I don't see her anymore, Magda. I guess they took a room."

"Of course they took a room. Why else would they come to a hotel?"

Bertha ignored her sarcasm and continued to search the lobby for Bessie. Still catching no sight of her, she turned around. "Isn't she the most glorious thing? And even prettier close up."

"That she is."

"Did you see the way men look at her? I never saw that many roosters on the prowl at one time."

"And all for squat," Magda said. "That chicken's been plucked. The little banty she strutted into town with has already staked a claim." She grinned. "He wasn't all that hard on the eyes himself."

Bertha frowned. "That strutting peacock? Besides his flashy clothes, she was the only thing special about him. Don't see how he managed to snare a woman like that. He must be rich."

Magda arched one tapered brow. "Did you see the rings on her fingers?"

"I reckon so. I'm not blind."

Magda stretched her back and heaved a sigh. "I guess that's it, then. Let's go."

Bertha grabbed her arm. "Wait. Where are you going?"

"Home. This show's over. They've settled upstairs by now."

Lacing her fingers under her chin, Bertha planted herself in Magda's path. "Won't you wait with me just a mite longer?"

"She's not coming out here, Bertha. Besides, you've seen enough for today."

"I don't want to see her. I need to talk to her."

Magda drew herself back and stared. "Are you teched? We can't just walk up and talk to someone like her. Why would she fool with the likes of us?"

"I don't know. I'll think of a way. I've got to." She bit her bottom lip—three words too late.

Looking wary now, Magda crossed her arms. "Got to? Why?"

"Just do." Bertha met her look head-on. She wouldn't be bullied out of it. Not even by Magda.

Resting chubby fists on rounded hips, Magda sized her up. "All right, what does this have to do with Thad?"

No one knew her like Magda. Still, the chance she might stumble onto Bertha's motives was as likely as hatching a three-headed guinea hen. Struggling to hold her jaw off the ground, she lifted one shoulder. "Who said it did?"

Magda had the gall to laugh. "Because, dearie"—she leaned to tap Bertha's forehead—"everything inside there lately has something to do with Thad."

"Humph! Think what you like. I am going to talk to her."

Magda glared. "Go ahead, then. I can see there's no changing your mind. But I don't fancy being humiliated by another of your rattlebrained schemes, thank you."

Bertha caught hold of her skirt. "Don't you dare go. I can't do this on my own."

"Let go of me. I said I'm going home."

"Please, Magdalena! I need you."

Magda pulled her skirt free and took another backward step. "No, ma'am. You just count me out this time."

She turned to go, and Bertha lunged, catching her in front of the hotel door. They grappled, tugging sleeves and pulling hair, both red-faced and close to tears. Just when Bertha got set to squeal like a pestered pig, from what seemed only a handbreadth away, a woman cleared her throat. Bertha froze, hands still locked in Magda's hair, and turned to find the bluebird beaming from the threshold—though *canary* seemed more fitting now that she'd traded her blue frock for a pale yellow dress.

"What fun!" Bessie cried, clasping her hands. "I feared this town might be as dull as dirt, but it seems I was mistaken."

CHAPTER 2

There wasn't much Thaddeus Bloom liked better than fishing, and he looked for any excuse to wet a hook. An uncommon passion for the sport took young Thad at an early age and plagued him till now. It started when he was barely old enough to sink a line in the muddy waters of Baton Rouge, and he'd trolled the lakes and bayous ever since. So it was no surprise that shortly after Papa moved the family to Jefferson, Thad discovered Big Cypress Bayou.

He decided early on that a man could solve most of the world's problems while dangling a cork from a cane pole. As it happened, he came to be standing at bayou's edge while in search of just such a remedy and a rest for his troubled soul.

As if life weren't burdened with complication and abundant challenge for a man his age, Thad found his forward motion of late impeded by a most fetching obstacle—in the person of Bertha Maye Biddie. In the whole of his nineteen years, he'd never beheld so lovely a girl. Many a young lady seemed determined to tempt him from his goals, but no matter how much they swished and swayed or how fast they batted their eyes, Thad remained focused. Now one comely Irish elf had turned his head with just the tilt of her dainty chin.

It would be a stretch to call Thad's college plans his dream.

As long as he could remember, his papa had spoken of places like Harvard, Boston College, and Yale in reverent tones. From the moment Papa heard they opened Texas Agricultural and Mechanical College in Brazos County, his ambition became obsession, and Thad's fate was sealed. Oblivious to the fact that it was his younger son, Cy, who loved the books, Papa worked tirelessly, saving toward the day when Thad would leave for the military college, vowing to let nothing stand in his way.

Nothing had until Bertha Biddie sashayed onto the scene, so small she could sit on the edge of a rug and her feet would still dangle, with dimples so deep he could swim in them and a smile so bright she didn't need candles. With every move, she had wriggled deeper into Thad's head and etched out a spot in his heart.

But he couldn't drag a bride along to military school, and he wouldn't ask a girl like Bertha to wait. Besides, he knew her father would never agree to such a lengthy engagement. Consequently, Thad's need to lose himself in fishing had increased tenfold of late.

He heard a splash and turned to look. Water rings played out in wide bands from the base of a big bald cypress. He searched the area just shy of the bank for clues. Too big for a bass. Probably not a gator. Could be a paddlefish, and if so, he wasn't interested. From the sound of the splash, it was a big one. Folks had reported seeing paddlefish as long as a man, weighing close to seventy pounds. Thad didn't much care for spear fishing and wasn't carrying a hook big enough to snag him.

The ripples stilled and with it Thad's interest. He shifted his attention to the gentle lapping of water against the tree. Submerged cypress trunks always reminded him of an overgrown foot, not unlike a giant elephant's or dinosaur's. He almost expected to follow the trunk up and find a brontosaurus lurking above. It wouldn't surprise him one whit to find such a curiosity in these waters. More than once he'd hooked and pulled to shore things he'd never laid eyes on before. Not just fish. There were creatures in those murky depths that had no name and defied description.

Thad picked up the bucket of worms, hoisted the rest of the

gear to his shoulder, and edged along the grassy bank, pushing aside streams of Spanish moss and a potbellied spider on a dew-beaded web. He lined up even with a dilapidated boat shack, just down shore from where he'd spotted the water rings. He leaned his cane pole against a tree then propped the net and his daddy's pole, which he'd taken without permission, against the side of the old building and sat down to wait.

The crunch of a broken twig behind him gave Thad a start, more so than it would have if his mind weren't crawling with monsters and bugaboos. He turned and gave a low whistle as he watched Charles Gouldy step into the clearing with a fishing pole in his hand. Charles picked his way over the ruts and cypress knees and joined Thad on the bank.

"Hey, Charlie. You came."

"Said I would."

"That don't always hold salt."

Charles sidled up beside him and baited his hook. Thad set to work threading a worm on his, hurrying despite himself. For some reason, they had an unspoken challenge to see who would be first to get a line in the water. Charlie bested him this time and started to whistle as soon as his cork settled onto the muddy surface. In no time his whistling became a quiet song.

" 'Had a fine reputation until he sold it. Liked corn liquor, but he couldn't hold it.' "

Thad laughed, his eyes still trained on his cork. "What's that you're singing?"

" 'Old Dan Tucker.' Don't tell me you never heard it?"

Thad looked at him. "Those ain't the words to 'Old Dan Tucker.' "

"Are, too."

"I'm telling you they ain't."

Charlie glanced up. "My papaw sings it thata way."

"He made it up, then."

Charlie shrugged and nodded. "Probably did."

"Well, try not to sing anymore, how 'bout it. You're here to catch fish, not torture them. And I know I can do without it."

"You wouldn't know a good singer if he sat on you."

"I know I'd rather you sat on me than sing."

Charlie grinned and gave him a light shove.

A quick flash of movement across the water caught Thad's attention. He studied the tree-lined bank until he caught another glimpse between the cypress trunks, just enough to identify two windblown shocks of red hair. The Taylor boys, sitting tall in their old beat-up skiff, skimmed along effortlessly, pulled by the flow, using only the occasional furtive dip of a paddle to steer.

When the faded blue boat pulled past a clearing, Thad nudged Charlie. "Looky there."

"Where?"

"That dinghy slipping up on us."

Charlie tensed. "Who is it?"

"T-Bone Taylor and that rogue little brother of his."

Beau and T-Bone, each barely out of knee britches, lived upstream a short row from town. They were known around Jefferson as the biggest thieves this side of the Red River. T-Bone had been asked, and not so politely, to forgo any further notions of an education at Samuel Ward's Paradise Academy due to unruly and downright naughty behavior. Beau, two years his junior, seemed destined to follow in his brother's footsteps.

Charlie craned his neck to see better. "What're they up to this far downriver?"

"No good, I'd wager. Look how much pain they're taking to be quiet."

Charlie leaned forward, ready to shout, but Thad stayed him with a hand on his arm. "Wait, let's watch what they do."

Thad pulled his line to shore, and Charlie followed suit. They ducked for cover under a yaupon bush and spied between its branches. The Taylor boys skimmed past and pulled stealthily beneath the shack, Beau lifting one hand overhead to drag the skiff well under. Thad watched them scurry around in the boat, both scrawny bodies bent under the suspended floor.

"What them rascals doing?"

"Hush, Charlie! Wait and see."

Before long, a skinny, freckled arm appeared from under the pilings to where the net was propped. Grimy fingers lifted it and disappeared. The arm was soon followed by a hand reaching for the bait.

When a smaller, more freckled version snaked out to grab Papa's pole, Thad sprang to life. "Hey, hold up there! That's right, Beau Taylor, I'm talking to you. Don't think I don't see you two scoundrels."

Thad hurried to the shack and ducked to look under, just in time to see Beau lower his hand, Papa's cane pole and all, beneath the water. "Nice try, Beau. Pull up my daddy's fishing pole and place it where you found it." He moved closer, trying to look fierce. "T-Bone, that there's my net and bait. Put them back or suffer the consequences."

"Didn't see you there," T-Bone mumbled. "Just reckoned somebody left it."

"If they had, it wouldn't make it yours, now would it? Save your excuses. Ain't no right reason to do a wrong thing."

Beau raised his ill-gotten bounty from under the water and eased it back onto the bank. Reluctantly, his older brother followed suit, propping the net against the piling then tossing the bait on the bank.

Charlie stormed up behind Thad, puffed like an adder, and chimed in: "What's the matter? You boys ain't familiar with the eighth commandment?" He clenched his fists and took one more menacing step. "What are we waiting for, Thad? Let's drag 'em out and teach 'em 'thou shalt not steal.' "

Thad grabbed Charlie's arm. "Didn't you just hear what I said about doing a wrong thing? They put the stuff back. It's over now." He turned to the boys. "You two get on home. You keep looking for trouble, it's bound to find you."

The brothers danced past each other, holding on to keep from falling in the drink. They found their seats and paddles then backpedaled from under the shack. When they cleared it, they turned the nose of the boat in the same direction they'd been traveling and left without another word.

Charlie shot an arm in their direction. "You see that, Thad? You just wasted your breath. Those two ain't headed for home. Their minds are well set on some thieving raid." He rested his hands on his hips and shook his head. "We should've beat them and sent them running home to Mama. Now they'll get their hides filled with buckshot."

Thad watched the boys catch the current, maneuver around a curve, and disappear. "I hope not, Charlie." He sighed. "I truly hope not."

"Why? Lord knows them two deserve it."

Thad gave him a long look. "Now you're an authority on what the Lord knows?"

Charlie glared and then feigned an elaborate bow. "I beg your pardon, sir. I get ahead of myself sometimes." He flashed a devilish grin. "We all know Saint Thaddeus is the authority on God. Too bad the Sisters of Charity sold Saint Mary's to them Jew boys and let 'em turn it into a synagogue. You could've joined the convent." He pulled his shirt up and fashioned a makeshift habit then pranced in a pious circle. "Sister Thad. Has a nice ring to it, don't it?" He stopped pacing and fell to the ground, howling and slapping his knee. "*Lord knows* you'd make a fine nun."

Thad felt rage boil up inside. "I'll excuse your ignorance concerning the good brothers of Sinai Hebrew and chalk up your lack of decorum to the one who raised you."

The last comment lifted Charlie's hackles, as Thad expected it might.

Charlie pushed off the ground. "What do you mean by that, Bloom?"

"Come on, Charlie, you know your sister's morals are questionable at best and her profession the talk of the town."

Charlie balled his fist. "Take it back! Isabella don't do those things no more. Not since Mama died. And who are you to talk?

Some folks think skinning every sucker dumb enough to sit across a hand of poker from you ain't exactly the Lord's work."

Thad shrugged and slung the two poles over one shoulder, picked up the bucket of bait, and turned to go.

"Where are you going?"

"It's not a good day for fishing, after all. I've got too much on my mind to wrangle with all this besides."

Thad started up the incline, careful to dodge the jutting roots on his way to the top. He heard rustling behind him and then running, stumbling feet.

"I take back what I said about you and the rabbis," Charlie panted, falling into step behind him. "I didn't mean no harm."

Thad stopped and turned to face him. "I had no right to bring up your sister's past. It ain't no concern of mine. And you're right. My life ain't been perfect." He held out his hand. "Truce?"

Charlie grinned and clasped his outstretched palm. "Truce. And here. You left your net."

Thad put his hand on the net, but Charlie held it. "Can I ask you a question?"

"Shoot."

"Why *did* you quit playing cards just when you got so good at it?"

Thad thought a minute then decided to tell the truth. "You ever have a coonhound latch onto the back of your shirt and go to tugging?"

Charlie chuckled. "A time or two, I reckon."

He nodded. "That's how gambling started to feel. Figured I'd better quit before it brought me down." He grinned. "Besides that, Mama found out. Needless to say, she wasn't very happy about it."

On the water behind Charlie's head, the blue dinghy shot from behind a stand of trees with Beau and T-Bone leaning into their paddles. Loud laughter and excited chatter sounded up the hill to where Thad and Charlie stood. Charlie whirled and watched with Thad as the boys skimmed past. Twin streams of smoke trailed behind them from the rolled-up tobacco that dangled from each boy's mouth. A large, misshapen bundle rested between them in the bottom of the boat, covered in stolen hides.

"There they go," Thad said. "Looks like some poor fool lost his tobacco tin."

Charlie chuckled. "Lord knows what they have stashed beneath those pilfered skins."

"And therein lies their fate," muttered Thad, flashing Charlie a somber smile. "The Lord knows."

CHAPTER 3

Sarah dipped two dark fingers in the murky bayou and sighed. Cold. Like the wind that whipped the bare tops of the sweet gum trees on the far bank before it skipped across the water and found its way up her dress. One thing for sure, it was too miserable cold to kneel in the mud pounding the stink out of Henry's britches. But no matter. Hands be numb, bones be chilled, her man needed clean drawers, and she'd see he got them.

Not that he appreciated it any. She could freeze stock-still and he'd just shrug and hang his hat on her, bothered not a whit until suppertime. He'd moan then but wouldn't lift a finger to change it. Henry King would sit down and starve plumb to death while waiting for her to thaw. Sarah was of the opinion that her husband set far too much stock in his family name.

She held the heavy denim overalls up to the sun to inspect her progress. The grass stains were still there. She could beat until the stones in her hands wore smooth, but the dirt ground into those old britches was there to stay. She dare not scrub the worn-out legs for too long. Already the only thing standing between Henry's knees and the world were a few crisscrossed patches of white thread. And the world wasn't ready for Henry's knees.

She lifted the soggy mess of cloth, heavily weighted by water, into her pail with a grunt. She'd draw a bucket of water to pour over them and let them sit till later. A good soaking could do them no harm.

"Woman! Where you be?"

Sarah gritted her teeth, wondering when in life's unfolding she'd find herself in a place where men didn't holler and order her about. She turned, shading her eyes from the sun. A shadowy outline of Henry stood atop the grassy knoll above the creek, his hands on his hips. Even with irritation crowding her throat, she couldn't help but mark the fact that her man cut a fine figure in silhouette.

She stood up and assumed his same stance. "What you doing bellowing at me like that? You ain't my daddy. 'Sides that, you know where I am. I'm down here washing your drawers, just like I washed his."

"Well, leave all that. I need you to ride into town with me."

Sarah bent and hoisted the heavy pail onto her hip then took her time walking up the hill. "What you be needing from town? We hauled in staples and dry goods on Wednesday, and this ain't but Friday. We still got potatoes and onions in the larder, and I made plenty of soap."

She stopped in front of him and tilted her head to study his face. He shifted his eyes at first but then gave her a bug-eyed stare. "Why you got to understand everything? Maybe I'd like the pleasure of your company. That's all you need to know." He reached around to swat her hard on the behind and then took the pail, laughing and dodging when she tried to hit him back.

"Go on, now. Quit acting up. And no more questions. Jus' get yourself inside and dress for town." He flashed a toothy grin with his audacious white teeth. "And hurry up, you hear? Don't hole up in that house and leave me here till my hair turns gray."

"I need water poured over them raggedy britches, Henry King. Make sure you see to that." She continued up the rise, tossing the last word over her shoulder like a pinch of salt. At the top she paused and turned her head. Not enough to see his face, but she knew she had his attention. "And I'll be ready when I'm ready. You look for me then."

Deep laughter rumbled behind her, causing warmth to spread through her core. Even being the exasperating man that he was, her husband could stoke a fire in her heart with very little effort.

The natural slope to the creek leveled out to a wide expanse of tilled ground running from where she stood to the edge of the backyard. To her left at the end of a long furrow, Henry's plow sat right where he'd left it, the blade still burrowed deep in East Texas soil. Just ahead, a line of young hickory trees marked the boundary of their yard.

A big oak with knobby, exposed roots shaded the house against the summer heat and provided a fine napping spot for old Dickens, Henry's hound. On a warmer day she'd find the dog sprawled on the cool, hard-packed dirt beneath the tree, growling and twitching in his sleep. But on such a blustery morning, he was more likely in the barn curled up in a nest of hay.

As she neared the porch, the hens left their pecking and pranced away, squabbling and complaining among themselves. They were meant to be inside the weather-beaten old coop, but Henry had given up on keeping them in, so they wandered the grounds at will.

On the top step, Sarah paused and glanced at the corner yard, wrinkling her nose at the odor wafting from the pigsty behind the picket fence. She and Henry had argued about bringing hogs on the place. She never wanted the smelly beasts, though she had to admit the occasional rack of bacon alongside her buttermilk biscuits was a mighty tasty addition to breakfast.

Once inside, Sarah didn't take long to get ready. She washed off the stench of bayou mud in the basin of water atop the dressing table handed down by her mama. Then she lifted her blue gingham day dress from a hook on the wall and pulled it over her head. Back at the dressing table, she smoothed her black hair into a tight braid, grateful again that she'd inherited Papa's manageable curls instead of Mama's wiry cap.

Henry waited outside near the rig. He glanced up and then

turned away smiling when she stepped out the door, but not before Sarah saw him trying to hide his grin. She joined him without a word and let him help her onto the seat. Whistling all the while, he gave Dandy's harness one more check before climbing aboard the wagon.

No doubt under heaven, her man was up to something, but she couldn't imagine what it might be. There was no special significance about the nineteenth day of January. No birthday or anniversary. No particular reason to mark a Friday morning, because one day on a farm was like the next, except for the Sabbath.

She wouldn't ask and ruin his pleasure. Whatever frog had Henry hopping, she'd know it soon enough. Because sure as sure was, it would croak when they reached town.

❧

"So tell me, girls. . .is this a private game, or can anybody play?"

Bertha's surprise at Bessie's bawdy laughter rivaled the shock of finding her watching from the doorway of the Brooks House hotel. Breaking free from Magda, she whirled to face her. "Yes, ma'am. I mean, no, ma'am. I mean—"

Magda pushed Bertha to one side. "Pardon my stuttering friend. We couldn't help but notice you've just arrived in town. We've come to say hello and to extend a sincere Jefferson welcome to you and your companion."

Surprise flickered in Bessie's bright eyes before she offered her hand. "Well, thank you."

Magda seemed to settle fast into her welcoming committee role. "My name is Magdalena Hayes, and this here's Bertha. Bertha Maye Biddie." Magda nudged Bertha hard with her elbow. "Say hello to the lady, sugar."

So amazed by the manner in which Bessie's broad smile enhanced her face, Bertha couldn't muster indignation that her name had inspired it. She took the proffered hand in her own and felt a current pass between them. "Hello," she managed. "I'm. . .so pleased to meet you."

"But you haven't really met me yet, now, have you, Bertha Biddie? I'm Annie. Annie Moore from Cincinnati."

Bertha blinked. "Annie? But I thought—" She started the question before she had time to think better of it. And the minute she asked, she remembered the man with Bessie had called her Annie, as well.

Annie arched one feathered brow. "I see you have the advantage over me. You know I go by more than one name, yet I don't know a thing about you." She smiled, but this time it never reached her eyes. "Your confusion is justified, so allow me to clear things up. You see, I've been called many names in the course of my life, and believe me, I prefer Annie to all the rest."

She took a few seconds to look around while tugging satin gloves onto her long, slender fingers. Up close, the diamonds were more impressive, in particular one very large gem surrounded by smaller stones. Annie turned back to Magda, her mood light again. "I must say this is a curious town. Do they always send brawling girls to welcome visitors?"

She laughed, and Bertha winced. She'd never heard a woman laugh so loudly in public. Not even Magda.

"Quite the mismatched scrap, too." She regarded them each in turn, the mischievous glint back in place. "One so tiny she can't block the wind, and the other descended from hardier stock. You two are friends, you say?"

Magda took Bertha's arm. "Of course we're friends," she said a bit defensively. "What's so peculiar about that?"

"Well, darling, I must say I'd never have guessed."

Bertha nudged Magda with her elbow. "She means because we were quarreling."

"Quarreling? It was a round of fisticuffs. And a very entertaining bout, I must say. You might've sold tickets."

Bertha knew Magda's sheepish grin likely matched her own.

Magda waved a dismissive hand in the air. "Oh, that was nothing, really. It's how we often settle things."

Annie laughed. "May I point out that it's an unlikely form of communication? When Abe communicates with me like that, I end up with beefsteak on my eye."

Magda frowned at Bertha, and Bertha returned the expression. In the silence that followed, Annie seemed entertained by their discomfort.

"Say," she said, breaking the spell, "can you girls point me in the direction of the general store? I've got a hankering for something sweet."

Magda looked relieved to change the subject. "Sure we can, considering we spend a good deal of our time there. I have a right demanding sweet tooth myself on occasion."

Annie leaned closer to Bertha and dropped her voice to a whisper. "The truth is, I could use a stiff drink"—she cast a nervous glance over her shoulder—"but Abe wouldn't like it. He don't like me drinking alone." She straightened and gave Bertha a wink. "So a sweet will have to do for now."

Bertha swallowed hard and nodded then squared around and pointed down the street. "Stilley's is just over there a ways, on Dallas Street. We can take you, if you like."

Annie tucked her velvet reticule inside her yellow sash and linked arms with them. "If I like? Well, I certainly do like, ladies. Lead the way."

❧

"Whoa, mule," Henry called, pulling back on Dandy's reins.

Sarah looked up to find herself in front of the last possible place she'd reckoned on going. She glanced over at Henry, but his purposeful blank expression offered not a clue. After securing the wagon, he hopped to the ground and came around to lift her down.

"Stilley's?" she asked, ignoring his outstretched arms.

He nodded.

The general store wasn't a likely setting for the caliber of surprise Sarah expected. She'd spent a fair amount of time inside those walls engaged in commonplace things such as sorting through flour sacks to find one without weevils or picking over packets of seed. To the best of her knowing, there wasn't a blessed thing behind those doors that would set a woman's tender heart to pounding. This made Henry's behavior quite a poser.

"Why can't you tell me what it is you might be needing in there?" Without waiting for an answer, she stood up on the seat and leaned into her husband's outstretched arms.

He swung her up and out of the wagon, set her down on the boardwalk, and reached to straighten her hat. "Girl, I guess you must be the nosiest woman in Marion County." He tweaked her nose and then tapped the end of it with his index finger. "It's a wonder this thing is still cute as a button and not stretched all out like a corncob."

Sarah slapped away his hand. "Curiosity ain't the same as nosy. Considering how hard you've worked to stir mine up, you have only yourself to blame."

Henry enjoyed a hearty laugh at her expense. "Funny, though, how it's always my business you get curious about, ain't it?"

She crossed her arms over her chest. "You reckon you're funny, don't you?"

He pulled her close for a hug. "Don't fret, now, Mrs. King. You gon' find out everything directly—that is, if I can get you to hush long enough to go inside."

She allowed him to nudge her across the boardwalk to the door. They passed beneath the sign reading W. F. STILLEY & CO. and stepped inside. Sarah stood blinking while her eyes grew accustomed to the dim light and her nose to the acrid odor of animal skins and cut tobacco, not a pleasant mix. She held her breath as they passed the racks hung with stiffened fox and coon-shaped furs and a shelf laden with bags and tins of chaw, the source of the cloying smell.

Barrels littered the floor, some filled with corn, some with wheat. Large sacks of flour and sugar were stacked on one side of the room, bags of beans on the other. On the counter, tall jars filled with licorice, peppermint sticks, and assorted penny candies were arranged in a lively display.

Sarah's inventory of the familiar room uncovered something new. Against the back wall, a row of bright colors caught her eye. Two steps closer revealed the only thing in the store she might be itching to get her hands on.

"Mr. Stilley! Why, looky here. You done got in a shipment since I was here last, ain't you?"

Behind the counter, the clerk smiled and nodded.

Sarah crossed the room and ran her fingers over the new bolts of fabric while a shiver of pleasure ran down her spine. They were pretty. Every single one. She'd take the plainest of the lot and still be as pleased as a suckling pup.

"These just come in from New Orleans?" she asked without looking up.

"Nope," Mr. Stilley called. "Brought 'em back from New York. Got a good buy that I can pass on to you folks."

She looked over her shoulder at him. "That so?"

Mr. Stilley nodded again. "Pick you out a nice color, Sarah." He winked over at Henry. "I'm sure me and Henry can strike a fair bargain."

Henry traded with Stilley on occasion, hauling in hides on consignment and corn to sell outright. But the money they got always went toward the bare necessities.

Sarah glanced at her husband. Might this be Henry's surprise? It wasn't the sort of thing he would think of. And she reckoned he knew nothing about her fondness for piece goods or her longing to have a new dress.

Henry stood shifting his weight back and forth, his cheeks nigh to splitting from the grin on his face. One thing was sure. Whatever they had come here for was about to take place.

Oh, please, please, Lord.

"I ain't come here for no trifling cloth," Henry announced, still grinning like a dolt. "I got something sweeter in mind."

Sarah's heart plunged to the muddy depths. She barely heard his next words.

"I come here to buy Sarah a slab of that chocolate."

Stilley beamed. "The new milk chocolate? I see word gets around." He reached under the counter, beneath the jars of candy, and pulled out a wooden box brimming with dark brown blocks in irregular shapes and sizes.

Henry beckoned. "Get on over here, sugar, and pick you out a nice piece. I got enough corn in the back of the rig to cover whatever you want."

Whatever I want? Sarah sighed. *If only you knew.* She forced a smile to her lips as fake as George Washington's teeth.

"Special occasion, Henry?"

Because Mr. Stilley had asked the question she'd wondered all day, Sarah looked up. The pleasure on Henry's face made his dark cheeks glow. "No, sir. No special occasion to speak of." His voice grew soft with embarrassment. "Jus' wanted to show my wife a little appreciation for how hard she been working. Heard about your chocolate and figured she might like some."

"A fine choice, Henry. I understand you can mix it in milk to make a sweet drink or eat it right out of your hand. It's all the rage up north." He winked at Sarah, and Henry turned to face her.

"Sarah?" Henry King had the look of Christmas morning on his face. "Ain't you coming, girl?"

She pulled her shoulders back, gave the bright bolts one last glance, and headed for her husband's side. " 'Course I'm coming. Mr. Stilley, scoot that box a little closer if you please, so's I can reach it better. I got to pick me out a piece of chocolate."

"Did you say chocolate?" someone bawled behind them. "That sounds like just the thing I need."

The bold, strident voice seemed better suited to a man, but when Sarah turned, she found a powerfully beautiful woman standing on the threshold, flanked by two girls. When they stepped into the store behind the woman, Sarah realized she knew them both.

It took one look to know their companion wouldn't be welcome to Sunday supper. But daring as day and big as you please,

Bertha Maye Biddie and Magdalena Hayes congregated with her like long-lost friends. If their mamas were anything like Sarah's had been, those two would feel the sting of a hickory switch before nightfall.

CHAPTER 4

Sarah watched the fancy white woman stroll to the counter, plant the tip of her parasol on the floor, and cross her delicate hands atop the handle. She aimed an unexpected smile and nod at Sarah then fixed Mr. Stilley with an amused expression.

"Am I to understand that there's chocolate for sale in this establishment?"

Mr. Stilley's face lit like sunshine. "Step back, folks." He waved a dismissive hand in Sarah's direction. "Make way for these good people."

Henry jumped as if poked with a hatpin. "Yessuh, Mr. Stilley," he mumbled then shuffled aside, pushing Sarah along with him, his eyes shifted to the floor.

Sarah gritted her teeth and turned away, too late to hide her disgust from Henry.

He winced as if he'd been struck and ducked his head again.

Mr. Stilley took hold of the wooden crate, pulled it from Sarah's side of the counter, and presented it to the three breathless women with a flourish. "You heard right, ma'am, but only half the story. It's not just chocolate I have here. There's genuine imported Swiss in this box, and at a reasonable price." He pushed the container a bit closer to the lively one. "Go on, then. Help yourself."

"Imported Swiss?" the swanky lady squealed, in a manner not fit for civilized company. "Perfect!" She rummaged, looking for the biggest of the lot, took a sizable wedge in each hand, and turned to the girls behind her. "Would you look at this? Have you ever seen as much pure pleasure?" She handed a chunk to Magdalena then tossed one to little Bertha, who juggled to keep from dropping it. "I do love this delightful concoction," she cooed at Bertha. "Don't you, honey?"

Bertha stared with big eyes at the wrapped brown block. "I've never tried it." She brought the confection closer for a sniff. "But it smells divine."

Sarah could smell it just fine from where she stood. All the stirring of the box had raised a rich, pungent cloud that hovered in the room, setting Sarah's mouth to watering. She tasted sweetness at the back of her throat.

The woman gasped. "You say you've never tried it?"

Magda leaned forward and stared at Bertha. "Come now, dear. Of course you have." She let go an uneasy laugh. "You'll have Annie thinking we're tight-fisted hicks."

Bertha gave a determined shake of her head. "I've had it mixed in milk before and once in cake. But never like this." She turned it over in her hands, leaving smeared spots beneath the clear wrapper where her fingers gripped. "What's it like, Annie?"

At first the woman named Annie looked at Bertha as though she didn't believe her. Then she spun around to the wooden box and set to scooping up sweet-smelling hunks with both hands. "There's a remedy for this cruel injustice, my dear. Never fear. You're about to be enlightened."

She unloaded the bundle of candy onto the counter in front of a beaming Mr. Stilley before reaching for one more piece. "There. That should just about do it. Now what do I owe for this child's education?"

Sarah had never seen Stilley with such a big smile. He reached behind him, producing a tablet and a fat leaded pencil. "Very good, madam. Will that be all?"

Annie nodded. "Yes, I believe it will."

The eager man bent over the pad, ciphering figures so fast Sarah waited for smoke to rise from his fingers; then he pushed the paper forward.

Without flinching, Annie reached for the reticule stashed at her side and pulled out more money than Sarah would see in two years' time. After counting out what she owed, Annie pulled the wrapped pieces toward her and asked Mr. Stilley for something to tote them in.

He smiled and shook out a flour sack. "Here we are. Allow me to wrap them for you." He opened the mouth of the sack and started to load her purchase, but she reached to stay his hand.

"Just a minute, if you please." She waved her finger over the mound until she decided which one she wanted. "Ah, yes! This one will have no use for your bag, good sir." She turned and flashed a smile with teeth as white as Henry's. "Will it, girls?"

The three of them laughed together, acting so silly over a fool piece of candy that it set Sarah's teeth on edge.

Annie took her bundle from Mr. Stilley and turned with a flourish. "Shall we go, ladies? We need to find a discreet spot and indulge ourselves to the full."

Bertha held one finger aloft, a glint in her eyes. "I know just the place."

Worry settled over Magda's face. "Bertha. . .you're not thinking what I think you're thinking."

Bertha dismissed her with a swish of her skirts. "Hush your fussing. You sound just like my mama. It won't hurt a single thing for us to go there for a spell. Besides, who'll know?" She shot a warning look over her shoulder. "Unless you tell."

No one need bother telling Sarah. She knew right where they were going. The fifty-foot bluff overhanging the Big Cypress Bayou drew all the youngsters around Jefferson, no matter how much their parents fussed. It was the only place that would arouse the cornered-fox look in Magda's eyes.

"Don't be silly." Offense straightened Magda's spine, and her nose went in the air. "I'd be daft to tell."

Despite her raised chin and put out tone, she seemed less than convincing.

Annie clutched both their arms. "Let's go, then. What are we waiting for?"

When they turned from the counter, Bertha's face paled, and Sarah realized the girl had forgotten she and Henry were there. Sarah watched her weigh the chance she'd been overheard. Then good nature overcame Bertha's fear, and she grinned in their direction. "Hey, you two."

Henry answered for them both. "How you today, Miss Bertha?"

"Just fine, and you?"

"Oh, we doing all right."

Bertha's kind eyes settled on Sarah. "And your papa?"

Her daddy's warm smile and merry eyes crowded Sarah's mind, and she grinned. "Much the same, Miss Bertha. Thank you kindly for asking. He still gets the crimps in his knees of a chilly morn. Slows him down some, but mostly he's all right."

Bertha gave a sympathetic nod. "My papa suffers something fierce with that old rheumatism. Makes him dread the winter."

"Tell him to carry a potato in his pocket," Sarah said eagerly. "Draws the misery right out of your bones."

Bertha's brows met in the middle. "A potato?"

"Daddy swears by it."

"Well, thank you kindly, Sarah." Bertha reached to pat her arm. "I'll pass that along to Papa." She lifted her chin toward the smiling stranger. "This here's my friend Miss Annie Moore from Cincinnati. Annie, meet Sarah and Henry King."

Annie's face lit with a sweet smile.

Sarah gave a brief nod of her head. Ill at ease in the company of the lady, she hurriedly changed the subject. "Been meaning to come by and tell you folks we got plenty of those turnips your mama be so partial to. Had a bumper crop this year. Come on around and pull some before they get stringy. You can take all you like. Henry just gon' plow them under soon." She glanced back at her husband.

"Ain't that so, Henry?"

"It sho' is." Obviously pleased with her gesture, he flashed all his teeth. "That goes for you, too, Miss Magda." His gaze lit briefly on the older woman before he squirmed and looked away. "Well, for all of you."

Sarah tried to picture this Annie person kneeling in a turnip patch, but her imagination failed her. She doubted the woman knew what to do with a turnip.

"We'll ride out and get some, then," Bertha said. "It's a generous offer." She winked up at Henry. "I see Sarah got wind of Mr. Stilley's new shipment. Bet your arm's fairly sore."

"My arm?" Henry rubbed his right shoulder. "Why you say that?"

Bertha grinned all over. "From the twisting Sarah gave it to get you in here."

Sarah watched the meaning of the girl's words fly over Henry's head like southbound geese.

Bertha didn't seem to notice. "Have you picked out something nice, Sarah? Something bright like you been pining for?"

Sarah shook her head. "We come for something else today. You see, Henry—"

"Don't hold these ladies up, Sarah," Mr. Stilley boomed behind them. "They want to be about their business."

The woman called Annie took a tighter grip on Bertha's arm. "You ready, sugar? It's time to go. My man won't sleep all day."

Bertha turned and stared up at her companion as though hexed. "Yes, Annie. I'm ready."

"Well, come on. Show me this mysterious place of yours so we can commence with your edification."

Arm in arm, the three turned and made their way to the door, and Sarah wondered how they'd pass through linked up like a chain. Forgetting herself in her concern for Bertha, she called after them. "You girls be careful, now, you hear?" When they left the store, she spun around and made big eyes at Henry.

He smiled.

Mr. Stilley turned from watching the door and swiveled the box in their direction. "All right, now, Sarah. I believe you were just about to have some of this for yourself."

Henry cleared his throat, anxious eyes on Sarah while he spoke. "Mr. Stilley, we've had a minute to ponder, and I believe we've changed our minds."

Sarah smiled and nodded her approval. Her broad-shouldered, straight-backed husband became a giant in her eyes.

His gaze locked on hers, Henry crossed the room and rested his arm around Sarah's shoulders. "We decided Sarah might better have some nice ice cream or a soda drink instead."

Mr. Stilley looked about, as if trying to figure how to produce the items Henry had named, his brows a puzzled line on his forehead. He nodded at the chocolate. "A minute ago, you had your mouth set for one of these." He pushed the box toward Sarah, as if a closer look might change her mind. "Don't you want to be the first of your kind in town to try it?"

Henry cleared his throat and pulled Sarah tighter against his side. "No, sir, she don't. I think we'll run on over to Mr. Nighthart's and buy her something from the fountain." He looked down at Sarah. "Ain't that right, sugar lamb?"

She nodded.

Stilley glanced between them. "You folks sure?"

Sarah beamed up at Henry, feeling proud enough to pop. "Oh yes, we right sure. Never been more sure of a thing."

Outside, Sarah stood on tiptoe and gave Henry a big kiss on the cheek.

He pushed her back and glanced around but had a wide grin on his face. "You ready for that soda drink now? Or maybe some ice cream?"

She cupped his strong chin in her hand, caressing the dimple with her thumb. "Reckon I already had myself a treat for the day. If I had my druthers, I'd sooner go back out to the house."

"Home?" Henry frowned at her and scratched his head. "But I ain't fetched you nothing yet."

Every ounce of her love for him pushed to the surface and spilled over into her voice. "What you gave me in there tasted better'n a whole box of chocolates with ice cream on top and a soda to wash it down." She lowered her lashes and dropped her voice to a whisper. "How about we go on home now and let me treat you?" She'd never said a thing so bold, and it brought a flash of heat to her cheeks.

Instead of the smile she expected, Henry tightened his jaw and brushed her aside. "I ain't did nothing that special."

"But you did. You—"

He put his hand on the small of her back and guided her, none too gently, toward the rig. "Go on, woman. You want to go home, let's get there. I got work waiting on me."

She stumbled along, hastened by the pressure of his hand, so taken aback she hardly felt her feet touching the ground. "Henry," she demanded over her shoulder, "what's wrong?"

"Ain't nothing wrong. I got work to do, that's all."

Sarah ground to a stop and dug in her heels. If he pushed on her back till day's end, she wouldn't mount the wagon without knowing what had turned his mood. She faced him, letting the set of her jaw and flash of her eyes tell him she'd brook no more. "Henry King, if you're swelled up because of what I said, then un-swell. I shouldn't have talked so loose, but—"

"It wasn't that."

"It's just that I'm so proud of you."

"I said it wasn't that!"

She took hold of his hands and peered up into guarded eyes. "Well, what, then?"

Henry jerked free and swept past, crossing to the rig and climbing aboard, leaving her to clamber up by herself. When he snapped the leads and Dandy pulled away from the boardwalk, Sarah sat so close to the far edge of the seat that she feared bouncing onto the ground at the first deep rut. But she preferred sprawling in the dirt to sitting next to her vexing man.

Not a word passed between them on the way. Sarah used the time to replay in her mind every detail of the day, desperate to pin down what she'd done to anger him. It had never set well with Sarah to have a body displeased with her. Especially Henry. But given her quick temper and saucy ways, life had proved a peculiar dance up to that point.

She spent an unreasonable amount of time waltzing on people's toes and then two-stepping her way out of trouble. Henry once said he considered her sassy mouth to be part of her charm and the very trait that first attracted him. But with the passage of time, he'd grown less enamored by her rowdy tongue.

When they turned down their lane, Sarah made a last cautious attempt to talk to him, but Henry offered a cold shoulder in return. By the time they reached the yard, hot rage had crowded out all desire to make up. She made her way down from her perch before Henry could offer his hand and swept out of the barn, leaving him to tend the rig and settle Dandy.

She stormed into the house and into their room, slamming the door behind her. Her shoes flew off one at a time with kicks that sent them crashing into the wall. Next came her dress, pulled overhead in angry jerks with the sound of ripping seams. She yanked her nightshirt from the hook and stomped into it, tossing the torn dress into a heap by the bed. By the time she locked the door and slid beneath the quilt, she heard Henry's heavy steps inside the house.

She listened while he walked from room to room. First the kitchen, then the parlor, and back again. He paused then crossed to the double windows that faced the side yard and outhouse. When next he moved, his determined stride led him just where she knew it would.

Least he could do is take off them muddy boots. I know he never wiped his feet.

Henry stopped outside the door and tried the knob. "Sarah?"

She turned away, hurling a string of insults in her mind.

He rattled harder. "Open up. What you doing in there?"

She knew if she didn't answer, he'd stand there asking addlepated questions all night. "I'm resting, Henry."

"Resting?" he called in a low voice. "It's midday. You ain't ailing, are you?"

How like him to act like nothing was wrong. "I'm just tired, that's all."

The long pause from the other side of the door said things she knew Henry couldn't find the words for. When he finally spoke, he said just the wrong thing. "What about dinner?"

She sat up and threw her pillow. "There's chickens running over the yard because you can't mend a fence. Pluck one and eat it. Frying pan's on the hook."

She'd have some apologies to make later, but for now Sarah hunkered down, swaddled in spiteful indignation, and tried to sleep. No more sound came from inside the house. In the silence, she listened to the racing pulse in her temple beat a rhythm against her pillow. She couldn't quiet it any more than she could silence the gentle voice in her head. Frustrated, she flopped on her back and kicked the covers to the floor.

Why should I, Lord? I don't care to feed that stubborn-hearted, perplexing man. Why would You ask me to? She had searched her heart and couldn't find a single excuse for Henry's bad behavior. If he couldn't offer her one, let him starve.

Sarah turned on her side again and huddled against the cold until it became more work to resist than to obey. Miserable, she spun around and sat up. Very well, she'd give him food, but that was all. There'd be no need to speak to him. She slipped a shawl around her shoulders and opened the door.

In the kitchen, Henry sat slumped at the table, but his head jerked up when she entered the room. He had already fetched the kettle of beans and ham she'd cooked the day before from the springhouse he'd built down by the bayou. He'd been right proud of himself for building the small house over the water to keep her vittles cool, but the thing had become a source of irritation for Sarah, considering Jefferson boasted an ice plant. The folks in town sat in their parlors and waited for the iceman to put blocks of ice in special wooden boxes sitting right in their kitchens. A pot of beans would last for days in a contraption like that.

Without a word, she took down the iron skillet and scooped in bacon grease from the jar near the blacktop stove. The solid grease turned to liquid as soon as it hit the pan, so she know the fire was hot. She hurried to mix the cornbread, poured the batter, and set the skillet on the stove with more force than was called for.

Behind her, Henry cleared his throat. "Did you see all the chocolate that woman had, Sarah? She done bought herself a whole mess of chocolate."

Sarah planted her knuckles on her waist and twisted to look over her shoulder. "I saw it all right, and some other things, too. I saw you looking mighty hard at that fancied-up white woman."

Henry drew back, and pain flickered in his eyes. "What you going on about?"

Sarah knew when she said it the accusation was unjust. In all the years she'd been Henry King's wife, she'd never once caught his eyes on another woman. She reached for the beans, slamming the pot on the stove. "You know just what I'm talking about."

It would be nice if she knew it herself.

"How could I be looking at a woman? You're all these eyes have wanted since they landed on you four years ago at Lawetta Draper's backyard social. You still in braids and looking so sweet in that pretty white frock we had to fight off the bees. From that day until now, I can't see past you to look at anyone else."

"The bees swarmed because Markas Scott sloshed cider on my dress." She kept a hard edge in her voice, but still Henry chuckled.

"Markas Scott was jus' trying to sit close to you. The man knows a good thing when he sees it."

Sarah longed to turn but kept right on stirring the beans. The scrape of Henry's chair on the pinewood floor told her he was coming to stand behind her. She steeled herself until his hands on her shoulders melted her resolve as fast as the skillet had melted the grease. When he pulled her close, she leaned into him despite herself.

"Girl, what's wrong with you?" he whispered. "Your man takes you into town to fetch you a surprise, and this is how you act?"

She picked up the dishcloth to wipe her hands and turned. "You the one acting up today. What happened to you down at Stilley's?"

The glow in his eyes faded, and waves of pain rolled in to take its place. He squirmed like he didn't want to answer her question, and his expression changed so many times she gave up trying to read him.

"Tell me, Henry."

"I don't care to start it up again, Sarah."

"Well, I need to know."

He shook his head. "You know I can't sort the words in my head good enough to say 'em aloud."

"Try."

Henry stared at the floor without speaking until Sarah pulled his attention back to her.

"Just say it."

He rubbed circles on his thick brows with his thumb and forefinger then looked up with anguished eyes. "All right, then. If that's what you want." His big chest moved up and down, and he opened his mouth twice before the words came out. "Sarah, today was the first time you ever said you was proud of me. Did you know that?"

She could only stare.

"And for what?" he continued. "For showing spite to Mr. Stilley? Never mind that I took you there in the first place to buy you something nice."

Sarah back-stepped and slung the dishcloth across the room. "I can't help it! I can't abide all that bowing and scraping! If you want to surprise me, Henry King, then live up to your name." She knew she'd gone too far but couldn't stop. "Looks like, you being a farmer and all, you could grow yourself a nice backbone."

She pushed him aside and moved about the room with gyrating hips, batting her eyes and spouting hateful words. " 'Yes, suh, Mr. Stilley, suh. Let old Henry move his big black bottom out the way for these fine white folk.' "

When she dared a glance his way, she saw his face was red, his fists clenched.

"That's enough, Sarah. You wrong, and you know it. I don't show out like that. And Mr. Stilley treats us good as anybody."

"Good as anybody?" She sneered and nodded. "Why, sure he do. When nobody's looking."

His fierce glare cut straight through her bones. "What you want from me, Sarah? This ain't St. Louis. I told you it would be different here."

When she didn't answer, he shook his head. "Small as you are, you got a sizable ornery streak. I love you, but your pride's gon' see me hanged."

Sarah returned to the stove, her back as rigid as her mind-set.

The door opened then closed behind Henry, and only then did the enormity of her words overwhelm her. She stood as if poured out and forged to the spot by the heat of her anger, until the acrid smell of burning beans and deep regret assailed her nostrils. She pushed the pot off the fire, untied her apron, and sank into Henry's chair. On a shelf above the sideboard, the ragged spine of Mama's Bible leapt out at her. A single verse from Proverbs seemed to sprout wings and fly out from the dog-eared pages.

"Death and life are in the power of the tongue: and they that love it shall eat the fruit thereof."

She sat for a bit, gingerly chewing the fruit of her words, finding it less than tasty. If she'd ever doubted that particular scripture, she didn't now. The pall that settled about her, heavy in the room, felt like the death of her husband's love.

What has my big mouth done?

She turned and stared at the place where he'd gone out, her pride, more than the solid oak door, an impenetrable wall between herself and Henry. A simple apology wouldn't do for this one, no matter how fast she danced.

Dear Lord, what have I gone and done now?

CHAPTER 5

Avoiding the main road was the smartest plan. One of the nosy old hens Bertha saw scratching about town might ask too many questions and then go squawking to Mama. If Mama caught her at Lover's Leap, it'd be the woodshed for certain. The fact that no one ever forbade her to go to the bluff was but a trifle, though one she'd use to her advantage should she be caught. Mama's unreasonable views on the subject were clear, voiced or not. But it was the only interesting place left in the whole of Marion County.

If they timed it right, they could catch Mose and Rhodie in an empty wagon, headed back to the bayou for more wood. Bertha squinted at Annie's fine yellow dress. "We have to run. Can you keep up?"

Grinning, Annie tucked her parasol under one arm and extended her hand. "Just try me."

Bertha returned the smile with an equal measure of glee and clasped Annie's hand. "Come on, Magda. Follow us," she cried and then darted between two shops with Magda's plaintive cry to wait echoing in her ears.

Bertha clung to her new friend and led her down the cluttered lane past discarded barrels, stacked crates, and piles of odorous trash. At the end, they cut to the left and ran behind staggered rows of shops along the back alleys of Jefferson with Magda panting far behind.

Bertha longed for her soft, low-slung boots instead of the bronze leather heels fastened by little buttoned straps that Mama insisted she wear that morning. They were far too tight with ridiculous pointed toes that pinched her feet. Bertha detested shoes and always had, much preferring the comfort of worn-in boots or bare feet. She wondered if the day would ever come when she might learn to tolerate fashionable shoes.

They passed behind Mr. Steinlein's clothing store on Walnut Street and cut across an open field before bursting onto the road in time to see Mose's rig approaching in the distance. Bertha and Annie doubled over in laughter, clutching their sides.

Magda, still hobbling across the field, gripped her waist in apparent pain and scowled her displeasure. When she reached them, her complaint was an accusation aimed at Bertha. "You didn't wait."

Guilt tickled the edges of Bertha's conscience. "I clearly said we had to run," she panted. "You heard me say it."

"But I asked you to wait."

"I don't have the wind to argue, Magda. Besides, here come Mose and Rhodie."

The boy spotted Annie from forty feet away. His wide eyes were fixed on her, and the freckles on his pale face stuck out like stars in a cloudless sky. The ever-unflappable Rhodie sat quietly beside him, hands folded in her lap. They drew alongside, and Mose reined in the horse. "Why, looky here, Sissy. If this ain't our lucky day."

His openmouthed smile reminded Bertha of a happy jack-o'-lantern. She moved closer, pulling Annie along for bait. "Hey, Mose."

He pulled his gaze from Annie long enough to address Bertha. "Well now, it ain't often I get to see the prettiest flowers in Jefferson, much less stumble upon them twice in one day." His eyes swiveled back to Annie. "And I see there's a mighty fair rose been added to the bunch."

"Hello." Annie stuck out her hand and clasped his palm as if it weren't calloused and covered in filth. "I'm Annie. Bertha's friend."

It wouldn't seem two simple words held the power to induce such joy, but they swept over Bertha in waves, leaving a rush of contentment behind. Her elation lasted as long as it took to catch the wounded expression on Magda's face.

Mose tipped his hat with his free hand. "Moses Pharr. Pleasure to meet you, ma'am. This here's Rhodie, my little sister."

Annie released his hand and beamed past him at the girl. "Oh, but this darling girl isn't so little. She's a young woman, and a pretty one, too. I always did envy girls with red hair."

Whether the compliment was genuine or a simple courtesy, it pleased Rhodie to no end. She returned a smile as sweet as hot cross buns, and a flush rose to her cheeks. "Thank you kindly, ma'am."

With a furtive glance behind her, Bertha decided they could exchange pleasantries later. "Mose, are you two headed back toward the bayou?"

A light flickered in Mose's eyes. "Why? You gals needing a lift?"

Bertha grinned back at him. "We sure are."

"Hop aboard, then. We got an empty wagon this time, so take all the room you need." He looked past them to Magda and spoke to her for the first time. "You can come, too, if you like."

Magda's frown darkened. "Really? Well, ain't I blessed?"

Bertha let go of Annie and caught Magda's hand. "Come, my beloved. Your carriage awaits."

The struggle not to smile played over Magda's face, but the effort proved too great, and she allowed Bertha to pull her toward the rig. "Save your sweet talk for those who don't know you so well, Bertha Biddie."

Bertha grinned and squeezed her fingers. "Just get in, you sour old crabapple."

Mose ordered Rhodie to the rear so Annie could join him on

the seat. Though Rhodie complied swiftly and without complaint, Annie refused to take her place even after Bertha tried to convince her. Instead, Annie hiked up her skirts and climbed into the wagon bed, seemingly oblivious to the cypress twigs and wood chips. When all was said and done, Annie, Bertha, and Rhodie sat cross-legged in back, and Magda wound up on the seat beside a scowling Mose.

Bertha leaned against the rail, watching the residents dwindle and the shops thin out as they pulled away from town headed west.

They'd gone less than a half mile before Magda leaned to whisper something to Mose, and he pulled up on the reins. When they came to a full stop, Magda gathered her things and stood up.

"What are you doing, sugar?" Bertha called.

"I decided not to go. It's time for the noon meal. Mama will be looking for me."

"You can tell her you ate with me. It won't be completely untrue." She winked and pointed at Annie's bag. "We'll be eating candy."

"Mama won't like it. She got mad the last time I did that. And she'll mention it to your mama. I know she will."

Bertha narrowed her eyes, causing Magda to lower hers. "You're scared, that's all."

Magda looked ready to make more excuses but then traded her wilted demeanor for a stamp of the foot. "All right, then. Yes, I'm scared. There, I've said it and feel no worse for it. You would be, too, if you had any sense at all."

Showing interest in the conversation for the first time, Rhodie leaned forward. "What you afraid of, Magda?"

Magda pointed an accusing finger at Bertha. "She's taking Annie to the bluff."

Rhodie came alive. "To Lover's Leap? I want to come!" Rhodie whirled to plead with her brother's back. "Oh, Mose, can we go?"

He shook his head. "Can't, Sissy. We got three more loads to get done before nightfall." He tilted to the left to gaze up at Magda.

"But there ain't nothing on the bluff to be scared of."

Magda regarded the top of his head with disdain. "What do you know, Moses Pharr? You're dumb as a box of rocks. The main thing I'm frightened of is Papa finding out. Bertha should fear the same."

Bertha sighed. "I told you they won't find out. If you don't come along, you'll miss all the fun." She plied the bait that always worked with Magda. Food. "And don't forget about the chocolate. You won't get any."

Magda reached inside her drawstring bag and produced the piece Annie had given her in the store. "Oh yes, I will."

Bertha shrugged and looked away. "Go on home, then. I can't stop you." She angled forward, propelled by a sudden troubling thought. "But you'd better not tell."

The words seemed to rock Magda as if a cannon had gone off inside. She flailed a hand in Bertha's direction while she struggled to find her words.

In a true act of fearlessness, considering she still towered above him, Mose smiled and nodded up at Magda. "Yep, she's bound to tell. Ain't you, Magda?"

Magda froze and fixed him with a disbelieving stare. Then she climbed down off the rig, muttering under her breath. When she reached the ground, she didn't say a word to Bertha or anyone else before she flounced away in a huff. They watched her cut across the field and duck into the dense woods that lay east of her house.

Annie's low voice broke the silence. "Will she be all right?"

Bertha glanced her way. "Magda? Of course she will."

"But she went off into the woods all alone."

Bertha laughed. "Ain't nothing in that grove of pine with the boldness to stand up to Magdalena Hayes."

Annie shifted her eyes toward Bertha. "You just did."

She nodded. "Why do you think she's so mad?"

Annie smiled. Bertha looked toward the spot where she'd last seen Magda's blue shawl bobbing through the trees, but all trace of her had disappeared.

"What's there to be so scared of?"

She squinted up at Annie. "At Lover's Leap, you mean?"

Annie nodded.

"Nothing, really. It's a dark and moody place, a sheer bluff fifty feet high that plunges straight down to the water's edge. The trees grow thick before it opens to the bayou, so not much light gets in. A lot has taken place there over the years. Even more things people talk about that never really happened."

Rhodie chimed in, her low voice laden with dread. "Rumor has it folks have taken their own lives by jumping off the bluff. And there was a murder happened there once." She peeked at Bertha. "Or so they say."

Annie's eyes widened. "A murder?"

"And a suicide," Mose said over his shoulder. "Some poor muggins caught his wife on the ridge with his own brother. Rolled them off the edge and then sailed in after them." He chuckled, raising his hand to the sky before dipping it low again. "Took him a leap, he did. I heard it wasn't the trip down he minded so much. Just the sudden stop."

Bertha raised her brows at Annie and shook her head. "That story's not true."

Mose turned around to look at her. "Sure is, too."

"Then why doesn't anyone know their names? If there was any truth to it, someone around here could say who it was. It's a legend, Mose. You shouldn't spread it about."

Mose looked from Bertha to Annie while a slow flush colored his cheeks. Without a word, he faced the front and flicked the reins, and the old horse eased into motion.

Rhodie reached to pat Annie's hand. "Don't worry your pretty self, ma'am. Even if it's true, nothing as bad as murder happens around Jefferson anymore."

"Why, thank you, darlin'. I'm comforted by that thought." The radiant smile Annie turned on Rhodie caused her to blush brighter than Mose and duck her head.

Bertha stewed about Magda for the rest of the trip. The others seemed lost in thoughts of their own, until Mose pulled to the side of the road at a spot where a small muddy clearing narrowed into an overgrown trail. He wrapped the reins around the post and jumped off to open the rear end and help Annie climb down. She thanked him then straightened her skirt and reached for her bag and parasol.

Bertha held up her hand. "Wait, Annie." She reached for Mose's outstretched arm and scooted to the ground. "Why don't you leave your things right here? Mose can pick us up when he's done. Can't you, Mose?"

"Sure, but I won't be back for an hour or so. And I'll be packing wood when I come."

Bertha looked at Annie. "I don't mind if she doesn't."

Annie shook her head. "It's better than walking."

Mose raised the tailgate. "Meet you right here, then. If you ain't standing on the road when I come, I'll send Sissy in after you."

Rhodie gasped and slapped her brother's arm. "Nuh-uh! I ain't traipsing through those woods alone."

Bertha chuckled. "Don't worry. We'll be here. And, Rhodie, mind Annie's nice things, won't you? Don't let Mose pile cypress on them."

Rhodie rose up on her knees and peered at the matching yellow parasol and reticule with anxious eyes. "I won't. But they're sure to get filthy in the bottom of this raggedy old crate. Give them to me, Mose. I'll hold them up front."

Bertha tried to pass the items to Mose, but he threw up his hands and backed away. "I ain't touching them girlie things."

Annie laughed aloud. "Go on. Take them. They won't bite."

He retreated farther and shook his head, staring as if facing down a copperhead.

"I swear," Bertha cried. "The more I learn about men, the more outlandish they seem." She shook her head and walked around to give the things to Rhodie. "Don't let any of this yellow silk touch your brother. We wouldn't want him to perish."

Rhodie grinned. "I won't."

Bertha turned to face Annie. "Ready now?"

"Ready as I'll ever be."

They were halfway across the clearing when Bertha remembered. She pivoted on the ball of her foot and ran toward the road.

"Mose, wait!"

He pulled the horse to a stop and turned on the seat. "Yeah?"

Bertha hurried to Rhodie's side of the rig and reached for Annie's reticule then held the bag aloft. "We forgot the chocolate."

Annie waved her hand. "Go ahead and get it, Bertha. I don't mind. And give them each a piece while you're at it."

Bertha rummaged inside, pulled out four pieces of wrapped candy, and handed one each to Mose and Rhodie. "This is for you."

Rhodie took it and turned it over in her hand. "What is it?"

"It's a block of candy. You're supposed to eat it. But you'd better hurry; it's starting to melt."

She tossed the bag to a still skeptical Rhodie and rejoined Annie. "*Now* we're ready." She grinned. "Let's go."

They dodged muddy ruts and boggy holes until they reached the end of the clearing and stepped into the mouth of the trail. Loblolly pine had succeeded in crowding out most of the sweet gum and oak along the edges, and underbrush threatened to overtake the sandy path. Bertha led the way, stopping occasionally to hold back a droopy pine bough or step on a vine laced with stickers so Annie could pass.

The summer sun in Jefferson blazed high and white-hot, but in the shorter, overcast days of winter, old Sol hovered in the sky like a dollop of fresh-churned butter. They made their way deeper into thick vegetation where the meager light began to lose its battle with the thick cover of trees and a cloudy sky.

As the forest dimmed, Annie hustled a few steps closer and took Bertha's hand.

Bertha grinned and peered at her. "Are you scared?"

She nodded and licked her lips. "A bit. All that talk of murder has me skittish. I keep waiting for some poor muggins to jump out with an ax."

They both laughed.

"Want to go back?"

A determined look replaced the worried expression. "After coming this far? Not on your life, dearie. Let's go eat some chocolate."

When the track opened onto the bluff, they linked arms and crossed to the edge. Once they stretched out Bertha's shawl and settled on the ground under a spreading oak, Annie seemed to relax and enjoy the view. They broke out the soft, squishy candy and divided a piece, laughing at the gooey mess it left on their fingers.

Bertha felt deliciously naughty reclining under wide-open sky in a forbidden place, nipping delicate bites from a decadent treat.

Annie seemed to have an endless supply of funny stories and epic tales. She told of her travels to faraway places and her house in Cincinnati. And about growing up in New York, though a shadow passed over her eyes when she mentioned her parents, as well as each time she mentioned Abraham Roth.

She described Edward R. Rice's production of *Evangeline* on Broadway so well Bertha could almost see the spouting whale, the dancing cow, and James S. Maffit's performance as the Lone Fisherman.

Annie paused to take a breath and glanced across at Bertha. "Have you ever been to the theater, sugar?"

She shook her head. "The closest I ever came was a poster on Mama's wall. It's a billboard from *The Magic Deer*, and it reads 'A Serio Comico Tragico Operatical Historical Extravaganzical Burletical Tale of Enchantment.' "

Annie laughed so hard she nearly choked on her candy. When she composed herself, she put the uneaten piece down and wiped her fingers on the grass. "Sounds like they covered all the bases."

Bertha grinned. "They didn't miss a one."

Annie scooted closer to the oak and leaned her head against the wide trunk. "Now then, darlin', how about telling me the real reason you brought me here."

Bertha stopped midbite and jerked her head around to meet

Annie's gaze. "What do you mean?"

Grinning, Annie studied the toes of her shoes. "Come on, now. Don't try to bamboozle me. I'm onto you."

"I beg your pardon?"

"Honey, you can't fool me. We're too much alike."

A surge of pleasure stole over Bertha's heart. "You think we're alike?"

Annie slid closer, took Bertha's candy, and laid it aside. "Allow me to demonstrate how much." She squared around to face Bertha and took hold of her hands. "Tell me you don't have a fire that burns inside all the time, pressing you to speak out when you don't agree with the general consensus, urging you to throw off antiquated conventions, the dictates of ceremony and social structure, and just be yourself."

Though she'd never have found such elegant words to describe her feelings, it seemed as though Annie had peeled back a layer of her skin and peered right down into her soul. She nodded dumbly.

"And tell me, little Bertha Maye, that you don't long to skip just because you feel like it, to dance a jig when no one's looking, and to run barefoot through the town square, sans bonnet, corset, or shawl."

Bertha felt undressed before Annie's wisdom and insight. "However did you know?"

Annie tapped her chest. "Because I recognize you. We're kindred spirits. And now that we have it all settled, answer my question, please. What's this all about? Why did you bring me here?"

Bertha ducked her head. "Well, you see, there's this boy. . . ." She looked up to find a knowing smile on Annie's face.

"I might've guessed. It's always a boy." She patted Bertha's hand. "Honey, you don't need my help on that subject. Why, look at you. You're lovely. Any man who can't see how wonderful you are, inside and out, doesn't deserve you."

Bertha shook her head. "I don't know what Thad sees, and that's the trouble. I go all trembly inside at the sound of his voice or the touch of his hand. But I can't tell how he feels about me."

Annie settled back and regarded her with soft gray eyes. "Well, if he's not mad about you, he's a fool."

Bertha shook her head again. "He's anything but a fool, but I don't think he wants me. I'd give anything to be like you, Annie. To have your enticing effect on men."

Annie released Bertha's hands and turned away. "Don't ever say that."

"But why? It's true. You're a splendid creature. Just looking at you makes people feel special."

Annie's laugh sounded harsh and hollow. "Is that a fact, little chicken? Well, not men. Looking at me makes men feel something else."

Warmth spread to Bertha's toes. "I know what you mean. Desire."

The lines of Annie's beautiful face turned to carved stone. "No, more than that. They feel the need to possess. To control."

It pained Bertha's heart to imagine what misdeeds had caused Annie to say such a thing. "Not all men. My papa would never treat a woman like that."

Annie smiled, but it didn't erase the hard lines. "Then I need to meet your papa. If it's true, he'd be the first of his kind I've run into."

"There are a lot of good men in the world. Thad's one of them."

Annie chuckled and held up her hand. "Don't be so hasty. He's too green to determine that yet. Let's give him a few years. Now tell me about your Thad."

They dwelled at length on Bertha's favorite topic. She described Thad in glowing terms—tall, with shoulders so broad she couldn't see around him, dark brown eyes, and sandy hair. A quick smile and rumbling laugh. She told Annie she'd been in love with Thad since the day Abel and Leona Bloom moved him into Jefferson. She shared that she longed to be his wife, said she knew in her heart he felt the same but something held him back.

"And I'm running out of time. He's leaving town."

"Leaving? Why?"

Bertha broke eye contact and stared at the ground. "College. He's going away to school."

"Oh, Bertha. When?"

Her voice broke when she answered. "I don't know for sure. Soon."

Annie picked up her hands and squeezed them. "I have no quick answers for you, honey." Annie's sincere gaze pierced Bertha's heart. "But I promise you this. I'll do my best to come up with a plan."

CHAPTER 6

A strong breeze kicked up, howling through the cut below and sweeping over the face of the water in a fury. Bertha watched it sway the oak and tangle the tops of the pine overhead while the branches complained aloud with ghostly groans and creaks. The brisk wind was the sort that ushered in a hard rain, so it seemed likely the gathering dark clouds on the far horizon were the cause of all the fuss.

Annie had stretched out on the shawl on her back and closed her eyes. She remained quiet for so long, Bertha thought she'd fallen asleep, until she spoke.

"Are you afraid to die?"

Bertha rolled toward her. "Mercy! What sort of question is that?"

Annie peeked at her from under her long lashes. "The nosy sort, I'm sure. But, well. . .are you?"

"Um, a little, I guess."

"Come on. You have to be more than a little. Isn't everyone?"

Bertha giggled. "Not everyone. My mama says she's scared of the process, but not what comes after."

Annie turned to her side and leaned up on her elbow. "But who's to say what that is?"

Bertha blinked. "You're joking, right?"

When Annie shook her head, Bertha knew she should proceed with caution. Raised by a Christian family in a Christian community, it seemed impossible to her that a person might not know and believe the Bible.

Before she could respond, Annie pressed her again. "So you're not absolutely terrified of death?"

Bertha swallowed hard and weighed her words. "I guess I feel the same as Mama. I don't want to suffer in death, but once it's over, I'll suffer no more."

Annie leaned back and rested her arm over her eyes. "Oh, I see. You're religious." The tone of her voice told Bertha that Annie considered "religious" as distasteful as warts.

"If by that you mean someone who believes the Bible, then yes, I am. Very much so."

Annie sat up and stared at the far bank while her tortured eyes revealed a struggle inside. Without warning, she shot to her feet and began to wrestle with something behind her. When she wiggled all over and then stepped out of her bustle, Bertha recoiled in shock.

"What on earth?"

Annie held the bustle up before Bertha's disbelieving eyes. "I can't abide this thing another second," she cried and then hurled it over the edge of the bluff.

Bertha stared in stunned surprise before she stood up and unfastened hers, as well. With an Indian whoop, she spun it overhead before letting it fly. They raced to the edge and watched the current carry the offending garments out of sight.

"Oh, Annie, I've always wanted to do that."

Annie beamed. "Well, darlin', now you have. Will you be in trouble when you go home without it?"

"From whom? Mama won't even notice. She still wears pantalets." Bertha had a sudden inspiration. "Now these infernal things." She leaned against the oak, unbuttoned her shoes, and slipped them off. Then she reared back as if about to fling them over.

Annie covered her face and squealed. "You wouldn't dare!"

Bertha sagged and tossed the pumps on the ground behind her. "You're right. I don't dare. As much as I'd love to see them floating downstream."

They giggled their way back to the shawl and slumped to the ground.

Annie sprawled on her back and sighed. "Now isn't this better? I have to say, though the bustle's a nuisance, the Basque bodice is worse. It wasn't enough to make the contraption so tight a girl can't breathe, they had to go and sew in rigid bones. I'd swear it was invented by a man." She laughed and rolled her eyes at Bertha. "Or spawned by the devil himself."

Bertha dropped her gaze and sat upright.

Behind her, Annie grew silent. Then she sat up, too, and touched Bertha's shoulder. "Did I say something to offend you?"

Bertha turned. "I'm not offended. Just surprised. We don't jest about the devil in our house."

Annie gave an uneasy laugh. "But that's silly, isn't it?"

"It's not silly at all. The devil is nothing to make fun about. We aren't frightened of him or anything, but we're sure not on speaking terms."

Annie laughed again, this time in earnest. "You think he's real?"

"Sure he's real."

Still in a frivolous mood, Annie held up one finger. "Oh, wait. Of course he's real. In fact, I've met him in person. I found him aimlessly roaming the lobby of Niblo's Garden during a revival production of *Seven Sisters*. I guess he was awaiting the last curtain call before taking the demon sisters back home to hell."

The loud Annie, the abrasive, boisterous Annie, was back, and Bertha didn't like it. She turned away and covered her ears. "Stop it. Don't make jokes. It's not funny."

She waited until Annie hushed laughing before raising her head to look. Annie sat and quietly stared at her, a puzzled look on her face. "It's absurd, Bertha. There's no such thing."

"Yes, there is. And it's serious business. Such matters aren't to be dallied with outside God's protection. Scripture says it like this. . . ." She leaned closer and lowered her voice the way Rhodie had earlier. 'Be sober, be vigilant; because your adversary the devil, as a roaring lion, walketh about, seeking whom he may devour.' "

Annie shuddered. "It says that?" She looked over Bertha's shoulder and then behind her. "That gives me gooseflesh."

Bertha felt guilty about scaring her. "Don't worry, Annie. There's a terrible end in store for him and all the workers of iniquity."

Annie stared back at Bertha with blank, hollow eyes. "Let's not talk about it anymore, please."

"Sure, if that's what you want. You brought it up, remember?"

"And I regret it." She glanced around anxiously. "Bertha, how long have we been here?"

"I can't say. Why?"

"I don't know. It suddenly seems as if a long time has passed."

Bertha gazed through the trees at the sun. "Oh my, it sure does."

"How much time, do you think?"

"An hour, at least."

Annie gathered her skirts about her and stood up. "Oh, Bertha. I think it's been more than an hour. Much more." She walked to the edge of the thicket and peered down the trail. "Where's Mose? He said he'd send Rhodie. We need to get back to town. Abe's sure to be awake by now, and he'll be wondering where I am." She clutched the sides of her head and moaned. "Why did I come out here? Whatever was I thinking?"

Bertha got the impression it wasn't the first time Annie had asked herself that question, or the first time her reckless nature had caused her grief. The way her face paled and panic crowded her eyes, she also gathered Annie feared Abraham Roth more than any threat of the devil.

"Bertha, I'm going. I can't wait for Mose."

Bertha stood and brushed off her backside. "It's too far. Let's wait a bit longer."

"No, I can't." She paced from the woods to the edge of the bluff. "You don't understand."

As if on cue, the sun dropped behind a cloud and the wind stilled. The trees and shrubs surrounding them seemed to lean close with Bertha to hear Annie's explanation, but the only sound was the whisper of the water below. The once-cheery spot had become the gloomy site of Mose's murderous story.

Annie swept past her and started up the trail. "That's it. I'm going right now."

Bertha hurriedly fastened her shoes and snatched up the shawl. "Wait, I'll go with you."

They struggled through the brush, this time with Annie in the lead. Bertha dodged swinging limbs and hurdled stickers in Annie's wake. They came onto a group of vultures huddled over a hapless meal. As the two approached, the birds abandoned their feast and took flight with a flutter of wings that startled Bertha but didn't even slow Annie's gait. She stumbled just ahead, muttering frantic words to herself, which Bertha heard in bits and pieces.

Bertha wished they could go back under the tree and recapture the merry mood. She knew she should ask what had Annie so upset, but she feared the answer, because somehow she already knew. So she plodded along behind her and said nothing.

When they broke into the clearing, Mose's rig lumbered toward them in the distance. Annie charged toward it, and Bertha followed.

"Where were you?" Annie demanded when they came within shouting distance.

"Sorry, ma'am," he called. "We got stuck."

He pulled alongside and tipped his hat, the only piece of cloth on his body not covered in muck. "Thought we'd be spending the night out in the woods until Julius Ney happened along in his oxcart." He wiped his sweat-beaded face with a handkerchief, smearing all the spots on his face, except for the freckles, into a pale muddy mask. He jerked his finger toward the back. "Nothing less than a team of oxen could've hauled us out with a load like that weighing us down."

The wood was stacked so high, Bertha didn't know whether to laugh or console the poor horse.

Mose saw the look on her face and hurried to defend himself. "You heard me say I still had three loads to get. We're running short on daylight. I was trying to make up for lost time."

Rhodie sat pouting on the seat. Muddy water had recolored her blue overalls and bright auburn hair to a dull grayish brown. "I told you not to cross that ditch, Mose. I knew we were bound to bog down." She raised her head long enough to scorch him with her eyes. "You don't never listen to me."

As if to prove her point, Mose ignored his sister. "I should be headed into town with this cypress, Bertha, but I figured we'd best come and fetch you."

Annie brought her hand down on the side rail so hard it had to hurt. "Let's go, then. Stop all this messing about."

"Sure thing, Miss Annie. Only. . ."

"Only nothing. Turn this thing around and let me get on."

Mose flicked the reins and spun around so tightly that Bertha held her breath until he straightened out again. She could just see Rhodie, Mose, and the wood becoming an oversized game of jackstraws in the center of the narrow road. When he pulled alongside them again, Annie headed straight for the tailgate.

Mose's eyes widened, and he stood up. "Wait, Miss Annie. Don't."

She stopped with her hand on the latch. "Why not?"

He shook his head. "If you open that, you'll be high-jumping logs. Besides, there ain't no room for a passenger now. Not in the bed, at least. Ain't safe." He inclined his head toward the buckboard seat. "And only room for one more up here."

Bertha watched while Annie figured it out.

When the truth dawned, she gasped and covered her mouth. "Oh no. Oh, Bertha."

Bertha placed an arm around her shoulders and walked her to the front of the rig. "You go on ahead. I'll come later."

"No, I couldn't."

"Yes, you can. You have to."

"But it's going to rain."

Bertha patted Annie's back. "Don't worry. I'll be fine. Mose will come right back, and when he does, he'll find me even closer because I'll be walking."

Mose scrambled down to help her, but Annie didn't wait. She lifted her skirts and clambered aboard before Mose could offer his arm. He jerked his gaze from her exposed legs and then leaned to check the load's balance.

Annie turned to wave her hand at him. "Leave that, Mose. Just get me back to town. And hurry!"

CHAPTER 7

Lightning, visible between the trees on the high bank of the bayou, prowled across the lowering sky. Standing on the bank, Thad did a slow count to five before thunder echoed over the tops of the tall cypress.

In the distance, T-Bone Taylor stopped paddling long enough to sit up straight on his seat and gaze toward the gathering clouds. Then he dipped his oar with renewed vigor while shouting to his little brother seated at the opposite end of the boat. Thad couldn't make out the words, but it became obvious what he said when Beau bent his shoulders to the paddle and dug in.

Thad nudged Charlie. "That storm is about a mile away. Looks like they're bound to get wet."

Charlie chuckled. "And all their loot, too. I hope that pilfered 'backy's in a tin, or tomorrow they'll be spreading it in the sun."

Thad joined in the laughter. "I heard there ain't nothing worse than soggy tobacco. Too smoky—if you can keep it lit."

Charlie peered up at him. "You ever smoke, Thad?"

Thad shook his head. "Never had a use for it." He looked back at the water.

The boys had rowed almost out of sight but still had a long way to go to reach their own dock. And the dark, paunchy clouds inched closer. Several fat droplets pelted the layer of pine needles at Charlie's feet with a muted *thwack*. Time to go.

Thad gathered the fishing poles then jerked his head at Charlie. "It'd be downright foolish to stand laughing at the Taylor boys while the same fate swirls our way. Let's get going before we're struck by lightning."

Charlie nodded and fell in behind him. They reached the top of the incline and hustled toward the spot where they'd tied their horses. On the way, Charlie kept up a panting discourse, and his topic made Thad weak in the knees. "So what did Bertha say when you told her you're leaving?"

Thad batted branches out of his way as he weaved through the slim, meandering trunks of a sapling grove. He dreaded answering, so he took his time.

Charlie took hold of his arm and hauled him around. "You haven't told her."

The flat statement held the same disbelieving tone Thad had endured from his conscience all week. He leaned his head down and massaged his brow. "There's nothing you can say to me that I haven't already shouted at myself."

Charlie took off his hat and dashed it against his leg. "Except maybe this—Sunday's the day after tomorrow, and then you'll be gone. Bertha will be looking for you, but she won't find you, will she? I hate to state the obvious, my friend, but you're out of time."

Thad turned pleading eyes to Charlie. "Tell me what to do." He paced the clearing, his booted feet causing a riot of sound in the blanket of dry leaves. "Charlie, I'm convinced I haven't told her yet because telling would make it real. And I just don't see how I'm going to leave that girl behind."

Charlie ducked the swinging poles slung over Thad's shoulder then grabbed them out of his hand on the next pass. "Why don't you ask her to wait for you?"

Thad shook his head. "Don't think I haven't considered it. But it wouldn't be fair. To Bertha."

"Don't Bertha deserve the chance to decide for herself?"

"There's more to consider. Her papa would never agree to such a long engagement."

"Marry her, then. Before you leave."

Thad stopped pacing and faced him. "I can't take a new bride with me to military school. And as hard as it will be to leave her now, it would be impossible if we were hitched." He turned on his heels and set off again in the direction of the horses. "I've thought this thing through, and I don't see any other way. I have to leave Bertha, and it's twisting my mind. I think about her every second of the day. I hear her voice in my head. I see her face around every corner."

"Hmm. Is that right? Say, Thad—"

"I tell you, the whole thing is driving me mad."

"Um, Thad?"

Irritation spiked through him. Clearly Charlie had no inkling of how Thad felt or he would allow no diversion from the topic at hand. "Heavens, man! Don't you see I'm in pain here? What is it?"

Charlie cleared his throat. "I'm thinking I must be a little smitten with Bertha myself."

Thad stopped so fast that Charlie ran into him. He turned on his friend, his back as stiff as a picket, and took him by the front of his shirt. "Why would you say such a fool thing?"

Charlie pointed past his shoulder. "Because I'm starting to see her, too."

Thad whirled and followed the direction Charlie pointed. The fleeting figure of a young woman came up the road in the distance, her image flickering as she passed in and out of sight between the trees and high brush. He might've discounted it as a vision, except Charlie saw her, too.

Thad stared hard at the woman's face. "You're right. It is Bertha. What the devil's she doing way out here, and on foot?"

Charlie nudged him. "There's only one way to find out. Come on."

Charlie walked fast toward the road, and Thad followed. They reached it just as the clouds started to make good on their threat and the occasional plump raindrop became a scattered shower.

Bertha, facing down with her hands up to shield her hair, picked up speed. She hurried their way, very distressed by the look of her, and didn't seem to see them yet. Thad cupped his hands around his mouth to call out to her when she raised her head and looked about, likely searching for shelter. Her gaze fell on Thad and Charlie, and she halted, staring as if unable to believe her eyes.

"Stay there, Bertha," Thad called. "We're coming."

He rushed to his horse and mounted in one fluid leap then whirled and rode hard in Bertha's direction. Drawing even with her, he slowed and reached for her hand. She latched on and allowed him to swing her up behind him. Thad felt her arms go around his waist and her cheek rest against his back, and he tasted bliss.

It seemed the space of a heartbeat from the time Bertha saw Thad until he pulled her onto his horse. She sat sidesaddle on the back of the galloping filly, clinging to Thad for all she was worth. The rain came down in sheets now, and she fought the improper urge to crawl up under his shirt. Instead, she cuddled close against the heat of his back and closed her eyes.

The rumbling thunder overhead, pounding hooves beneath her, and the rapid beat of Thad's heart against her face made her feel giddy and reckless. She had no notion where he might be taking her, or why. Such earthly details held no merit. She wanted only to cry out for Saint Peter to open wide the Pearly Gates, because surely the mare would carry them straight into heaven.

Too soon the road to Beulah Land became the trail to Crawford Street when Thad reined firmly to the right and into Julius Ney's pasture. The horse roared up the path to Mr. Ney's barn.

Bertha clung so tightly to Thad she feared for his ribs, but any less of a grip and she'd spring off into mud and certain disaster. No matter how marshy the surface, the harsh summer sun had baked a brick-hard crust on Jefferson's soil. Bertha doubted she'd bounce if she went down.

With Charlie fast on their heels, Thad galloped the horse past the barricaded front of the structure and around back where the wide doors faced the open fields between the barn and the main house.

In the distance, Bertha saw Mr. Ney running from the outhouse, suspenders down off his shoulders and shirttail flapping. He waved a permissive hand in their direction just as they ducked beneath the threshold and dove inside.

Thad eased Bertha to the ground and dismounted. Charlie led his horse to a post in the corner and tied him up. Thad did the same with the mare. When Charlie turned, Bertha couldn't help but laugh. Mud spattered him from head to toe in big gray blotches like the markings on a dappled hound.

Thad followed Bertha's gaze to Charlie then halted and stared. "Followed a mite close to my heels, didn't you, old friend?"

Charlie looked down at himself and grinned. "Never intended to follow. I was trying to gain the lead." He brushed at his clothes. "I'll think better of it next time."

Thad took the handkerchief from around his neck and began blotting raindrops from Bertha's head and shoulders. She watched him while he worked, his face close and intent on the task. When he dried her to his satisfaction, he took a rolled-up blanket from behind his saddle, shook it out, and spread it on the hay. Then he took her arm and led her to it. "Sit on this side. It's still mostly dry." After he saw her well settled, he sat beside her on the blanket, a shy smile on his lips.

He loves me.

The truth of it washed over Bertha, making her feel weak and warm, as if her bones were melted butter. There'd be no more wondering, hoping, praying. Thad loved her, all right, and now she knew.

His actions hadn't confirmed her belief that he cared—any gentleman would do the same for a lady in distress—it was more the manner in which he went about his ministrations. The way he touched her, led her, succored her, with the tenderness a mother might show toward a beloved child. These things gave Thad away, no matter how distant he kept his feelings or how hard he tried to deny them.

Thank You, God.

"Bertha?"

She averted her gaze. She'd been staring. "Yes?"

"Are you cold? I can close the doors."

She shook her head and met his eyes again. A water droplet found its way past his hairline and started a slow trek down his face, pulling her attention to his tanned cheek. Her finger twitched with the urge to touch it. "I'm fine. No need to fret."

He grew suddenly stern. "What in the dickens are you doing out in the woods by yourself? You might've been lost or shot by a hunter." He stopped and raised his brows. "Say, how did you get here anyway?"

"Mose brought me."

His face iced over. "Moses Pharr left you standing in the woods in a thunderstorm? I'll need to say a few words to that bump-headed boy."

She held up her hand. "There's no need, Thad. He's coming right back for me. He promised."

Thad looked skeptical, so she tried to soften him with a smile. "He should be here any minute, in fact."

Charlie loped over to join them, a welcome distraction. He dropped onto the blanket beside Thad and reclined his lanky body, placing both arms behind his head for a pillow. "Sure is cozy in here." He stretched and closed his eyes. "Wouldn't take me a minute to fall asleep."

Thad nudged him. "Wouldn't take you a minute to fall asleep if you were balanced on a broom handle." He winked over at Bertha. "I hear tell Charlie slept his way through the last two years of school."

Charlie poked him back. "Don't believe everything you hear, pilgrim. More like the last three." They laughed together, and then Charlie turned on his side as if ready to demonstrate the virtue of his statement.

Bertha watched him turn and shared a smirk with Thad. But the smile that began as shared amusement blossomed into an intimate meeting of eyes and soul. The encounter caused Bertha's breath to catch. Flustered, she turned away to exhale.

When her breathing settled, she tried to ease the strain between them with small talk. "Mr. Ney did a right fine job on this barn, didn't he?" She let her gaze follow the neat row of new planks along the wall to the sturdy overhead beams. Above their heads, a wide hayloft seemed bursting at the seams with bales, and matching tied bundles lined the walls on the floor.

The smell of fresh-milled pine and cut hay filled the room, mixed with the odor of wet clothes, damp earth, and the headiest scent of all, Thad's hair balm. It smelled of nameless spice and pomade. Mingled with the odor of soap on his cheeks from his shaving mug, it wove an intoxicating halo about him. She grew hesitant to turn his way, because when their eyes met, she felt herself sway toward him against her will.

She stole a sly glance and discovered Thad seemed rattled, too. He focused on his hands, which wouldn't stay still in his lap. She expected at any minute he might sit on them.

Instead, he reached for her hand, pulling her shy fingers with his determined ones, gently tugging until her hand was close enough to gather up and squeeze. The simple gesture made her stomach lurch. The warmth and pressure of his strong hand around hers thrilled her and related how he felt without his saying a word.

"Bertha, there's something I—"

Sloshing footsteps outside cut him off. Mr. Ney appeared in the door of the barn with a feed sack held over his head.

"You kids all right in here?"

Thad struggled to his feet. "Mr. Ney, sir. Yes, we're fine. We just ducked in to wait out the storm." He jabbed a finger toward the slumbering Charlie. "The three of us, I mean. Sure hope you don't mind."

Mr. Ney stepped inside and shook the water from his sack.

"The missus sent me out here to fetch you." He glanced behind him at the pouring rain. "Says you're welcome to sit in the kitchen until this thing blows over."

For some reason, Thad had become as edgy as a cat the moment Mr. Ney appeared. He smoothed one hand through his wet hair and shook his head. "No disrespect intended, sir, but we'll stay put until it slacks off, if it's all right with you. We'd just repay her kindness by tracking half of Texas onto her floors."

Mr. Ney shot a look toward Charlie, who hadn't moved. Then his eyes swept to Bertha. "That all right with you, child?"

Bertha gave him a wide-eyed stare. "Why, yes, sir."

Mr. Ney cleared his throat. "All right, then. I guess that'll be acceptable. But leave this door open, Thad." His attention returned to Bertha, and he pointed behind him at the house. "We'll be just inside. . .if you need us for anything."

Bertha wondered why Mr. Ney acted so stern about such a trifling thing as sitting outside in the barn. She guessed she might never understand the ways of men. She offered Mr. Ney her brightest smile. "Give my best to the missus, won't you?"

He said he would, then with one more weighted look toward Thad, covered his head with the sack and darted for the house. Bertha giggled at the nervous look on Thad's face as he watched him leave.

"I can't imagine how difficult it is to be a man." She had his attention. Likely more by the way she squinted up at him than by her words.

"What do you mean by that?"

"Oh, just that men spend so much time guarding the virtue of women that they forget to safeguard their own."

His mouth drooped in shock. "Bertha Biddie. What a forward thing to say."

"Oh, pooh. It's only the truth. Annie would agree if she were here."

When Thad looked blank, she remembered he didn't know about her new friend. She scurried up and dashed to his side.

"I didn't tell you, did I? I've met the most wonderful person. Her name's Annie Moore, and she's lovely. And elegant. And mysterious. And ever so wise. I've never seen anything like her. I'll wager you haven't, either."

She paused to gulp air then continued. "In a very short time we've become fast friends. Annie's offered to help me with—" She felt her cheeks heat up, so she lowered her lids. "With a most vexing dilemma." Her voice dropped to a whisper. "Annie's just the one to help me, too. I know she is."

She found his eyes again. "I do want you to meet her. Oh, promise you will."

Thad took her by the shoulders and laughed down at her. "Whoa there, sugar. Dig in your spurs. I'll meet Annie twice if it means that much to you."

A cloud fell over Bertha's excitement, heavier than the one over Julius Ney's barn. "The only thing is, I don't know when I'll see her again. The last time I saw her, she was very upset."

Thad's brows puckered in the middle. "What about?"

She gazed up at him, trying to decide if she should speak the whole truth. After all, it was Annie's affair and none of her own. So despite the concern in his big brown eyes, Bertha made up her mind not to tell. "I believe Annie's in terrible trouble. That's all I'm at liberty to say. And I don't know how to help her."

Thad lifted her chin. "I can't imagine what sort of trouble might put such a worrisome look on your face, but there's no trouble in the world bigger than God."

His words struck Bertha's heart like a thunderbolt and kindled fire in her muddled mind. "Oh, Thad, that's it! Annie needs God's help, not mine." She pulled him low and kissed him on the cheek, surprising him by the look on his face. "It's so clear to me now. I know just what to do."

They heard the sound of an approaching wagon at the same time and moved to the door. Voices shouted Bertha's name from the road at the end of Mr. Ney's lane.

"Bertha!" The deep bass bawl had to be Mose.

"Bertha Biddie, where are you?" The high, tinny mewl belonged to Rhodie.

"See! I told you they'd come back for me."

She started out the door, but Thad clutched her arm and pulled her back. "Bertha, wait. I'll take you home."

"I'm not going home. I need to see Annie first."

"Then I'll take you to see Annie."

"It's out of your way."

He held up one hand. "I don't mind. Honest."

It sounded tempting but made no sense. Thad's clothes were soaked through. He needed to get straight home before he came down with a fever. She shook her head. "There's no reason to put you out. Those two are here for me, and they're headed straight into town."

The rain had stopped, but heavy drips fell from the eaves over the barn door. She waited, timing her exit to avoid getting splashed on the head.

Thad moved up behind her, his voice unsettled. "Bertha, there's something I haven't told you."

"We'll talk later. I promise. Don't forget you still have to meet Annie." She turned and patted his arm. "Good-bye, Thad. And thank you ever so much for your advice." Darting out the door, she ran around the barn just as Mose and Rhodie rolled past.

"Wait! I'm here!"

Rhodie whirled on the seat. "Stop, Mose. There she is. Bertha, where were you? We've looked everywhere."

Bertha pointed back at Julius Ney's barn. "I took shelter in there. It started to rain."

Mose gave her a disgusted look. "I guess we know that." He and Rhodie sat atop the unprotected buckboard as wet as two bedbugs on wash day.

Bertha pressed a hand to her mouth to hide her smile. "Let's get going, then. Before it starts up again."

Rhodie moved aside to let Bertha board then elbowed her brother. "Don't get stuck this time."

Mose clucked at the horse and pulled away.

Bertha looked back to find Thad standing outside the barn with a curious look on his face—part longing, part desperation, with a touch of sadness around the edges. She leaned to peer closer, but the jostling wagon had put too much distance between them. She raised her hand in a last merry wave, but Thad didn't wave back.

As she watched, Charlie came around the side of the barn and joined him. He patted Thad on the back with what could only be described as sympathy. Charlie's gesture was the last thing she saw before the two men fell out of sight around the bend of a tree-lined curve.

CHAPTER 8

Sarah leaned closer to the window, so near her breath fogged the glass. She stretched to her tiptoes to peer over the misty spot and checked the road again. No sign of Henry. When he first slipped out, without angry words or slammed doors, her shame and pride had pronounced him weak. With the passage of time, his meekness turned to strength against the memory of her railing fit.

She traded her nightdress and shawl for the torn dress and boots and set out to find him. She soon learned he didn't ride away, because Dandy stood in his stall munching hay. The indisputable sight of the big gray mule meant the wagon would be in its place. Though Henry's rage may have given him the strength to pull it, he'd lack the inclination.

He wasn't in the fields. She roamed the yard and peered in every direction, at first sashaying in a casual way, stealing furtive glances in case he lurked somewhere and watched. The longer she searched, the more scared she became, fear turning her easy sway into determined strides.

Though it made no sense, he had vanished. Unless the Lord had come for his children and left her to stew in her sins, Henry had departed the place on foot—walked when he had a perfectly fine means of transportation lollygagging in the barn.

After one more rambling search of the place, Sarah stumbled back inside to begin her vigil. A glance at the stove reminded her she had placed a towel over the corn bread and set the beans off the fire a good two hours ago. She lifted the lid and stared into the pot. The mingled odor of pintos and ham hock wafted up. Her favorite food. Another day she'd give in to the grumble in her stomach and dish up a bowl, but dread had taken her appetite. She needed to put them away before they spoiled—*Lord knows we have no food to waste*—but she couldn't muster the strength to care. Henry was all that mattered. She had to find him, confess her sorrow over how she had treated him. Again.

Her mind settled, Sarah pulled off the blue gingham dress just long enough to sew up the seam she'd ripped under the arm in angry impatience. Another casualty of her unbridled temper. If she hadn't stripped down and hopped into bed in the middle of the day to pout, she'd never have torn her dress. She held it up, surprised to see a neat row of stitches despite her haste. Slipping it overhead, with more care this time, she ran out the door, without stopping to return the sewing kit to the drawer in the console table or to store the corn bread and beans.

Dandy stood in the same place she'd found him earlier, pulling lazy bites of hay from a handcart in the corner. She slid the bridle onto his head then jerked him away from the hay and over to the saddle rack hanging on the wall. Sarah's size and Dandy's interest in the hay made the task hard, but she got him saddled and led him from the barn, where Henry kept a stool near the fence just for her. She stepped on it and slipped her foot in the stirrup then swung up on Dandy's back and gave him a swat. "Let's go, mule."

Dandy heaved a rebellious sigh against the straps on his belly and listed to the side. Sarah knew what came next. The ornery cuss would side-step to the fence and try his best to rake her off, a trick he knew not to play on Henry. She outsmarted him by lifting her leg just in time, but it was a close call.

"Blast you, Dandy! We got no time for your shenanigans today. You best smarten up and recall who feeds you. If you don't help me find Henry, I'll let you starve, I swear it."

As if he understood every word, the mule took off down the lane, lit out for the road, and gave her no more trouble on the way into town.

The distance to Jefferson was walkable for sure but an easier ride, and Henry had no reason to go there. They only rode in earlier in the day on account of his notion to buy her a treat, the foolish idea that started the whole dreary mess. Common sense said he would be down by the bayou, skipping stones across the water or lying sprawled under a tree to pout. No matter how unreasonable, something led her straight to Jefferson as fast as Dandy could plod.

Once there, Sarah had no idea where to look. She relaxed the reins and let Dandy follow his nose. She hardly expected him to snuffle the ground for his master's scent like old Dickens would've done before he led her straight to Henry. But she reckoned Dandy could put forth more effort than it took to follow the same route he trod every trip into town. She couldn't rightly blame him. It did seem like just another trip to Stilley's to trade skins. She closed her eyes and allowed herself the luxury of pretending it was.

Her eyes flew open when a high-pitched squeal from nearby startled her. Dandy, too, by the way he flinched. She looked toward the grating sound and found it came from Charles Gouldy's sister, Isabella, her face puffy and red, her hair a wild nest of tangles. A strange man, somebody's husband no doubt, had Belle pressed against the wall in a nearby alley. Sarah wondered how much he had paid for a bit of time with her.

Belle turned her painted face toward Sarah as she passed. Her eyes were glazed and her mouth a big red smear. She offered a brazen smile. "Afternoon, Sarah."

Embarrassed, Sarah turned away. Dandy passed up the alley just as the man pulled Belle deeper into the shadows. Sarah shuddered. For all her problems, she wouldn't trade places with Isabella Gouldy if they threw in fame and fortune to sweeten the deal.

Up ahead, Jennie Simpson stepped off Lafayette Street onto

Polk, looking none too spry. She wore a stiff black dress and white apron, but the woman inside the dress had lost her starch. Doc Turner insisted all his help wear the same sort of clothes, except the men, who pranced around in black bow ties and knickers. Most likely Jennie had spent the morning changing beds and cleaning floors behind Doc Turner's paying guests over at Brooks House.

The thought of it caused guilt to twang in Sarah's heart like a chord from a busted fiddle. She knew if not for Henry, she'd be a chambermaid at Brooks House, too. Or maybe the Commercial Hotel. She worked as hard as anyone, but when she smoothed fresh sheets on a bed, she and Henry slid between them that night. And when she wiped a table and served food, she got to sit right down and eat. For all of her trouble, Jennie Simpson got a bent back, calloused hands, and a pitiful, pinchpenny wage. Jennie was another poor soul with whom Sarah wouldn't agree to trade fortunes.

Since her man had given her so much in life, Sarah wondered why she seemed driven to throw it all away. And why she continued to hurt him. She sighed. All roads in her mind led right back to Henry. She wished the one Dandy trudged down now would do the same.

Sarah rode up even with her friend just as she started to cross the street. "Afternoon, Jennie."

Jennie looked up at her with tired eyes. "Why, Sarah King, don't I see you in town most every day of late? Ain't you got enough at home for to keep you busy?"

She waved her hand. "Pissh! Got me more'n enough, thank you kindly. Say, you ain't seen Henry around anywhere, have you?"

Jennie gazed all about as if she expected to see him then shook her head. "Naw," she said, drawing the word out the length of Dandy's ears. "Not since yesterday." She scrunched her chubby face. "Don't see how you managed to lose a man that size. Didn't he ride in with you?"

Sarah cleared her throat. "Not this time."

"Then how'd he get here?"

Sarah avoided the question by standing up in the stirrups and making a show of searching the street. She'd be careful not to say anything more to set off Jennie's curiosity. "Don't fret yourself. I'll find him."

Jennie opened her mouth to speak, but Sarah cut her off. "Girl, you look plumb tuckered. Are you finished for the day?"

Jennie shook her head in exaggerated fashion. "Uh-uh, honey. Don't I wish? I jus' come to fetch a jar of molasses for Doc Turner's tea. He swear by it as a restorative for the blood." She rested the back of her hand on her hip. "S'pose I need some myself to get me through this day. When I get back, I still got me a mess of laundry and two more rooms to clean."

Sarah's heart went out to her. "Sound like you gon' be there most all night."

Jennie reached to stroke Dandy's neck. The old mule's coat trembled in pleasure at her touch. "Don't know why I bother to drag myself to my room some nights, when I got to be back in the main house before sunrise to start all over again."

"Forget about molasses. What you need is a good tonic. Ride out to the house, and I'll give you one made from blessed thistle. It's the best thing there is for the droops."

Jennie's eyes bulged. "You never said you practiced healing arts, Sarah."

"I know how to steep herbs and make remedies. Mama taught me. I have a store of them in fruit jars sealed with wax. Come by when you can, and I'll give you some for what ails you."

Jennie smiled as brightly as if Sarah had offered to dole out redemption. "I'll walk out in the morning a'fore I starts my day at Brooks."

Sarah nodded. "That'll be just fine. I'll look for you."

She glanced around again for Henry but caught no sign of him, so she turned her attention back to Jennie. "Doc Turner have a full house this week?"

"Jus' mostly the usual. The judge and a few more."

"Judge Armistead?"

"Tha's right. He staying a few days." Her eyes grew wide. She pressed against Dandy's side and motioned Sarah closer. "Honey, you ain't seen nothing in your whole life like what done checked into number four upstairs."

Sarah leaned farther down. "Is that right?"

Jennie rolled her eyes "Well, I ain't never seen the like. Them two be a special breed of folk."

"Which two?"

"Some highfalutin couple out of Boston, New York."

"Boston, New York?"

"That's what the gentleman say. I asked him where they come from, and he say, 'We's from Boston, New York.' "

"I thought Boston was in Massachusetts State."

"I don't know nothing 'cept what he tell me. The woman, she ain't said much. Jus' sat there and looked sorrowful. Saddest, most prettiest woman I ever laid eyes on. All done up in floozy clothes like a high-dollar coquette."

"I reckon I know just who you mean. She come into Stilley's today with Magdalena Hayes and little Bertha."

"What you mean, 'with' them?"

"I mean walking in just as big as you please, laughing and talking like long-lost friends. They left together, too."

Jennie clucked her tongue. "What they doing gallivanting about with the likes of her?"

"I can't say, but when they mamas get wind of it—and they will 'cause the whole town's talking—mercy, the fur gon' fly."

Jennie smiled. "The place I'm thinking of ain't got no fur. Missy Hayes and Missy Biddie won't sit to supper for a spell." Jennie's gaze left Sarah and fixed on something across the way. She raised her finger to point. "Looky there. I believe I found something what belongs to you."

Sarah's heart lurched. She peered back over her shoulder to find Henry standing outside of Stilley's. He gazed back at her, but she couldn't read his mood. At the sight of his dear, familiar face, shame washed over her. She lowered her eyes.

"Sarah King."

At the sound of her name, she jerked up and fixed her gaze on him.

He motioned with his head. "Come on over here."

She nodded without saying a word and turned back to Jennie. "All right, then. We'll see you in the morning. You take care, now, you hear?"

"Tha's right, you run on quick when yo' man call. I don't blame you none a'tall. I wish I had me a man to take care of me the way Henry do you." She gave a hearty laugh that jiggled her broad bodice.

Her words pricked Sarah's conscience, but she hid her shame with a bright smile. "Get you some rest, Jennie. Lord knows you need it."

"No, ma'am, not till Sunday." She had already turned to make her way up the street, so Sarah barely heard her last words. "I'll get me some rest on the Sabbath, but not a minute before. Bye, now."

Sarah turned Dandy, which wasn't hard to do now that he'd caught her husband's scent, or maybe the smell of what Henry had stashed in the wrapped package tucked under his arm. When they pulled up beside Henry, his eyes swept her face, as if searching for traces of her spiteful anger. The realization cut Sarah through the middle, especially when his shoulders eased.

They both knew what came next, and it embarrassed her. She would plead for his forgiveness. He would say she'd done nothing to forgive. She hated Henry's tolerance the most. If he'd fuss, hurl accusations, even admit how badly she'd hurt him, and then forgive, she'd feel forgiven. . .instead of unworthy.

Henry peered at the sky. "You shouldn't be here. Get on home. It's clouding up to rain."

"Ain't you coming?"

"I'll be along directly."

She knew she should just go, obey him for once like she'd vowed on their wedding day. "I don't want to go without you. I was so worried, Henry. You ain't never just took off like that." She pleaded with her eyes. "Can't you go with me now?"

He dipped his head and raised a finger toward the horizon. "Woman, them clouds are ripe. They ain't gon' hold off much longer."

"All the more reason for you to come now."

"Dandy's back can't hold us both, and you know it. Somebody be heading our way soon, and I'll hitch a ride."

"We can take turns on Dandy. Better still, I'll walk the whole way if you like. Since you already walked it once."

Henry sighed. The first sign of his dwindling patience. "Fine, Sarah. I guess I'd best go if I want any sleep tonight."

She cringed at the familiar sound of cross resignation in Henry's voice. But it didn't outweigh her relief. She needed her husband at home.

Henry opened Dandy's saddlebag and pushed the package he held deep inside. Then he took the reins from her and set off down the street leading the mule.

Sarah watched his back with a mixture of pleasure and pain. Pain because of the wide sweaty blotch on his shirt, already dry at the edges, which meant he'd walked hard and fast into town despite the sultry heat. Pleasure because he'd agreed to return home with her.

She glanced again at the white-rimmed stain. "Henry, come get up on Dandy. You've walked enough today. Your bunion must be throbbing."

He trudged ahead at a slow, steady pace. "That's all right. I'm fine."

Sarah studied his feet but saw no sign of a limp. Still. . . "I don't mind walking. Honest. I want to."

"I said no."

She bit her lip and focused her anxious energy elsewhere. "It's coming up a mighty blow sure enough. From the north, too. There'll be cold weather in behind it. I figured this heat couldn't last."

Henry raised his head to the darkening sky and mumbled a reply, but she couldn't make out his words.

She tried again. "Guess I never will get used to the mixed-up weather in Texas. In St. Louis, you don't see folks breaking a sweat in the middle of January. Most unreasonable thing I ever saw."

When Henry failed to respond, Sarah decided to hush. They made it a quarter mile in silence until curiosity won out over caution. "Say, what is it you got in this package back here?"

"It'll keep."

The tone of his voice said he'd abide no more questions on the subject, so she held her tongue. But whatever Henry had wrapped in paper and tied up with twine seemed to heat up inside the saddlebag and spread enough warmth through the bag to scorch Dandy's fur, singe the leather saddle, and light a fire in her gut.

She imagined every possibility, from the part Henry ordered for the plow to a new pair of trousers to replace his worn-out pair. He may have bought a bullwhip to keep his ornery wife in line. But knowing Henry, she doubted it.

"Sarah?"

She startled at Henry's sudden, strident voice and all but toppled from Dandy's back.

Before she could answer, he continued without turning around. "I know you'll want to talk things out like always. So if it's all the same to you, I'd rather hash it out before we get home. I need myself some peace at the house." He cleared his throat. "I mean, if it's all right with you."

She winced at Henry's guarded tone. It cast a shadow of condemnation squarely on her head. She'd heard Mama and her aunties whisper about a coarse, abusive wife who kept her husband on a short lead, carrying his dignity chained about her neck. Other husbands ridiculed such men and called them names behind their backs. The thought of herself as one of those women, of Henry as one of those men, made her blood run cold.

"We don't need to talk at all if you'd rather we didn't." Shame rendered her voice so low she wondered if Henry heard her at all.

"No, Sarah, I'd rather get it over and done with. Go on and start."

She tried to comply but found she couldn't speak. She knew her silence might anger him but found it hard to muster the will for a conversation her husband wanted over and done.

Henry glanced over his shoulder. "Fine. If the cat got your tongue, I'll start."

The words stunned Sarah. Henry King mostly kept his emotions dammed up tight. Getting him talking about his feelings generally took a three-day pout followed by two days of nagging. She guessed he must need peace at the house in the worst possible way.

Henry cleared his throat. "When I left the house, I had no place in mind to go. Jus' walked without thinking. When I come to myself, I seen I'd walked all the way to town, but I wasn't even tired. Felt like I'd done sprouted wings and flew."

Henry put a hand back on Dandy's nose to bring him to a stop and came around to stand at Sarah's knee. He stared up at her without speaking at first then reached for her hands where they were clasped together over the saddle horn. "I looked up and saw I done walked a beeline to Stilley's. Then I knew why I came to town."

In one quick move, Henry lifted Sarah down from the mule and stood her in front of him. He clung to her hands, and his eyes bored into hers with fierce emotion. "Today I set out to give you something special to show how I feel about you, and I intend to finish the task." He let go of her hands and reached behind her into the saddlebag.

When he came up with the package and handed it to her, Sarah frowned at him and then at the tied bundle. "What is this?"

He stifled a grin. "If you open it, you might see."

She held his eyes for three heartbeats then got to work on the twine. Impatient with her slow and careful fingers, Henry reached to tear a hole in the paper. When Sarah lifted the other end, white fabric poured out and settled in his hands like woven snow. She jerked her eyes to her husband's face. "What you got here, Henry King?"

His familiar smile warmed her heart. "I ain't completely daft. . .or blind neither. I seen the way you fingered those bolts at Stilley's."

She wiped her palms on her skirt then held them up to receive the soft folds. Struggling to believe she really held it in her hands, she lifted the shimmering cloth in his direction. "Why would you buy me a gift after the way I treated you?"

He wrinkled his brow and gave his head a little shake. "I ain't stopped loving you, woman. I never will. No matter how you treat me."

She cringed and lowered her head. "Why'd you choose white?"

Henry moved closer and cupped her face in his nimble hand. "I know you like all them bright colors. But I sure like to see you dressed in white." He traced the line of her jaw with his finger then lifted her head with one knuckle. "It looks so nice against your skin."

His words reminded her of their conversation that morning, when he'd spoken of the first day they'd met at Lawetta Draper's backyard social and the white dress she wore. From the yearning in his eyes, he remembered, too. He nodded at the cloth. "Hope you don't mind."

She reached up on tiptoe and pressed a soft kiss to his cheek. "Not one bit." She opened the paper to tuck his gift inside but paused and rattled the package. "There's something else down in here." She tucked the fabric under her arm and then reached in and brought out a smaller parcel. She held it up. "Now what's this?"

Henry took it from her hand. "Almost forgot about that." He tore it open to reveal a small chocolate block.

Sarah squealed. "Candy, too?" She reached to grab it, but he held it just out of reach.

"Uh, uh, uh. This one I bought for me." He peeled back the clear wrapper and took a huge bite. Then he closed his eyes and threw his head back while he chewed and swallowed, his face a mask of pleasure. "Ooo-wheee! If that ain't the best thing since pure sweet honey."

Sarah lunged and tugged at his upraised arm. "Stop, now. Give it here!"

He laughed and backed away. She followed until she'd chased him in a wide circle around the mule. He finally stopped and turned.

Still holding the candy far overhead, he pinched off the tiniest bite and pressed it into her mouth. "There," he teased. "Now you know what you're missing."

The small piece delivered a strong, delightful taste, reminiscent of the potent smell and taste in the back of her throat at Stilley's. She wondered at what a full-sized bite would be like.

"Don't tease, Henry. It's mean."

A strong gust of wind bore straight down on them from out of the treetops, followed by a distant clap of thunder. Dandy laid back his ears and shuffled his feet. Sarah felt a raindrop hit the top of her head.

Henry looked to the sky then crossed to Dandy and held up the stirrup. "Climb up, Sarah. Let me get you home before your pretty cloth gets wet."

She rolled the paper around the fabric and hurried to his side. "Put it back in the saddlebag, quick."

He took the package from her and fastened it inside the leather bag then hoisted her into the saddle. He took up Dandy's reins and they started up the path.

"Good thing we almost home." Henry looked back at her with raised brows, winked, and patted his pocket where he'd stashed the candy. "A good rain might ruin my toothsome chocolate."

She waited until he glanced back again, a huge grin on his face.

"Your chocolate, is it? We'll just see about that, Henry King."

CHAPTER 9

Bertha held her shawl above her head, but it proved pointless. She surveyed the mess that made up Mose, Rhodie, and herself and stifled a laugh. Mose's battered hat hung like a woman's bonnet, channeling sheets of water past his chin. Rhodie, so drenched her eyelashes drooped in streaming tangles, sat upright next to Bertha. She had no shawl, given she wore her usual tattered overalls, no longer spattered with mud because the rain had washed them clean. Rhodie accepted the downpour, pelting her head and running off her braids in twin rivulets, the way she accepted most things—with quiet dignity.

The sky had opened up a quarter mile back, just when Bertha figured she'd make it to town high and dry. And no matter how hard Mose flicked the reins or how loudly he bellowed, the overburdened horse had given his all. A slow, lanky pace proved the most the poor creature could muster, hardly enough to save them from a good soaking, though the weather did seem to perk him up. The way his head had lifted and swung from side to side, Bertha reckoned his refusal to hurry might be on purpose, as if he were bent on taking revenge.

Mose raised his voice to be heard over the roar of the pounding rain. "We have to turn here, Bertha. Can't take you clear to town.

Our pa will be watching for us in this weather."

Rhodie picked up Bertha's hand. "Come, go home with us. You can dry off and change into something warm. Our baby sister's garb should fit you fine."

Bertha shook her head. "Just drop me by Magda's place. I need to see her anyway."

Rhodie scrunched up her face. "Are you sure?"

Bertha smiled at the wringing-wet girl. "Yes, but thanks."

They lumbered to the lane up ahead, hardly more than a rut that had been cut through the trees on each side. Overgrown branches crowded the entry, causing recent travelers to veer to the right, if the circle of tracks in the high grass were any sign. Past that point, what had been the long byway to Magda's house now appeared to be a wide, shallow lake.

Bertha placed a hand on Mose's arm. "Stop here. You'll just get stuck if you turn down there. I can walk across the pasture where the ground's higher."

Mose pulled back on the reins, and she climbed down and sloshed around to where he leaned over waiting to speak to her. "You gonna be all right? I sure don't like leaving you out here."

Bertha looked to the sky where the cloudburst had dwindled to a hard shower. The murky clouds that once swirled over their heads had slid off to the southern horizon and piled up over the town of Marshall like a billowing swarm. "It's slacked off now. Looks like it's blowing to the south."

Mose stared down at her, chubby bottom lip laced behind his top row of teeth. "Ain't you cold?" he asked, releasing it. "Feels like a norther's done snuck in behind that front."

As if to underscore his statement, a strong gust howled through, shaking the wagon and raising the hair on Bertha's neck. She wrapped her arms around herself and shivered.

Mose shook his head then turned around to dig under the seat. "Ain't we got a blanket under here somewhere, Rhodie?"

Rhodie nudged him with her shoulder. "It's wet, Mose."

Bertha pointed up the path to the tumbledown shack where

Magda lived. "Don't fret yourself, Mose. Look. I'm nearly there."

Rhodie leaned behind Mose's back to point at Bertha's shoes. "Don't see how you plan to make it in them infernal things."

Bertha looked down at her feet. The low leather pumps were soaked and filled with muck where they gaped at the ankles. Wet grass plastered the pointed toes, and rust-colored pine needles threaded the delicate buttoned straps in a scattered crisscross.

She smiled up at Rhodie. "Better than bare feet, but just barely."

Rhodie giggled. "Sounds like a limerick."

Mose nodded toward the field. "Be watchful of snakes out there." Then he faced forward and released the brake. "We'd best get going. Pa will be in a stew."

He jerked the reins, and the wheels started to roll. Without thinking, Bertha stepped back to avoid being splashed with muddy water then smiled at the futile notion.

Rhodie turned on the seat and raised her hand to the sky. "Bye, Bertha."

Bertha waved back. "Much obliged for the ride."

She waited until they'd gone a respectable distance then lifted her soggy skirt and pulled plastered petticoats away from her legs. Holding the whole sodden mess in her hands, she jumped the ditch, nearly landing on her bottom on the other side. She fought for balance then picked her way to higher ground, came close to losing her shoe in a soft spot, and shuddered when more thick mud spilled over the instep.

Halfway across the pasture, dodging crawdad mounds and roving clusters of homeless ants, she wished she'd been less stubborn and taken Rhodie up on the offer of shelter and dry clothes. Or Thad's offer to take her home, for that matter. He'd have seen her straight to her doorstep, dry as gunpowder. And it might've given him the chance to say what seemed to be gnawing at him.

The last few yards to Magda's house put her in floodwater up to her ankles. She thought of her new bronze heels and tried not to imagine the look on Mama's face when she saw them, but at least the water sifted the sludge from between her toes. Thankfully, there was no sign of snakes.

The door opened before she reached it, and Magda's mama appeared on the stoop with a blanket. She rushed to Bertha the second she stepped up on the porch, enveloped her in scratchy wool, and hauled her inside as if pulling her to safety.

"Ach, Bert'a! Your *mutter* knows you're out in *das schmuddelwetter?*"

Bertha drew the cover closer and stamped her feet before she entered the house. "Foul weather, indeed, Mrs. Hayes. Bless you for taking in a poor drowned wretch."

Mrs. Hayes scurried to the hearth, scooted a low stool in front then waved Bertha closer. "*Bitte kommen.* Sit by the fire, *kleine.* Ve roast dem feets lest you're taken vit fever."

Bertha smiled. *Kleine* meant "little one," yet Magda's mama stood no taller than Bertha, her body as slight as a hummingbird. And the braided blond ropes that crowned her head made up a fair portion of any weight she carried.

Tiny Gerta Fricks had traded the home country and her German culture for big Jacob Hayes of Nacogdoches before coming to settle in Marion County. Magda took after her big-boned papa's side of the family and could easily lift her mama straight off the ground. Magda's papa came from mixed culture himself, his father a Texan, his mother a Sicilian immigrant.

For the first time, Bertha noticed Magda at the stove. She stood with her back to them and seemed in no hurry to turn around. Bertha knew she would still be miffed because they called her a talebearer. But Magda's mishandling of a confidence reminded Bertha of a quote she'd read by C. C. Colton: *"None are so fond of secrets as those who do not mean to keep them."* Only Magda never betrayed a trust on purpose. It seemed the weight of the secret pressed the words right out of her mouth.

Still, Magda was Bertha's dearest friend, and she felt bound to make amends. She sidled up behind her. "Hey there."

No answer. Magda lowered her left hip and shifted her body away.

Bertha tried again. "Say, what's in the pot? Sure smells tasty."

Magda paused her stirring and raised her face to the ceiling. "It's sauerkraut, Bertha. You hate sauerkraut."

"Sauerkraut? Why, fancy that. I'd never have guessed." She moved a bit closer. "You must've done something clever to make it smell so nice."

Magda didn't speak. Just went back to pushing the pungent shreds of cabbage around a skillet with a broad wooden spoon.

"Come, Bert'a. Sit and take off dem shoes, *liebchen*. Dey are soaked clean through."

Bertha waved toward Mrs. Hayes, her attention still on Magda's back. "Yes, ma'am. One second, please." She took a step closer to the stove. "I came to talk to you, Magda. It's real important. Come sit by the hearth for a spell, won't you?"

Mrs. Hayes scurried to her daughter and took the spoon from her hand. "Dis kraut is done, Magdalena. You von't make it any more so by vorrying de life out of it." She set the spoon on a saucer and shoved the heavy pan to the back of the stove. "Go now, *Tochter*. Stoke the fire for your friend and sit vit her." The tiny woman nudged Magda aside with her hip. "Dat's right, go on. Go help Bert'a vit dem shoes. And fetch hot vahter for her feet."

Magda scooted to the side at her mama's urging but stood like a headstrong statue, as rigid as the cast iron stove.

Bertha gathered the blanket tighter under her chin and closed the space between them. "Very well. If you won't come sit with me, I'll stand with you. Of course, there's a draft through here, and it's caused me quite a chill. My teeth are starting to chatter." She edged closer. "It's likely you can hear them if you listen. I'm sure to come down with lung fever."

She leaned around to look. Magda still scowled, so she tried again. "My feet are so cold I can't feel my pinkie toes or their nearest neighbors. I imagine they're as blue and shriveled as dead toads." When this brought the hint of a grudging smile to Magda's face, Bertha went on. "If I find them loose inside my shoes, I'll save them for Thad. They'll make good catfish bait."

The words melted Magda's resolve like honey in hot tea. Her

stingy smile became a generous toothy grin that brightened her eyes and lifted the apples of her cheeks. "Hush your crazy talk and go over by the fire before your silly words come to pass." The power of her smile dimmed a bit when she turned to stare into Bertha's eyes. "I'll fetch water for your dirty feet, just like our Savior did for His betrayer." She flipped the hand towel from the counter over her shoulder and lifted a washtub from the corner. Then she glanced back at Bertha, her smile completely gone. "But you owe me an apology, Bertha Maye Biddie. I intend to get it if you'd like me to ever speak to you again."

Thad turned his horse. He couldn't just ride home and let another day pass without telling Bertha he was leaving. He never should've let her get away from him again. But she'd been so upset about whatever bee buzzed inside her bonnet, the weight of her excitement pushed aside his important news. But the time had come to fess up. He had handed off the fishing gear to Charlie along with a promise to tell Bertha before the sun went down. He pressed the edges of his heels to the horse's side. If he hurried, he could catch up to them.

He thought of Bertha unprotected in such heavy rain and winced. If she became ill, he'd blame himself. He never should've let her go off with that scatter-thought Moses Pharr. The boy only paid attention to cypress wood and a well-turned ankle and had trouble juggling between the two. He lacked the common sense required to find shelter for Bertha and Rhodie.

As if to confirm his thoughts, the fresh wagon tracks never veered from the road, where they might've sought relief at a farmhouse or under a thick grove of trees, but carried on straight through the mud.

He glanced up the road and sighed then felt his jaw tighten.

Wait'll I get my hands on that careless boy.

CHAPTER 10

Bertha's gaze followed the row of bundled herbs that hung drying over the mantelpiece from a length of twine like laundry pinned to a clothesline. She recognized some, like the puccoon Mrs. Hayes used for red dye and the root of Dutchman's-pipe, a remedy for snakebite. Most of the fragrant bunches she'd never seen before but guessed they played a big part in the wonderful German meals Magda's mama stirred up.

The chimney corner in Magda's house had become the hub of the family wheel. The fireplace took up most of one wall in the tiny two-room dwelling and served the household well. The women used it to roast meat and vegetables, boil water, even make coffee when they had the stove tied up with other chores. Along with the wood-burning stove, it provided a source of heat when the weather turned cold. Magda, an only child with no warm siblings to curl up with, slept near it for warmth in the wintertime.

To the left of the fire pit, in back of the low, sturdy stool where Bertha perched, stood a box filled with split oak, fuel to feed the benevolent fire. On the right, behind where Magda stood, barrels of dried corn were pushed into the corner, the drums so full a few ears spilled out onto the floor. Staggered in front of the corn was a collection of baskets overflowing with plump new pecans, some in husks, others shucked down to their mottled shells.

Bertha loved the room. The sights and smells that dwelled in the Hayes kitchen always set her stomach to rumbling even if she'd just had a respectable meal.

"Watch out, now. It's hot."

Bertha snapped to attention and lifted her feet so Magda could set the pan of water on the smooth stones of the hearth. But she barely got her toes wet before she jerked them back. "Too hot!" She held the sides of the stool to maintain her balance while her feet dangled precariously over the steaming water. "Did you do it on purpose?"

Magda slid the pan to the side so Bertha could lower her legs, sloshing at least a quart of the scalding water onto the floor. It ran along the mortared lines and deep cracks, spilling over into the flames with a snap and sizzle. "Don't talk foolish. I'm not mad enough to disfigure you. Though I may have the right to be."

"Aus einer Mücke einen Elefanten machen," Magda's mama called over her shoulder. She leaned against the sideboard across the way, cutting venison into lean red chunks.

Magda rose up and frowned at her. "You're supposed to take my side, Mama. I'm your daughter, remember?" She pointed at Bertha. "This here's a neighbor child." She crossed to the table and returned with a pitcher of cold water to pour into the metal pan on the floor. Still pouting, she cast a sullen look at her mama. "Honestly, sometimes you act like it's the other way around."

Bertha peeked up at Magda. "What did she say?"

Magda laid the back of her hand on her hip. "She said I'm making an elephant out of a mosquito. Her way of saying I'm blowing things out of proportion." She took a poker from the corner and bent over to stir up the fire but twisted around to look at her mama while she worked. "Another German proverb. Just what we need around this house. Thank you, Mama."

"Yer velcome."

Magda tossed the poker aside and flapped her hands in frustration. "Mama! Why do you always defend Bertha? You don't even know what our quarrel is about." She gave Bertha a meaningful stare then leaned down next to her ear. "That's right," she hissed in a forced whisper. "She doesn't know a thing about it. Just like I promised."

Bertha considered it most prudent not to respond. She busied herself with checking the heat of the water then eased her feet down into the pan.

Mrs. Hayes scraped the diced meat into a wide stew pot and replaced the lid. "I go now and give you girls a little privacy. Only keep one eye on dis Rehragout, vill you, Magda? Don't allow your little spat to ruin your papa's meal." A satisfied smile softened her face. "You know how Papa likes my venison stew." She took off her apron, wiped her hands with it, and left it in a heap on the table. "Look, dere's no more rain. I tink I go help Papa vit chores."

She lifted her coat from a peg by the door then turned for one last word before she went out. "Have yourselves a nice little talk, girls." She squinted one eye and leveled it on Magda. "But have dis ting over and done before I come back vit Papa. Ja?"

The obstinate look on Magda's face told Bertha she felt no pressing need to settle the *ting* between them. But she lowered her head and regarded her mama with raised brows.

"Yes, ma'am."

As soon as the latch clicked behind Mrs. Hayes, Magda stalked into her parents' tiny bedroom and came out with another stool. She dropped it in front of Bertha so hard the three legs did a clattering dance, until Magda's weight settled them onto the floor. Seated directly across from the pan, she stripped off shoes and stockings, pulled back her dress, and crowded her sizable feet in alongside Bertha's.

Bertha watched her until she looked up. "What are you doing?"

"Soaking my feet. I never meant this water for you. Not in my heart. I only let Mama think I fetched it for you."

Her smile reminded Bertha of an overindulged child.

She flicked her first finger in the direction of Bertha's feet. "So kindly withdraw yourself from my foot soak."

"Magda. . ."

Magda wriggled her feet around Bertha's until she had forced her ankles to the sides. "Fine. Keep them there, but you'll have to take whatever room is left and be happy with it. I drew this water for me."

Bertha eased her toes from under Magda's. "For corn's sake. This is silly."

"Oh? Silly, is it? But I thought you liked silly. After all, you like silly city women well enough. You like their silly laughs, their silly clothes, and their silly candy. Seems to me silly would set just fine with you." Magda spouted her tirade in a low, even voice, but the pain laced through it struck Bertha's heart like a piercing shout.

"I came here to apologize."

Magda crossed her arms. "Did you bring a list? Because you'll need it."

Bertha hung her head. "Where do I start?"

"With not trusting me, maybe? Or forgetting who happens to be your best friend?"

Bertha rose up and gasped. "I'd never forget that."

Magda's feet stopped warring for position in the pan, and her whole body stilled. She turned her face to the fire and seemed to study the dancing yellow flames while tears on her cheeks glimmered in the reflected light. "You made me feel like a bother, like unwelcome company." She took a ragged breath and shook her head. "I've never felt so bad in your presence, Bertha." She looked up and sought Bertha's eyes. "I don't ever want to again." Magda's tears flowed freely now that the dam had burst, and she wiped her nose on her apron.

Bertha stood up in the pan and leaned to wrap her arms around Magda's neck. The awkward angle of her feet, still curled on each side of Magda's, rendered her bent and bowlegged, but she didn't care. "I'm sorry, sugar. I never meant to hurt you. Can you ever forgive me? I'll do whatever it takes to make it up to you. I swear."

"Don't swear. You know you're not supposed to."

"Promise, then. I promise on my life."

"You don't have to go that far. I'll just take your word that you'll never do it again. A mite less costly than your life, don't you think?"

Bertha laughed and nodded. "Just a mite."

"But you have to mean it, Bertha. If I know you mean it, I'll forget it completely and not hold it to your account."

Bertha drew back to look her in the eye. "I mean it. On my honor, I mean it."

Magda gave a solemn nod. "All right, then."

Bertha leaned to kiss her ruddy cheek. On impulse she kissed her cheek again then twice more on the other side.

Magda squealed and pushed her away. "You don't have to get me all soggy. And speaking of soggy, kindly sit down before you land bottoms-up in this bucket."

The words had barely left her mouth when Bertha lost her footing, and her toe slid hard against Magda's side of the pan. She squealed in pain and thrashed wildly to regain her balance. Magda caught both her hands and held on while she lowered her backside onto the stool.

She picked up her foot and scowled down at the throbbing big toe. "Look what you made me do. If this thing puffs, it won't fit into my shoe." She looked up at Magda and found her smiling. "Stop it, now." She held her toe higher. "This hurts to beat all."

Magda's grin turned to a belly laugh. "I imagine it smarts, all right, but I'm not laughing at your toe. I'm laughing at your ruckled-up face." She pointed at Bertha's shoes drying in front of the fire. "It's about as puckered as those poor things, which, by the way, will never fit you again, swollen toe or not."

Bertha followed Magda's gaze to the crumpled brown shoes on the hearth. "And that will be a bother to everyone but me. Those things were fashioned in the pit of perdition."

"But what will your mama say?"

"Oh, she'll be scandalized. She'll pester and fuss for days and make me work off their cost with chores." Bertha winked at Magda. "And it will be a small price to pay to never have them on my feet again."

He had found her.

Thad knew the deeper ruts meant Mose had stopped long

enough for the weight of the wagon to sink the wheels a bit in the soft mud, and there were marks on the ground from restless hooves. They'd stopped, all right, and the lone set of footprints that led to the swollen ditch in front of Magdalena Hayes's house meant Bertha would be inside.

Runoff rain poured into the trench, causing it to crest. Bertha had jumped it before it filled; otherwise she'd never have made it across the rushing surge. And the lane was completely gone, swallowed up by standing water. She may have walked up to the house, but she'd never make it out on foot.

He turned his horse, jumped the ditch, and rode across the pasture to the house. Magda's parents came out of the barn and picked their way across the higher ground in back of the property. Thad waved and they waved back; then he rode up to where they waited on the porch.

Tall, potbellied Mr. Hayes wore the same wide grin on his face he had plastered there the first time Thad ever saw him. According to local legend, he was born with it and couldn't change expressions if he tried. The man pushed back his hat with two fingers and beamed in Thad's direction.

Thad worked hard not to look straight at him, because the infectious nature of the jolly gentleman's smile made it impossible to keep a straight face. He returned the wife's nod instead. "Good day, folks."

"Thad," Mr. Hayes said, as if apprising Thad of his name, "what you doing way out here on a day like today?" His brows, raised in twin peaks over laughing eyes, told Thad he already knew.

Thad squirmed in his saddle and pointed back over his shoulder. "Me and Charlie—Charles Gouldy, that is—were over yon way, fishing."

"Catch anything?"

"Not this time. Seems we were the ones caught. Out in the storm, I mean."

"Where's Charlie now?"

"Well, sir, he rode on home." In his nervous state, Thad allowed his gaze to linger too long on the older man's face and right away felt his mouth begin to twitch.

"And you didn't?" Mr. Hayes found so much humor in Thad's discomfort, the tops of his cheeks reddened from the strain of overtaxed muscles.

Thad lowered his head. "No, sir, I didn't. I came out here to see about—"

Mr. Hayes held up his hand. "Don't tell me, now. Let me guess. You started out this day a-fishing, and now you've come a-hunting." He pointed back toward the house. "A mighty fine tracker you are, too, since your prey sits cornered inside that door. Get on in there, boy, and flush her out."

Thad looked to Mrs. Hayes for help but found no comfort in her toothy smile.

"Ja, go inside, Thad. A bowl of venison stew should sit vell on such a day."

Thad tipped his hat. "I won't likely turn down such a fine offer on a good day, ma'am, much less on this dreary afternoon. If you're sure there's enough. . ."

"There's more than plenty, son," Mr. Hayes boomed. "And I can smell it from here. Get down from there and come on in."

Thad dismounted and tied his horse to the porch rail. By the time he made it to the top step, Mr. Hayes had opened the door. From somewhere past the entrance came shrill laughter and a spate of uproarious giggles.

Mr. and Mrs. Hayes exchanged a look.

"What them gals up to, Gerta?"

She gave him a vacant stare. "I couldn't say, Yacob."

Grinning, Mr. Hayes led the way past the entry with his wife on his heels. Thad, burning with curiosity now that he'd recognized Bertha's laugh in all the glee, brought up the rear. When Jacob and Gerta Hayes parted before him like the Red Sea, Thad smiled every bit as widely as Mr. Hayes.

CHAPTER 11

It started to rain in earnest as Sarah and Henry pulled past the gate. They barely got Dandy inside the barn before the sky opened all the way up. Behind the rain came a chill, blustery wind that rattled the wide doors and raised the hair on Sarah's neck.

She left Dandy in Henry's care and hightailed it to the house to kindle a fire. When the flames blazed high and hot, she put the kettle on and ran shivering to their room, pulling the gift from Henry out of the saddlebag as she went. Dropping the wet leather bag on the floor outside the bedroom door, she stepped inside and carefully placed the wrapped parcel in the middle of the bed.

She peeled out of her blue gingham dress and threw it over the door to dry, certain she'd never changed in and out of the same garment so many times in one day. The square of linen cloth she pulled from the bar on the washstand to blot her wet hair reminded her of her new fabric, so she crossed to the bed where the package lay. Wiping her hands on the linen rag, she laid it aside to open the end of the wrapper and shake the material out onto the quilt.

She wondered at Henry's choice. Not that the sight of it didn't set her heart racing and make her limp with joy. But she couldn't imagine where in their dusty country house she might store it, much less where in their dusty Texas town she might wear it. If they were still in St. Louis, it would be different.

Sarah smoothed one finger over the glistening white weave.
The cloth was truly the most beautiful thing she'd ever seen, much
less owned. What a lovely dress it would make.

And I know exactly which one it should be.

She dropped to her knees and reached under the bed, using the
feel of the boxes against her fingers to find the right one. When she
had hold of it, she pulled it out into the light. The wooden crate
held every favorite gown that ever belonged to her or her mama. Of
course they weren't really garments anymore, just the cut-out parts.
The tied-up bundles resembled stacks of puzzle pieces more than
clothes—an arm here, skirt there, a bodice and back. Whenever
Sarah got ready to make a new frock, she'd choose from one of the
old fabric puzzles and cut out a pattern. Sometimes she mixed and
matched just for fun.

Near the bottom of the box she found the right one and slid it
from under the rest. The dingy pieces were wrinkled and smelled
of camphor, but no matter. She'd wash and press them before she
started. The pattern would fit her too small now, but she would
adjust for that when she traced.

A tender smile stole over her face when she held up the stack of
cloth pieces that had once been a sassy white dress, the same one she
wore to Lawetta Draper's house the day she first laid eyes on Henry.
It might need a touch here and there to make it more stylish, but
she'd chosen the perfect pattern.

When the kettle on the stove began to whine, she shoved the
crate back under the bed away from Henry's prying eyes and tucked
the new fabric in the bottom dresser drawer. Then she shimmied
into her housedress and scurried into the kitchen.

In the darkest corner of the pantry sat a small red tin where
she kept the last of the tea leaves given to her by Miss Susan Blow,
her former mistress and teacher. Miss Susan gave the tea to Sarah
during her last visit home to see Papa. The kettle came from Miss
Susan, too. Sarah brought it with her when she first left the French
settlement in St. Louis and moved to Jefferson.

The most precious gift her teacher gave her was an education, a prize with no value in her new hometown. It seemed the longer she stayed where people considered her ignorant, the more ignorant she became. Some days she wished Miss Susan hadn't bothered.

Sarah picked up the tin, pried off the lid, and drew in a deep whiff of the pungent plant. The familiar smell built a bridge in her mind from Texas to Missouri. It carried her along the river, past St. Louis to the wide streets of Carondelet. There it wound through the rooms of Miss Susan's fine house then straight to the Des Peres School, Miss Susan's kindergarten where Sarah used to cook for the children.

She sighed and pulled a small wad of dried leaves from the can. Before closing it, she peered inside and mourned the fact there was barely enough left for one more pot. Relaxing her fingers, she allowed a few leaves to fall back into the can and dropped the rest into the steaming kettle. Closing the lid, she set it aside to steep.

Henry stepped up onto the porch, whistling and stamping the mud off his feet the way he always did when he came in from the barn. The screen door squealed behind her.

"Get yourself out of those damp clothes," she said without looking back. "And don't bother hanging them up. After the way you sweated today, they'll be stinking without a wash."

Sarah waited for him to grumble. The trousers he wore were his favorite pair, the only britches he owned without holes in the knees. When he didn't say a word, she turned to see why. Henry stood by the door unbuttoning his shirt with one hand and gnawing on her chocolate with the other.

"Put that away now. You're bound to ruin your supper."

"Can't hep it. This ain't ordinary candy. It's black magic." He used the back of his hand to slide a stray piece from his bottom lip into his mouth. "Once you start in on it, you lose the power to stop."

"Let me help you with that." She hustled over and swiped the sweet treat out of his hand, wound the wrapper around it, and took it to the pantry—picking up the red tea can on the way. When she came out, Henry's gaze latched on and followed her around the room. Sarah grew fidgety under his meddlesome stare and spun around to face him. "What is it now?"

"What's what?"

"Why are your peepers glued to me? Has my face turned blue?"

His big brown eyes, still so intent, narrowed and crinkled. "Naw, your face still dark and sweet like that chocolate but stronger magic than any old candy."

A warm flush crept up her neck, but she kept her guard up. "Fine. Now answer my first question. Why you looking at me in such a way?"

Henry lifted one broad shoulder. "Jus' noticed you making tea, I guess."

She stiffened. "And what of it?"

"Means you homesick again, that's all."

"What you going on about, Henry?"

"Woman, I didn't meet you yesterday. You go to making that tea, it means you thinking 'bout St. Louis and Miss Susan's house."

Sarah turned back to the sink. "What a fool thing to say. When I make tea, it means I have a hankering for a cup, that's all. Don't go readin' things where there ain't no writin'. Go wash for supper, now. I'll have food on the table before you're done."

Henry laughed and raised his hands in surrender. "Yes'm, Missy King. I'll do like I's told."

He pulled off his shirt and wadded it into a ball then started toward the hallway door. When he stopped just short of it, Sarah cringed. It would be nice if he'd just leave it be, but she knew he wasn't about to.

"I reckon I know why you act how you do 'bout folks 'round here."

She snorted. "I know, too. They're cruel, narrow-minded bigots, every last one of them."

He turned from the door, big hands busy rolling his shirt. "You seem right fond of little Bertha."

"Miss Bertha's different, her and Magda both. They speak to

me no matter who's watching. They don't wipe their hands on their skirts if our fingers touch. Least not where I can see them."

"You act like Bertha and Magda the only good folks in this town. They's jus' as many good apples in the barrel as bad."

Sarah feigned shock. "Where they hiding the good crop, then? All I come across are sour and wormy."

Henry's face puckered like sun-dried corn. "Like I said, I know why you act how you do. I reckon you're jus' mad all the time. But it ain't the people 'round Jefferson you're mad at."

She dropped her dishrag on the sideboard and propped one hand on her hip. "It ain't, huh?"

"No, ma'am, it ain't."

"Well, who am I mad at?"

"Me."

He might've said Dickens and made more sense. Sarah waited to see if he meant the witless words. He stood not moving a muscle, his face a blank wall. She cocked her head. "Why would you say so foolish a thing?"

He uncoiled the shirt ball and slung it across the kitchen. "Weren't it me what took you away from St. Louis? From your papa, Miss Susan, and the schoolhouse?"

"Henry, St. Louis is over and done. Jefferson's my home now."

He challenged her with a look. "You can't tell me you don't miss it every day."

Now he'd sashayed too close to the truth, his prying words plundering near that place in her heart she kept all to herself. She picked up the rag again and went to work cleaning the stove. "Quit spewing nonsense. If you don't let me get supper done, you won't eat tonight."

He closed the gap between them and grabbed her arm. "You told me I'm reading what ain't wrote. Well, now you wiping up what ain't spilt." He took the rag from her hand and tossed it in the corner along with his shirt. "Stop all this dancing around the truth. You wish you'd never left St. Louis. I know you do."

The pigheaded man had stumbled right onto it—the only place

in her heart he didn't belong—and his blunder made her mad enough to tell him.

She jerked her arm free. "You want to know so bad? Well, here it is. Miss Blow treated me like a person. Like I mattered in this world. She taught me to read and write, cipher numbers, to talk like a lady, not the child of a slave." Sarah glared up at him. "I don't miss St. Louis. Or Carondelet, or my house, or the school. Not even Miss Blow, though I love her with all my might." Pushing his hands away, she backed into a tight wad. "I miss feeling good about myself, Henry King. I miss walking proud along the street instead of slinking like a hang-tailed dog."

Henry pressed her to the stove and pulled her struggling body close. "Hush, baby girl," he cooed against her hair. "I'm so sorry. I didn't know you hurt this bad. God, help me, I jus' didn't know." Shame masked his face. "You was happy in St. Louis, and here I come along and take you away from there. You followed me to Jefferson without a peep or a mutter, and look at what a sorrowful trade you done made. A broken-down farm and two sorry old mules for your trouble."

Sarah sniffed. "Two?"

He nodded toward the barn. "One out yonder with his face in a feed bag and the other right in front of you."

Her stomach lurched. She unfurled from the wretched place she'd allowed herself to go and took hold of his face with both hands. "Don't you say that, you hear? I could do without Dandy, but my life would be a wearisome mess without you."

Henry tried to pull away, but she held him fast. "Look at me, now. Don't you know I can survive any sorrow as long as you're by my side?"

He looked down at her, the challenge back in his eyes. "Anything?"

She stilled. "I thought we agreed not to talk about that."

"I reckon it's a good day for airing things out."

Sarah pressed her forehead to his bare chest and ran the palm of her hand down the back of his head. Stopping at his neck, her fingers lingered there and caressed the smooth, warm skin. "There's no way of knowing why we haven't had children, Henry. It could just as likely be down to me."

She raised her head and sought his eyes. "Mama always said these things are best left to the wisdom of the good Lord, and I agree. It's only been four years. We could still—"

His finger on her lips stifled the rest. "Don't say no more. Four years is enough time to give it. I ain't wasting no more hope. But I can't help thinking you'd have settled in better if we'd had a child."

Seeing his tears flooded her eyes. She pushed away and wiped her cheeks with her palms. "How'd we get back on this same old tired subject?"

Henry shrugged. "Don't we always?"

"I guess we do." Lifting on her toes, she kissed him on the cheek. "Will you kindly go wash for supper now? You've stirred enough trouble for one day, even for you."

He swatted her behind, the old Henry once again. "If I clear my plate, can I have me some more of that chocolate?"

Sarah went back to her stove. "I believe you've had quite enough. Besides, I might like one more little taste before it's all gone."

"I reckon Dandy would, too."

She glanced back at his too-innocent face. "What did you say?"

"I said Dandy might want him one more bite. That old mule sure liked it."

She swiped at him. "You ain't fed my candy to that no-'count critter!"

Henry laughed and dodged. "Jus' a taste. But he sure was hankering for more."

"Well, I hope he enjoyed it, because neither one of you sorry mules will see another morsel of it." His words from moments before came back to her, and she wanted to whack off her tongue. But he still grinned like he didn't notice, so she hit him with the towel.

"Git on, now. And don't come back until you're fit for the table."

Smiling, Sarah watched him leave the room. Their talk had lifted some of the weight from around her heart. They should try it more often.

She turned back to the stove and gasped. *The tea!*

Lifting the pot, she raised the lid to peer inside at the oily dark brown liquid.

Ruined.

It had been left to steep far too long, and the result would be a bitter, distasteful brew. Given the way the day had gone so far, it seemed a fitting addition to scorched beans and crumbly, dried-up corn bread.

CHAPTER 12

T had tried hard to turn away. His mama would expect no less of him. But it wasn't every day he saw two grown women—though the scene before his eyes made him question that estimation—standing in a bucket of water. There they were, Magda and his own little Bertha, up to their calves in a washtub. They clung to each other, inching their way in a tight circle and laughing like addlepated loons.

Gerta Hayes reacted as if miles of skin were showing, instead of the two inches of bare leg above the line of the pan. "Girls! Vot on earth? Cover yourselves!"

The two froze and looked her way, but the hilarity didn't leave their tear-streaked faces until they spotted Thad. Then the jostling in the pail increased tenfold as they worked their way around to their stools and sat down hard. The visible skin disappeared to the point where Thad knew their hems had gone under.

Mr. Hayes, evidently content to let his wife fend for their modesty, never flinched. But his curiosity proved less restrained. "What y'all doing, Magda? Ain't never seen that jig danced before. Least not in a tub of water."

The red-faced girls, still feet-first in water like a pair of wading ducks, watched owl-eyed as their audience drew near.

"Answer your papa, Magdalena, and be quick about it."

Magda averted her eyes and lowered her head. Bertha, cute as a newborn calf even with her mouth agape, gawked at Thad.

When Mr. Hayes cleared his throat, Magda dared to raise her eyes. "Sorry, Papa. We were turning, see?" She twirled her finger in the space between them. "To opposite sides."

Bertha awoke from her daze and pointed behind her. "The fire. It got too hot on the one side."

Magda nodded. "So we turned."

"Yes, to the cooler side."

Thad groaned at the manner in which they had stumbled into Mr. Hayes's web. Innocent lambs to the slaughter.

The older gentleman stepped forward, nodding his head. "Oh yes, I see it now." He glanced behind him, his expression sincere. "Don't you see it, Thad?"

Thad could only grin and wait.

"So, girls. . .what you're saying is you were done on the one side, so you flipped over to roast the other'n." He fell forward, clutching his knees to stay upright, and laughed at his own joke. He pointed at the pan and all but shouted as he delivered the kicker. "I see you saved some time by sitting in your own basting sauce."

Mr. Hayes's laughter turned out to be more contagious than his smile, and Thad felt his good breeding start to slip. His own grin turned to a chortle then a full-blown howl. He leaned into Magda's papa to stay upright, and the two braced each other while they laughed. The girls pouted at first, but a quick glance at each other's faces set them off, too. The only sane person in the house stood scowling from the stove.

"You two best be glad this stew's not ruined. Now hush, all of you, and come to supper."

Thad followed Mr. Hayes to the table, still wiping his eyes. He tried to avert his attention from the circus ring near the fireplace but found the performance too engaging. His headstrong gaze wandered there against his will.

Magda pulled her skirt free from where she had wadded it under her sash and stood up. Bertha, the most fetching clown in the show, freed her dress, too, but remained seated. Magda stepped out on a towel, dried her feet, and slid her shoes on.

Bertha broke eye contact with Thad and tugged on Magda's skirt. "What about me?"

"What about you?"

"I don't have shoes to wear."

Magda handed her the towel. "Dry your feet before they prune up. I'll see if your shoes are dry."

Bertha swung her feet to the floor and stared down at them. "Too late. They've been wet so long they're pickled."

Thad covered his mouth to hide his grin.

Magda bent over a pair of button-strap shoes and lifted one from the hearth. "Still soaked clean through. They might be dry by Christmas."

Magda's mama glanced at her from the stove. "Ve just had Christmas."

"I know."

After Mrs. Hayes laid another place at the table, she crossed to her bedroom door. "Vait, dumpling," she called to Bertha. "I think my shoes might fit you, ja?"

Bertha discreetly turned and wrung out her drenched hem over the towel. Then she leaned toward the fire pit and held the damp fabric closer to the flames.

Thad found something else to look at until Mrs. Hayes returned with a pair of worn black boots.

"Not so pretty, but varm and dry at least."

Bertha took uncommon pleasure in the sight of the boots. Smiling as though she'd been granted a wish, she looked them over. "Oh, these will do fine, Mrs. Hayes. Much obliged."

Mr. Hayes slapped both beefy palms on the table. "Enough about shoes, womenfolk. That venison tastes good from here. Serve it up, Gertie, before my lint-catcher caves."

As if her husband hadn't spoken, Mrs. Hayes stood over Bertha while she tried the boots. "Dey fit you nice. *Das gut.* You may keep dem, Bert'a. Too big for me."

Bertha gaped up at her. "Oh, I couldn't possibly." Thad watched the idea flit around in her pixie eyes. "But suppose we trade?" She pointed at the bronze shoes, her voice high-pitched with excitement. "Those will never fit me again, I'm sure of it."

Mrs. Hayes stared toward the hearth. "You give me dose nice shoes?"

"With pleasure."

Mrs. Hayes gave a quick nod and held out her hand. "Ve have us a deal."

"Gert, you'll have more than a deal if you and your daughter don't start shaking those pots. I'll give you a knot on the head."

"Hush, Yacob. We're coming." She waved him off as she passed but hustled to the stove with Magda on her heels.

Bertha finished lacing her new boots and stood. Patting her stringy hair and smoothing her mud-caked skirt, she eased toward the table.

Thad leaped to his feet to pull out her chair, and she sat down with a shy smile.

Mrs. Hayes ladled the stew with a flourish. She passed between them nodding and winking, grinning down at each bowl as though she'd birthed rather than cooked the pleasant-smelling dish. Magda brought a basket of hot, crusty bread and a saucer of soft, churned butter and then returned to the stove for a large bowl of sauerkraut and sausage. She placed it in front of Mr. Hayes and surveyed the spread with a practiced eye.

"Need anything else, Papa?"

"Just space for my elbows and a little time, sugar."

When they settled around the big oak table, Mr. Hayes bowed for prayer, and Thad followed suit. The amen was barely said before clanking spoons and spirited conversation commenced.

Mr. Hayes lifted his face from his bowl long enough to nod at his wife across the bread basket. "Fine vittles, woman. Mighty fine vittles."

Thad winked at Bertha and smiled at the older woman. "Your husband's right, ma'am. This here's good eating."

Mrs. Hayes beamed so brightly she lit up the room. "You really tink so?"

"Oh yes, ma'am. You could serve this with pride to Ulysses S. Grant."

Mr. Hayes stopped eating and glowered at Thad. "Watch your tongue, boy. Don't go putting crazy ideas in the poor woman's head. There ain't no way she could serve this stew to President Grant."

Thad's gaze jumped back to Mrs. Hayes. She had lowered her head and folded her hands in her lap. All trace of her pleasure had vanished.

Magda, red-faced and scowling, rose to her mama's defense. "And just why not, Papa?"

"I don't intend to leave him any, that's why!"

Mrs. Hayes, who Thad reckoned should know her husband better by now, tittered with relief and picked up her spoon. "Aw, go on, Yacob Hayes. Eat your stew and behave."

The tension eased around the table and a spell of quiet, companionable eating followed. The venison stew really was hands-down the best Thad had ever tasted. Especially when he dipped the soft middle of the fresh bread in the thick, dark broth and followed it with a bite of chewy, buttered crust. Never one for eating cabbage, the savory kraut and sausage surprised him. He sat contemplating seconds when Gerta Hayes broke the silence.

"Your mama vill be vorried about you, Bert'a?"

Bertha swallowed a bite and wiped her mouth on her napkin. "Yes, ma'am. I expect she'll be on the porch craning her neck when I get home."

Thad took his chance. "Bertha, I'll be glad to take you straight home after supper."

Mr. Hayes shook his head and spoke with bread-stuffed cheeks. "No sense in you young people riding horseback in the rain, not when we got Gert's two-seater in the barn. I'll see her home, Thad. But you kin tie your horse to the back and ride with us."

Thad raised a finger to protest, but Mr. Hayes cut him off. "Won't be no trouble a'tall."

"I'm coming with you, Papa."

"No, daughter. You stay put and help your mama. I won't be long."

Magda settled back in a pout while Bertha leaned forward to help Thad. "Won't we bog down in the surrey, sir?"

Mr. Hayes shoved another broth-soaked piece of bread in his mouth and proceeded to talk around it. "Never been stuck a day in my life. A body just has to recognize when it ain't smart to push your luck." He slapped the table near Thad with his free hand. "Get it, son? You ain't got to know where to go, just where not to."

He ducked his head to peer under the tasseled shade on the window. "Most the water's run off anyway, now that the rain's dwindled. The ground under that lane is packed solid, little Bertha. Take a bigger cloudburst than we had today to soften it up." He dismissed any more discussion with a wave of his hand. "Eat up, now. Let's get this young lady home before they round up a search party."

Thad went back to his bowl, but his heart found no more pleasure in venison stew. He comforted himself with thoughts of sitting next to Bertha in the surrey on the way to town. If Mr. Hayes cooperated by focusing his attention on the road ahead, the trip presented the chance to cuddle close to her on the rear seat, maybe even hold her hand. The prospect caused a chill down his back that had nothing to do with the steadily plummeting temperature outside.

The rain had ushered in a cold snap no one had prepared for, especially Bertha. She wore a lightweight dress with short sleeves and no stockings inside her boots. After they finished the meal and cleared the table, Mr. Hayes went around back to hitch up the horse while his wife found Bertha a suitable wrap. When the wagon pulled to the front door, Thad thanked Mrs. Hayes for dinner and helped Bertha into her borrowed coat. Bertha kissed the still-pouting Magda on the cheek, and they ran outside.

Mr. Hayes had arranged purchase of the ten-year-old surrey and the horse to pull it at the same time. Thad reckoned the seller knew he'd never unload the poor creature otherwise. The gelding looked white some days, gray on others, depending on the quality of the light. The grayish cast of his skin extended to the rims of his smallish eyes, his overlarge mouth, and the insides of his droopy ears in such a way that he always appeared slightly dirty. His overlarge teeth, which he displayed with amusing regularity, were stained brown as if he smoked a pipe.

Despite being hard on the eyes, the aging horse was a favorite with the locals. More than sixteen hands tall with the disposition of a kitten, he made up in size and character what he lacked in good looks. Mrs. Hayes had rigged a straw hat for him to wear, cutting two large holes in the sides for his ears, and insisted on braiding his tail. To his credit, the old gentleman never seemed to mind.

When Mr. Hayes jumped down from the surrey and lifted Bertha onto the leather seat beside him, Thad's mood bottomed out. A ruinous trick of fate, somehow stronger than his love for Bertha, was determined to keep them apart. He exchanged a grim look with her as he climbed into the backseat alone. Her mournful eyes told him she must be thinking along the same lines.

True to his word, Mr. Hayes expertly guided them down the long drive and onto the street without mishap, and they set off toward town. Bertha lived on the other side of Jefferson, near the bridge on the road that led to Marshall, so Mr. Hayes turned off Broadway and headed south on Polk.

Bertha started to fidget, and Thad leaned to touch her arm. "What is it, Bertha?"

She stared west toward Vale Street, her eyes narrowed, brows drawn. Instead of answering Thad's question, she squared around to face Mr. Hayes. "Excuse me, sir. Would it be too much trouble to cut over and drive past Brooks House? There's someone there I need to see."

Mr. Hayes reached a finger to scratch a spot up under his hat. "Well, I don't know, darling. Didn't you say your mama would be watching for you? We don't want to fret her none, do we?"

Up ahead and one street over, the back side of the hotel

appeared through the trees. Bertha swiveled on her seat as they passed it by, squirming as though she might jump off and run if the surrey didn't stop. She latched onto Mr. Hayes's arm so tightly her fingers turned white. "Please, sir. It will only take a minute. I have an urgent errand to attend."

Thad scooted to the edge of his seat and cleared his throat. "I'll gladly go along to see that she returns in a timely fashion."

Mr. Hayes pulled up on the reins, and the horse eased to a stop. He looked back at Thad, still not convinced. "I don't know, boy."

"I assure you it will be quick, right, Bertha?"

Her head bobbed up and down. "Oh yes. Very quick."

Before Mr. Hayes could say anything more, Thad hopped to the ground and turned to help Bertha down. He untied his horse from the back and climbed into the saddle, pulling Bertha up behind him. The next idea came to him before he had time to feel guilty. "As a matter of fact, there's no reason for you to wait. I'll help Bertha with her errand and see her straight home. You have my word."

Mr. Hayes spun around on the seat. "Now wait a second, Thad."

Thad tipped his hat. "You can count on me, sir. I won't let you down." He tapped the horse with his heel and reeled into the street with Bertha clinging to his middle.

They rode the short distance to Austin Street and turned back up toward Vale before Bertha started to laugh. "Shouldn't you be ashamed of yourself? You left him with his mouth gaped so wide he'll be catching flies."

Thad chuckled. "As fond of the man as I may be, it's worth him eating the odd fly to have a moment alone with you. It's right hard to steer you away from prying eyes, you know." He patted her hand. "Besides, I got you a chance to go see your friend."

She tightened her grip around his waist, and he could hear a smile in her voice. "You most certainly did. And for that, Mr. Bloom, I thank you."

Within a few feet of the next crossroad, he felt Bertha tense behind him. "Speaking of Annie, there she is now."

Thad's head swung around. "You see her? Where?"

She pointed past the horse's nose. "There. Coming out of the Rosebud."

At the corner of Austin and Vale crouched a saloon of dubious reputation. Said to be "the rendezvous of judges, lawyers, and men with notched guns," the Rosebud was a lively watering hole, and it nagged Thad a bit that someone Bertha cared so much for would find the gin mill worthy of her time.

The woman Bertha indicated was in the company of a tall, dark-haired man. Unaware of Thad's approaching horse, they clung together and lurched toward Vale Street. When Thad and Bertha drew alongside them, it took the couple a moment to realize they were there. But by the time Thad dismounted and helped Bertha down, the two stood swaying and staring their way.

Without waiting for Thad, Bertha hurried toward them. "Annie!"

The woman glanced at the man with panicked eyes. Then she shoved him aside and started to walk away, but he clutched her arm and held her.

"Whoa, now! Where you going in such an all-fired hurry?" He dragged her around to face him, but she wouldn't meet his pointed glare.

"Where do you think I'm going, silly? Back to the hotel."

Her companion gave her a little shake. "S'matter, you deaf? This little lady's speaking to you."

Annie flung her head from side to side. "No, Abe. You're mistaken. She isn't."

He shook harder. "You know right well she is."

Thad sensed trouble and crossed to stand beside Bertha. Annie pulled free, and Bertha closed the gap between them and touched her arm. "Wait, Annie. Don't go. It's me."

The "Abe" character tilted his chin toward Bertha. "Who is this? How does she know you?"

"I tell you, I don't know! I never seen her before in my life."

Abe grasped both of Annie's shoulders and leaned close to her ear, hissing every syllable through gritted teeth. "I asked you a question, Bessie. Who is this girl?"

Annie winced under his cruel hands. "I swear I don't know."

"Don't give me that. That's twice now she's called you Annie."

"I don't know what her game is," Annie shouted. Her voice lowered to an ominous tone. "I bet she heard you call me that." She leaned close and attempted to focus bleary eyes on Bertha. "Go away, little girl. I don't know you. Why are you trying to make trouble for me?"

With that she pulled away from Abe's grip and reeled down the street. "Come on, baby. I thought you were in a hurry to get back to the room. We ain't getting no closer standing around here."

The man watched her go with narrow, flashing eyes. He gave Bertha another suspicious scowl then followed Annie up the road.

Bertha stood on the grass where she had backed away from Annie's angry words.

Thad joined her there and slid one arm around her shoulders just as Annie's voice floated back to them on the night air. "Don't be silly, sugar. Why would I waste my time on that foolish child?"

Bertha turned and burrowed her face against Thad's shirt. "Oh, Thad. That's exactly what I am. A foolish child."

He tightened his hold around her. "Don't take it to heart, Bertha. Your friend's so pie-faced she could enter her profile in the county fair. She'll remember you tomorrow, when she sobers up."

Bertha looked up at him, her lips trembling. "That's what you don't understand. She remembered me, all right, but for whatever reason, she doesn't want him to know. I think I just got her in terrible trouble. Lord knows what he'll do to her now."

She shuddered and pressed close to him again. "Did you see his eyes?"

Across the top of Bertha's head, Thad watched the man named Abe wrestle the woman named Annie up the steps of Brooks House. He breathed a prayer of thanksgiving that Bertha didn't see it. In the distance, the struggling couple disappeared through the door, and Thad tacked on one more prayer.

He asked the Lord to send an angel for Annie.

CHAPTER 13

Saturday, January 20

Sarah stepped out the back door with every intention of feeding the chickens. The second her feet touched the cold, damp boards of the porch, she scampered back inside for her shoes and a wrap to lay over her shoulders.

Most days the weather stayed so warm and dry she wandered the place barefoot, especially the hard-packed trails leading to the barn and the chicken yard. Sarah loved feeling the smooth dirt under her feet. Some mornings the earth would be cool against her skin. On others the heat from the day before lay just below the topsoil.

Walking barefoot outdoors was a new experience. Folks in St. Louis wore shoes all the time, from field workers to scullery maids, and it disgraced the household to be caught without them. Things in Jefferson were different, and Sarah had to admit she liked going without her shoes.

But not today. Yesterday's storm had chugged through like a steam engine pulling a chilly caboose. And from the looks of the dark swirling sky, the tail end of the rain-train was in no hurry to leave the station.

There would be no sunrise setting for her clothesline daydreams, no bright rays dancing through her garden rows. She would slap the clothes on the line willy-nilly then ply the hoe in haste. She prayed that the rain held off till her laundry dried and that the cold would spare her greens.

But first came those chickens. The wayward, self-centered fowl were confused about the sort of bird God made them, considering they skulked near the back porch each morning like vultures. Squawking and sparring, they followed her to the chicken house where they belonged to start with and pranced around with jutting necks and impatient mutters while she dished out a bowlful of feed.

"Wait your turn, sisters." She swatted a speckled red pair away from her legs. "First one to peck me winds up on the table."

She had a good mind to leave them to scratch out a breakfast of crickets and worms the way the good Lord intended. Except she feared finding the lazy critters on their backs, drumsticks aimed at the sky, stone dead of starvation. And there would go Henry's eggs.

At the thought of her husband and his eggs, she stood up and scoured the surrounding fields. He'd been up since daybreak hoeing trenches to drain standing water and trying to plow the grassy rise, so she knew he'd be mighty hungry by now.

She covered the feed and slipped out of the chicken yard, fastening the gate behind her. As she neared the porch, she spotted Dandy in the distance, plodding on the east side of the farm. Henry couldn't be far behind.

Sure enough, he passed into her line of sight from behind the house, shoulders bent, head down, and far from a point where he might stop anytime soon. She still had plenty of time.

Sarah hoisted the metal tub full of washing off the porch and struck out for the bayou. Her thoughts flew to the day before when she'd complained about cool water and a breeze up her skirt and realized folks never knew when they had it easy. She reckoned she'd trade the nip she felt that day for the teeth-chattering chill she suffered now. When she reached the water's edge, she dumped the laundry on the ground and kneeled down to let cold, clear water run into the pail.

Henry had shown her how to dip just the rim of the pan so she wouldn't take up sludge or the muddy bottom water, but she still had to watch what streamed in at the top, or she'd fill it with floating debris.

She smiled. Her first time to try she'd dipped so low she caught a perch. The poor fish didn't know what to think about swimming with dirty overalls, but it pleased Henry to no end. He'd held it aloft and declared it "eating size" then set out to prove it by laying his chores aside and catching a stringer full to fry alongside hers for supper.

Sarah pushed the memory back and dragged the sloshing washtub to shore. She decided it wouldn't hurt the bundle of clothes a bit to soak until after breakfast. The day should be warmer by dinnertime.

She crested the rise and sighted Henry again. Looked like she still had time to hoe, but pure laziness crept in, so she decided against it.

Dickens had moseyed out to find her. When the old hound saw her top the hill, he lowered his lanky body to the ground and wriggled up to meet her.

"Morning, boy. What you doing way out here?" She scratched behind his ears, and he thanked her by curling his long tongue around her wrist. When he tasted bayou water on her arm, he sat upright and got busy drying her off. He had to be starved, or he'd never have moved from the porch. She drew her shawl around her shoulders and set out for the house to feed him.

Despite his hunger, Sarah beat old Dickens to the yard. She ducked into the kitchen and poured bacon grease over stale bread, threw on the scraps of beans and corn bread left from supper, then spooned the slop into the rusty metal dish beside the steps.

She stood up, her mind on starting Henry's breakfast, and heard a low whistle. Jennie Simpson lumbered up the road in the distance. She waved, and Jennie waved back.

The tonic. Jennie's energy tonic had entirely slipped Sarah's mind. Thankfully, she had a batch made up in the pantry.

Dickens lifted his droopy snout from the dish and rolled onto his side with a groan. Sarah shook her finger at him. "You might try chewing, Dickens. Make it last longer."

He didn't respond and appeared half asleep, his nose just inches from the plate. The old hound could do with a shot of restorative himself.

Jennie made it to the far corner of the yard and cut across to the back of the house.

When she got within shouting distance, Sarah shaded her eyes against the cloudy-day glare and smiled in her direction. "Morning, stranger."

"Morning, Sarah," she called, breathing hard. "It sho' nuff cold out here."

"You poor soul. I can't believe you walked all this way in such grievous weather."

Jennie laughed her good-natured laugh. "Honey, don't you worry. I's bundled up real good." She patted her ample thighs. "And got all this extra paddin' to keep me warm. 'Sides, I ain't had no choice. I needs that tonic to keep me going." She made a wrinkled face and shook her head. "Gots a tiresome workday ahead at Doc Turner's."

Sarah couldn't help thinking the get-up-and-go Jennie used to walk from town would've taken her through two days' labor, but she kept such thoughts to herself. "Well, I'm sure glad to see you, at any rate. You're just in time for breakfast."

"Breakfast?" Jennie stopped at the bottom step, panting and clutching her side. "Well, I already took me some biscuit and gravy right 'fore I left home, but I wouldn't want to offen' you none."

Sarah stifled a grin and turned to open the screen. "Come on in and let a body cook for you for a change. You can just sit back and watch."

Laughter rumbled in the big woman's chest. "I ain't that shiftless, chile. I might be able to crack an egg or two." She stopped and winked. "But I'll let you fry 'em."

Once inside the kitchen, Jennie seemed to forget even the promise to help. She perched her behind in a cane-bottomed chair and caught Sarah up on all the doings at Brooks House while Sarah did all the cracking, frying, and serving of eggs—alongside bacon, biscuits, and grits.

Henry trudged through the door and hung up his coat and hat just as Sarah slid a sheet of golden-topped biscuits from the oven. He took one look and hustled to wash up, with a grin and a nod toward Jennie as he passed.

Having just arrived at the scandalous part of her tale, Jennie offered him only a scanty tilt of the head. She was still talking when Henry came back in and settled across from her. Not just with her mouth—thrusting shoulders, waving hands, and rolling eyes stressed the finer points of Jennie's stories, not to mention the constant bob of her head. And she prattled with nary a break throughout the meal.

Sarah smiled across the table at Henry as Jennie wound up her latest yarn with a slap to her knee and a laugh to rival Dandy's bray.

"I'm tellin' you," she crowed, "I ain't never seen a body run so fast. And his wife right behind him with a broom. Funniest sight I ever seen."

Henry nodded in agreement, his cheeks too full of egg to laugh, but his manner laughed along with her. He swallowed and beamed at Jennie. "And the funniest thing I ever heard."

It rested Sarah's heart to see Henry appear so carefree. Far too soon, he sopped the last bit of running yolk with his last bite of biscuit, stood up, and reached for his coat.

"Pains me to leave good company, but I got a few acres standing between me and quitting time."

Jennie gazed up at him with big eyes. "How you working that soggy ground, Henry?"

He shrugged. "Ain't no way to plow the dirt. Too wet. Thought I'd try to turn over the grassy hill on the east field. Hard work, though. Too much rain, I guess." He tugged his hat down on his head. "Old Dandy don't much cotton to it."

Jennie cackled. "Cain't say as I blame him. You take care, Henry. It sho' was good talking to you."

Talking at you, more like.

The spiteful thought came to Sarah's wayward mind in the time it took to blink. She felt ashamed for thinking it, but it was nothing short of the plain truth. Jennie Simpson could talk a soup bone from a dog's mouth.

The door shut behind Henry, and Sarah's heart gave a tug. Her husband worked too hard. That was the plain truth, too.

"Wish he'd stayed a mite longer," Jennie said, echoing Sarah's own thoughts. "He won't get to hear me tell 'bout Miss Bessie."

"Who?"

Jennie leaned closer and raised her voice, as if shouting would give Sarah better recall. "Miss Bessie Monroe, over to Brooks. Number four?"

Sarah gave her a blank stare.

"We talked about her yesterday. That highfalutin couple what come in on the northbound train."

"Don't you mean Miss Annie Moore?"

"Who Miss Annie?"

"The woman in Mr. Stilley's store. Don't you remember? I told you I saw her in Stilley's with those two reckless girls?"

Jennie shook her head. "I don't know nothing 'bout no Annie. The gal what's staying in number four's named Bessie."

Sarah's brows knit together. "I'm certain they called her Annie Moore in the store. We must be talking about two different folks."

"Can't see how. Ain't but one woman staying at Doc Turner's."

Sarah shrugged. "Never mind. Go on with the story you're busting to tell."

Jennie's eyes opened up and her voice dropped to a whisper. "It's about Miss Bessie and her man. Sarah, them two spar like wet cats."

"They have a squabble?"

"Honey, squabble don't tell it all. You could hear them all over the house. I heard her crying from the third floor."

"What was it all about?"

"Something 'bout he woke up from a drunk and she ain't wearing her bustle, and so where is it. And then he find her fancy parasol in the closet, soaking wet and covered in mud, and her jus' finished swearing she ain't never left the room."

"My, my."

"When I went up to clean, she still be crying. And when she cry, he jus' sit hisself in a chair and read. The louder she bawl, the more he read. Beat all I ever seen."

Sarah shook her head. "He sounds hard."

"Cold as ice. Shame, too, 'cause she's a pretty little thing. I asked her how long they been married"—she gave a wide-eyed nod—"you know, to take her mind off it. Only she don't say a word. He up and say they been married two years. So I asked him how long they been traveling, and she say three weeks. But when I asked where her folks be from, she started crying again."

Sarah clucked her tongue.

Jennie leaned back and stared at the ceiling. "So I asked the gentleman if they be traveling for her health." Her gaze jumped back to Sarah. "You know, 'cause she acting so poorly like. He say yes they is, 'cause she has a spleen in her side."

"A spleen?"

"Tha's right." Jennie placed two fingers beneath her ribs. "It's right here, next to your gizzard."

Sarah nodded.

Jennie continued, "After that, I don't know nothing else they said, 'cause my eyes done lit on her hands. Sarah, that woman be sporting diamond rings so big she can't hardly lift her hands."

Sarah leaned forward. "Diamond rings?"

"Big ones. That's why folks around here call her 'Diamond Bessie,' on account of all her diamonds."

"So it is the same woman I saw in Stilley's."

"You reckon?"

"It has to be. Fancy parasol? Diamond rings? Pretty? Ain't

two strangers wandering Jefferson at the same time to fit that description."

Jennie touched a finger to her chin. "Wonder why she go by two names at once?"

"Jennie, they ain't no telling why white folk do like they do. You know that same as me."

"Hmm. I suppose so."

Sarah snorted. "Sounds like Diamond Bessie brought her problems on herself, what with lying lips and missing bustles."

Jennie shook her head. "Don't know what she trying to hide from that man, but they ain't nothing that woman done to deserve how he treat her. She jus' kindhearted as they come, Sarah. I can see it in her eyes. Around the hotel she treat everyone the same, black or white. Don't seem like she see color at all."

The words hit Sarah hard. Had she misjudged the dark-eyed stranger?

Jennie pushed her plate away and leaned back, eyes wide and blinking as though she just woke up. "Say, what's the hour getting on to be? Doc Turner say he gon' shut the door in my face if I be late one more time." She turned to look out the window, and panic gripped her face. "How long you reckon I've been here flapping my jaws? Can't rightly tell with those clouds hiding the sun. If it's too late, I'll be high-stepping clear to town."

Sarah laughed and got up from the table. "If that's your plan, you will need a tonic." She crossed to the dimly lit pantry and rummaged around the bottom shelf until her fingers closed around one of the last two bottles in the batch.

She handed the brown glass container to Jennie. "Take one teaspoon in water every morning. Not boiling water, but it can be hot. Sip it like tea until it's all gone." She tapped the cork with her finger. "You'll feel spry as a girl before you can say Pete's pig."

Jennie raised the bottle and peered at the dark brew. She gave it a shake, but the thick potion just oozed like cold molasses. "You sure I can't jus' take a swig right now? It's an awful long walk back."

Sarah scowled. "No, you can't take a swig. It's too potent. You liable to take off and fly from here to Brooks House."

Grinning, Jennie started toward the door. "That be all right by me. My feet hurt."

Sarah walked outside with her and gazed in Henry's direction. "I could whistle for Henry and have him harness the rig."

Jennie waved her off. "Let that man work. If I'm late, I'll tell Old Doc I came out here after an energy tonic. He'll be so busy trying to get some of it for hisself, he won't notice the time." Chuckling, she stashed the bottle in her pocket and made her way off the porch, lowering one leg at a time and settling her weight before taking the next step. With both feet firmly on the ground, her gaze went to Dickens, still sprawled in the dirt beside his pan.

"Mercy me! Them's the biggest ears I ever seen on a hound."

Sarah looked over her shoulder at the dog and laughed. "Ain't they, though? Henry says if we propped up Dickens's ears with sticks and pushed him off the house, he'd soar from here to Longview."

Jennie's shrill laughter cut the morning stillness, sending the chickens scrambling. "Girl, he'd pass right by Longview and sail clear to Dallas." After a giggling fit, she turned with a warm smile, wiping her eyes on her sleeve. "Sarah, thank you kindly for the tonic. And for breakfast. That was some fine eatin'." She took a couple of lumbering steps. "If you ever need work, I can vouch for you in the Brooks House kitchen."

Sarah stared across the field where Henry struggled behind the mule. "I hope I never need take you up on that offer, considering my husband swore to care for me as long as he's able."

Jennie followed her gaze. "Can't see as you have anything to fret over in that case. Henry's a fine figure of a man." She turned to go with a backward wave. "I better git if I'm gon' beat that storm back to town. Take care, now, child. And thank you again."

"You're welcome anytime," Sarah called. "To breakfast and my tonics."

When Jennie crossed the yard and passed from sight, Sarah gazed toward Henry and pondered the woman's last words. She allowed herself to consider, just for a moment, how life would be without him. Startled, she pushed away the image of St. Louis that fluttered to her mind. She loved her husband too much to entertain such wicked thoughts.

Didn't she?

A cold, wet nose against her ankle gave her a start. "Dickens! You old rascal—I thought you was sleeping." Sarah nudged him with her foot. "You might warn a body before you slip up behind them." She looked down at his droopy, pleading eyes and shook her head. "You don't need no more to eat, but I reckon I can scare you up some breakfast scraps."

Feeling guilty, she glanced toward Henry and wondered if she'd have jumped so high if she had a clear conscience. Luckily, there was no time to dwell on it. A dish-cluttered table and greasy stove awaited her inside. She pulled open the screen door and stepped into the kitchen. The smell of bacon and biscuits hung heavy in the air, less enticing on a full belly.

Life on a farm revolved around food. Sarah no sooner got breakfast cleared than it was time to start dinner. Most days she planned supper while they ate the noon meal. Hard work honed Henry's appetite as sharp as his plow. Thankfully, she worked just as hard, or she'd be as wide as the barn door.

She pulled on her apron and set to work on the dishes, scraping bits of bacon, egg, and biscuit in a pan for Dickens. Then she heated water and washed dried yolk and grits from the plates, milk and coffee from the tin cups. Lifting the heavy cast-iron skillet with a grunt, she poured bacon grease into a ceramic jar on the stove. Dickens would be hankering after the fresh drippings, but she had to save them for dinnertime biscuits.

The screen door squealed and slammed behind her.

Sarah jerked around. "Henry. You scared me out of ten days' growth. What you doing back at the house two hours before the noonday meal?"

He chuckled and held out his hand. "I come to get me some salve."

She left off cleaning the skillet and joined him by the door. "What happened?"

"Jus' a little cut. Me and Dandy got crossways 'bout which way to go."

Sarah reached for his big hand and with her apron wiped away the blood flowing from a spot between his thumb and forefinger. She held it up to the sparse light struggling through the kitchen window. "It's a poke, not a cut, but it ain't reached the bone." She rubbed her thumb over his knuckles. "At least he left your fingers."

Henry grunted. "Only 'cause I got out of his way. When that old mule reckons it's time to quit, it's a hard sell to turn him."

She ruffled his hair. "Maybe he's smarter than you. Sit at the table. I'll get my poultice powder."

She opened the pantry door and lit the lamp. She needed light to find the powder because she wasn't sure where she'd left it. It could be on the top shelf near the cough syrup she boiled up for croup and the grippe or behind the pokeweed tonic she kept for putrid sore throat. Maybe on the lower shelf next to the last two bottles of energy tonic. She reached to move them aside and froze.

Two bottles? She'd given one to Jennie not one hour ago.

Her eyes shifted to the identical brown containers next to the tonic, and her heart reared up in her chest. She dashed out of the pantry and stood staring at Henry, one twin vessel in each hand.

"We got to get ourselves to town right this minute."

Henry looked up, and his eyes bulged. "What happened, Sarah? You look like you seen a spirit in there."

Dazed, she shook her head. "Not yet, but I might get the chance. I've done killed Jennie Simpson."

CHAPTER 14

Bertha opened her eyes to a darkened room. She thought she'd awakened early until distant thunder pealed, and she realized stormy weather still lingered over Jefferson.

She reached with her big toe to push aside the tasseled shade. The roiling black sky promised rain, but the threat had yet to come through. No new raindrops sprinkled the windowpane, no fresh puddles dotted the path, and Papa puttered with his roses near the trellis, though he wore a heavy coat.

The chill in her room made her loath to give up her quilt, and in her head were memories of Thad she wanted to linger with a bit. He'd been so tender on the ride home, so mindful of her feelings. He even tried to explain away Annie's rebuke in an effort to lift Bertha's spirits. When they arrived on her porch, she knew he itched to tell her his important news. Instead, he pressed his lips to her forehead and insisted she get some rest.

But rest hadn't come easy. After tossing all night on her cotton mattress, she wound up encased in a blanket cocoon. In the early morning hours, she finally surrendered to drowsy lids and fell into a fitful sleep where she and Annie skipped arm in arm through town dressed in nightshirts and corsets, chased by a menacing Abe.

"Bertha Maye!"

She cringed. The tone of Mama's voice meant she'd found Gerta Hayes's boots—Bertha's boots, now—and would require an explanation.

Last night Mama had been so busy scolding her for coming home late, she never noticed her feet. Though Bertha preferred getting all the fussing done at once, she hadn't the heart to rekindle Mama's ire once she finally settled down. So she left the boots on the porch and hustled to her room without mentioning her trade with Mrs. Hayes.

She would pay for it now.

The door swung open and slammed against the wall. Mama stood on the threshold holding the boots away from her with two fingers, as if afraid they might bite.

Bertha took her stature from Papa's pocket-sized family. Emeline Biddie, a foot taller and pounds heavier than Bertha, struck an imposing figure hovering in the doorway.

"Bertha Maye Biddie, did you hear me call?"

She swung her feet to the floor. "Yes, ma'am."

"Why didn't you come?"

"I was about to."

It would do no good to explain that between Mama's call and her appearance, there hadn't been enough time to come. If Bertha had tried, she'd be crumpled in a heap between the door and Mama's prized William Morris wallpaper in the Daisy pattern. Such logic generally escaped the woman's notice.

Mama held the scruffy black boots higher. "Would you care to explain?"

Bertha pointed. "Those are boots." Not a wise response.

Indignation swelled Mama to twice her size. "I know what they are, Bertha Biddie. What I don't know is how they came to be in your possession." She widened her eyes as a warning. "Don't try to deny them. Not even your papa's feet are this small. You're the only one here who could wear them."

She hadn't planned to deny them but decided not to mention it.

"I've tolerated your old lace-ups because Papa said you need them for chores. But I won't abide a second pair." She took a closer look at the footwear dangling from her hands. "And these are even more horrid. Where on earth did you get them?"

"They were a gift."

Disbelief shaped Mama's posture from tilted head to jutting hip. She took advantage of the protruding hip and rested her free hand on it. "Do you intend to sit there and break three of God's commandments at once?"

Bertha drew back in shock. "How have I managed that?"

Mama ticked them off on her fingers. One finger. "Your answer is clearly not the whole truth, which makes it a lie by default." Two fingers. "I believe your attitude toward me in this matter is far less than honorable." She shook the boots at Bertha and held up the third digit. "Your evasive answer about these monstrosities gives me cause to believe you stole them."

Bertha grinned and nodded. "That's three, all right."

"Don't be fresh, Bertha Maye." She tossed the boots in a corner and lifted a rigid shoulder. "I never imagined a daughter of mine would have such an aversion to shoes."

It seemed a cruel twist of fate on both their parts. The fashionable shoes Mama loved to the point of obsession, Bertha considered instruments of torture. In the past she'd tried to conform but had never found comfortable footwear that pleased her finicky mama.

"I'm sorry." Bertha stood up and walked around the end of the bed. "I didn't lie or steal, and I never intend to dishonor you. It just happens."

Mama jabbed her finger toward the corner. "No more nonsense, then. Tell me where those came from."

Bertha steeled herself and plowed ahead. "Magda's mama gave them to me in exchange for my shoes."

It took a full three seconds for the news to sink in before Mama turned around and stared in disbelief. "Your beautiful bronze pumps?"

She held up both hands. "Before you bust a gut, just listen. They weren't beautiful when I gave them."

Mama sagged against the door frame. "What do you mean? They were brand new."

"Yes, they were, but not anymore. I got caught out in the storm and wound up tramping through muddy floodwater." She nodded at the boots on the floor. "Those look better than the shoes did when I finally made it to high ground."

Mama cringed but didn't speak, so Bertha went on.

"The boots don't fit Mrs. Hayes, so she offered them to me. And they're ever so comfortable, as if made for my feet." Mama scowled, so she ducked her head. "Mrs. Hayes took a liking to my shoes, though I can't imagine why."

Mama crossed her arms and raised one dubious brow.

"They were puckered and ruined, I promise. When she offered the boots, I suggested an even trade. It seemed only fair."

This brought Mama ramrod straight. "So the lovely pumps I saved weeks of egg money to purchase—shoes in the latest fashion, I might add—were an acceptable exchange for. . .for. . ."

Papa, who had come to stand behind Mama without her knowing, started to mimic her stiff posture and wild gestures. When he broke into a jaunty Irish jig, Bertha plastered both hands over her mouth. Laughing would be the ruin of them both.

Still oblivious to Papa, Mama stopped waving her arms and glared. "What are you doing, Bertha?"

Papa tugged his twisted vest into place and stepped forward with a poker-straight face. "The girl's speechless with remorse, my dear Emeline."

Mama whirled. "And well she should be. I'm glad you're here, Francis. You need to deal with this girl. I've reached the end of my tether."

"Ah, me lady, surely there's an inch or two left. What dastardly thing has the wee snippet done?"

"Ask her yourself. I'm taking leave of the situation before I lose my temper."

If Mama hadn't already lost her temper, Bertha would just as soon see her go.

Papa put on his pious face. "It can't be that bad. Can't we afford her a bit of Christian charity?"

Mama waved off his suggestion. "Francis, I fear your daughter has depleted my ration of Christian charity for the day and with the sun barely over the horizon." She shoved past him and started down the hall then turned for one last remark. "This time see to it you're not overly lenient, Francis, or you'll answer to me." She left in a huff, still muttering.

Papa raised his hands to his throat and mimicked strangling himself, causing Bertha to erupt in stifled laughter. He waited until the angry clack of heels faded toward the kitchen before he winked and grinned at Bertha. "Stretch out on the bed so I can beat you, daughter. I'm getting too old for the chase."

She clutched her head and moaned. "Can't you do anything with her?"

His cheeks reddened. "Been trying for years. Haven't made much headway. It's my penance for marrying a city girl." He sighed. "Let's get your punishment over and done."

"Do we have to?"

"If you want to save me hide, we do." He touched the end of his chin. "Let me see, now. Can you live with adding Mama's chores to your own until the Sabbath?"

"Tomorrow?"

"Not so easy, me girl. Sabbath next."

She winked. "Can't fault me for trying."

"You would, you rascal. Do we have a bargain?"

She nodded. "We do."

He raised both shaggy brows. "You're sure? It's not too late for a beating."

Bertha laid her cheek on his shoulder, one of the few shoulders she could reach. "The extra chores will do nicely, thank you."

He patted her back and gave her a tight squeeze. "Fine, fine. Now squeal a bit or work up some tears—else you'll land me in trouble, too."

She giggled and pulled away. "Stop it, now. And kindly take leave of my room. I have to dress and get started on all those chores."

He held up his hands. "I'm going, lass. I have to get dressed meself."

She looked him over. "You are dressed."

"Aye, for the barn, not for town."

She widened her eyes. "You're going into town?"

"Right after breakfast."

She clutched his hand. "Oh, Papa, I need to go with you."

He screwed up his face. "I don't know, lass. What about your work?"

"I'll do all I can before we leave and the rest when we get back. I promise." She grabbed both of his arms and pleaded with her eyes. "I need to see about a friend of mine."

Concern creased his forehead. "Is your friend ill?"

She looked away. "She needs my help with a problem."

"I see."

She put both arms around his neck. "Oh, please. It's very important or I wouldn't ask."

His staunch resolve crumbled before her eyes. "This will get us both a lashing, but very well. We'll slip away after we eat."

She kissed his ruddy cheeks. "You're a wonderful papa."

His rosy face turned crimson. "So it's flattery you're up to, is it? Save yourself the trouble, lass. No bit of trickery or slip of the silver tongue can sway Francis Biddie." At the door, he spun on the ball of his foot. "Ah yes, and those extra chores can wait. You may start them Monday morn."

She tried to hide her grin. "Thank you, Papa."

He winked and turned to go.

"Papa?"

"Yes, wee girl?"

"Why are shoes and such so all-fired important?"

He cocked his head and squinted both eyes. "Ah, Bertha, me love. One barefoot day spent dealing with the trials of those too poor to buy shoes and you'd be begging to wear them. Trust your old papa on this one. Now ready yourself for breakfast and be quick about it."

Quick she was, with chores and with breakfast, and in no time they were ready to leave. Mama scowled when Papa announced Bertha would join him on his trip to town, but she held her tongue. Bertha slipped out of the house fast when he pulled the horse and buggy to the door, before Mama decided to make her stay home.

In the two hours since daybreak, Jefferson had come to life. Nearly all of the locals shopped and ran errands on Saturday in preparation for Sunday rest. Lone riders on horseback and families on outings swarmed the streets, and the boardwalks teemed with farmers, merchants, laborers, and backwoodsmen. Gentlemen planters stood in clusters bemoaning the price of cotton and lamenting the decline of trade brought on by the dwindling steamboat traffic.

The ladies, unmindful of their husbands' woes, pranced about in high-dollar duds. Not the elaborate gowns reserved for balls and garden parties or the chaste and unassuming frocks set aside for church—these colorful dresses were their town clothes, topped off by matching parasols and feathered hats.

The carriage from the Commercial Hotel rumbled past, and the toothy driver tipped his hat at Bertha. Papa frowned at the young man then shook his head and winked when Bertha grinned. He reined in the wagon in front of Rink Livery Stable and set the brake. "Won't be a minute, sugar. When I come back, we'll head over to Sedberry's Drugstore." He patted her hand. "I'll let you pick out some nice penny candy."

Bertha pulled her hand free and placed it over his. "I hate to tell you this, Papa, but I'm not ten years old anymore."

He leaned nose to nose with her and scrunched up his face. "Is that a fact? When did it happen?"

She swatted his arm. "A good while ago. A detail you'd notice if you paid better attention."

He pulled her close and chuckled. "Daughter of mine, a man can't see what he ain't looking for." He leaned back and regarded her from a distance. "So that's why the young upstart driver's eyeballs popped?" He stretched his arms out in front of his face. "Out to here, they were."

Her face flushed with heat, and she lowered her head. Papa chuckled and lifted her chin. "You turned into a right bonny lass while me head was turned."

His words flooded Bertha's soul with warmth. "Thank you, Papa."

He kissed her cheek and climbed down then peered up from the ground, scratching his head. "So you're not ten years old, you say? Funny how you never grew."

"Oh, go on with you," she sputtered.

His laughter rang out in the morning air. "Sit tight, then. I'll be back directly. I just need to check on Sol."

"Is Mr. Spellings ill?"

He pushed out his bottom lip. "Nothing any doctor can fix. He's having a hard time dealing with Carrie's loss, is all. If he didn't have the livery to keep him busy, I expect he'd go clean out of his mind." He furrowed his brow and stared toward the livery door.

"Papa?"

Lost in his own thoughts, he regarded her with dazed eyes. "Yes, love?"

"I still have the errand of my own to attend." She pointed. "It's just over on Vale Street. Is it all right if I walk?"

He tilted his head and stared across the distant treetops. "I suppose, since you're not ten anymore, I won't ask what your errand might be." He shook his finger at her. "Go on, then. Just don't cause me any more trouble with your ma."

"I won't. I promise."

He finished securing the reins and helped her to the ground. "I'll pick you up at the corner of Lafayette and Polk in one hour. See that you're there."

"Yes, Papa." Bertha smoothed her bodice and straightened her skirts around her. She looked back, but he had already disappeared through the wide doors of Mr. Spellings's livery.

It took all of her strength to walk in a dignified manner to Brooks House. She longed to break into a mad dash and run, the way Annie described on the bluff—sans bonnet, corset, and shawl.

After last night, the need to ensure her new friend's safety swelled in her heart, pushing reason aside. She didn't know how she would go about it, but she had to speak to Annie away from her frightening companion.

Bertha drew near Brooks House, a grand yet inviting place where the white picket railing and four columns on the ground floor perfectly matched the wide balcony and four columns up top. Inside its walls, weary travelers who could afford it found comfort and rest under the vigilant eye of the hotel's owner, Dr. J. H. Turner.

She had no idea how to find Annie inside or how to get her away from Abe when she did. She just knew she would do it if it took all day and night, although squeezing so much time into the hour Papa had given her might pose a challenge.

Dr. Turner's omnibus approached from the opposite end of the street and pulled to a stop near the steps. Judge Armistead and another man, engaged in quiet conversation, stepped down from the big carriage and strolled to a spot by the front steps. The door of the hotel opened, and Bertha's heart ricocheted in her chest when Abe stepped out on the porch and lit a fat cigar.

Ever so slowly, so as not to attract his attention, Bertha pulled her shawl up over her head and faced the other way. As naturally as she could manage, she took three steps to put a shrub between her and the porch. From the cover it provided, she watched Abe while he watched the judge and his crony. When the two older men sauntered into Brooks House, Abe tossed his cigar over the rail and took the two steps down to the street.

For one heartrending moment, Bertha thought he would head her direction, but he turned right instead and strode down the street whistling, his hands shoved deep in his pockets. Sending a prayer of thanksgiving toward heaven, she made a beeline for the hotel but kept her gaze fixed on Abe's back until she reached the entrance and ducked inside.

Brooks House seemed quiet for a Saturday morning. Bertha expected to find staff buzzing about the dim lobby and guests lounging in the well-appointed parlor. But the judge and his friend must have retired to a room, and there were no porters or maids in sight. Surprisingly, Dr. Turner himself manned the front desk.

Bertha pulled back her shoulders, licked her lips, and sauntered toward him as fast as she dared. "Good morning, Dr. Turner."

He looked up from the copy of the *Jefferson Jimplecute* he had spread open across the desk. "Bertha Biddie. How nice to see you, child. How's your father? We've missed him at the lodge."

"He's well, Doc. Mama's been a mite under the weather, but she's fine now."

He closed the newspaper and crossed his arms on it. "Good, good. Now what can we do for you?"

Bertha cleared her throat. "I need to see a friend of mine. She's one of your guests, but I don't know what room she's in."

Doc pulled the hotel register around so he could see it. "Well, of course, dear. Which guest?"

"Her name is Annie Moore."

When he frowned and flipped the page, Bertha waved her hand at the book. "Forgive me. I guess you know her around here as Bessie Monroe."

Drumming on the desk until Bertha wanted to scream, Doc stared at her as though trying to cipher a disturbing puzzle.

"I'm sorry, Dr. Turner, but I'm in a bit of a hurry."

Frowning, he awoke from his ponderings. "I have a couple of guests registered as A. Monroe and wife. I believe the wife might be the person you seek, considering she has a trunk labeled 'A. Moore.' "

Bertha nodded. "Yes, that's her. Please tell me what room she's in."

He cocked his head. Bertha could almost read in his eyes the questions he wanted to ask. She supposed he thought Annie Moore wasn't exactly the sort of friend she should have.

"I guess it'll be all right," he finally said then pointed behind him. "Go right down the hall to number four. I think you'll find your friend inside."

She pushed away from the desk but stopped and turned back

after only a few steps. "Can we keep this between us, please? I don't want anyone to know I was here."

He pulled on his mustache. "Somehow I can believe that, Bertha. You be careful, now, you hear?"

She nodded then rushed down the ornate hall. She found number four with no trouble and knocked. No one answered, so she knocked again, this time louder. Though she saw Abe leave with her own eyes, her flesh crawled as she pictured him standing behind the door.

"What now?" Annie blustered from inside. "You have the key." She opened in a rush, and all the blood washed from her face. With wide, darting eyes, she looked down the hall before yanking Bertha inside. "What are you doing here? You can't be here."

Bertha's legs threatened to give out, so without an invitation she hurried to sit on the end of the bed. "I'll only stay a minute. I had to see for myself that you're all right."

Annie pointed at the door. "Abe—"

"He's gone. I saw him leave."

She pulled Bertha off the bed by her wrist and herded her toward the exit. "Trust me, he won't be gone long. You have to get out of here before you get us both killed."

The warning sent terror spiking through Bertha's heart. "Killed? Oh, Annie. . ."

Annie seemed surprised by her own choice of words. She waved her hand back and forth, as if the gesture could erase what she'd said. "A figure of speech, silly girl. People say it all the time. It doesn't mean. . . Abe would never. . ."

Bertha wasn't convinced. Annie's lips were smiling, but her eyes were afraid. "Let me take you out of here. You can hide out at my house until he leaves town. Please, Annie."

Annie's put-on confidence crumpled, and she gathered Bertha in her arms. "Oh, sweetie, I'm so glad to see you. I really am. I've wracked my brain for an excuse to leave this room and come find you." She leaned back and peered into Bertha's eyes. "Can you ever forgive me for the way I treated you last night? I felt so bad about it, but I had to pretend I didn't know you. I did a foolish, impulsive thing by running off to the bluff. And then I lied to Abe about it. Only he caught on that I left while he was sleeping. He thinks I'm holding out on him."

"Holding out?"

"Money. He thinks I—"

She bit back the words and turned her face aside. "Well, it doesn't matter what he thinks. I should've told him the truth from the beginning. Now I have to hold my ground, no matter what. Abe hates it more than anything when I lie."

Bertha took hold of her hands. "You can tell me, Annie. He hits you, doesn't he?"

Annie swiped a tear from her cheek with her finger. "Hits me? Don't be silly." Sudden panic crowded her eyes. "Bertha, you have to go now. Please."

She hurried to the door, opened it a crack, and peered out. "Come on. The hallway's empty."

Bertha crossed to her and touched her trembling arm. "I'll go. But there's something we need to discuss. Can you get away from him? Just for a little while?"

She nodded. "Tonight. I'll wait till he's soused and sneak out."

"Is it safe?"

"I've done it before, and I'm still here, ain't I? I'll be fine as long as I don't stay too long, all right?"

"All right."

"We can't go far, though. I need to stay near the hotel. Somewhere out of sight."

"Remember where we met up with Mose to hitch a ride to the bluff? The spot at the end of the alley?"

Annie nodded.

"Meet me there. I'll look for you at sunset, but I'll wait no matter how long it takes."

"I'll be there." Annie peeked out again and pulled Bertha to the door. "It's now or never, sugar. Please go."

Bertha paused long enough to give her a tight hug then slipped out the door. Annie had no sooner closed it than Bertha heard approaching footsteps. She dashed across the hall and stood in front of another room, her hand on the doorknob as if she'd just come out. She feared he'd be suspicious if she lingered, so she headed toward the lobby, though he came right toward her.

They passed in the corridor. Bertha kept her face turned away, her shawl pulled tight against it. Abe mumbled a greeting, and she managed to nod and return it in a low voice. When Annie's door opened and closed behind her, relief flooded her bones.

As she passed the front desk, Doc Turner cleared his throat. "Everything all right?"

She swallowed her tears and nodded.

He picked up his paper and gave it a shake to straighten the pages. "Then good day to you, Bertha."

She smiled at him. "Thank you, Doc."

He winked at her across the *Jimplecute* as she backed toward the door and stepped outside.

CHAPTER 15

Dense clouds had managed to hold the light over Jefferson at bay for the better part of two days. Sarah thought it fitting when the overhead sky parted and the sun fired an accusing ray through her kitchen window, as if God had aimed the light of judgment full in her face. She sagged against the pantry door in tears. "What have I done to that poor woman?"

Henry got up from his chair and took her trembling body in his arms. "Slow down, baby. Jus' tell me what happened."

Sarah pointed in the direction of town. "The tonic I sent home with Jennie Simpson. It ain't no energy tonic at all."

Now Henry looked scared, which scared her more. "What'd you give her, Sarah?"

She held up one of the vials. "Aloe and sacred bark. With some other cleansing herbs."

Thunder sounded, and somewhere overhead a cloud doused the sun ray, drenching the kitchen in shadows again. When the light left, a cold draft rushed in to take its place.

Henry stared at the tonic and swallowed. "Poison?"

"Maybe. If she takes too much. . ." She shook her head. "I don't know for sure."

"What's it gon' do to her?"

She blinked up at him. "Remember those stewed prunes you liked so much at Miss Blow's house last Christmas?"

He tilted his head and answered real slow. "I do."

"Remember what it done to your insides?"

He made a face. "I sho' do."

"Henry, if Jennie mixes the tonic in water like I told her, she might as well done ate ten pots of those prunes all by herself. She left here ready to drink it straight from the bottle."

This time he blinked. Then came the slightest twitch at the corners of his mouth.

Sarah gave him the eye. "Don't you dare laugh."

And that was all it took. Henry laughed so hard the plates rattled. He laughed until tears rolled down his cheeks. He laughed until he doubled over, holding his sides.

Sarah longed to join in, but she couldn't because she still held the terrible mistake in her hands.

He finally rose up and looked at her, likely to see how mad she would be.

She stifled a grin. "I never knew you to be a cruel man, Henry King."

He wiped his eyes with his shirttail. "I'm sorry, Sarah. I jus' keep seeing Miss Jennie running along Polk Street, trying to make it home in time." Saying it must've brought the picture back, because he fell into another howling fit.

Sarah pushed him toward the door. "Go bray it to Dandy whilst you hitch him to the wagon. We should've been halfway to town already."

Henry turned at the door when he heard her gasp. "What now?"

"Jennie said Doc Turner would be itching to try her tonic, too. Said she'd bribe him with it if he saw her coming in late."

He wiped his forehead with his sleeve, no trace of laughter left on his face. "Then you best pray she ran the whole way."

On the porch, Bertha took her first easy breath since she'd entered

Brooks House. After a glance back at the door, she scurried down Vale with plenty of time to spare before she had to meet up with Papa. She reached Lafayette and headed for Polk Street, where Papa said he'd be waiting. A loud whistle sounded behind her, and she turned to find Magda coming up the road in her mama's red surrey.

The two-seater pulled next to her, and she grinned up at Magda. "Remember, ladies don't whistle in the streets like common pitchmen. Your pa will take a strap to your legs."

Magda snorted. "Fine. He can borrow your papa's strap. The one he doesn't have. What are you doing alone in town this early on a Saturday morning?"

Bertha climbed up on the seat beside her. "I reckon I could ask you the very same."

"I ain't alone. Papa's at the barber. Mama's at Stilley's." She dug in the pocket of her dress and produced a sheet of paper. "Meanwhile, I'm to hustle on over to the drugstore and fetch everything on this list."

"Sedberry's? I'm headed there to meet Papa."

"Where've you been this morning?"

Bertha glanced around them before she answered. "Can you keep a secret?"

Magda drew back and glared. "Did you just ask if I could keep a secret?"

Bertha laughed. "Don't get your bustle in a bunch. Long-standing habits are hard to break."

Magda waved a dismissive hand. "Just get on with it."

"I've been to see Annie over at Brooks House."

Magda stiffened. "Oh?" she asked with an air of indifference. "How is she?"

"Truth is, she's in terrible trouble. I can't go into it now, but I'm awfully worried about her."

Magda gave her a look. "It's that man she's with, isn't it?"

Startled, Bertha looked into her knowing eyes. "Goodness, how'd you guess?"

Magda sniffed. "I know trouble when I see him."

Bertha gripped her friend's hands. "Oh, Magda, I believe he's dangerous. Annie's scared witless of him. There has to be a reason."

A wagon veered close, driven by an agitated woman and loaded down with rowdy youngsters. Six stair-step boys, all with runny noses and unruly shocks of brown hair, stared up from the wagon bed.

Bertha nodded at the poor mother then watched them rattle off down the road.

Magda tugged on her fingers. "What are you going to do?"

"There's nothing I *can* do. I'm smart enough to know that much. But God can do plenty, and I intend to tell Annie so."

"Think she'll listen?"

"Her life may depend on it. Her eternal life, at least."

Magda sat back against the seat and crossed her arms. "At least it's given you something to worry about besides what's happening to your own life. You seem in awfully good spirits, considering."

The baffling statement didn't bode well. Magda knew something Bertha didn't. Something bad. "Good spirits considering what?"

"Papa was ever so mad when he got home last night. Ready to skin Thad and hang him in the square for running off with you. But today Charles Gouldy explained why. Now Papa understands completely."

Bertha gripped the sides of her head. "Understands what? What are you going on about?"

Magda heaved an irritated sigh. "You know. About him leaving tomorrow."

"Who's leaving tomorrow?"

"Thad, of course."

The three words rushed at Bertha in a fuzzy white fog, and her ears started to ring. The noisy, bustling town around her faded to the far distance. She tried to shake the haze enough to understand. "What did you say?"

"Thad." Magda's tone sounded less sure. "He's leaving for school first thing tomorrow morning." She covered her face with both hands until only wide-open eyes were visible above her fingertips. "Oh, sugar, you didn't know."

Bertha struggled for her voice. "Who told you that outlandish story?"

"Charlie." She pointed behind them. "I just left off talking to him and his sister in front of the barber shop. He said Thad swore to tell you last night."

A seething cauldron of rage tipped over inside her chest. She writhed with shame at how she'd lingered in bed nursing fanciful notions about Thad's motives. He hadn't put her feelings above a desire to share his news. He'd simply run out on her. She'd mistaken cowardice for consideration and careless disregard for concern.

"Turn this thing around," she demanded, pointing back over her shoulder.

Magda, pressed into the corner of the surrey waiting for her reaction, seemed taken aback. "Why?"

"I'm going to see Thad. I need you to take me."

Magda looked more thunderstruck than when she'd first let the news slip. "That's the most improper suggestion I'll ever hear. You won't do any such thing. You can't."

Bertha met her scandalized gape with gritty determination. "I can, and I will."

Magda's head rocked back and forth. "I won't be a party to it. It's too reckless bold, even for you."

Bertha waved her finger in the direction of Thad's house. "Thaddeus Bloom can show you a thing or two about reckless bold. The deceitful scoundrel held my hand in Julius Ney's barn. Kissed my forehead on my own front porch. He's dangled me like a love-struck marionette for the sake of his ego, all the while knowing he'd be riding away tomorrow. Nothing I do at this point can stack up to the shameless thing he's done."

Magda tilted her head, compassion clouding her dark eyes. "Oh, Bertha. . ." Steeling herself, she held up her paper and waved it. "What about my list? I'll be in trouble with my folks."

Bertha patted her hand. "Don't fret, then. I understand. I'll find my own way." She started climbing down, but Magda latched onto her skirt and pulled her back.

"No, you won't, blast you." She released the brake and whipped the surrey around in the middle of the street. "I must be teched in the head, but we're on our way. We have to hurry, so sit tight and hang on to your corset."

As they raced through town, Bertha's thoughts went to Papa, waiting for her in front of the drugstore, and her promise not to get him into any more trouble. Then her jilted heart took over again, crowding guilt aside. She took the reins from Magda's hands and urged the horse to go faster.

❧

Henry pulled to the servants' entrance behind Brooks House, and Sarah scrambled to the ground without waiting for his help. She left him to tether Dandy and, with no thought to who might be watching, lifted the hem of her dress and ran. After a series of undignified knocks, she lost all patience and reserve and pounded the door with clenched fists. The door jerked opened at the same time Henry bounded up to join her.

Thomas Jolly, Doc Turner's head porter, scowled at them from the threshold. "Well, if you two ain't the last folks I expected to see making a ruckus behind this door. Why you be trying to beat it down, Henry?"

Traitor Henry pointed her way. "Ain't none of me. It was Sarah."

Thomas shifted his lazy gaze. "You, Sarah?"

"Yes, me. Now stand aside. I need to see Jennie Simpson right away."

Still blocking the door, he gave her a puzzled look. "You heard already? Can't see how. It jus' happened."

Sarah and Henry shared a look.

"Poor old Jennie," Thomas went on. "I's loath to see harm come to such a fine, hardworking woman, but the good Lord done decided it be her time to rest."

Sarah clutched Henry's hand so tightly her fingers ached.

Thomas stepped aside. "I guess you come for to see her. Step right this way. We laid her out on the kitchen table."

Sarah's world spun. Sweat popped out on her lip, and all the sap drained from her legs. Henry's hand on her back was the only thing holding her in place. If only he'd just remove it, she could ease out of there and find the strength to run.

Thomas's voice echoed in her head. "Well? Is you coming in or not? I got to shut this door before Miss Jennie draw flies."

Sarah's stomach lurched. She turned and buried her face in Henry's shirt, but he gently guided her to the door, whispering in her ear all the while.

"Stop it, now. Straighten up and act natural. Don't attract no attention to yourself."

Trying to say yes and no at the same time, her head bobbled like a fishing cork. "I can't go in there, Henry."

"Yes, you can," he hissed. "We come to see, and we gon' see. If we leave now, it won't look right. You got to carry through."

It felt like Henry had ten arms at work behind her, pushing, prodding, and lifting, until she made it down the long, dim corridor outside the kitchen. Thomas, who led them the whole way, opened the door and went inside.

Sarah dug in her heels. "I can't, Henry. I won't stand looking down at her, knowing it's all my fault."

He gripped her arm hard. "Shush your mouth, Sarah. It was an accident." He let go of her arm and cradled her face in his hands. "Whatever happens, we face it head-on. I ain't gon' let nothing bad happen to you. But you got to hush saying it's your fault, or I can't protect you."

He ran his fingers through her hair. "Straighten your back, now. Raise your chin. That's right. Now follow me."

He took her wrist, his hold so tight she couldn't break free if she tried. When he opened the door and pulled her inside, she closed her eyes, dread squeezing her chest. She heard milling footsteps and low murmurs in the room, and a woman's clear, steady voice rising above the others.

When Henry gave a low chuckle beside her, Sarah thought she must be hearing things. She opened one eye and peeked at him. A mixture of glee and sheer relief warmed his face, and his firm grip on her waist became a caress. The next sound was the loud bray she'd last heard at breakfast.

"Dat's de funniest story I ever heard, Miss Bessie. Go on, tell another."

Sarah opened both eyes and spun toward the sound. Jennie sprawled on the sturdy oak table, her jolly face aglow. All activity in the usually bustling kitchen had ceased, and the staff stood in a quiet circle around her. Everything that once graced the table— assorted utensils, a lantern, several baskets, and a set of nested bowls—they had placed beneath the table or pushed to the floor. One of Doc Turner's maids had a rag and a pan of water and was washing Jennie's legs, while the woman she called Miss Bessie, but Sarah knew as Annie Moore, sat at Jennie's feet prodding her bruised and swollen ankle.

Before Miss Annie could speak, Jennie caught sight of Henry towering above the others and sent her roaming gaze in search of Sarah. "Why, looky who come to see about me. Ain't that nice. You two heard about my fall, then?"

Henry cleared his throat. "We heard a little, but not the whole story. Why don't you tell us what happened?"

The woman needed no stronger bidding. "All right, den. You see, I was hurrying to get to work on time, only I know'd for sure I's gon' be late. So I crawled under a fence and struck out over a pasture, thinking to save time travelin' as the crow flies. I got clear to the other side of the field when I stepped in a hole, and down I come, right on a fresh cow patty." She rolled her head on the table and laughed, her cheeks so round they hid her eyes. "I was a funny sight, I'm tellin' you. Busted my ankle up real good, though."

Jenny rose up and motioned for Sarah. When Sarah came close, she understood why the young maid who scrubbed Jennie's legs held her nose and why Thomas had fretted over flies. Jennie had brought most of the cow pie back with her.

"I'd be laid there still, wallowing in my mess, if Mr. Ney and his boys hadn't come along. They helped me up and loaded me on their big old wagon then brung me all the way here."

Jennie waved toward Miss Annie with the handkerchief she held in her hand. Pale blue embroidered silk. Sarah knew it didn't belong to her.

"This sweet soul got wind of my troubles and come all the way downstairs, fussing over me and wiping my brow with this nice little hankie." She held it up for Sarah to see. "Then insisted on tendin' my broke ankle herself."

The well-dressed woman glanced up from her work, a smile in her bright eyes. "Jennie, my dear, you have a sprain, not a break. You'll be fit as a fiddle in a few days. But you need to stay off of it until then."

Jennie leaned up on her elbows with alarm in her eyes. "What you mean stay off it? I cain't stay off it. How am I supposed to work standing on one foot?"

Miss Annie flashed Sarah a wink and a smile. "A sprain is good news. Have you forgotten you believed your ankle to be broken just a moment ago?" She finished winding long strips of white cloth around Jennie's injury then patted her leg above the wrap. "I'd say this means you're not supposed to work, for a while at least."

Thomas stepped closer, nodding his head. "I jus' said the same to Henry by the door. The good Lord must done decided you been working too hard, Miss Jennie. The scripture do say, 'He maketh me to lie down. . . .' The good Lord means for you to rest a spell."

Henry surprised Sarah by speaking up from his place by the door. "God ain't struck this woman in the leg, Thomas. He don't do such things."

Jennie fell back and commenced to thrashing and wailing. "I cain't rest for a spell, Thomas. I'll find myself wanting a job if I do." She covered her face and started to cry. "What am I gon' do? Doc Turner gon' fire me now for sho'."

Miss Annie stood, her lacy blue gown out of place in the greasy, cluttered kitchen. "Now, now, dear lady. Dr. Turner seems a reasonable man and a kindly sort. I doubt he'd be inclined to fire you for getting hurt."

Sarah eased out of the way as Miss Annie moved to Jennie's side. When Jennie uncovered her face and stopped her tossing, Miss Annie smiled down at her. "If you think it'll help, I'll be happy to say a word to him on your behalf."

Jennie blinked away her tears. "You'd do such a kindness? For me?"

Annie leaned down and patted her wet face. "And why not? I'll go tend to it right away." She picked up Jennie's hand. "Will you be all right now?"

Jennie gazed up at Miss Annie as though she'd sprouted a halo and wings. "Oh, yes'm. I will, now you done fix me up." Smiling, she held up Miss Annie's handkerchief. "Here's your pretty hankie back."

Miss Annie patted the hand holding the delicate scrap of cloth. "Would you like to keep it?"

Jennie's eyes bulged. "Oh yes, ma'am. If you really don't mind."

"I don't mind one bit."

It amazed Sarah how comfortable Miss Annie seemed, how at home in a messy hotel kitchen filled with Sarah's people. She marveled at how Annie listened to them with interest, how she touched Jennie with genuine affection. Sarah had never seen such behavior from a white woman before, not even in St. Louis.

The fancy woman. . .no, the special lady met Sarah's eyes. "Don't I know you? Sarah, from the dry goods store, isn't it?"

Sarah tried to lower her gaze, but the soft gray eyes held hers. "Yes'm. That's right."

Miss Annie held out her hand. "It's good to see you again."

Astonished, Sarah reached a timid hand and let the lady take it in her own.

"May I leave our Jennie in your care? You'll see she gets up to her room, won't you?" She raised her brows at Henry. "You'll help her?"

Henry nodded. "Yes, ma'am. We'll see to it."

"Thank you both," Miss Annie said and gave Sarah's fingers a gentle squeeze.

When she started for the door, Sarah watched her closely, because she needed to know. Miss Annie crossed the whole length of the kitchen, pausing once to give last-minute instructions to Thomas, then left the room, without once wiping her hand on her skirt.

Jennie tugged at her sleeve. "You want to hear the worst part, Sarah?"

Fighting tears, she pulled her attention from the door. "What's that?"

Jennie patted a wide stain around her skirt pocket. "I done broke my bottle of tonic. Now what am I gon' do?"

Sarah smiled down at her childlike pout. "Sounds to me like you ain't about to need no energy tonic. But if it makes you feel better"—she reached into her own pocket, pulled out a brown bottle, peered closely at the contents, and then slipped it into Jennie's waiting hand—"just so happens I got another one right here."

At the door, Henry started to laugh. "Miss Jennie, take some advice from old Henry. No matter how much you like the first helping, don't go for seconds. Some things is better in small doses."

CHAPTER 16

Halfway to Thad's house, Bertha pulled the surrey to a stop along the dense wall of pine by the side of the road. She met Magda's gaze and answered her unspoken question. "Go back, Magda. I've changed my mind."

When she handed over the reins, Magda's confused look changed to bewilderment. "After all this? Why?"

"I shouldn't have asked this of you. It's bad enough I've brought down calamity on my own head. Poor Papa's, too, more than likely. I have no right to pile it on yours, as well. Go on back and see to your errands. I can walk to Thad's from here."

Magda sighed. "I've come this far. It's no more trouble to take you the rest of the way." She flicked the reins and whistled, goading the horse back onto the street. They rode in silence until Magda cut her eyes at Bertha. "I am still wondering if this is a good idea. I mean, it is sort of. . ."

Bertha twisted on her seat. "Sort of what?"

Magda swallowed and faced forward, taking her time to answer. "You know."

"Please quit studying that horse's behind and say what you're itching to say."

Magda glowered at her. "Brazen. It's downright brazen."

The words caused anger to rise in Bertha's throat. She whipped around and slapped the wooden seat so hard it rattled her bones. "You just don't know when to hush, do you?" She pointed at the ground. "Let me off this thing right now."

Magda hauled back on the reins. The surrey rolled to a stop and the two sat facing each other in angry silence. Magda crossed her arms. "Well, go ahead. Get down and run off. It's why you stopped, ain't it?"

Bertha managed a nod.

"Well then, why don't you?"

Grief crowded Bertha's throat, blocking her answer. The weight of her predicament pinned her to the seat, so heavy she could barely lift her shoulders in a helpless shrug. Tears stung her eyes, tears she couldn't stop if she tried. When Magda's startled face dissolved into a reflection of her pain, she released the pent-up flood.

Magda scooted beside her and gathered her close. "Don't cry, sweetie. Please don't." She smoothed Bertha's hair and rocked her on the seat while she fished a hankie from her bodice. "Here you go." She tucked the cloth in Bertha's hand. "You're right. I should learn when to keep my mouth shut." She leaned back and tilted Bertha's chin. "Dry your face, now. I'll take you straight to Thad's and won't say another word about it."

Bertha wiped her eyes and tried to swallow the hedge-apple-sized lump in her throat. "No, you were right to speak up. Running after him is the wrong thing to do. If Thad cared about my feelings, he'd have told me himself. Not let me hear it on the street."

"Honey, I think he tried."

Bertha banged her fist on one knee. "No, he didn't. He had plenty of chances to tell me."

Magda raised her hands in surrender. "All right, then. Thad's a scoundrel of the first order."

Bertha whirled on her. "Don't say such a thing. He wanted to tell me all along. Isn't that what Charlie said?"

Magda patted Bertha's clenched fists. "Whoa there. Remember, I'm on your side—whatever side it is. But you have to make up your mind." She lifted her chin toward the road. "And you have to decide if we're going to Thad's house. Otherwise I'm turning this contraption and heading back to town."

❧

The easy stride of Thad's horse didn't match the determination in his soul, yet dread had gathered and settled in the pit of his stomach, preventing him from urging the mare on. The task ahead weighed heavily, pulling him so tight his bones ached.

His thoughts turned to the words King David cried while in distress. *"Have mercy upon me, O LORD, for I am in trouble: mine eye is consumed with grief, yea, my soul and my belly. . . . My strength faileth because of mine iniquity, and my bones are consumed."*

The ancient words twanged a familiar chord with Thad. His joints hurt as much as his empty, knotted stomach.

He should've told Bertha days ago. Putting it off had spared him seeing her upset, but waiting only stacked up the pain and gave him so little time to say good-bye.

Well, no more. Though long overdue, today was the day. He swore to himself he'd not return home until he spoke with her.

He came to the cutoff that led to a shortcut into town, a path the mare always took without his bidding. When she plodded right past and kept with the road, he wondered briefly why she chose the long route but didn't bother to rein her back. Then he wondered at his willingness to let her go the long way and hoped his cowardice hadn't returned.

He didn't have far to go before he understood why the mare didn't turn. Around a bend in the road, Magda's surrey came into sight, pulled to the side with Magda and Bertha aboard. His mare must've smelled the old gray horse and decided a visit was in order. Or maybe God Himself desired a swift end to Thad's procrastination.

Heart pounding, he approached the carriage. The two girls sat with their heads together, Bertha leaning toward her friend. When Thad saw her wipe her eyes, his heart stopped pounding and crawled up his throat.

She knew. Somehow Bertha knew. It was the reason they were on the road to his house and the reason she cried. He shoved down the yellow-bellied urge to flee and rode their way.

Magda saw him first. She watched him come with a mixture of sorrow and anger on her face. Then she sat up, nudged Bertha, and pointed over her shoulder. He came alongside and Bertha stared into his eyes with a look he couldn't describe.

He gave her a curt nod. "I was on my way to see you." It sounded weak, even to him.

She blinked a few times, as if to convince herself she really saw him there. "I was, too. Until I came to my senses."

He hated himself for her tears, her red-rimmed eyes, the pain so evident on her face. "I should've told you myself, Bertha. I tried."

She looked away, and the rebuff twisted his stomach in knots. He glanced at Magda for help, but she shook her head and put her arms around Bertha.

"Magda, can you leave us alone? I need to talk to her."

The balance of sorrow and anger shifted, and Magda glared at him over Bertha's head. "I won't leave unless she tells me to."

The wind picked up, whipping and bending the overhead trees, chilling Thad's poor scattered bones. His insides danced and tossed in time with the treetops while he waited for Bertha to speak, and for the first time that morning, he felt glad he'd had no stomach for breakfast. When her silence stretched on, he thought to turn the mare and ride away, but his heart insisted he stay.

"I'll beg if I have to, Bertha, but you can spare me muddy knees if you'll climb down and come here."

"Why should I spare you anything?" she asked without looking up. "The sight of you on your knees might be just what I need to feel better."

Thad swung his leg over the horse and dismounted. "Then it's a small price to pay."

By the time he reached the surrey, Bertha had turned. "What do you think you're doing?"

He knelt in the cold, miry clay beside the road. "Making you feel better."

"No, don't!" She scurried to the edge of the seat and dropped her legs to the step. "Thad, you stop it right now." She came even with him and took his arm, trying with little success to pull him to his feet.

Down on his knees, his face wasn't much lower than hers. "Do you feel better yet? This ground is mighty cold."

"All right. I feel better."

"Will you stay awhile with me and let me explain?"

"Whatever you say. Just get up from there."

The look she returned as he gazed up at her gave him courage. He got to his feet and pulled her in front of him. "I have so much I need to say to you. I just don't know where to start."

Magda cleared her throat. "While you're trying to sort it out, kindly get out of the way so I can turn this thing around."

Thad eased Bertha off the road, and Magda urged the horse around. She stopped beside them and leaned down. "I suppose you'll get her safely home, then?"

Thad nodded, and she flicked the reins. He tucked Bertha under his arm, and they stood together while the surrey moved along Line Street toward town. He watched Bertha's face as she stood staring after Magda. He had powerful feelings for the girl beside him, feelings that had gone unspoken for too long. So many nights he'd wrestled with his thoughts and his sheets, wondering if she felt the same. But he knew then what he knew now. He had no right to ask her.

"Bertha?"

She lifted teary eyes to his. "Yes?"

"Can you ever forgive me?"

"It's true, then. You're leaving Jefferson."

"You knew one day I would."

"Yes, one day. Just not tomorrow." She blushed. "I thought we had more time."

He reached to touch the soft spot under her chin. "I have no choice. My fate was decided a long time ago."

Her brow furrowed. "Your fate? You make it sound like a trip to the gallows." She whirled away from him with a swish of petticoats. "Surely a man can decide for himself if he's ready for hanging?"

He took her by the shoulders. "You don't understand, sugar. It's Papa's dream that I attend a good school and be the first college graduate in our family. I can't let him down."

Her frown deepened. "So it's your Papa's dream, not yours?"

"The man's talked of little else since I can remember, planned and saved for years. I've watched Mama and Cyrus do without while he stashed away money for school." Desperate for her understanding, he gripped her arms. "When Papa got wind of Texas AMC opening right there in Brazos County, it was all it took to send him over the edge."

Thad let go of Bertha and began to plod back and forth. "You should see him when he talks about it. I tell you, his face lights up, and he looks ten years younger. The last few days. . .well, you'd think he was the one leaving for school in the morning."

Bertha grabbed his arm to stop his pacing. "Do you hear yourself?" She tightened her grip on his arm. "Has any of this ever been about you?"

Her simple words leapt to life, striking hard and boring to the center of his gut, to the secret place where he'd buried the same ungrateful, disloyal question. Bertha, by voicing it aloud in her sweet, sincere voice, had rooted straight through and exposed it and somehow shed a different light on his betrayal.

"What are your dreams?" she persisted.

"My what?"

"Every man has dreams, Thad. What do you want out of life?"

He sighed. "Not much, really. All it would take to make me happy is some farmland, a pond for fishing, and a place to raise dogs." He blushed and grinned. "And a good woman to share such bounty."

"Dogs?" She laughed, but not at him, and he loved the throaty sound.

"Hunting dogs. Men pay top dollar for good hunting dogs.

With proper breeding and training, there's money to be made." Just talking about it stoked a fire deep in his heart. "Like Henry King's bloodhound, for instance. Old Dickens is one fine-looking animal. Did you ever get a good look at him, Bertha?" He cupped his hands beside his head. "Ears on him like an elephant's."

She laughed louder. "Thaddeus Bloom, you're glowing. You sure don't shine like this when you talk about going to school."

Thad looked away. He'd never clear his head by staring into her bewitching eyes. "Bertha, I should've told you I had to go before now. I have no excuse for such ill treatment, and I hope you'll forgive me. But no matter how much I love you, only one thing really matters. I'm leaving tomorrow, and I don't know when I'll be back. Nothing can change it."

A hurt looked erased her glowing smile. She crossed her arms over her chest and presented him with her back.

He reached to touch her shoulder. "Bertha?"

She jerked her shoulder from under his hand and walked a few steps away. "You really think your leaving is all that matters, Thad? Well, you're wrong." She spun and ran at him, burrowing into his shirt. "I think loving each other should be what matters most."

He didn't trust himself to hold her the way he wanted, so he patted the top of her head as if she were a sister and then felt silly for having done it. Bertha loved him, too. She'd just said so. And he had nothing to offer for her trouble.

Thad moaned at the sky. "I don't want to leave you, Bertha. Especially now. But I have to go, and I can't take you with me."

She nodded in his arms. "I know you have to go, and I understand. I really do. Though I can hardly bear the thought."

"Will you write me? Your letters will make the time go by faster." He mentally kicked himself. He had no right to expect that sort of commitment.

"I'll write to you every day. I promise."

"No, sugar. No promises. I can't ask you to keep them. I can't even ask you to wait for me. It wouldn't be fair."

She opened her mouth to speak, but he pressed his finger to

her lips. "Bertha, let's not think about what comes later. If your Papa will let me come see you tonight, I'll stay with you as long as I can."

"Oh, Thad. That sounds so nice. I'm sure Papa will let you stay late if I tell him you're leaving tomorrow. And Mama will want you to come in time for supper."

He grinned. "You sure know how to sweeten the pot."

She laughed, and the lighthearted sound of it lifted the anchor from his heart.

"I wish I'd known sooner I could lure you with food. How about if I ply you with cobbler for dessert?"

"I'd say it sounds like I'd better rush home and pack. I won't have time later." He pulled her to him for a chaste hug, as chaste as he could manage, at least. "Bertha, I want us to be together every minute until I leave."

She leaned back and focused on his eyes. "We will be. If I have to move heaven and earth to be with you tonight, I'll make sure it happens."

CHAPTER 17

No two ways about it, Miss Annie had the gift. Wonder of wonders, she convinced Doc Turner to put Jennie in a room upstairs at Brooks House while she mended. Thomas, who witnessed the whole thing, said Miss Annie insisted he would be doing her a great kindness, considering she wouldn't need to walk clear back to the servants' quarters to tend Jennie's ankle. Thomas claimed that Doc Turner, who didn't stand a chance against Miss Annie's beguiling ways, just lifted his hat and nodded while grinning like a love-struck boy.

When the shock from the unlikely arrangement wore off, Sarah had Henry and Thomas brace the jabbering Jennie between them and help her to the foot of the stairs. Then Henry took over, winding her arm about his neck while she hopped on one leg up the steps. A wide-eyed Thomas followed, holding his fidgety arms out front as if ready to catch Jennie's tumbling body. Sarah figured he might as well save himself the trouble. If Jennie fell, she'd take them all to the bottom with her.

Sarah brought up the rear, one hand laden with a bowl of Cook's hot broth, the other with fresh linens. At the top landing, Jennie nodded to the right, too busy talking to stop and give directions. Henry guided his cumbrous burden around the polished banister post then along the hall to the first door. Thomas bobbed in front to turn a key that dangled from the lock.

Henry glanced back at Sarah and shook his head. By the look on his face, she knew what he had on his mind. He often pondered white folks' uncommon fixation with bars and bolts, considering his people had fought so hard to be free of them, so a key stored on the outside of a locked door would be just the thing to vex his mind. But Sarah knew the reason. Jennie once mentioned it let the maids know which rooms were empty and needed cleaning.

Thomas swung the door open onto the prettiest room Sarah had ever seen, even counting Miss Blow's house back home. The walls, so high you could stack two and a half men against them head to toe, were covered in wallpaper the color of a sunset, like pink stirred up with orange peels. Rows of tiny flowers, the shade of eggshells, dotted the pink. Tall mahogany posts of equal height jutted to the ceiling from the four corners of the high bed. The same molasses-colored wood as on the posts, rubbed with carnauba wax to a high shine, made up every stick of furniture in the room.

Jennie pointed at a spindly-legged bench that looked too fragile to hold her. "Jus' drop me on the settee, Henry, while Sarah makes the bed. Thomas, pull up the stool yonder for my poor old foot. Sarah, you can put my broth on the side table to cool, but lay a napkin over it so no dust settles on top. And by the by, hold the pillow out the window and beat it good a'fore you covers it. Nothing I hates worse'n a dusty pillow." She chuckled. "Less'n it be dusty soup." She frowned at Thomas, who had done her bidding but now edged toward the door. "Come back over here and pull in this stool so I can reach it better. My leg ain't made of rubber."

Sarah stifled a grin but couldn't help raising one eyebrow at Henry, who seemed to have a harder time hiding his amusement. He busied himself by taking hold of the other corners of the sheet Sarah held, raising his side high overhead and flapping so hard she nearly lost her grip. As the sheet settled to the bed between them, he gave her a playful wink. She turned away and bit her lip to hold in the laughter.

Henry rescued her by drawing Jennie's attention over to him. "Mighty nice of Doc Turner to open up this room for you, Miss Jennie."

Jennie sat on the edge of the settee turning her ankle back and forth, studying it from every angle with puckered lips. At Henry's words, her fretful look turned to joy, and she beamed up at him. "You got that right, Henry."

She gazed around the room as if she'd never seen it before. "All the times I swept and dusted in here, I never once imagined I'd be sleeping in that bed." She turned a squinty eye on Henry. "But it weren't really Doc's idea, you know. He didn't have the starch to stand up to Miss Bessie, that's all."

They all nodded and mumbled their agreement.

Jennie drew her shoulders back and raised her chin. "Not to say Doc don't hold me in the highest regard." She lowered her voice and peered at the three of them in turn. "But we all know things don't happen this way 'round these parts. If Doc hadn't been plum bothered and befuddled by Miss Bessie, none of us would be sitting here in this nice room."

Sarah cast a quick look at Henry. Sure enough, Jennie's talk about the way things were around Jefferson had him squirming.

He grabbed a feather pillow and blustered over to throw open a window. Leaning on the bustle bench under the sash, he pounded the pillow until soft tufts of down formed a cloud around him and drifted like snow to the street. "Hard to believe it's jus' past noon," he called over his shoulder. "This storm got it dark as gloom out here. Cold, too."

Jennie pulled the afghan from the back of the small sofa and wrapped it around her shoulders. "Hurry up and close off that draft, Henry. All I need is the croup to go along with this ankle."

Henry shut the window and tossed the pillow to Sarah. "There now, Miss Jennie. Your bedding's dusted, and all danger of the croup is past."

Sarah slid on the crocheted pillow slip and patted out the lumps then turned to give the room a careful look. "I guess that about does it, Jennie. Unless you can think of anything else you might need."

Jennie took a look around and smiled up at Sarah. "Seem like you done thought of everything."

Sarah placed an extra blanket at the foot of the bed. "You sure I can't stay and sit with you tonight?"

Jennie waved her hand. "My sister's girl gon' be here directly. Should've been here by now, in fact. Don't worry—I got Thomas to care for me till she come." She peered past Henry to where the startled man still lurked by the door. "Ain't that right, Thomas?"

He spewed and sputtered, backing toward the door and shaking his head.

Jennie shook her finger and fixed him with a warning look. "Hush, now. Bring yourself over here and sit down. You ain't gon' no place till my niece show up."

Sarah picked up the broth and handed it to Thomas, who reacted as if she'd handed him a skunk. "This is cool enough to sip now. See she drinks it down."

Laughing, Jennie took it from the stricken man. "It's my ankle what's ailing, Sarah. Not my hands. You two git on home to your chores. You've wasted enough of this day foolin' 'round with me. Not to say I ain't grateful."

Sarah leaned down to hug her. "I'm just glad you're all right, that's all." *Powerful glad.*

Behind her, Henry cleared his throat. Sarah guessed he must be thinking along the same lines, remembering what they feared had happened to Jennie. She decided if he laughed, she'd skin him.

Outside, Sarah drew in fresh air laden with sweet relief. It felt good to be headed home instead of to the jailhouse. She sat tall and proper in town, but when the wagon rolled past the Polk Street Bridge, giddy laughter bubbled to the surface. Henry stole a look behind them then pulled back on the reins, climbed down, and ran around to her side. She stood up, fit to bust, and soared into his arms. He swung her around in circles, both laughing so hard their tears mingled each time he kissed her.

"I never been so relieved of a thing in my life!" Henry yelled.

"I thought sure I'd be watching you hang."

Still clinging to his neck, she jerked her gaze to his face. "But you said—"

"Never mind what I said. I'd done give you up to the noose. Figured nothing on earth could save you. 'Specially if you'd done killed Doc Turner, too."

If not for his rascally grin, she'd have throttled him. "I've never been so scared in all my born days."

His arms around her waist tightened, and his grin disappeared. "Neither have I, Sarah. I always figured I could protect you from any harm that came your way. I learned today they's some things only the Lord can shield you from. Don't think I didn't call on Him."

Sarah leaned her head against Henry's broad chest and let him hold her. She couldn't tell which of them trembled the worst, but she felt his heart pounding against her cheek.

Henry kissed the top of her head. "I'm jus' grateful the Almighty took care of you."

She rose on her tiptoes and kissed his chin. "Me, too."

He pulled back, a glint in his teasing eyes. "You reckon it's the first time the good Lord used cow manure to save one of His own?"

Sarah laughed again, and he pulled her close for a tender kiss, but they sprang apart at the sound of approaching hooves. Henry tightened his arm around her waist at the sight of three men on horseback headed their way. One of them, a pale-skinned man with long, stringy hair the color of jerked beef, rode out in front. Henry took her arm and gave her a gentle shove toward the rig. "Get aboard, Sarah. Those men are strangers."

The edge in his voice set her feet in motion. Without waiting for him to lift her, she grabbed the side rail and clambered onto the seat. In his haste, Henry made it around Dandy and into his place before she ever sat down.

"How do you know they're strangers?"

The men were close enough now to hear, so Henry whispered his answer. "The horses they're riding came from Rink Livery." As he spoke, a winsome smile slid over his face, and he raised his hat in greeting. "How ya'll doing?"

The men had started reining in their mounts before Henry said a word. Sarah sensed it didn't bode well. Her legs tensed under her, ready for flight.

Up close, the first man wasn't much taller than the others. He only seemed so from a distance because he held himself high in the saddle and wore a proud smirk on his face. He turned cold eyes on Henry and called back to his men in a sassy tone, "What we got here, boys? This uppity whelp thinks he can address us without permission, like he thinks we're one of his kind." He turned to a portly man with thinning hair. "Do I have anything black smeared on my face, Edward?"

Edward laughed. Sarah figured he spent a lot of time laughing just to please the haughty man. She seethed inside, but Henry's leg pressed hard against hers sent a clear warning to behave.

As for Henry, he kept right on grinning. "You folks lost? 'Cause if you was lost, you ain't no mo'." He pointed over his shoulder. "Not a mile back sits Jefferson, right there where you left it."

The scrawny man on the right, actually more of a boy so thin Sarah thought he could use a pot of beans, attempted a smile that became more of a grimace. She reckoned he needed more practice.

The tall leader pulled a gold watch from his breast pocket. Not to tell the time but to twiddle it between his fingers while he seemed to mull over something in his head. His next words shot fire through Sarah's heart. "You two stole that rig, didn't you?"

Henry's senseless grin faded. His Adam's apple rose then fell. "Excuse me, suh? What did you say?"

Pocket Watch Man swept Sarah's body with a downright meddlesome gaze, so slowly her skin crawled, and then fixed soulless eyes on Henry. "You ain't deaf, boy. I said you stole the rig. The mule, too, because that there's my mule. Been looking for my animal all day, ain't I, boys?"

The grinning dullards alongside him nodded.

"And here you come, riding up with my mule hitched to my wagon, sitting there pretty as you please on a stolen rig."

Terror melted Sarah's bones. Her dress was all that held her useless sack of skin on the seat. Henry's face looked the way it had the time Dandy kicked him in the stomach and laid him out on the ground gasping like a trout.

"No, suh! Ya'll mistaken. We ain't no more stole this rig than fly." He jabbed his finger at Dandy. "I've had this here same mule going on three years now."

The fearsome stranger waited while the stillness behind Henry's words settled around them like pitched hay. Then he rose up in his stirrups and eased back with a grunt. His squirming seemed to set off the other two riders, because they leaned over their saddles, watching his face and waiting. Sweat pooled at the base of Sarah's spine.

The man cocked his head at Henry. "Know what I say to that, charcoal boy?"

Henry trembled beside her. His face shifted from fear to terrible rage then relaxed to show no emotion at all. . .until he smiled. Sarah stared up at his even row of shiny white teeth and decided he'd lost his mind.

"Naw, suh, I don't know what you might say. I sho' don't." Henry leaned back against the buckboard seat and adjusted the raggedy brim of his hat to cover his eyes, which made his broad grin stand out like a polecat at a party. "But I know you sho' 'nuff 'bout to tell me."

The man's eyes narrowed, and his face flushed red. "I say you're a low-down liar and a thief!" Flecks of spit spewed from his mouth into the air.

All three horses lurched toward them at the same time. The skinny, pock-faced boy, who hadn't yet said a word, reached for the pistol strapped to his side.

Sarah stood up and screamed then lunged forward to cover Henry with her body. A shot rang out, the exploding boom loud in Sarah's ears. She'd heard that gunshot wounds burned like melted lead poured in an open sore, so she stiffened and waited to feel hot pain.

When her body spun, she opened her eyes to see if Henry or Jesus held her. Through the haze of fear muddling her mind, she realized Henry had turned his back on the men. Puzzled, she followed his gaze to the edge of the woods.

T. M. Bagby, the sheriff of Marion County, sat astride his horse in a clearing not ten yards off the road. Sheriff John Vines, who held the office just before Bagby, stood next to him, the reins of his dun pony in one hand, a rifle pointed to the sky in the other. Wisps of smoke still streamed from its barrel.

"What's going on here?" Sheriff Bagby growled.

Sarah's shaky legs failed her, and she slid down Henry's body to the seat. Sheriff Vines mounted his horse, and the two men rode their way. Never in her life had Sarah been so glad to see two white lawmen.

Sheriff Bagby came alongside the wagon, his angry glare aimed at the strange men, a fact that greatly eased Sarah's mind. "I asked you men a question. What the devil's going on?"

Edward, the fleshy one, lowered his head like a hang-tail dog and backed up behind the others. The hungry-looking boy pulled his hand away from his holster, but by the snarl on his face, it pained him.

The prideful man in front lost no trace of his swagger. He took his time answering while he circled the face of his timepiece with the thumb of his smooth white hand. For the first time, Sarah noticed his slender fingers looked more like a woman's than a man's. He pointed at Henry. "This business is between this man and myself. No one else. How about you two ride on off and let us get it settled?"

Sheriff Vines tightened the grip on his rifle and eased closer. "I'd sure like to oblige you, mister, but"—he pointed over his shoulder at the clearing—"from over there it appeared your business had gotten a little out of hand."

Sheriff Bagby looked even madder than before. "What say

you let us in on the details? We'll decide whether or not it's our business."

Sarah nudged Henry hard. He gave her a look like nobody was home but came around in time to speak up in a jumble of words. "Sheriff, this stranger say I done stole my own wagon. Old Dandy, too." He straightened his shoulders and scowled at the man. "Ain't stole nothing. He knows it same as I do."

The sheriff glanced back at Henry. "Why, that's foolish talk. Henry here is no thief."

Pocket Watch Man regarded Sheriff Bagby with one raised brow then spat on the ground between them. "Suppose I want to contest? It's the word of three white men against one colored boy."

Sheriff Bagby frowned at each accuser in turn. "Gentlemen, I know this man well enough to say he's the owner of this rig and the animal pulling it. I can vouch for him myself."

Sheriff Vines snorted. "So can I, which means you need to refigure your math. Looks like it's the word of three white men against one colored man and two officers of the law. By my ciphering, our sum's higher."

Pocket Watch Man's jaw worked in circles. "What if I said I bought the rig from him fair and square, paid good money for it, and he slipped around and took off with it again?" He sneered over at Henry. "I know he don't look smart enough, but he's got himself quite a racket going down by the docks." He sat back with a haughty smirk, clearly proud of his lying story. "Now then. What avenues for justice does this town afford?"

The two lawmen shared a grin. Then Sheriff Vines's amused look turned hard. "Sir, one of the avenues for justice around here is the truth. So I'm sure you won't mind giving me a truthful answer to a direct question."

"Not at all. Ask what you will."

Sheriff Vines tipped his hat. "Let's start simple. You got a name?"

"Indeed I do. Frank Griswald, from the Boston Griswalds, at your service."

The sheriff raked him with doubtful eyes. "If you don't mind, I have a few more questions, Mr."—he paused and raised one brow—"*Griswald.*"

Sarah and Henry shared a knowing glance.

Sheriff Vines edged closer on his horse. "You boys staying here in town?"

The lead man nodded. "We are. We're paying guests over at the Commercial Hotel."

The sheriff nodded then leaned forward on his saddle horn. "The Commercial Hotel, you say? Well, tell me this, didn't I see you three get off the *Maria Louise* when she put into port not an hour ago?"

Griswald opened his mouth to answer but closed it again when Sheriff Vines held up his hand. "Since I know right well I did see you crawl off the *Louise*, I'm wondering how you found time to negotiate purchase of a rig, manage to lose it again, book a room, find the livery, and hire these horses, then track down this man to accuse him. That's a busy hour, my friend. It just don't sound reasonable."

Sheriff Bagby interrupted before the black-hearted scoundrel had a chance to answer. "If you don't mind, John, I have a couple questions of my own. First, your name isn't Griswald at all, now, is it? Fact is, you're Jack Thibeau, a two-bit gambler out of New Orleans. You stole the Griswald name just like you were about to steal from this man. . .after murdering him and his wife in cold blood."

Sarah tensed as the three scoundrels started to fidget, but they stilled when Sheriff Vines lowered his rifle. Sheriff Bagby unsheathed his own gun and lifted the business end in their direction. "Before you boys start lying and denying, what say I escort you into town and lock you up for attempted murder?"

CHAPTER 18

Bertha slid a satin ribbon around her neck and pulled it up into her hair then wove it through the tied-up curls and fashioned a pretty bow in front. The dusky green fabric against her black hair set off her eyes to perfection. Leaning closer to the looking glass above her dressing table, she ran her finger back and forth over her two front teeth. The resulting squeal sounded loud inside her head. Twice since dinner she had scrubbed her teeth with tooth powder until they gleamed.

She picked up the container of Sozodont and read the label. *"For relief of impure breath caused by catarrh, bad teeth, or use of liqueur or tobacco."*

Catarrh? Bertha glanced at her reflection and sniffed. No runny nose.

Bad teeth? She drew back her lips to check. Not yet, thank the Lord.

Liquor? No, thank you.

Tobacco? Never!

Still, the powder promised sweet breath and pearl-like teeth. With Thad coming soon, she wanted her breath as sweet as possible. She ran her finger across her mouth again and listened, grinning at the satisfying squeak.

She crossed the room to her wardrobe and threw open the doors. As she thumbed past her everyday frocks to find her favorite green dress, the lyrics to the song she hummed came to her mind.

Oh! why am I so happy,
Why these feelings of delight?
And why does gladness cheer me?
Why everything so bright?

To say things were bright would be false. The very gloomy fact of Thad's leaving hung around her neck like a millstone. But she couldn't mourn today, not when Papa had given permission for Thad to come for supper and stay as long as he liked. A dangerous offer, considering the two of them had so much time to make up.

Bertha sang aloud as she slipped into the lacy dress.

"Why am I so happy,
Why these feelings of delight?"

Why? Because at long last Thad admitted his love for her. After the many times she had thought of it, prayed for it, daydreamed about it, Thaddeus Bloom would stand on her doorstep, come to court. She wouldn't allow herself to think beyond tonight.

Bertha checked herself in the looking glass. Though she had taken extra care getting ready, the image staring back surprised her. Her hair never looked so glossy or her eyes so bright, as though the joy churning in her heart had oozed its way to the surface.

Only one thing missing—jewelry to accentuate the plain, high bodice of the gown. She reached inside her collar and found the chain around her neck. A few years past, Moses Pharr had found the beautiful silver necklace by the docks and given it to Bertha, an act of generosity Rhodie had never forgiven. With two fingers, Bertha pulled the necklace free, kissed the filigreed cross, and centered it on her chest. Perfect.

Perfect necklace, perfect dress, perfect night.

"Perhaps I should change me mind. If Thad sees you like this, he's bound to carry you off, and I'll never see you again."

Bertha smiled at Papa's reflection in the glass then turned to where he stood in the doorway. "Oh, Papa, thank you for letting Thad come."

"Allowing such a fine boy to court you is easy. Telling your mother he'll be staying past respectable was the hard part. Well, that and sitting up half the night playing chaperone. I admit I don't look forward to it."

"You, Papa? You'll be my chaperone?"

Papa lowered his head. "Aye. 'Tis a woman's place, I know. I might as well don a skirt and corset." He lifted pleading eyes to Bertha's. "But what can I do? Your mama refuses. Will you be very ashamed of me?"

Bertha put her arms around his neck and kissed his cheek. "Ashamed? I'm glad. You'll make a much better chaperone than Mama."

When he made a face, she laughed. "Comfort yourself with knowing tonight is the first and last time I'll be courted."

He pushed her to arm's length. "What folly is this?"

She squeezed his shoulders. "I mean it, Papa. If Thad leaves tomorrow without proposing first, I'll live out my days a spinster."

He flashed a roguish grin. "Then I'll keep you to meself forever? So much the better." He cupped her chin in his hand. "But I fear it's too much to ask for with a daughter as lovely as you."

Warmth crept up her cheeks. "I only want Thad, Papa."

"Aye, and from what you told me this morning, I suspect he wants only you."

"Then why is he so stubborn? We've wasted too much time already, and he refuses to ask me to wait."

Papa pulled her down on the bed beside him. "We men are complicated creatures, me love. Matters you can't understand consume our hearts, but these things nurture traits you will someday find of great value. Traits like honor, self-sacrifice, and commitment. Thad loves you, and you love him back. This is the foundation of a good relationship. The rest are minor details. Can you trust God with the details, Bertha?"

He wrapped his arms around her, and she leaned her head against his shoulder. "Your words encourage me, Papa. Until now, I've been afraid to hope."

He patted her head. "Never fear hope, me girl. Not with the Great Hope in your life. He's well able to work out the details of a surrendered life." He took hold of her shoulders and raised her up to face him. "The cantankerous man in question will arrive any minute. Are you ready?"

Bertha grinned. "Oh, Papa, I've been ready for months." Then she held up her finger. "Except for one last thing." She picked up the Sozodont powder from the dressing table and held it up for him to see. "I need to clean my teeth."

He covered her hand with his and pushed the bottle down. "Your teeth are fine, Bertha. Too much of this stuff will eat away at them."

Groaning, she set the can aside. "I just want everything to be perfect tonight."

"*You* are perfect, dearie, and the only thing old Thaddy Boy will notice."

Mama leaned inside the door. "Francis? Here you are, for heaven's sake. I've been calling until my ears rattled."

"If you'd rattled the windows instead, I might've heard you. I take it you're ready to go?"

Bertha sought Papa's eyes. "Go? You can't go. Thad will be here any minute."

Mama unfolded and pulled on her gloves. "Don't fret, Bertha. We'll be back before he arrives. I promised Dr. Eason I would look in on Mrs. McKenzie and her new baby. Supper is ready to serve, and we'll return before Thad comes. Set the table while we're gone, would you?"

"Yes, ma'am, I will."

"And remember. . .should Thad happen to get here before we get back, serve him hot tea on the veranda."

Bertha pointed toward the window. "But it's cold out there."

"Just do like I say. Don't dare take him inside the house. Understand?"

"No, ma'am, I won't."

Papa grinned past Mama at her. "Heaven forbid I should have to shoot the poor lad the first time he comes calling."

Bertha herded them toward the door. "If you're going, then go. I won't leave Thad to languish on the porch until he dies from exposure."

When they left, she turned back to the mirror for one last check of her appearance. Satisfied with how she looked, she ran her tongue over the roof of her mouth and glanced at the tooth powder.

Papa's reflection appeared in the glass, peering around the doorpost behind her. "Ah, ah, ah! Leave it alone, now."

She burst into giggles and tossed the Sozodont container. He dodged it then disappeared, but she heard his hearty laughter until the back door slammed.

∽◈∾

On the road to Bertha's house, Thad made up his mind. Considering the situation in which he found himself, maybe, just maybe, the trait his mama often cautioned him about had waylaid him again. She claimed Thad had a habit of deciding too soon about the expected outcome of a situation and, once he decided it would turn out one way or the other, lacked the flexibility to consider a different end.

Might self-imposed blinders have blocked his sight? If he could wait however long it took to be with Bertha, why shouldn't he believe the same applied to her? And Francis Biddie's willingness to receive him tonight, knowing full well he'd be leaving tomorrow, cast new light on whether the man would be agreeable to a long engagement for his daughter.

Thad allowed the decision to settle around his heart. He would ask Mr. Biddie for Bertha's hand in marriage. He wouldn't leave their place tonight without the man's blessing and a promise from Bertha to wait.

The murky clouds had folded back in the last couple of hours, allowing sunshine on Jefferson soil for the first time in several days—not that it warmed things up any. Thad approached the turnoff to Bertha's just as the sun settled onto the horizon and began its slow ride down. An orange haze spread over the western sky, and Thad entertained the pleasing notion that it was the last sunset he would see before he and Bertha were betrothed.

He turned down the lane, leaving the painted sky at his back. Up ahead, the Biddie place sat back about a quarter mile off the road. In the fading light, the house and tall trees surrounding it stood out in sharp relief, like black cutouts on a gray background. Excited and impatient, he gave the mare a light tap with his heel to speed her along. As he neared the yard, he noticed the Biddie wagon approaching from another direction.

"Hail, Thad!" Mr. Biddie called.

Thad raised his hand in greeting. "Evening, sir." He nodded toward Bertha's mama, who sat straight and proper on the seat. "Mrs. Biddie."

The woman nodded back but waited until her husband helped her down and Thad joined them on the front walk before she spoke. "Good evening, Thad. We're ever so glad to have you tonight. I hope you're hungry."

Thad took off his hat. "Yes, ma'am. And thank you for the invitation."

Mr. Biddie shook Thad's hand then motioned toward the gate. "Come inside out of the cold. Bertha's waiting for you."

Mrs. Biddie nudged him and frowned. Mr. Biddie lifted his shoulders at Thad and grinned. She turned and offered her arm to Thad then nodded toward the horizon as they made their way up the walk. "How pleasant to see a sunset, no matter how unexpected and brief. I do detest wet weather. I like the snow, mind you, but not the rain. Have you ever witnessed the sunset on a snow-covered hill, Thad?"

The Louisiana boy ducked his head and grinned. "Can't say that I have, ma'am."

"Well, it's a sight to behold."

"Yes, ma'am, I imagine it would be."

Mr. Biddie ducked around them to open the door. Thad allowed Bertha's mama to pass through; then he followed her inside. His stomach jumped as he entered the hall, and he couldn't corral his searching eyes.

Mrs. Biddie touched his arm. "Show our guest to the parlor, Francis; then summon Bertha from her room. I'll bring in hot tea. We'll relax a bit and get acquainted before we eat." She fixed a bright smile on her face. "If it's all right with you, Thad."

"Oh yes, ma'am. That'll be fine." As long as they hurried to the "summon Bertha" part, everything about the evening held promise.

Mr. Biddie left Thad perched expectantly on the edge of a high-backed chair. He sat alternately drumming on the arm then gripping it, crossing and uncrossing his legs, and biting his lower lip until it hurt. The door finally opened and he jumped to his feet.

Instead of Bertha, Mrs. Biddie came in alone and set a tea service on the low, claw-foot table. She glanced around, surprised. "They haven't returned?"

He shook his head. "No, ma'am. Not yet."

"Well, goodness." Pulling her anxious gaze from the door, she smiled at Thad. "We'll just have to start without them. I'm sure they'll be along directly."

When Mrs. Biddie served him, he wished she hadn't. His hands shook so much, the delicate cup clattered against the saucer until he braced it on his knee. Thankfully, she pretended not to notice. But he caught her casting worried glances at her china when she wasn't staring nervously at the door.

Bertha's mama gave him a shaky smile. "I can't imagine what's keeping those two."

She'd no sooner spoken than Mr. Biddie entered the room. His wife glared up at him, and Thad stood, so nervous he nearly tossed the lady's china in her lap. Mr. Biddie remained just inside the doorway, frowning and gnawing on his lip.

Mrs. Biddie leaned forward. "Francis? What on earth? Where's Bertha?"

"I can't say."

For the first time, Thad noticed that all color had drained from the man's face, and at his words, Mrs. Biddie's paled to match it, her bright smile long gone.

"What do you mean?"

"I mean I can't say, because I don't know. Your daughter's not here, Emeline. Not in her room, inside the house, or anywhere on the grounds. I've search the whole place. Bertha's gone. Just plain gone."

CHAPTER 19

Bertha rode hard toward town, her attention drawn to the setting sun. She'd already lost too much time by circling around the usual route, but she had to avoid the road to miss Thad.

Her spirits sank lower at the thought of him. What would he do when he arrived to find her gone? She'd bungled things before, but never with such heartrending consequences.

As she stood staring at the cross around her neck in the looking glass, her heart had seized in her chest and she'd stumbled back to sit on the bed before she fell. To her shame she considered forgetting her promise to meet Annie just as fast as she'd recalled it, and after a few deep breaths to settle her nerves, she'd gone right on preparing for Thad's visit.

Until the reminder came that the time she planned to spend with Thad didn't belong to her. The evening belonged to God in sacrifice for Annie. But when she'd offered it, she'd had no way of knowing how dear the cost.

The last bit of daylight faded to the point where Bertha could hardly see, which made it necessary for her to pick her way with caution through the woods. She would be late. What calamity if, after all of this, Annie gave up on her and went back to her room.

Suppose Annie didn't show? Bertha had to admit she'd be glad.

She already hoped the meeting went fast enough to get her home early, though she'd have some explaining to do when she got there. If she didn't see Annie standing in the alley, she'd hightail it back and enjoy her evening with Thad, her conscience clear.

"I'll look for you at sunset, but I'll wait no matter how long it takes."

They were her words, spoken with conviction just hours before. At this latest reminder, anger welled up along with sudden hot tears. "Very well, God!" she cried aloud. "But I don't understand why You're doing this to me."

Thad would be hurt at losing so much of their time, especially after her promise to move heaven and earth to spend the evening together. When she got back, she'd have to make him understand. Her determination may have succeeded with moving the earth, but she found her stubborn streak no match for God's heaven.

At the last turn into town, Bertha slowed her horse so she wouldn't attract attention but rose up in the saddle and peered toward the alley. "Where is she?" she whispered to the horse. She leaned over the saddle and strained her eyes. *Where is she?*

There!

Annie stood in the shadows near the corner building, huddled against the cold. She faced away from the road and the streetlamp, and away from Bertha. To keep from scaring her, Bertha got off the horse, tied him to a post, and walked the rest of the way. "Annie?"

Startled, Annie's shoulders jerked, but she didn't turn around.

"It's me. Are you all right?"

Annie turned, and Bertha saw why she hadn't at first. Tangled hair fell around her head and shoulders in a stringy mess. Powder and paint ran in streaks, and her face appeared swollen and wet with tears. She wore a coat over what appeared to be her nightdress. In the dim glow from the nearby gaslight, Bertha noticed the nightgown had been ripped off one shoulder.

Her steps faltered. "Oh, Annie. What has he done to you? "

Annie stumbled close and fell against her. "He hurt me. He always hurts me. I hate him so much."

"Did he hit you?"

She rocked her head from side to side. "Not with his fists. Not this time. He can't afford to mar the merchandise."

"Merchandise? What do you mean?"

Annie tugged her coat around her and looked away. "Nothing. Never mind." She cleared her throat and licked her smeared red lips. "Abe pushed me around a little, that's all. Pinned me to the bed and screamed insults in my face. When he let me up, I ran." She fingered the tattered fabric on her arm. "He made a grab at me but missed and ripped my gown." She rubbed her shoulder. "Twisted my arm a bit, too."

Bertha groaned. "Is this my fault? Did he catch you trying to leave?"

She shook her head. "Oh no. His anger's been building for hours. He started guzzling right after you left today, and Abe just gets meaner with every drink he pours down. I took his abuse for as long as I could before I made a run for it."

Bertha crossed her arms over her chest. "Well, you can't go back."

Annie gave a nervous little laugh. "Sure I can. I just have to wait until he passes out. If I'm lucky, he won't remember a thing by morning." She snorted. "You think it's the first time this has happened?"

Then she leaned to peer into Bertha's eyes. "I'll be fine, I promise. But thank you for caring, huh? And thank you for being here for me. You're the best friend I have." Her laugh sounded bitter. "What am I saying? You're the only friend I have. Abe won't allow anyone to get close to me."

Bertha felt a tug in her heart. This was her chance to say what she'd come for. She took a deep breath and forged ahead. "Annie, I'll always be your friend, for as long as you'll have me. But I know Someone who'll make a better friend to you than I ever could." She reached to smooth tangled hair from Annie's face then plucked at the torn fabric of her gown. "He can help you out of this mess, too, if you'll let Him. What do you say, Annie? Would you be willing to meet Him?"

A hard look crossed Annie's face and her hand came up. "Stop right there. I've had my share of those kinds of friends. Got me one now, in fact. And, honey, I don't need another. You can tell him so, too, whoever he is." She tilted her head slightly and narrowed her eyes. "Is that why you're here? Some two-penny hustler put you up to conning me?"

"Of course not! Oh goodness, you don't understand."

Annie turned her back. "And I don't care to, thank you."

Bertha gripped her shoulder. "You've got it all wrong. Or rather, I didn't say it right. Let me try again." She swallowed hard and said a silent prayer for courage. "You know yesterday at the bluff, when we talked about the devil and dying?"

Annie's eyes changed, as if a curtain dropped inside her head. "What about it?"

"I believe God can protect you from both of those threats."

"Whoa, there. Abe's pretty bad, I'll admit, but he's not the devil." She smirked. "At least, I don't think so." She took a few steps away. "Look, I know where you're going with this. I've heard it all before. I'm not interested."

Bertha cringed. "But why? God just wants to care for you. Why would you reject such a loving offer?"

Annie stared off into the dark alley behind them. "Sugar, your God doesn't want someone like me."

"Yes, He does."

Annie's tense shoulders slumped in an attitude of defeat. "Then He doesn't know what all I've done."

Bertha cocked her head to the side. "I wouldn't count on it. God knows things you can't even remember and those you wish you could forget."

Fear paled Annie's face. "Bertha, I don't want to talk about this anymore. I mean it."

"But—"

"I mean it."

Bertha felt heartsick. Begging Annie to accept God's grace seemed like force-feeding a starving man. But if she didn't want to hear it, Bertha could only do as she asked.

When the idea came, Bertha knew it wasn't hers any more than standing in the dark streets of Jefferson while Thad stood on her porch was her idea. Without trying to reason it out, she reached behind her neck to undo the clasp of her cross necklace and held it up to Annie. "Very well, I won't say another word. But take this as a reminder of what I did say."

Annie's startled eyes followed the motion of the swinging necklace. "I can't take that."

"I want you to have it. Turn around and let me fasten it for you."

Annie backed away as though the chain would burn if it touched her flesh. "I could never wear it."

Embarrassment burned Bertha's cheeks. Maybe she hadn't heard from God, after all. Why would someone who owned diamonds wear her secondhand silver? "I'm sorry, Annie. You don't like it."

Annie's mouth gaped. "What? Don't be silly. Of course I like it."

"What, then?"

Tears clouded her tortured gray eyes. "It's a cross, Bertha. I'm not worthy."

Bertha's own eyes blurred. "Stop it. Why would you say that?"

Annie started to cry in earnest. Great splashing teardrops hit the front of her coat and rolled down her cheeks, making watery tracks through already-smudged makeup. "Because I do things with men. Shameful things. Things that make me feel sick."

Bertha's insides recoiled in shock, but for Annie's sake she held her ground. "Why would you. . .with those men. . .I mean, if you don't want to?"

"He beats me, all right? Abe beats me if I say no. He slaps me and drags me by my hair. He pushes me down and hits me with his fists until my eyes swell and I can't see."

Bertha covered her ears with her arms. "No, Annie. I can't bear to hear this."

Too wound up to stop, Annie paced the alley and sobbed. "After he's finished with me, he gets even madder when he realizes what he's done."

"Because he's sorry?"

"Oh, he's sorry enough. Sorry he won't get as much money now that I don't look so nice."

Annie cried so hard by then, Bertha feared they'd hear her clear to Dallas. She took three steps back to peer up and down the dark street but saw nothing. "Annie, why do you stay with him? How can you even think of going back there tonight?"

Annie sniffed and swiped her arm under her nose. She spoke, and her voice held a mournful tremor. "I have nowhere else to go. No one to take care of me."

Bertha frowned. "Why can't you go home?"

Annie shuddered. "That's impossible."

"Why?"

She crossed her arms and paced back and forth again, this time in a calmer stride. "I left home when I turned fifteen. Ran off with an older man I thought I loved. He claimed to love me, too. Even said he wanted to marry me." Shame flashed in her eyes. "But he left me high and dry. My parents were so angry, and I couldn't go back after disgracing them."

"What did you do?"

She looked at the ground. "The only thing I knew how to do at fifteen. I turned to strange men for money and love." She looked up, and her eyes had welled again. "I'm not the least bit proud of it, but I was alone and so scared. When Abe came along, I took him to be my ticket out, and in some ways he was. He treated me good at first. Still does when he's not drunk or broke." Annie leaned against the building and continued to pour out the dreadful story of her ill-fated life, complete with all the desperate, wretched things she'd ever done.

Bertha longed to stop her ears, to run away from the vulgar tale, but she sensed Annie needed to confess her past in order to cleanse herself from its hold. So love held Bertha fast.

Annie's halting words drained her so that by the time she finished talking, her body slumped against the wall and her voice sounded strained. When it seemed nothing else festered inside,

Annie raised her head. Water droplets glistened on the hood of her coat. Whether beads of rain or dew from the heavy night air, Bertha couldn't tell, but they sparkled like Annie's tears in the glow from the gaslight.

She breathed a hopeless sigh. "Now do you understand why I'm not worthy to wear that cross?"

Anger stiffened Bertha's spine. Not anger toward Annie, but toward the man who abandoned her so long ago, toward her parents for doing the same, toward the cruel-hearted Abe, and toward every other beastly circumstance of Annie's life that had robbed her of hope.

Bertha dangled the necklace in front of her eyes. "Annie Moore, you listen to me. The gift this cross represents is more powerful than any laundry list of sins you may be guilty of, no matter how heinous. The cross covered them all." Annie turned her face away, but Bertha cupped her chin and pulled her back. "All, Annie. You just have to accept it for yourself in order to be free."

Annie wrung her hands and searched Bertha's face with anxious eyes. "I just don't know how to believe that."

"Don't take my word for it, then. Ask God yourself if He's able to forgive the things you've done." Bertha opened Annie's hand, pressed the necklace into her palm, and closed her fingers around it. "Hang on to this for now, while you think about what I've said. Will you do that much?"

Annie nodded. "I'll hang on to it. Thank you, Bertha." She held up her closed fist and looked at her rings. She wore two on that hand, lovely pieces with big diamonds that sparkled even in the sparse light. "How I wish I could repay you in kind. I'd love for you to have one of these."

Bertha gasped. "For heaven's sake, Annie, those are far too costly. I could never accept."

Annie met her eyes. "Sadly, I could never offer, or Abe would kill me for sure. He's tried every trick in the book to get his hands on my diamonds." Her jaw tightened. "Not that I care two hoots about any of my jewelry, but it's the only thing left he hasn't taken."

She gave a twisted smile, her gaze on the rings. "Besides, if he ever walks out on me, I'll have these to fall back on. I could at least trade them for a meal."

"They're worth a sight more than a meal, Annie."

Annie closed her eyes and shook her head, as if coming out of a trance. "I think it's getting late. How long have we been here?"

Bertha stepped to the end of the building to look at the empty street. The chill wind whipping around the corner almost took her breath, and a light drizzle had started. "Way too long." She ducked in the alley and took Annie's arm. "Come. Let me take you home with me. You can have my bed, and I'll take the chaise. Don't worry—I can fall asleep anywhere, even sitting upright in a chair."

Annie gave her a sidelong glance. "What are you thinking, Bertha? Your folks won't allow you to drag someone like me in off the streets, and you know it." She waved at her clothes. "Especially in a getup like this."

"They will if I explain."

"Oh, sugar, can't you just hear that? 'Mama, I've brought this beaten, half-dressed trollop home to sleep in my bed. I just know you won't mind.' "

Bertha imagined explaining Annie to Mama. She couldn't conceive of it. Still. . .

Annie must've read the struggle in her eyes. "Don't give it another thought. I know it's out of the question. Besides, if I don't go back, it'll just make matters worse."

Bertha clutched at her hands. "Annie—"

"He's asleep by now. Passed out, I should say. He won't hurt me any more tonight."

"What about tomorrow night? And the next?"

"Stop worrying about me, little Bertha. I've been taking care of myself for a long time. Let me get back to the room before Abe wakes up. With any luck, he'll be sick in the morning after all he drank and stay in bed all day. That'll be fine with me, because there's nothing better to do in this horrid rain. You get up on that horse and go home before your parents send a search party."

Bertha hugged her and for some reason hated to turn her loose. "Let me walk you back to the hotel, at least."

"No, sweetie. I can't be seen with you."

The words made Bertha's stomach ache. "If you say so, but please be careful."

"I thought we decided you'd stop fretting over me."

Bertha shook her head. "I decided no such thing." She squeezed the hand where Annie held the cross. "Do you promise to think about what I said?"

"I promise. We'll talk some more tomorrow. All right?"

Bertha tried to hide her pleasure but couldn't. She smiled so widely her cheeks hurt. "I'll hold you to that. Good night, Annie."

"Good night, little Bertha. Now go!"

Back in the saddle, Bertha mouthed a silent prayer when Annie waved and then slipped into the darkness. She whirled her horse into the street and headed for home at a full gallop, unsure of the hour or how much time had passed while they huddled in the alley. She only knew she had fulfilled her duty to God and Annie, so whatever remained of the night belonged to Thad. She'd find a way to make it up to him, and they'd spend every possible hour together until he left.

Nearing her lane, she jumped the narrow ditch to cut the corner and thundered toward the house. At the gate, she leaped to the ground and led her horse to the porch. She expected Thad would have tied his horse out front, but it wasn't there. She told herself it had to be in the barn, had to be somewhere.

"Bertha?"

Her hand froze on the hitching post. "Papa, I didn't see you. What are you doing out in this weather?"

"You took the words right out of me mouth. I hope you have a reasonable explanation for turning our hair gray this night. Mama is beside herself, Bertha. She's taken to her bed."

Bertha rushed to join him on the porch. "Where's Thad?"

"And that's what frets you, daughter? No spare word of concern for your dear mother, after what I've just told you?"

Bertha ducked her head. "I'm sorry. I didn't mean to worry her."

He didn't answer, so Bertha sneaked a peek at his face then recoiled in shock. "Oh, mercy. You're not crying—?"

He swiped angrily at his eyes. "Mama wasn't the only one worried, you know." He took her by the shoulders and gave a gentle shake. "Where were you, girl? With you all a-flutter over young Thad's visit, it made no sense that you'd leave."

"Where is he, Papa?"

Papa looked grim. "Where is he, you wonder? Well, that makes two of us."

Her stomach lurched. "What do you mean? Didn't he show up?"

"He came, all right, and found you gone." He tucked in his chin and furrowed his brow. "Are you saying Thad never found you? That you haven't been with him this night?"

"Of course not. You're making no sense at all."

"Bertha, Thad rode off to search for you but never returned. For his dear mama's sake, I pray he's at home warming his backside at the hearth."

Bertha's head reeled. She tried hard to grasp what he had said, to lay all the facts in a neat row and sort them out, but they wouldn't line up. Each time she tried, the only important detail rose to the top and consumed her. She had to find Thad.

"I'll explain everything. I will. The minute I return. But I have to go bring him back." She brushed a hasty kiss across Papa's cheek and rushed down the steps, making it clear to the hitching post before he bellowed from the porch.

"Bertha Maye Biddie! Kindly march yourself right back. You won't be going anywhere else tonight."

Unwilling to believe her ears, she turned. "You can't mean it."

"Oh, I mean it."

She shook her head. "But I must."

"No, miss. Not without good reason. And I've heard not a reason, explanation, or apology from you tonight."

An apology would be easy. She hadn't meant to hurt them. If

he wanted an explanation, she had one of those, too. Could she find fit words to give it?

She hustled back to the porch and blurted out a short account of her story with the promise to fill in the gaps later. Papa's hurt, angry expression changed to sympathy and understanding as she spoke of her mission to save Annie.

When she finished with another plea to go after Thad, Papa set his stubborn jaw and shook his head. "Mama will have my gizzard on a spit."

"Papa, please. This is the most important night of my life. Can't you at least ask?"

Releasing his breath in a rush, he nodded. "All right, then. I'll speak to her. I suppose I need to tell her you're home before she frets herself sick."

Bertha wanted to mention he'd bawled her name loudly enough to alert Mama and half of Jefferson of her whereabouts. One look at his face, and she decided against it.

Papa opened the door then turned and wagged his finger. "Don't expect miracles."

She raised her brows. "Too late. I need a miracle with all that's at stake."

He disappeared inside but returned right away, his heavy footsteps echoing through the house. It didn't bode well for her cause. It meant Mama wasn't in the market for Francis Biddie's blarney.

The screen opened and Papa joined her on the porch. "Her mind is made up. She absolutely forbids it."

Bertha's head expected the answer, but her heart clung to hope. "No. Please go try again."

"She's in no mood for it, daughter."

Bertha stamped her foot in anger, and frustration loosened her lips. "Who wears the trousers in this family anyway?"

Silence. Papa held her gaze, but shame veiled his eyes. Bertha bit her bottom lip and wished she'd bitten her tongue. When she uttered the unimaginable words, she'd leaped a forbidden line and didn't quite know her way back across.

She touched his arm. "Oh, Papa, I'm so sorry."

He patted her shoulder. "No, sprite. It's a fair question. And here's your answer, since you asked. Your mama herself wears the trousers and holds me on a short tether. I allow it because otherwise it's impossible to live with her."

Considering the amount of time Bertha spent dancing around Mama's ire, his words plucked a familiar chord. She'd never considered her papa a fellow survivor of Emeline Biddie, the whirlwind. Seeing him as such forged a kinship that had little to do with blood ties.

"I did try, Bertha. I even asked if I could fetch Thad for you. She said it's unseemly to disturb the family at this hour."

Bertha crumpled onto the porch swing. "Blast unseemly! When I'm mistress of a house, I'll make my own rules. I'll talk as I wish, dress as I wish, go where I want, when I want, and never, ever wear shoes. If my daughter asks for something important to her, I'll care more about her feelings than the opinions of others." She lifted wet, sorrowful eyes to his. "I will, Papa. I swear it."

He laid a heavy hand on her shoulder. "Don't stay out much longer, darlin'. There's a cold wind a-blowin'." Then he stepped quietly to the door and went inside.

Bertha sat on the damp, drafty porch remembering how glad she'd been such a short time ago. The song she'd warbled to her empty room while dressing for Thad rose up to mock her.

Why does gladness cheer me?
Why everything so bright?

With a heavy heart, she crowded the song from her mind with more fitting lyrics.

Wilt thou be gone, love, wilt thou be gone from me?
Gone, I must be gone, love, I must be gone from thee.

She stood up and walked into the house, furious with her parents, Annie, and God.

CHAPTER 20

Sunday, January 21

Bertha opened her eyes and grimaced. Her tongue was stuck to the roof of her mouth and covered with a thick, unpleasant coat—one part mint and three parts glue. The Sozodont. The peppermint-stick flavor of the tooth powder never hinted at the hideous aftertaste. She groaned and struggled to free her arm from the quilt pulled up to her shoulders and saw the green cotton sleeve of her favorite dress. Why was she in bed fully dressed?

A strong sense of urgency fairly lifted her from the mattress, but she couldn't imagine why. She threw back the cover she'd fumbled for sometime in the night and swung her feet to the floor, shaking the fog from her head so she could think.

"Papa!" she shrieked, scrambling across the cold floor for her shoes. "Papa, come quick!"

Her parents' startled faces appeared at the door. Papa, still barefoot and dressed in his nightshirt, rushed to her side. "What is it, child? Are you ailing?"

"I need you to take me to Thad's house right away."

Mama, her robe pulled hastily over her gown and her hair tied up in curls with strips of cloth, slumped against the door frame. "Bertha, for heaven's sake."

"I got the idea last night. If we get there before he leaves for the station, we can go with the Blooms to see him off. Mama, I knew you wouldn't allow me to go alone, but Papa can drive me."

Papa rubbed the stubble on his chin. "It's a mite early, darlin'. What time does Thad's train leave?"

"I don't know. That's the trouble."

Mama squinted down at her. "Don't tell me you slept in your clothes."

Embarrassed, Bertha looked away. "With time so precious, I didn't want to waste it getting dressed." She finished fastening her shoes, a pair she'd picked to gain her mama's favor. "I must see Thad before he goes—to explain about last night and ask him to forgive me."

She stood up and reached for her shawl. "Hurry and dress, Papa. I'll go hitch the wagon."

Mama clamped a hand on her arm as she passed. "Just a minute, young lady. No daughter of mine will go calling on a young man uninvited, and so early on a Sunday morning."

Papa, who had watched from the door without comment, cleared his throat and leveled a warning look at Mama.

Mama watched his face for a second then nodded and gave Bertha a weak smile. "I meant to say, no daughter of mine will go calling on a young man at this hour—without first washing her face and combing her hair."

Bertha cried out and jumped up to hug her. "Thank you, Mama."

Mama pulled back and made a face. "You might want to use some of your minty tooth powder while you're at it, dear."

Bertha covered her mouth. "I'm afraid the powder might be part of the problem. I'll rinse with water and chew a sprig of parsley on the way." She gave her papa a gentle push toward the door. "Go dress, please. My entire future hangs on how quickly you can slip into your trousers."

He grinned and rocked on his heels, his thumbs hooked in imaginary suspenders. "I'll go, but did you happen to notice who's back in rightful possession of his trousers?"

Mama frowned, so he gave her a playful swat on the bottom. "No sass out of you, Mrs. Biddie. And by the by, I'll expect breakfast on the table when I return. Eggs, fried bread, and black pudding will do nicely." He planted a kiss on her cheek and sauntered to the door.

Horrified, Bertha froze, waiting for the anger, the shock and outrage, the whirlwind to spin off and consume him. To her amazement, Mama's face softened, and she smiled like a smitten girl. When she saw Bertha watching, she ducked her head and followed Papa out the door, as tame as an autumn breeze.

Somehow Bertha managed to close her gaping mouth. She returned to the basin to splash water on her face and arrange her hair, determined to find an explanation for the miracle she'd just witnessed. She'd start by asking Papa about his astonishing conquest on the way to Thad's house. Perhaps he could offer a few tips on how she might approach Thad. After last night, she'd need them.

Papa rushed past her door in a whoosh. "Let's go if we're going. I'll fetch the rig."

"Yes, sir. I'm coming."

With no time to get warm water, she picked up the ceramic pitcher left there from the night before and poured a cold stream into the basin on her dressing table. She dipped a rag and wiped her face, tucked back a stray curl and pinned it then hurried to the kitchen.

Mama stood at the stove warming milk for black pudding. Still wary, Bertha pushed past her and pulled a few sprigs of parsley from the cold box. Unsure what to make of the strange woman in the kitchen, she tucked the parsley into her mouth and opened the door. "We're going now. Please say a prayer we reach Thad in time."

The stranger pointed at Bertha with her ladle. "Speaking of prayer, try to be home in time for church. And don't forget your wrap. It's still cold out."

"Yes, ma'am," she called then grabbed her hat and coat from a hook by the door and scurried out to the wagon.

Papa stood waiting. She rushed over and hoisted herself up before he had time to offer a hand. He gave her a mock frown then hustled around to board on his side.

They were quiet on the ride to the Bloom house. Planning what she would say to Thad distracted Bertha from asking Papa how he'd reclaimed his trousers. By the time she remembered, they were nearly to Thad's and Papa seemed lost in his own thoughts. Sitting tall on the seat, he wore a silly grin on his face, and Bertha wondered if he sat basking in his recent victory. More in keeping with his character, he likely sat basking in expectation of fried bread and black pudding.

A lump rose in Bertha's throat as they neared the big white house northwest of town. She twisted on the seat and latched onto Papa's arm. "What will I say to him?"

He patted her hand then loosened her fingers. "Don't fret, darlin'. The words will come."

She rubbed the red marks on his forearm. "Sorry, Papa. I'm just so afraid."

He tilted her face up to his. "Remember the thing I asked you? About trusting God with the details?"

She nodded.

"Well, if you have a mind to ever trust Him, this is your chance."

Bertha nodded again and leaned against his arm, her heart too full to speak. Her breath caught when they pulled up and stopped in front of the low picket fence surrounding Thad's yard. She sat up and stared past the tall magnolia, past the smaller Eve's necklace, and down the cobbled path to the two-story house, wondering which window stood between her and Thad.

Papa set the brake and shook his finger under her nose. "You sit tight till I come 'round. We'll have no more hurtling into wagons, young miss. You'll wait for help like a proper lady."

"Yes, Papa. But hurry, please."

He grumbled but climbed down and hastened around to her side. Together they rushed up the walk to the white double doors. Papa questioned her with his eyes and she nodded, so he lifted the heavy brass knocker and let it fall. As the door swung open, Bertha thought her heart would burst. She held her breath and readied the words she needed to say.

"Mr. Biddie. Little Bertha. What a nice surprise to find you on our doorstep."

Bertha's body wilted. She couldn't answer Mrs. Bloom because Thad's words still pressed her tongue. Papa cleared his throat then slipped past Bertha and lifted his hat.

"Mornin' to ye, me lady. Apologies for disturbing your fine household so early on the Sabbath morn. But we fancy a short chat with your boy, if you don't mind."

Leona Bloom lifted her brows. "Of course. One moment, please." She left the door open and slipped away. Bertha stared at the entry, waiting for Thad's broad shoulders to fill the empty space.

"You all right, love?"

"Yes, Papa."

After a wait that lasted forever, Thad's lanky little brother appeared with his mama on his heels. Cyrus looked nervous and clearly couldn't imagine what Papa might have to do with him. He squinted out the door, pushing his wire-rimmed glasses higher on his nose. "Yes, sir, Mr. Biddie?"

Disappointment and impatience warred in Bertha's gut like cats in a bag. Papa gave a nervous little laugh and addressed Mrs. Bloom. "While we're double-blessed by young Cy's handsome face, I fear it's Thad we mean to see."

Cy stepped back, his cheeks going crimson. Mrs. Bloom tented her fingertips over her lips and shook her head. "Of course you do. How silly of me. It's not as if I didn't think of Thad first, but since. . . Well, you see. . ."

The door swung wider, and Thad's papa appeared behind his wife.

"Why, Francis, how nice to see you." He leaned past his family to clasp Papa's hand then frowned at Mrs. Bloom. "Leona, where are your manners, dear? Don't leave our guests on the stoop."

She flushed a bright pink and moved away from the entrance. "Oh my. Forgive me, Abel. I'm not myself with all that's gone on around here."

Mr. Bloom motioned them inside. "Come in, come in, before you ice over." He held out his hand. "This way to the parlor, folks. Leona, brew some tea to warm their bones." He glanced at Papa. "Unless you prefer coffee, Francis."

Papa waved off the coffee and the parlor. "Don't go troubling your good wife, sir. The warmth of your foyer is sufficient. We can't stay long."

They stood discussing foul weather and trading good-natured remarks until Bertha feared her pounding head might explode. At long last Papa pulled her forward, and Mr. Bloom turned his attention her way.

"Look who this is." He accepted the hand she offered and kissed it. "Bertha, you're lovelier each time I see you."

"You're too kind, sir. I wonder if I might be allowed to see Thad now?"

Papa cleared his throat again, louder than before, and laid a restraining hand on her shoulder. "What my wee daughter means to say—"

"Hold up. You came to see Thad?"

Mr. Bloom wore a puzzled look. Behind him, Mrs. Bloom pressed a hankie to her lips and spun away from the door, leaving Cyrus staring after her with startled eyes. Mr. Bloom lowered his head and frowned then took hold of Bertha's hands. "I thought if anyone knew, it would be you, dear. Thad's gone."

Bertha peered into eyes so like Thad's and tried to make sense of his words. "Gone? You mean he left for the station without you?" She looked from Mr. Bloom to Papa to Cyrus, trying to work it out. She couldn't imagine Thad's family not seeing him off to school. Well, no matter. She would. A renewed sense of urgency pulsed through her heart. "It's so early I doubt the train has arrived. There's still plenty of time to catch him before he leaves, and we can all ride to the station together. Won't Thad be surprised?"

Mr. Bloom came toward her with his mouth open, about to speak.

Done with talking, Bertha rushed for the door and opened it. "Forgive me, Mr. Bloom. We have to be quick or we won't make it." Outside she made a mad dash for the rig.

"Better stop her, Francis." Mr. Bloom's voice behind her sounded strained.

"Bertha, wait right there," Papa ordered.

She stopped and turned.

Papa, Cyrus, and Mr. Bloom gaped at her from the porch.

"Wait? For what? We're going to miss him if we don't hurry."

Compassion softened Mr. Bloom's eyes. "You won't find my boy at the station, Bertha."

Papa asked the question for her. "Why's that, Abel?"

"Thad left last night. Seemed in a powerful hurry to go, so I let him take one of our horses. He planned to ride to Longview, sell the horse for spending money, and take the first train out to Bryan."

Bertha knew she stared openmouthedly but didn't care. "What did you say?" she asked, her voice a feeble croak.

"I said he's gone, Bertha. Thad's already gone."

∽℘∾

Something had Henry's long johns in a knot. Sarah knew it for a fact after he shoveled food around his dish at supper then left the breakfast table without cleaning his plate. Anything that interfered with her man's vittles would be no light matter, but Henry wasn't talking—and it scared her.

Worse still, he'd left early that morning without her. Said he had business in town. Said he wouldn't be back in time to fetch her for Sunday service, but he'd stop along the way and ask a neighbor to bring her. On his way out the door, Henry promised to finish his dealings in plenty of time to join her at the meetinghouse.

The reason these things troubled Sarah?

Henry never did business on the Sabbath. When Sarah asked him outright what he planned to do, he mumbled and shuffled then dashed out the door.

By the time Thomas Jolly pulled into the yard, the bed of his wagon overflowing with laughing children, worry had curdled Sarah's stomach. After giving him a wave out the door, she went to her room for a wrap. Sarah wore a dress made of heavy fabric but didn't own a proper coat, so she grabbed the warmer of her two good shawls and dashed outside, braced for a cold morning ride.

Thomas raised his hat. "Miss Sarah."

Sarah nodded. "Thomas." She stepped to the back of the wagon and grinned at the turned-up faces. "Children! How spry you look, all washed and polished."

"Morning, Miss Sarah," rang out from eight different voices.

Sarah tried hard never to question God, but as her hungry eyes roamed the tiny faces, she wondered about His ways. Why bless some folks with more babies than they could feed yet withhold one tiny suckling mouth from her barren breasts?

Thomas leaned to wipe off the seat while one of the older boys handed Sarah up beside him. She thanked him and settled the skirt of her Sunday dress around her. "Where's Arabella this morning?"

"Sent her on ahead with Thomas Jr."—he jerked his thumb behind him—"so you wouldn't have to ride in back with those ruffians."

She laughed. "I wouldn't have minded that a bit. I hope I'm not putting you out."

He winked and grinned. "Not a whit. We more'n happy to help."

"Well, the Lord gon' bless you. I know I sure do appreciate it. I bet you're glad Doc Turner lets you off on Sunday mornings to go to worship."

Thomas snorted. "He know I'll quit before I work on the Lawd's day." He gave her a sidelong glance. "Say, what's old Henry up to this morning? He come by my house in a right big hurry. Didn't say where he had to get to so quick."

Sarah's clabbered stomach lurched. She wasn't about to admit she didn't know what business her own husband was about. She squirmed and glanced away. "You know Henry King. Probably found him a good trade or some such. I don't pay no mind to that man's mischief."

Just as she hoped, Thomas laughed and asked no more questions. They didn't talk much after that because the teasing, giggling children made it impossible. Sarah settled back and tried to forget Henry's strange doings. She set her mind instead on thoughts more suited to the day.

Thomas began to hum a gospel hymn in a deep baritone. The clamor behind them ceased, and several small voices rose with the lyrics of the song. The tension in Sarah's body melted. She turned on the seat and joined her high soprano to the swaying angel choir clustered in back.

Just as her heart rose up and soared to the throne of grace, the thundering hooves of an approaching rider reached her ears. A boy on horseback galloped toward them, shouting and waving his arms.

She looked at Thomas. "What's that about, you reckon?"

Thomas stared at the rider and shrugged, but worry drew lines over his brow.

When the frenzied rider reined up so fast he almost landed in her lap, Sarah's back stiffened, and her stomach forced bile to her throat. One glance at the boy's frightened eyes—his gaze locked straight on her face—and she knew. Something bad had happened to Henry.

"Best come quick over to the Commercial Hotel, Miss Sarah. There's trouble out back." Without another word, the boy, who turned out to be Cook's son, dug his heels in the horse's flank and sped away.

"Is it Henry?" she called after him, but he raced away as if the weight of the disaster rested on his young shoulders.

She stood up in the wagon. "Wait! You come back here!"

The wind picked up her useless cry and blew it behind her as the rider disappeared in a cloud of dust.

"That foolish boy. I could've taken his horse or rode with him at least. Oh, Thomas!"

Thomas gripped her hand and pulled. "Sit down, Miss Sarah. We'll get you there." He slapped the reins hard and roared, and the horse took off as though he'd been stung.

Holding on to the seat, Sarah twisted to look behind at their precious cargo. Fear had the children as wide-eyed as a basket of owls, especially the little ones. She gave them a steady smile while she lifted up a prayer.

I know I deserve it, but don't take Henry from me. And please don't let harm come to these babies on my account.

CHAPTER 21

Thad rode into Longview in the wee hours, cold, hungry, and heartsick. The only accommodations available at that time of night happened to be a shabby little room above the saloon—a fact he'd forget to mention to his mama. He paid the bartender in advance then slipped past a drowsy dance-hall girl and a cluster of men engaged in an all-night poker game.

The so-called room consisted of little more than a cot hidden behind a curtain in an alcove off the hall. The plain cotton mattress smelled of a hundred unwashed bodies, and the fetid pillow turned out to be a drool-stained sack stuffed with hay. Thad feared bedbugs and lice, but rather than sit up all night or risk a crick in his neck, he pulled a clean shirt from his travel bag to cover the pillow and slept on top of the quilt. He was cold, but better cold than share a warm bed with crawling critters.

The woolen curtain across the cubbyhole smelled so musty he couldn't breathe. He pushed it aside, which allowed the gaslight on the wall to burn a path past his eyelids straight through to the back of his head. He turned his face to the wall and buried his nose in the shirt-wrapped pillow that now smelled mostly of the lilac water mama sprinkled on her wash. The familiar scent made him want to cry like a boy in knee pants.

He finally fell into a troubled sleep that didn't last. He drifted in and out between brawls among the gamblers and fits of shrill, tinny laughter from the saloon girl, who must've found her second wind. He spent the wide-awake parts of the long night wondering why Bertha had let him down.

As soon as Mr. Biddie had discovered her missing, he headed off one way to search while Thad went another. Bertha's mama stayed behind in case she came back. Thad deliberately chose the road toward town. Despite her papa's insistence that Bertha would never go there alone at night, something told Thad that Annie Moore had everything to do with her disappearance.

He rode straight for Vale Street and Brooks House but found Bertha standing on a street corner with Annie before he ever got that far. He held back and waited to talk to her until watching from the shadows made him feel like an intruder. Feeling miffed and more than a little hurt, he had eased his mare around and headed for home.

Not many deeds in Thad's life had caused him shame, but the disgrace of running away from Jefferson without seeing Bertha safely home or easing her parents' minds made him cringe. He'd focused on his own hurt feelings, disappointment, and jealousy until his bruised heart had swept him away. All the way out of town, in fact. Now regret over not asking Bertha to marry him or even telling her good-bye gnawed holes in his soul.

The remorse tumbling in his gut mixed with the racket from below made his jerky attempts at sleep more of a chore than actual rest. He gave up trying and spent the last hours before dawn praying for forgiveness and direction. When the sun rose high enough to light the dim hallway, Thad rose, too, and set about finding a buyer for the Appaloosa.

He stepped out of the livery a few minutes later, one horse lighter and a few dollars richer. He gave the silver coins another quick tally then tied them up in a red bandanna and tucked it deep inside his pocket. Now to find breakfast and locate the depot.

"Good morning, my good man. A bright and beautiful day, is it not?"

The loud, cheerful voice and curious remark set Thad on his heels. He frowned up at the overcast sky then turned to see who would say such a thing. A tall, smartly dressed man in a bowler hat stood not three feet away.

The gentleman winked and tipped his hat. "All a matter of perspective, my boy." He pointed toward the sky. "Up there it's dim and gloomy. But in here"—he tapped his temple with a long, slender finger—"it's sunny all day long."

Thad returned the tipped hat gesture, nodded, and turned his back on the unfamiliar person. Couldn't be too careful.

Undeterred, the man sidled closer. "Hope you won't mind my saying, but I couldn't help noticing you've come into a bit of good fortune there." He jabbed a finger toward Thad's pocket. "Monetarily speaking, that is."

Thad's body tensed. *Dolt!* Who but a dolt would flash his money on the streets? He decided it best to ignore the inappropriate comment. "I hope you'll forgive my rudeness, sir, but I have a train to catch." He hitched his bag higher on his shoulder and stepped down off the boardwalk.

"You'll not catch one in that direction."

Thad turned, feeling foolish.

The fancy man grinned and pointed his index finger. "That way."

Thad nodded his thanks and set off again.

"I'm afraid you won't find a train to board for hours yet," the man called out behind him. "Looks like you're stuck here for a spell."

"That's all right. I'll wait at the depot."

The inquisitive stranger hurried along the boardwalk to draw even with Thad. "So where you headed?"

Thad frowned to show he resented the question. "South, to Bryan."

"Bryan, eh? Signed up at the new school there, unless I miss my guess." The dandy held on to a post and vaulted off the boardwalk directly into Thad's path. "What's your handle, son?"

"My what?"

"Your handle. Your name."

"Name's Thad," he answered, not sure why he had. "Thaddeus Bloom."

The stranger stuck out his hand. "Darius Q. Thedford at your service, Thad. Now I ask you, good son, why would a young man full of spit and vinegar choose to spend his morning in a dusty old train station? Especially when I can point the way to more"—he raised his brows and winked—"*stimulating* activities."

On a different day—a day his heart didn't throb in his chest, a day he hadn't just left behind everything he cared about, a day he wasn't mad as spit at his papa, even a day he hadn't been up all night—Thad would've been smart enough to turn and walk away. Instead, he peered at the smiling face across from him, and though he recognized the look of a man who'd just hooked a fish, he took a step closer.

"Did you say stimulating?"

The fisherman's dark eyes twinkled. "Downright exhilarating." He looped his arm around Thad's neck and led him up the boardwalk steps in quick little hops. "Ever try your hand at cards, lad?"

The words set his heart racing and tickled a memory to the surface. Thad knew where he'd seen the man before. The same mustachioed face had smiled up at him from the circle of poker-playing men in the saloon.

The taste of bait in his mouth, Thad dug in his heels and held up his hand. "Stop right there. I want nothing to do with gambling."

Darius removed his arm from around Thad's neck and backed away, looking him over. "So that's the way it is, eh? Very well, boy. I understand where you're coming from. Don't give it another thought." He pulled a pouch from his breast pocket and commenced to pouring tobacco in a line along the edge of a thin sheet of paper. With a practiced hand, he rolled it into a cigarette and licked it to seal the end. "Sorry I asked."

Confused, Thad stared at the man. He hadn't expected him to give in so easily.

Darius leaned against a pole and tucked away his tobacco. "When you're ready, I'll direct you to the train. Wouldn't want to worry your mama none."

The stress Darius placed on the word "mama" raised Thad's hackles, especially since he'd hit the nail right on its head of silver curls. At the mention of cards, Mama's face had drifted into Thad's mind, her voice warning him of the perils of flirting with Lady Luck and dabbling in games of chance.

He pushed her image away and swaggered closer to Darius. "What do you mean to imply, sir?"

Darius shrugged. "Only that a fine, strapping boy with a pocketful of money and a lot of extra time should be ripe for a little action. Of the competitive sort, I should say." He lit his hand-rolled smoke and shook out the match then gave Thad a sideways glance. "I figured the only thing holding you back from our little game must be a pressing need to mind your mama."

Thad saw himself standing on the bayou playing out the line on his Kentucky reel, teasing a fat catfish to shore. He had enough sense to know that Mr. Darius Thedford, still fishing, had just used the same maneuver. Enough sense to know it, but not enough to care.

The hook had set. Nobody called Thaddeus Bloom a mama's boy.

⌘

Thomas's bucking, skidding rig clattered across the Polk Street Bridge so fast Sarah feared soaring off into the bayou. They cut across on Dallas Street to Vale then took the turn over to Austin on two rumbling wheels. Sarah abandoned her place beside Thomas and crawled in back to help shield and comfort the babies. When they bounded up to the rear entrance of the Commercial Hotel, she did a quick head count for fear one of the children had bounced right over the side.

Satisfied they were shaken but all right, she gathered her skirts and clambered out of the wagon. It didn't take long to locate the trouble. A crowd of men stood out back of the building, their waving arms and raised voices pointing the way Sarah needed to run. She slowed to keep from mowing down onlookers at the rim of the circle then started elbowing her way through.

"Make way, now," she cried, realizing how deep her anguish flowed by the sound of her own voice. "Oh, please. Move out my way."

On the other side, a worse sight than Sarah could imagine met her eyes. She took it all in then slapped a hand over her mouth to keep from crying out. Henry slumped in the saddle, hands tied behind his back and a noose around his neck. Bruises covered his face, and blood flowed from a busted nose. The only thing standing between Henry's legs and empty space, between life and certain death, was the most cantankerous mule in the good Lord's creation.

Dandy, don't you move.

The three dreadful men from the day before, laughing like drunken hyenas, hovered around her man. Skinny Boy held a handgun on the crowd. The one called Edward waved a scattergun with shaking hands. The man claiming to be Frank Griswald stood on the bed of a wagon tightening the noose around Henry's neck.

"This ain't right," a voice called out behind her. Sarah looked back to see who spoke, but it could've been any one of ten frowning white men standing among the other locals and shopkeepers who had gathered, most of them red-faced with anger.

"We don't do things this way in Jefferson," a distant voice cried.

"No problem, then," the thin one growled in a stone-cold voice. "We ain't from around here."

"What crime did this man commit?"

Sarah glanced to her left. This time she recognized the scowling owner of Sedberry's Drugstore. Frank Griswald leaned away from Henry and pinched the butt of a drooping cigar from his mouth. He answered without looking at Mr. Sedberry, squinting through his smoke at Henry instead. "This boy's a thief." He pointed at the rope. "Where I come from, this here is a thief deterrent."

"You fellows won't get away with this," Mr. Sedberry shouted. "That man deserves a fair trial."

Thomas and his two older boys pushed in behind Sarah. Thomas gasped and laid a hand on her arm. "Did anyone go for the sheriff?"

Sarah clutched his hand. "It don't matter. By the time he gets here, Henry will be dead."

She weighed her options. Despite the guns, despite the cold look in the men's eyes, she longed to rush headlong in Henry's direction. But if she did and lived through it, what would it accomplish? Dandy would bolt for sure, leaving Henry to dangle.

Desperate, she turned around to search the crowd for help. A cluster of her people stood off to the side, the men puffed up and spewing, the women wringing their hands. A closer look at their faces told Sarah fear had them by the throat. She'd find no help among them.

Too scared to cry, Sarah clung to Thomas and hid her face in his stiff woolen shirt. "We have to do something quick, Thomas. Henry's gon' die if we don't."

Please help us, Lord! Please spare my good-hearted man.

Sarah raised her head when the babble around her died. Certain it meant the dreadful men were about to finish their grizzly task, she jerked her head in Henry's direction, but he still sat slumped on Dandy. Her gaze darted, searching for the reason the crowd had stilled.

Drunken singing swelled from the alley, lifted on the morning breeze, and carried into the hotel's backyard. A man's voice, loud and getting louder, neared the back corner of the building. Even Henry's tormentors paused and stared.

Thomas craned his neck. "What's going on? What is that?"

Sarah stood up on her toes. "I don't know. I can't see."

The source of the racket shot bobbing and weaving from the shadows, singing an Irish chantey in a rowdy bawl. Behind Sarah, a woman gasped and a youngster giggled. Muttering voices uttered shocked surprise.

"Is that Mr. Stilley?"

"Sure is!"

"Can't even walk a straight line."

"Drunk as a skunk."

"Can't be. The man's a deacon."

"And a teetotaler."

Mr. Stilley wore his hat shoved down so far it covered his eyes. The buttons of his coat were fastened into all the wrong holes so that the lapel flapped under his chin on one side and the tail hung to the ground on the other. He carried a big bottle of scotch in his left hand and a broken umbrella in his right. He plodded with a lurching, halting gait, still singing the sailor's song at the top of his lungs.

Sarah prayed for God Himself to steady Dandy.

Oblivious to the meaning of the scene he had stumbled upon, the stodgy owner of the dry goods store meandered straight toward the thin, pock-faced young man and his pistol.

Skinny Boy raised his free hand. "Hold up there, grandpa. Where you think you're going?"

Mr. Stilley tipped his head back and peered from under the brim of his hat. "Heard a party," he slurred in a loud voice.

By the way they snickered and shot each other looks, this tickled the men's funny bones to no end. Their evil leader stooped down on the wagon and jumped to the ground. "Don't think you want an invite to this party, old man." He nodded at the nervous Edward, who waved Mr. Stilley away with the barrel of his gun.

"Move along, now, pop," Edward ordered in an important voice. "Go somewhere and sleep it off."

Sarah bit her lip and tasted blood when Mr. Stilley lumbered past the mule, headed straight for Edward. "Now see here, young man," he slurred. "I won't be spoken to like that. Don't you know who I am?"

With the quickness of a striking snake and the boldness of a senseless man, Mr. Stilley clutched Edward's shotgun and raised the business end toward the sky. In the same instant, he grabbed Dandy's halter and held him fast.

Her eyes busy with this spectacle, Sarah missed how Doc Turner and Sheriff Vines got the jump on the other two. By the time she thought to look, both bad men had dropped their weapons and raised their hands out of respect for the guns buried in their backs.

Mr. Stilley, cold sober and looking right proud of his acting skills, glared at the crowd. "Don't stand there gawking like fools. Someone go fetch Sheriff Bagby."

Cook's boy, who had remained on his horse the whole time, most likely to see better, whirled his poor horse and sped away in the direction of the jailhouse.

Sarah felt the knot in her stomach unwind like a child's whirligig and feared she might lose control of her bowels. She rushed toward Henry, fully expecting one of the white men to order her back. They didn't, and she made it to the wagon bed, scrambled on, and stretched up to remove the loathsome rope from around Henry's neck. When she couldn't quite reach it, she began to cry for the first time since laying eyes on her husband's plight.

Thomas leaped up beside her and gently pulled her hands away. "Here, let me, Miss Sarah."

She hadn't been able to look at Henry's battered face since that first horrid glimpse but dared a peek while Thomas lifted off the noose. What she saw stabbed grief to the center of her heart.

Henry stared straight ahead, as he had since she first saw him. His busted face wore shame forged there like a mask. His lips, chin, cheeks, all trembled, and silent tears welled in waves that spilled over and tracked down his face.

Unable to look any longer, Sarah pressed her belly against Dandy's back and tore at the ropes on his hands. "Don't you fret, Henry King. You hear me, now? Don't you fret no more." She heard her own babbling voice, teetering on the edge of hysteria, but couldn't stop. The need to comfort raged too strong. "Don't let them whip you down. Don't you dare let them win. Those men gon' be at someone's mercy now. They'll be bound in cuffs and shackles, but you'll be free."

She got his hands loose and cringed when his arms fell to his sides like wilted celery stalks. Thomas jumped down and wrapped Henry around the waist to pull him off Dandy's back. Several other men, black and white, rushed to help lower him to the ground. Not until Henry's knees buckled did Sarah realize he had injuries she couldn't see. She leapt to the ground and rushed to his side to help Thomas hold him up.

Cook's son rode up with Sheriff Bagby. The sheriff sprang from his horse and joined Sheriff Vines where he held Griswald at gunpoint. "Thought sure you fellows would take fair warning and clear out of town." He glanced around at each of them. "Ain't too bright, are you?"

After all she had suffered at the hands of the haughty gang leader, Sarah deemed him above the law and impossible to break. She held her breath and waited for him to spin like a whirling dervish, guns blazing. Instead, he ducked his head and gave in without a peep. Sarah's jaw went slack.

The two lawmen shared a guilty look; then Sheriff Bagby stepped closer to Henry. "I'm real sorry this happened, son. But like I told you this morning, we had nothing solid to hold them on. Had no idea they were capable of something like this."

Sheriff Vines took the handcuffs from the other lawman. "We know now, and we have enough to hold them for a very long time."

Sarah stared up at a stone-faced Henry. So that's where he'd gone that morning. But why? And how did he wind up on Dandy's back with a noose around his neck?

Thomas left the job of holding Henry to Sarah and the others and moved out front to clear the way. "Let us pass, folks, so's we can get him over to my wagon."

Dr. J. G. Eason, in his long black coat and stovepipe hat, pushed through the crowd waving both hands in the air. "Hold up there, Thomas. Where are you taking this man?"

Thomas looked baffled. "We 'bout to take him home." He sought out Sarah behind him. "Ain't that right, Sarah?"

The doctor shook his head. "He needs medical attention." He glanced at the owner of the Commercial Hotel. When the man nodded, Dr. Eason pointed toward the rear entrance. "All right, you men take him inside so I can examine him."

The gang of helpers shifted directions and carried Henry toward the door. As they passed where Mr. Stilley stood holding the spineless Edward captive with his own gun, Sarah gazed over her shoulder and met her hero's eyes. "Thank you," she whispered.

Mr. Stilley winked and gave her a warm smile then returned his attention to Edward.

Sarah surrendered her place at Henry's side to a man for the hard trek up the steps. The last thing she saw before ducking inside was a parade of men—Mr. Stilley, the lawmen, and some others—marching the prisoners off to jail.

Sarah expected the men who carried Henry to go straight to the kitchen and put him in a chair near the servants' pantry, but they trudged on through to the parlor. Henry shook his head when they steered him toward the pretty settee, nodding instead at a straight-backed wooden chair. It angered Sarah that even in his busted-up state, he felt unworthy to sit on the beautiful couch. When they settled him on the chair, he found a spot in the corner and fixed his eyes there, refusing to face them.

Besides the two who bore Henry's weight, a group of curious and concerned folks had followed them inside. Sarah stepped around them to tend to her husband, and Henry tilted his head toward hers, muttering something she didn't quite make out.

She leaned closer. "What's that?"

He shifted his eyes to hers then right back to the corner. She bent down and put her ear against his lips. "What is it, Henry? Tell me."

She felt him shudder. "Take me home."

Before she could decide how to answer, Dr. Eason swept through the parlor door with his medical bag under his arm. He stopped short and looked at Henry sitting upright. "What's going on here, gentlemen? I can't examine a man in a chair. Let's get him stretched out on this couch."

Henry didn't protest this time, and Sarah wondered if the pain he felt had anything to do with it. She sent up a quick prayer that nothing serious might be going on inside him.

Thankfully, Dr. Eason ordered all but Sarah to wait outside. When the last of them shuffled through the door, the doctor pulled up a chair, raised Henry's shirt, and commenced to poking and prodding his chest. Henry winced and rolled away from his hands, and the doctor nodded. "Thought so."

Sarah moved closer. "What, Doctor?"

"It's a fractured rib, Sarah. Maybe two."

"Is he gon' be all right?"

He mashed Henry's stomach for a long time before he answered. "No sign of injury to the internal organs." He asked a few questions, and Sarah felt relieved when Henry answered every one.

Finally, the doctor stood up and smiled. "He'll be all right. Just sore for a spell. We'll wrap him up tight and send him home to bed. You make him rest for a few days, you hear? Don't let him get out there chasing behind that mule tomorrow. It'll be a month or so before he's fit for hard work."

Henry frowned.

The doctor pulled a roll from his bag and wound yards of white cloth around Henry's chest then offered a hand so his patient could sit up. He grimaced before moving gentle fingers over Henry's nose. "Nothing much we can do for this sort of thing, I'm afraid. Just clean it up when you get home and pray it heals without causing you any problems."

Sarah searched his eyes. "Problems?"

The doctor shrugged. "Trouble breathing, excessive snoring." He glanced back at Henry. "You won't be as pretty as you were before if it heals crooked or bumpy."

Sarah cringed at the thought. She liked her husband's nose just the way it was.

Dr. Eason lowered his voice to a whisper. "I'll be happy to bring out a bottle of wine to cut the pain, Henry. I make it myself on my own winepress. The grapes come from a vineyard I set up near the old Welch Bridge."

Henry struggled for something to say. Sarah said it for him. "No, thank you, sir. We're abstainers."

He gave her a thoughtful nod. "Well, it's there if you need it."

Henry raised his pain-filled eyes to the doctor. "Can't I go now?"

Dr. Eason nodded. "I'll get someone to help you to your wagon. Go home and rest, now. You hear?"

Henry nodded.

The doctor picked up his bag. Sarah couldn't imagine what other instruments lay in the depths of the shiny black satchel and didn't care to know. Not if it came to using them on Henry.

Wincing, Henry scooted to the edge of the settee so Sarah and the doctor could help him to his feet. She couldn't help wondering why he seemed so weak if his injuries weren't that serious.

Dr. Eason seemed to read her mind. He gripped her husband's arm and gave him a gentle shake. "Henry, the human body wasn't designed to suffer what happened to you. In episodes of great pain, fear, or humiliation, the mind shuts off, like when your old mule decides he won't take another step."

He waited for Henry to speak. When he didn't, the doctor carried on. "Just like that mule, as soon as you get a little food and plenty of rest, you'll be good as new again. Do you understand what I'm trying to say?"

Henry nodded and even tried to smile. The sight of it lifted Sarah's heart.

Dr. Eason left after giving her a few more instructions but kept his promise to send someone to help Henry out to the wagon.

Thomas and his usually rowdy sons slipped into the room, the boys so hushed at the sight of the fancy parlor that Sarah didn't recognize them. The oldest, though only sixteen, stood as tall as Thomas and likely weighed more. Plenty big enough to help support Henry's weight. Thomas's eyes lit up to see Henry acting more like himself. He hustled over, ready to brace him.

Henry held up his hand. "I'm obliged, Thomas, but I can make it on my own now."

Sarah clutched his arm as he passed. "Wait, Henry. Let them help you."

He turned—slowly, deliberately, with eyes so scary her scalp tingled. "Don't touch me, woman. I said I can make it." He limped around the settee and stumbled for the door, leaving Sarah unable to breathe.

CHAPTER 22

T had picked up his bag and strutted closer to Darius Thedford. "On second thought, mister, I reckon I got some time to kill. Where's this poker game of yours?"

Darius tried in vain to hide a satisfied smirk. "That's my boy. Follow me."

Something told Thad he'd regret heeding those words. He fell in line with Darius and retraced his steps to the same place where he'd spent the night. No surprise when Darius slowed his stride and pushed past the swinging doors into the saloon.

A collection of men still huddled around the card table. Likely the same bunch, considering their bloodshot eyes and stubbly chins. Gone the boisterous laughter and loud arguments of the night before—fatigue had reduced them to nods and grunts. When Darius approached, the gamblers squinted up at him through a haze of cigar smoke and nodded.

"What you got there, Thedford?" growled a man in a wide-brimmed black hat. "Did your cur throw her pups?"

None of them spared the energy to laugh, but they all grinned and nodded their approval. Darius clutched Thad by the shoulders and guided him closer to the table. "Make room for two more players, gents."

A scruffy man, tobacco-stained teeth visible behind a bushy gray mustache, tilted his head up at Darius. "What you doing back here? Thought you was all tapped out." His voice ground out like iron on gravel, probably hoarse from smoking, if not from shouting all night.

Darius poked a sleeping man in the ribs then moved in to take his seat when he stumbled away. He motioned for Thad to take the empty chair next to him.

Thad complied, tucking his travel bag securely between his feet.

Darius picked up a deck of cards, shuffling so fast his hands blurred, and nodded at Thad. "My good friend here has enough to guarantee my stake."

Thad's head whipped around. "What?"

Darius leaned close to whisper. "Just a few dollars until I'm back in the chips. Don't worry, old boy. I'm good for it. Now ante up."

Before Thad could protest, the other players had their money down. The raspy-voiced man tapped the end of his cigar on the leg of the table and scowled. "Well, pup? You in or out?"

Thad glared at Darius.

Still shuffling, he winked and smiled. "Go ahead, boy. We'll be all right."

Feeling snookered, Thad turned his back on the players and dug out his kerchief-wrapped bundle. He counted out double the required amount and slid it into the pot. He'd scarcely drawn back his hand before cards were flying and the first bets were placed.

Just as fast, Thad found himself down to his last silver dollar.

He never expected the excitement of the game to snare him, never expected the same old flutter in his stomach or the familiar surge of heat through his body each time he held a fair hand of cards. As a boy, he'd read of Homer's Sirens, beautiful women who perched on the shore and lured sailors onto the rocks to shipwreck and enslave them. Sitting at a card table in a gaudy, smoke-filled saloon, Thad could hear the Sirens' song. And it scared him.

More than that, it stripped him of every last coin in his

possession, save the one in his hand. Hardly enough for a train ticket south.

Mama's scowling face rose up in his mind, but her pointing finger and well-earned "I told you so" paled in comparison to Papa's angry eyes.

He opened his mouth to tell the men he'd made a dreadful mistake, that he hadn't meant to play, and could he please have his money back. But the ruthless gamblers seated around him weren't kids playing Lanterloo for buttons. His money would pad their pockets, and he wouldn't be seeing it again. The realization struck that he'd simmered other men in the same stew he found himself in, and it shamed him.

Thad felt the weight of the dollar he held, enough to see and call the last wager. Should he fold and leave the table with enough for a much-needed bath and a plate of food or throw all his lot toward recouping some of his losses? He stared at the pair of kings in his hand and decided they weren't good enough.

When he moved to lay down his cards, he felt a bump against the side of his boot. Convinced it was an accident, he moved his foot. A pointed toe followed and nudged him again, so he stole a glance at Darius's unreadable face. Without looking at Thad, he gave a barely perceptible nod.

Since Thad couldn't exactly lean over and ask what Darius meant for him to do, he had to assume he should stay in the game. He grimaced and laid down his dollar. "I see your bet, and I call."

"That's it, then," Darius announced and threw out a pair of jacks. "Beat those or fork it over, friends."

With grumbles and rude remarks, the others folded their cards and threw them facedown on the table.

Thad stared at the cards in his hand until the spots ran together. Then his gaze moved to the mounded pot. He'd won. All his money back and then some. Grinning like a youngster at a birthday party, he slapped down the two kings with a satisfied shout and reached to draw in his loot.

A hand shot out and latched onto his wrist so hard he winced.

"Hold up there, partner. I think there's been a mistake."

His arms still stretched around his winnings, Thad blinked at the man's scowling face. "What mistake? You all folded, and two kings beats two jacks last time I checked."

Fingers still locked on Thad's arm, the cigar smoker glared at Darius. "Well, I reckon there's some sort of a mix-up. Right, Thedford?"

Darius went on shuffling with his quicksilver hands then slid the deck toward Thad. "Son, I believe it's your deal."

The angry man stood to his feet. "I asked you a question, Thedford."

Darius shrugged and leaned back. "I suppose everyone's luck runs out after a while, Billy." He scooted to the edge of his chair and calmly scooped up the money. No one made a sound while he counted and stacked the coins. Then he reached for Thad's neckerchief and tied the money into a wad. "Let the kid take his winnings, Billy. He won them fair and square."

Billy's brows met in the middle. "Oh, I follow now. You and the tadpole struck a bargain of your own." He leaned over the table, shifty eyes bouncing from Thad to Darius. "But I got news. Nobody cuts Billy Eddy out of a deal." With a furious roar, he shoved over the table, sending cards and money flying. Thad and Darius leaped out of their chairs, and Darius backed away from the swarming men, one hand held up as a shield.

"Now, Billy, you know I'd sooner kiss a rattler than cross you boys."

Thad spun and shot Darius a fierce look. It all made sense. Thad hadn't been an angler's fish. He'd been a swindler's pigeon. Darius Thedford was a crook. A crook burdened with a sore conscience, but a crook nonetheless. He'd brought Thad to this saloon to double-cross him.

Thad wasn't about to risk his neck for the no-'count cheat. He snatched up his travel bag and inched toward the exit.

The gamblers, intent on a pound of Darius's flesh, didn't notice.

When Thad's groping hand connected with the swinging doors, he eased out and quick-stepped to the corner then ducked down the alley. He picked up speed as he neared the back of the building, but his mind lingered inside on the bandanna filled with lost money.

Why hadn't he listened to his mama?

Why? Because insufferable arrogance had tripped him up, and temptation had brought him on down. Darius's challenge had pinned Thad to the wall by his own weakness. He'd really thought he could use his skill at cards to fleece those men but found himself stripped of wool instead.

"Pride goeth before destruction, and an haughty spirit before a fall. Better it is to be of an humble spirit with the lowly, than to divide the spoil with the proud."

The words from the Bible rocked inside his mind. In his case, pride had brought such a great fall that there would be no spoil to divide. He lowered his head before the eternal truth of God's Word.

Forgive me for the sin of pride. And for gambling when I know it's wrong. I'll try and do better next time.

If not for the need to hurry, he'd slip to his knees and say a proper prayer. Under the circumstances, his whispered plea would have to do. He'd be sure to thank his mama for her wise counsel when he got home—and apologize for not heeding it.

The burden inside him lifted as the wall beside him exploded. He jerked around in time to see Darius soar from a boarded-up window. His body landed and rolled with the grace of a dancer, and he wound up on his feet next to Thad.

"Let's see how fast you can run, boy. Follow me."

The same two words had gotten him in this fix to start with, but Thad had little time to consider the wisdom of following. The band of gamblers fired two shots from the window behind him then scrambled through the opening shouting curses. Thad burst out of the alley on Darius's heels.

They thundered down the narrow passageway behind the row

of buildings, turned into the back door of a livery stable, and came out the front. Then up the boardwalk a ways, weaving between disgruntled pedestrians, before turning down a side street just past the mercantile.

By then, Thad couldn't tell where he was going or where he'd been. The rest of their escape passed in a blur of shops and startled faces—until they ran to the end of a block, cut across a field, and wound up in front of the train depot. Darius wheeled to a stop near the ticket window and bent over, panting to catch his breath. Thad dropped his bag and leaned against the wall, breathing hard.

Darius recovered enough to speak and rose up grinning, his lips pulling the edges of his handlebar mustache into twin peaks. "A close one, my boy. We gave them the slip, though, didn't we?"

Thad glowered. "I get the feeling you've had plenty of practice."

Darius reddened and glanced away. Still, Thad had little pity to offer the man. He'd left his compassion in a dingy saloon tied up in a worn bandanna.

Still clutching his side, Thad straightened and looked around. A big Texas & Pacific passenger train loomed on the tracks beside them, boarding travelers of every description. Thad frowned at Darius. "What are we doing here? I don't expect they're giving away tickets today."

His wide grin back in place, Darius held up the knotted kerchief. "You didn't think I'd leave without this, did you? Go on. Take it."

Thad shook his head. "It's not mine."

Darius dangled it closer. "Why, sure it is."

Thad pushed his hand away. "I didn't win that money. You cheated those men out of it."

Darius raised his brows. "I just cheated enough to get back your investment. Since I took it by cheating to start with, I figure that makes it all right."

Thad gritted his teeth. He didn't want any part of the stolen money, especially Billy Eddy's or the other men's tainted loot. He reckoned he deserved to lose his portion for going against his parents' advice. "I'm telling you, I don't want it."

Darius shook his arm. "Come now, Thad. How else will you get to school?"

When Thad didn't answer, Darius grunted and pushed him out of the way. He stepped up to the ticket window, spoke to the smiling man behind the bars then slid a few dollars under the window. Before he walked away, he paused and asked the agent for a pen. Using the protruding ledge as a desk, he pulled a piece of paper from his pocket, scribbled on it, then stashed it again. He returned to Thad, picked up his hand, and slapped the ticket into his palm. "Take this, at least. It's your passage to Bryan."

When Thad didn't close his hand, Darius folded his fingers for him. "Thad, even a mule knows when to quit being stubborn."

Thad lifted his gaze to the man's earnest face and grinned. "Thank you."

The conductor for the noon train headed their way shouting the last chance to board. Darius placed his hand on Thad's shoulder. "You're a fine young man. I envy the direction you've chosen for your life and regret any action on my part to hinder you. I pray you'll forgive me."

Thad searched his eyes and found true sorrow there. He gave a little nod.

"And, son," Darius whispered, "my mama tried to sway me from gambling, too. I only wish I'd listened."

Thad laughed aloud, and Darius pounded him on the back. "Time to get on that train, unless you plan to chase it."

Wiping the dust off on his trousers first, Thad held out his hand.

Darius winked and gave it a hearty shake. "Wait right here. I'll get your things." He took two sliding steps to the wall, returned with the travel bag, and laced the strap over Thad's arm.

Thad shifted the weight of it and tucked his arm around the middle. "Thank you, sir."

Darius gave the bag a thoughtful pat. "It's the least I could do, son. Good luck to you."

"I appreciate it, Darius, but I rely on a Power more dependable than luck." He ducked his head then lifted a sheepish grin. "Well, most days, at least. I'm sorry my actions didn't bear witness of Him." He gripped Darius's shoulder and held his gaze, wanting to say more, to tell him the Power he depended on was a better way.

The last whistle blew beside them, the haunting blast so loud they both jumped. Darius beamed, lifting the edges of his mustache again. "Better go, son."

Thad returned his smile then ran for the open door of the passenger car. Handing over his ticket, he hopped aboard just as the wheels began to turn. He lumbered down the aisle, found an empty seat, and eased into it.

Darius shouted his name, and Thad leaned out to find him trotting alongside the train waving a folded piece of paper. When he saw Thad, he picked up his pace and ran up next to the window. "Here! Take this before I change my mind."

"What is it?"

Darius tucked the document into Thad's outstretched hand. "Maybe a worthless waste of ink, but maybe enough to soothe my sore conscience and settle our score."

"There's nothing left to settle."

He grinned and stopped running, cupping his hands to shout, "Let's just say I have a lot to atone for."

Thad thrust it at him, but Darius had fallen too far behind and didn't seem inclined to take it back. He lifted his hand in a mock salute and turned away. Thad stared after him until the track curved and he could no longer see the platform.

Puzzled, he settled against the seat, unfolded the paper, and tried to make sense of what he had. At the bottom, a name had been crossed out and Darius's penciled above it. Then Darius's name was struck through and Thad's printed on top. His eyes lit on the word "property" then the word "deed," and his breath caught in his throat. He leaned out the window, as if Darius might still be there to explain.

Why would Darius give it to him? He said it might be worthless, so he'd never seen the property, which meant he'd likely won it playing cards.

Thad held it in a shaft of light to read the small print. The official sounding words described a parcel of Texas land in a place called Humble, somewhere north of Houston. Was it really his? From the look of it, after a trip to the courthouse to record the deed, it would belong to him, worthless or not.

Could he accept such a valuable gift? A gift Darius won at poker, no less? A better question, how would he go about giving it back?

Didn't the Bible say the wealth of the sinner was laid up for the just? Well, he hadn't behaved very justly by disobeying his parents and risking Papa's money in a game of chance. But God also promised to forgive a man's transgressions when he asked.

He hauled his bag from under the seat and undid the loop from the button holding it shut. Pulling aside a stack of trousers and his long johns, he tucked the deed beneath them. When the pile of clothes fell back, a flash of color in the opposite corner caught his eye. Heart racing, he pulled the red bandanna from its hiding place, untied it, and counted out the coins. They totaled every dollar of the money he'd lost playing cards, less the price of his ticket south.

Darius.

Another scripture, this one from the book of Romans, drifted through Thad's mind.

"Be not forgetful to entertain strangers: for thereby some have entertained angels unawares."

Did he really believe Darius Thedford, a cigar-smoking, card-cheating dandy was an angel? Hardly. But God had used the man to teach Thad a valuable lesson and even turned to good what had been a very bad offense on his part. He lifted a prayer of thanksgiving then tacked on a plea on Darius's behalf. Thad wondered if he'd ever see the man again.

Lost in thought, he jumped like a frog when the train whistle blew at a crossing. Grinning, he patted the bag still clutched in his hands and thought about the deed inside. In His mercy and grace, the Lord had chosen not only to forgive Thad but to bless him right out of his socks.

CHAPTER 23

Monday, January 22

Bertha laid her needlework aside. A good thing, really, considering the mess she'd made of it. Tiny stitches were hard to see with tears in her eyes.

She sat with her mama in the parlor, a basket of sewing between them—Bertha huddled in a corner of the settee, Mama perched in a straight-backed Windsor chair. The fireplace crackled beside them but did nothing to warm Bertha's heart.

She raised her head and met Mama's sorrowful gaze. "Stop watching me, please. I'm all right."

Her mama flushed. "How did you know with your chin on your knees?"

"I feel your eyes on me like twin brands. They've seared holes in my head."

Mama poked her needle into her pincushion. "Well, you don't seem all right to me, dear. You hardly touched your dinner, even after sleeping straight through breakfast."

Bertha grimaced. "I wasn't sleeping. Hardly slept all night." She rubbed her midriff, fighting tears. "And food makes the ache worse."

Mama winced and ducked her head. She'd tiptoed around the house since yesterday morning, shamefaced and apologetic. "Try to drink something, then. Let me steep you a cup of chamomile tea. It'll ease your stomach and relax you."

Bertha stood, her bleary eyes going to the window again. She couldn't stop searching the lane for Thad, though she knew he was long gone.

"Gone, I must be gone. . . ." The words sounded so final.

She moved behind Mama's chair and patted her shoulders. "I know you mean well, but tea won't help. Nothing short of Thad's return will make me feel better."

Reaching back, Mama squeezed her hand. "I'm responsible for all of this. Can you ever forgive me?"

A catch rose in Bertha's throat. "There's nothing to forgive. I know you didn't realize how much it meant. I would've told you, but—"

She paused so long that Mama twisted around to look. "But what?"

"You'll think me fresh."

Mama waved her hand. "You go right ahead and speak your mind."

"It's just that you're so different now. I don't remember you ever apologizing to me before." She gave a nervous laugh. "Or allowing me to speak my mind, for that matter. If you'd been like this that night. . ." She couldn't finish. The boldness of her words sealed her tongue to the roof of her mouth.

Mama sighed. "You're free to say it. It's only right that I hear what I've done to you."

Bertha pressed the backs of her fingers to her mouth. "I can't," she whispered when she could speak.

Mama took her wrist and guided her around in front of the chair. "Let me say it for you. If I'd been approachable, as I am now, you'd have come to me, told me about Annie and Thad, and together we'd have worked things out. But I was rigid and inconsiderate instead, and I failed you." Her voice broke on the last three words.

Bertha knelt and pressed her forehead to Mama's calico-covered knee. "It doesn't matter. Please don't cry."

With a trembling finger, Mama lifted Bertha's chin. "It matters. So I ask you again. Will you forgive me?"

Despite the fact they belonged to her mama, Bertha stared into warm, caring eyes she'd never seen before. "Of course I will."

Bertha rose up and fell into the first real hug she could remember them sharing.

When they parted, both smiling and wiping their eyes, she stole a long look at her mama's serene face while Mama fished a hankie from her waist pocket. Drying her cheeks, she shifted her gaze to Bertha. "Now you're staring."

Bertha giggled. "I've been wondering what Papa did to, well. . ."

"To change me?"

Speechless, she nodded.

"Simple. He threw the Bible at me."

Bertha clutched her lace collar. Throwing the Holy Book seemed extreme, even for her feisty papa. Mama tittered and waved her hankie. "Not literally, dear. He merely pointed out the scriptures directing a wife to submit to her husband and a husband to love his wife." Her eyes lost focus. "Funny how a verse can be right under your nose, or in this case right before your eyes, yet you can't see it. I must've read those passages a dozen times and never recognized it as the formula for happiness I'd been seeking."

Mama shook herself from her daze and motioned for Bertha to sit across from her. "So we struck a bargain." She stared at the ceiling and smiled, as if reliving the moment. "Francis promised abundant affection from here on out if I promised to honor his place in our home." Her slender white throat worked with emotion. "That silly man's devotion is all I've ever wanted. I just never knew how to get it."

Bertha leaned forward, confused. "I don't understand. Papa's such a loving man."

Mama nodded and delicately blew her nose. "Of course you'd perceive him that way. Besides the fact he adores you, when I built a wall to shut him out, he still had you to lavish attention on. Your father confessed that he's longed to show me the same love, but my rigid insecurity and lack of respect held him back."

She glanced at Bertha with grief-stricken eyes. "I shut you out, too. I don't know how I allowed it to happen. Now we've lost so much time."

Bertha rushed to embrace her. "Just think. We'll have a fresh start. It's never too late for love, you know."

Mama caressed her cheek. "Bless you, daughter." She kissed her then held her at arm's length. "And that's what you must remember about your Thad. It's never too late for love."

Bertha straightened and peered at the window again. "I do hope you're right. But we have a long wait to prove it. Thad won't be home for months."

"You'll see him soon. He'll come back to Jefferson on breaks and holidays. The time will pass quickly—you'll see."

Bertha stood, hoisting her basket and the frock she'd been hemming to her hip. "May I be excused? I can't sit in this house moping for another second." She walked around and rested her hand on Mama's shoulder. "If you don't mind, I'm going to ride into town to try to see Annie. I left her in such a terrible state."

Mama took Bertha's basket from her hands and placed it on a side table. "I hate to see you go into town alone. Wait and let Papa take you."

"I don't need to trouble him."

A stirring at the door caught their attention. "When in time have you caused me a mite of trouble, me girl?" Papa boomed. "I've a matter or three to see to in town meself. Let me fetch an overcoat, and we'll be off."

He disappeared, returning to peek around the corner at Mama. "Be ready to warm me supper then warm me bed, Mrs. Biddie. I'll be back in a trice."

Mama blushed like a girl. "Francis! Not in front of Bertha."

He winked and went away chuckling.

Mama busied herself with a sock and darning egg, her red face almost in her lap.

Bertha tried hard not to laugh. She turned away and covered her mouth with both hands.

Behind her, Mama let loose a small titter. They both giggled softly until Mama stood and gathered her sewing. "The man is scandalous," she announced.

"That he is."

"I can't do a thing with him."

Bertha grinned. "He may be a lost cause."

Mama beamed back and pinched Bertha's cheeks. "Yes, but in the most charming fashion." She cupped Bertha's chin in her palm. "Don't forget your wrap, dear. It's cold out."

Her papa, small in stature with a giant's presence, filled the doorway again. "Ready, me girl?"

Bertha pushed past him, planting a kiss above his scruffy beard on the way. "As soon as I fetch my shawl."

Papa stood by the wagon when Bertha came out, ready to lift her aboard. "Where to, young'un?"

"Brooks House. I need to see that Annie's all right."

He nodded. "I'll take you right to her doorstep. Just let me swing by the livery on the way."

"Isn't Mr. Spellings coping any better with losing Miss Carrie?"

Papa looked grim. "He'll be fine if loneliness and grief don't kill him. We just need to rally 'round him and keep him in our prayers."

Bertha sat silent for a moment then cleared her throat and sought his eyes. "I don't mean to show disrespect, but it's been awhile since Miss Carrie passed. Shouldn't he be getting on with it by now?"

Papa studied her with a somber look. "I'm afraid husbands don't fare well after losing a wife." He nudged her with his elbow. "If you ever tell I said this, I'll deny it. Understand?"

"Yes, sir."

"Womenfolk are far and away stronger creatures than men. It's how the good Lord fashioned you because of all you're required to endure."

"Like what? You seem stout enough to endure anything."

He drew back and made a face. "Can you see me birthing a babe?"

She blushed and grinned. "So you reckon we're stronger, do you?"

He gave a solemn nod. "Without doubt. You're the glue that binds us together. Thankfully, Sol's not yet forty, so youth is on his side. We older men don't last long after our wives pass. I think over time we forget how to care for ourselves."

She sat back and pondered his words. She had to admit she knew of many elderly widows but hardly any widowers. She stole a look at Papa, chewing on his mustache while deep in thought, and tried to imagine him alone, fending for himself. They rode the rest of the way in silence, Papa distracted and Bertha fighting tears.

When Mr. Spellings limped out of the livery to greet them, Bertha saw him with new, more compassionate eyes. He waved and lumbered their way, dodging mud holes and scattered piles of manure. Just before he reached them, he took off his battered Stetson and beat it against his leg, sending hay straws flying. "Francis Biddie and little Bertha. To what do I owe such a pleasure?"

Papa raised his derby and let it settle back onto his head. "The pleasure's ours, Sol. Stopped by to see if we can do anything for you today."

Mr. Spellings's cheeks rose in a warm smile. "Can't think of a thing. I take most of my meals over at Kate Woods's restaurant, and I hired a girl to see to my wash. Much obliged, though."

Bertha leaned past Papa. "Are you certain, Mr. Spellings? What about sewing? Do you have any clothing in need of repair?"

He scratched his head. "Now that you mention it, I do have a bag of tattered duds at the house. Some things Carrie never got around to." Tears clouding his soft brown eyes, he peered up at Bertha. "I'll bring them by the house, then. If you really don't mind."

She swallowed the lump in her throat so she could speak. "I'll be proud to do it."

He swiped his eyes with his sleeve and tucked his hat on his head. "Thank you kindly, Bertha."

Papa propped his boot on the side rail. "How's business, Sol? This weather must be pinching your purse."

A look of disgust came over Mr. Spellings's face. "Nothing to brag on, that's for sure. Folks don't much care to ride around in the rain." He raised one finger. "Except I did rent out a few horses on Saturday to some fellows just off the boat. And a man came in that day inquiring about a rig for Sunday. But when he came back for it yesterday, I decided not to let him have it."

Papa frowned. "Didn't like the color of his money?"

"Never saw his money. Didn't want no part of it, whatever the shade. Something about him I didn't trust."

Papa propped his arm on his knee and leaned closer. "Local fellow?"

Mr. Spellings shook his head. "Out of Boston, I think. Staying a few days over to Brooks House."

A sensation of dread wriggled fingers in Bertha's belly. "Excuse me, sir. I don't mean to interrupt, but what did he look like?"

Mr. Spellings took off his hat again, as if he couldn't think with it on. "What'd he look like? Well, let me see." He rubbed the top of his head as though he was trying to coax the memory back. "Sort of a fancy dresser, with a high-blown manner. Tall but not too thin. Had an overlarge mouth, if I remember right. A surly mouth, at that."

Her stomach lurched. *Abe Monroe.* "Did he say why he needed the rig?"

"Claimed he wanted to take a lady around town." He widened his eyes and curled his top lip. "In this weather, if you can believe it. I asked him to put up collateral, and he offered very little. Didn't like it a whit when I insisted he'd have to do better."

Papa smiled. "What'd he say to that?"

Mr. Spellings mimicked a haughty voice. "He said, 'I guess, then, that we can walk,' and took off down Polk Street."

She scooted forward on the seat. "Was the woman with him, sir?"

"No, darlin', she weren't. I asked who his lady was, thinking

232

she might vouch for him. He told me I wouldn't know her, and anyway he left her over at Kate Woods's place."

For some reason the news unsettled her. If Abe knew Saturday evening that he planned to take Annie around town on Sunday, why didn't Annie know about it on Saturday night?

What was it she'd said? She hoped Abe would be sick from drinking and rest in bed all day. Obviously, Annie had no idea Abe planned to take her anywhere on Sunday. Why hadn't he mentioned it?

Bertha scarcely heard the rest of Papa and Mr. Spellings's discussion. She squirmed like a netted fish until Papa finished his business. When they finally said good-bye and pulled out of the muddy yard in front of the livery, a mixture of relief and worry weakened her knees.

"Can't we go faster, Papa?"

"What's the hurry, love?"

"Nothing really. Just anxious, I guess." She bit her lower lip. "There is one thing I haven't yet mentioned."

He swiveled to face her. "Well, mention it."

"I won't be able to see Annie if her companion is there."

Papa scowled. "What are you saying?"

"Just that we'll have to make sure he's nowhere around the hotel."

His eyes popped. "And why is that?"

She bit her knuckle and searched for the right words. "Abe won't allow Annie to see me. He doesn't let her have friends."

He swung his head back and forth. "You can forget it, then. Sneaking behind a man's back was never my style, and I won't start now. We'll walk up and knock on the door like proper guests or not at all."

Fear crawled up her spine. "You don't understand, Papa. We can't. Abe Monroe is mean to the core."

His hand shot up. "Stop right there. What sort of person speaks ill of a friend's spouse? It's not how we raised you, Bertha." A crop of blotches sprouted on his cheeks. "What were you thinking, coming between a man and his wife?"

Bertha looked away, her face on fire. "Annie's not his wife."

Papa cleared his throat. When she glanced at him, he appeared as red as she felt. "I don't like it, Bertha Maye."

She swallowed hard and peered into his face. "I don't either, Papa. But I told you some of Annie's story. Can't you see? She needs my help."

He looked straight ahead again, his face grim. His mustache twitched as he chewed one side of his bottom lip then the other. "You know it's a mighty heavy burden you've shouldered. Are you certain it's your load to bear?"

Her heartbeat quickened. "It's cost me dearly. I need to see it through."

He released a heavy breath, gave a curt nod, and spurred on the horse. They rode up Vale Street in silence, Papa's Irish temper still seething beside her.

When they pulled up to Brooks House, Bertha started to climb down. "Wait here. I won't be long."

Papa latched onto her arm. "There'll be none of that."

Frustrated, she plopped back. "Sorry, I forgot. Hurry, please."

"I ain't referring to helping you down." He pointed at the door, his face crimson and mottled like a ripe red plum. "I mean there'll be none of you going inside there alone."

She heaved a sigh. "Papa, listen. I'll inquire at the desk first. I promise not to go near her room until I'm sure he's gone out."

"I'm going with you, Bertha. To the lobby, at least, until I'm satisfied you'll be safe."

"Papa—"

"Else we leave here right now!"

Bertha winced and drew back. Papa never raised his voice to her. Defeated, she nodded. "Very well, then. Let's go. But please. . . let me do the talking."

After looking around the grounds in front, they passed through the doors of Brooks House and checked the lobby and parlor and then the dining room out back. Feeling like a player in one of Annie's Broadway shows for all their skulking about, Bertha gingerly approached the desk.

Thomas, Dr. Turner's porter, leaned over the registry, his lanky elbows planted on each side. He glanced up as they drew near, his face lighting up at the sight of Bertha's papa.

"Well, well, well. Mr. Biddie, suh. How you? You catched any mo' dem big old catfish?"

At the mention of his favorite subject, Papa's bright face matched Thomas's glow. "I ain't been fishing any more since that day. Too much work around the house."

"What? Too busy to fish? Mr. Biddie, that's way too busy." He chuckled then pursed his lips, the picture of innocence. "Well, dat's a shame, ain't it? I reckon since you ain't using yo' secret catfish bait, ain't no reason you cain't tell me what goes in it."

Papa jabbed his finger in Thomas's face. "A worthy attempt, laddie. You'll not be gettin' it out of me that easy."

They laughed together; then Papa leaned in toward the desk. "Doc Turner around?"

"Naw, suh. Went home fer a spell. He be back over here directly." He pointed at the well-appointed parlor. "You folks mighty welcome to wait."

Bertha stepped closer and lowered her voice. "Maybe you can help us. Do you happen to know if the gentleman staying in number four is in his room?"

Thomas started around the edge of the desk. "No, ma'am, Miss Bertha, but I'll be glad to find out."

Papa clutched his arm. "Let's not do that, son. We don't necessarily want to see him, just wanted to know if he's home."

Thomas gave Papa a blank stare. "Yes, suh, Mr. Biddie. But it won't trouble me none to go see if he's in there."

Footsteps in the hallway sent Bertha's heart rumbling like loose boulders. She jerked around to find Jennie Simpson limping into the foyer. Jennie stopped to stare, probably because none of the Biddies ever came inside the hotel.

"Well, I swear, if it ain't little Miss Bertha. Afternoon to you, as well, Mr. Biddie, suh."

Bertha hurried to her. "Afternoon, Jennie. Tell me, have you been cleaning the rooms?"

Her long lashes fluttered, and she pointed at her ankle. "No, ma'am, I ain't s'posed to."

For the first time, Bertha saw it was swathed in white cloth.

Smiling, Jennie turned her foot back and forth so Bertha could get a better look.

"Mercy, what happened?"

"Twisted it. Near to broke. Wouldn't be standing here now 'cepting I be about to starve to death upstairs." She glared at Thomas. "A body could lay up and die for all they care around here."

Thomas made a tent with his brows. "How you gon' starve when you find your way down those stairs in time for every meal served in this place? If you ask me, you're fit enough to work if you're fit enough to trot around huntin' up food all the time." He nodded at her feet, his lips curled in a smirk. " 'Sides, I just seen you limp out here on the wrong foot. Better not let old Doc see you do that."

She planted her knuckles on her hips. "Shush your mouth. Why you gon' lie on me like that?"

Bertha ducked in front of her scowling face and pointed down the hall. "Do you know if Miss Annie Monroe's, um, husband is in the room with her?"

It seemed a dreadful struggle, but Jennie pulled her attention from Thomas to Bertha's question. "Who?" Then her frown became a slow grin. "Oh, I know. You mean Miss Bessie's man."

"Miss Bessie. Yes, that's right."

"He ain't here. And she ain't neither."

Disappointment swelled. Bertha hadn't considered that possibility. "She's not here?"

"No, miss. Ain't seen her since they went off together yesterday morning. The mister, he come back all by hisself that afternoon."

"By himself?"

"Yes'm. When I went to fetch them for dinner"—she shot a

vengeful look at a grinning Thomas—"Mr. Abe say he already ate over to Miss Woods's place. So I asked him, 'What about Miss Bessie?' He say he left her at the restaurant, and she gon' be home that night." She stopped to draw a breath. "Only this morning at breakfast"—a glare at Thomas—"she weren't there."

"Not there?" Bertha felt like a parrot but couldn't stop repeating.

"No, miss. Mr. Abe be sitting at the table by hisself wearing those two big rings of hers." She touched a finger to her lips. "Or did I see that on Saturday night? Can't recollect which time, but I seen it."

The front door opened behind them, and Bertha whirled. Dr. Turner stood in the foyer hanging his coat. Relieved, she clutched at her collar and drew a ragged breath.

Doc turned with a playful frown. "Does anybody work around here when I'm gone? Francis, don't give these two any more reason to lollygag, if you don't mind. They manage quite nicely on their own." He widened his eyes at his two employees. "I'm back now, so get to work."

Panic gripped Jennie's face. "Dr. Turner, what about my leg?"

"I reckon you've nursed that excuse plumb to death." He studied her mournful face then slumped his shoulders. "Very well, get upstairs and rest your leg. But I expect you for light duty tomorrow morning."

Jennie backed away with a sullen look on her face. "Yes, suh. I'll make it. . .somehow."

When Jennie turned to follow Thomas from the room, Bertha was almost positive she favored the wrong foot.

Dr. Turner frowned. "Where you going? I said to get upstairs."

She whipped around. "I's hongry. Thomas ain't tended me no way like he should."

Before Thomas could protest, Doc nodded at the stairs. "Get on up there. I'll have him fetch your supper in a bit."

She cut sulky eyes at Thomas and smiled. "Yes, suh, Doc."

Laughing, Doc shook Papa's hand. "What can I do for you, Francis?"

Papa nodded toward Bertha. "Nothing for me. It's my girl here. She's worried about her friend. Thought maybe you could tell her where she is."

He turned. "Your friend Annie?"

Close to tears, she only managed a nod.

"Sorry to say she's not here. We haven't seen her since early Sunday morning."

Papa spoke up in Bertha's stead. "That's what Jennie said. Do you have an idea where she might've gone?"

"I saw her gentleman friend around two or three o'clock yesterday. The lady wasn't with him. After dinner I asked if she had returned from wherever she'd been, but she hadn't. So I asked from where he expected her return. He said he left her across the bayou visiting friends."

Bertha's head reeled with the information. Annie had friends across the bayou? She'd never once mentioned it. She found her voice. "When she comes back, will you tell her I'm looking for her?"

"I will." He tilted his head toward the row of rooms down the hall. "For now, you'd best not let him see you here. It'll just make more trouble for that poor girl."

Bertha clutched her papa's arm. "He's here? Jennie said he wasn't."

"Oh, he's here all right. Not answering the door is all. Paced his room all through the night, according to the other guests. Came down for breakfast this morning but didn't eat a bite. Said he was sick last night. Stinking drunk, more like it." He hooked his thumb toward number four. "Been moping in there all afternoon." He grinned and winked at Papa. "Just between us, I think she finally wised up and left him."

Bertha couldn't get outside of Brooks House fast enough. Even with Papa beside her, the thought of coming face-to-face with Abe Monroe raised the hairs on her neck. In her nearly eighteen years, she'd never had to fear a living soul, but something about Annie's companion stuck pure terror in her heart.

She thought of the day on the bluff when she first saw Annie's fear of Abe reflected in those lovely gray eyes. Annie had dreaded Abe's wrath more than an encounter with the devil himself. Then the night outside the Rosebud, even with Annie's senses deadened by drink, Bertha had witnessed the depths of her terror.

Maybe Dr. Turner was right. Maybe Annie had found a way to escape.

Bertha jumped when Papa touched her arm.

"I'm talking to you, Bertha. Haven't you heard a word of it?"

She gave him a tight smile. "Sorry, Papa."

"I asked if you knew of a place Annie might be hiding."

She shook her head. "She never mentioned knowing anyone in Jefferson. Of course, we weren't friends before she came. Annie's so kindhearted and outgoing, I can't assume I'm the only person in town who was drawn to her, now, can I?" Bertha had to admit the thought brought a peculiar sensation to the pit of her stomach. A sensation a little too close to jealousy. Jealously blended and stirred with anger and a generous dose of hurt feelings.

How could Annie turn to someone else after Bertha's offer of help? How could she up and leave town without even saying good-bye? Especially after Bertha's considerable sacrifice.

Then again, while grieving for Thad, she'd let a whole day pass without finding out what happened to Annie after she left her standing on a street corner in her nightdress.

God, forgive me. I've made a real mess of things.

"Bertha, what's ailing you, lass? I might as well be talking to a picket."

"Please forgive me. What did you say?"

"I asked you what's next, then."

His question ricocheted through the empty chambers of Bertha's heart, once so filled with fond affection from a friend and abiding love from a man. The same question applied to both Annie's fate and Bertha's future with Thad.

She drew a shaky breath. "What's next? Papa, if only I knew."

CHAPTER 24

Henry hadn't spoken to Sarah since the ugly words he spat at her in the hotel parlor. All the way home he sat silently in the back of Thomas's wagon, pale and gritting his teeth. When they pulled into the yard, he managed to thank Thomas and the boys, even greeted Dickens on the porch. But then he walked straight to their room and climbed into bed with nary a spare word left for Sarah.

Desperate to be near him, she followed him inside. "Henry?" she whispered. "Don't you want to eat something?"

He turned his face to the wall and drew up his shoulders. She knew he wanted her to leave, but she couldn't. Instead, she pulled the shade without making a sound, eased her way to the corner rocker, and sat so quietly in the dim room that he didn't seem to know she was there.

She watched while he tossed and turned, cried and groaned, twitched and moaned. When his breathing deepened and his face relaxed in sleep, Sarah finally dared to move. Easing her body from the chair, she crept out of the room. To keep the old hinges from squeaking, she left the door open and tiptoed down the hall.

In the kitchen, she sought the comfort of her red tea can. She took it down from the shelf and shook it, and only then remembered she had enough left for one last cup. While the water heated, Sarah wracked her mind. What had happened to make Henry so angry? What had she done to cause his hateful glare? To lace his voice with spite?

Dr. Eason said Henry's mind had shut down like a stubborn mule's. Well, she didn't believe it. She knew what a stubborn Henry looked like. The sullen man in the bedroom was a stranger she'd never laid eyes on.

Sarah lifted the kettle just as it started to whistle and sprinkled the last bit of her tea leaves over steaming water. Before closing the lid, she watched as swirling color leeched from the dried leaves. Some nameless disaster swirled about her in much the same way, threatening to stain her marriage and darken her happy life.

She found no consolation in the tea and let more than half the cup go wasted while she sat at the kitchen table lost in thought. She knew she should fix something to eat. They hadn't had a bite since breakfast, and Henry barely touched his plate then.

Leaning over the table, she folded her arms and rested her forehead there. The day had been the hardest of any she could remember. Of course, it would've been unthinkably worse if Dandy had bolted from under Henry. Still, she felt like those men had strung her up and beaten her right alongside her husband. She wondered if Henry's beating hurt worse than the heartache she felt.

Beneath the table, her stomach growled. She sucked it in as hard as she could, but it rumbled again in protest. They had pork chops left from supper last night, with baked beans and stewed apples to go with them. She could stir up a batch of biscuits fast, though skillet corn cakes would taste better.

Startled, she realized how quickly she'd gone from pure misery to thoughts of feasting. How odd the workings of the mind.

"I need a poultice for my nose."

Henry's voice brought Sarah to her feet as though she'd been bucked from the chair. "You're awake?"

He ignored her foolish question. "I can't abide this pain another minute."

She longed to reach for him. Comfort him. Instead, she scurried for the pantry and brought out jars of salves and herbs. "Your nose, you say? What about your ribs? You'd think your ribs would be giving you fits instead of your nose. 'Course, I ain't never had a broken rib, or a busted nose for that matter, but it just seems a rib would be bound to hurt worse."

Why was she babbling like Jennie Simpson? A better question— why was she talking to Henry as if he hadn't ripped the heart clean out of her chest?

He settled at the table and sat quietly while she tended his nose. When she finished, she got up without saying a word to pull out the pork chops and beans. After she warmed them and they ate, Henry pushed his empty plate aside. "I reckon I owe you some answers."

She put down the bite of apple between her fingers and met his eyes. "I only need one."

He looked away. "I'm sorry I treated you so poorly, Sarah. I had no right, and I hope you'll forgive me."

She felt her heart start to mend. "Can you tell me why?"

He wrinkled his face. "I think so. I'll try."

"Good enough."

He shifted in the chair and cleared his throat. "Yesterday, on the road when those men harassed us jus' for sport, I got real mad. When that little one pointed his gun straight at me and you jumped between us, I had so many thoughts swimming in my head I couldn't keep 'em straight." He scooted to the edge of his chair. "First thing, I ain't never had no gun in my face before. I wasn't ready for how it made me feel. Second thing, I realized if he had shot that gun, you'd be dead. Maybe both of us. That's when I passed up mad and went to crazy. Stayed crazy all the rest of the day."

She gave him a look. "You didn't seem mad."

He nodded. "I kept it pent up, like I always do. But I tossed in bed half the night thinking. When I woke up this morning, I had it figured you'd been right all along. White folks jus' plain mean and no 'count. Ain't a one of 'em care a whit for any of us, and I was wrong not to defend you better in this town."

"Oh, Henry."

"So I decided I wasn't about to let them men get by with what they done. I'd go see the sheriff and make sure he doled out proper punishment on those mongrels." He snorted. "Come to find out, the sheriff done turned 'em loose." He leaned over the table, looking at her with bulging eyes. "Turned 'em loose, Sarah. Like they ain't done one thing wrong." He slapped his hand down so hard he rattled the dishes. "There ain't no justice in that."

Remembering, his eyes glazed. "I didn't know what I was about to do next. I was in such a state by then I couldn't think. Wouldn't you know it, about that time I happened up onto them dogs. Instead of going the other way, like a man with any sense, I pranced past 'em glaring like I owned Austin Street." He flexed his jaw. "That's all it took to set those devils off. Next thing I knew, I was trussed up like a butchering hog on Dandy's back."

Sarah shuddered at the memory. "But that still don't explain—"

"Sittin' up there on Dandy, I think I went insane for a spell." He chewed his bottom lip. "All sorts of crazy thoughts took over my mind."

"What sort?"

He gave her a sheepish glance. "For one thing, I thought I was about to die, and I decided it was your fault."

She swallowed. "My fault? How'd you come up with that?"

He puffed his cheeks then released his breath in a whoosh. "Before you come to Jefferson, I didn't have no problems with these folks. I minded my business and stayed out of their way. Shucks, I even cared about most of them and believed they cared about me."

"Henry, I—"

He held up his hand. "Let me finish. Sarah. You put all these uppity thoughts in my head. You the one had me looking at white folks different. That's why I wound up talking back yesterday on the road. If I'd handled those men the way I know to, they would've gone on and left us alone. Jus' like today when I passed them on the street. If I'd ducked out of their way, I never would've wound up with a rope around my neck."

"So you think doin' things the way you always have makes it right?"

He slammed his hand on the table again, harder this time. "I don't know what's right anymore, Sarah. That's what I think. I jus' learned how to make it, that's all. I've been ducking and dodging for so long, I don't know any other way."

She knew she shouldn't lose her temper, too. Not now. Not with Henry hurt and already in such a state. But she did anyway. "If I'm the cause of all the problems in Jefferson, why'd you ever bring me here in the first place?"

He lifted cold, hard eyes. "I've been asking myself that same question lately."

They stared, neither giving an inch until Henry propped his elbows on the table and gripped the sides of his head. "All my life I've tried to believe what I read in the Good Book, where it says we supposed to love our neighbor like ourselves. That they ain't no race or color in Christ.

"When I was a boy, I remember thinking the white folks' Bible must have different words than mine, because the men coming out of the meetinghouses holding Bibles were the same ones buying and selling our people, cursing and whipping 'em. The Good Book say we all free in Christ, but the last thing they wanted was to see us free. None of it made sense to me then, and it still don't now."

"Henry, slavery didn't start here, with these people. Papa said slave trade has existed in Africa for thousands of years. He said our own brothers brought us down to the ships, bound and gagged."

Henry's eyes bugged. "Your papa's been yanking your leg."

"No, it's true." She patted his hand. "And not only white folks have owned slaves. He told me many colors and races of people are guilty. You want to know what I think? I think slavery's not a white or black problem, or even a people problem. It's a sin problem."

He snorted. "Well, it sure is a Jefferson problem. They jus' won't let us be free."

Sarah reached across the table and held his hands. "We don't need them to *let* us be free. Or haven't you heard about emancipation?"

He shifted his gaze to her. "That's an awful big word around these parts, Sarah."

"Maybe, but now I feel like there's hope for a life in Jefferson. I didn't feel that before today." She stood up and walked around the table, kneeling at his side. "Didn't you see who came to your rescue?"

"No. I mean, I don't know." His forehead wrinkled. "I don't remember much about it."

"Well, I do. They were our white friends and neighbors."

He drew back and stared. "When did you ever have a white friend or neighbor in this town?"

"Since today, and from here on out." She gripped his arm. "I'm trying to say I've been wrong. Well, partly, anyway. Like you said before, it's wrong to lump everybody into the same barrel. It's still true that some are wormy, but most of the apples in this town, though they be lumpy and blemished on the outside, are sweet at the core."

He made a face, and she stood. "This is so peculiar, Henry. About the time I change my mind, you go and change yours?"

He gazed up at her with doubtful eyes. "What has you talking like this, Sarah?"

She didn't have to think about her answer. "Miss Annie."

"Miss Annie?"

"The pretty lady we first saw in Stilley's, the one tendin' Jennie yesterday."

"I know who she is. She'd be right hard to forget. What about her?"

Sarah stared past the kitchen window. "I learned something from her. I ain't never seen a kinder soul in anyone, black or white. And that's what I'm starting to understand. It's the heart that matters, not the color of our skin. Miss Annie taught me that."

"So about the time I get you figured out, it's time to start all over?" He pushed away from the table. "I don't want to talk about this no more. My whole body hurts. I feel like I done been—" His startled eyes flashed, and he bit off the rest. Sarah knew what he'd almost said, a phrase he used all the time, especially after a long day in the field.

"*I feel like I done been whipped.*"

His jaw worked, and he swallowed, hollow eyes focusing just over her head. "Move out my way, Sarah. I'm going to bed."

CHAPTER 25

Tuesday, January 23

Bertha awoke the next morning with Dr. Turner's words ringing in her ears. She scooted higher in the bed and propped herself on her pillows. After weighing the facts half the night, she decided it would take a lot more to convince her that Annie ran off without saying a word. In fact, she refused to believe it until she had proof. Something definitely wasn't right, and in the light of a new day, another visit to Brooks House seemed the only option.

More than likely she'd find Annie shut up in number four, Abe's prisoner again. If not, she'd talk to every person there, even knock on Abe's door if need be and question him on Annie's whereabouts. And she'd stand right behind Papa while he did the knocking and the asking.

Her punishment for losing the horrible bronze shoes had started the day before. While pining for Thad, she forgot and barely got done with her regular work. Mulling over Annie's plight made her aware of how God had blessed her, so she made up her mind to honor her parents with a more obedient daughter. Maybe the extra work and the mystery surrounding Annie's disappearance would take her mind off Thad for a bit and provide a welcome distraction from her wounded heart.

She kicked off her quilt and sat up. The odor of fried bacon hit her nose as soon as her feet hit the floor, eliciting a deep groan from the pit of her stomach. Surprisingly, her appetite had come back. She dressed as fast as she could and hustled to the kitchen. "Morning, Mama."

Flipping hotcakes, by the warm, buttered-wheat smell in the room, Mama stood by the stove. She looked over her shoulder and smiled. "Good morning, dear. Sit down and I'll pour your milk."

"Don't trouble yourself. I'll do it. I wouldn't want to hinder your efforts. It smells like you're doing a fine job."

Laying her spatula aside, Mama turned. "Why, look at you. If I didn't know better, I'd say you're a different girl."

Bertha grinned. "No, it's me. I saw myself in the mirror."

Mama's stunned look turned to alarm. "Are you all right, Bertha? After the state you were in yesterday, your mood is unnaturally light. You're not feverish, are you?"

"I'm fine, Mama. In fact, I'm starving, so don't let my hotcake burn."

Mama crossed to the table and flipped the golden circle onto Bertha's plate. "I must say, I'm finding this nothing short of miraculous, dear."

Bertha served herself two strips of bacon. "It's no miracle. I didn't touch a bite all day yesterday."

"Not your hunger. Your upbeat mood."

Bertha swallowed a big bite then smiled. "Oh, that. Well, I've had some time to think and pray, so I have a whole new outlook. Papa counseled me to trust God with the details. After pondering some of those, I've come to a few conclusions."

She counted them off. "As you mentioned yesterday, Thad does live in Jefferson. He has to come home sometime, doesn't he? Meanwhile, there's less chance of a girl stealing his heart at a military school. Despite his anger, if he misses me a fraction of how I miss him, he's still miserable. And last but really first, if God wants us together, we will be. I have to believe that."

Mama laughed and forked another steaming flapjack onto her plate from a stack on the stove. "I knew we raised a sensible daughter, but I had no idea of the depths of your wisdom." She squeezed Bertha's shoulder. "I'm very proud of you. Papa will be, as well."

She grinned. "Oh, pooh. You'll embarrass me saying such things." She reached for the ceramic pitcher and poured a glass of milk. "Speaking of Papa, where is the old rascal?"

At the stove again, Mama poured more batter into the skillet, lowered the empty bowl into a dishpan, and leaned against the counter. "You just missed him. He ate enough breakfast to stagger a horse then rushed out."

Bertha craned her neck and looked out the window. "Is he out in the barn?"

"No, dear. He's gone off on an errand."

Her heart sank. "Without me?"

"Had you planned another trip into town? Lately you spend more time there than at home. I don't think you should go today." Standing with her hand on her hip and a disapproving look on her face, Mama resembled her old stormy self.

Fearing the damaging winds of the past, Bertha dared to protest. "I plan to do all my chores first, including the extras. I won't be long, and you can pick which shoes I wear." Mama's slight grin gave her courage. "Please?"

Understanding dawned on Mama's face. "You're going to look for Annie again, aren't you?"

When she nodded, Mama stiffened. "You can't go alone. Wait for Papa."

"That won't work. There's no telling when he'll be home."

"Magda, then."

Bertha wiped her mouth and stood. "We have a bargain. Thank you, Mama. Now move aside and let me at those dishes. The morning's getting away from me."

By the time Bertha completed every task, her hands were sore and her back ached. She longed to slip into the parlor and put her feet by the fire, especially since the temperature had steadily dropped all morning. Instead, she fetched her hat and warmest wrap, saddled her horse, and struck out for Magda's house northwest of town. She ran into her coming out of the end of her lane.

Magda reined in the big gelding and stared at Bertha as if she had spots. "Well, fancy that. I was just coming to your place."

Bertha nodded at the surrey. "Do you live in that thing? You're sitting up there every time I see you."

"It beats walking. What are you doing here? Are you all right? I mean, about. . ."

"I need a favor."

Magda nodded. "Sure, if I can."

"I need to go into town. Will you take me?"

She shrugged. "I was headed there after I left you. Ride your horse back to the house. I'll turn around and get you."

The surrey sat waiting when Bertha closed the barn door. She pulled herself up opposite Magda and smiled. "I'm grateful. Mama wouldn't let me go alone."

The morning chill had Magda's lips a deep cherry red and her cheeks a bright pink. The striking color against her pale skin and brown hair made her resemble a china-head doll. As soon as Bertha settled on the seat, Magda gathered her up for a hug. "I'm so sorry about Thad, sugar."

Bertha leaned against her shoulder. "Why haven't you been around to see me, then? Before now, I mean. I could've used a friend."

Magda pulled away and looked at her. "I did, Bertha. I came around on Monday. Didn't your mama tell you? She said you were in town seeing about a"—she raised her brows—"friend." Twisting around straight, she gathered the reins and signaled the horse to go.

They rode a ways before Bertha could think what to say. "I was worried about her. You don't know what Annie's been through."

Magda quirked the corner of her mouth. "And how could I? Since I'm not counted worthy to keep company with the two of

you. Why hasn't Annie worried about what you've been through?
I know I have."

Bertha cut her eyes at Magda then made up her mind. "Pull
this thing over in those trees there. We have to talk."

It surprised Bertha when Magda did as she asked without
argument. When the surrey came to a stop in the shaded grove,
Bertha reached under the seat for a blanket to cover them then
settled back on the seat and began to talk. She told Magda about
believing God may have arranged for her to meet Annie in the first
place and the reason why. She confessed how hard it had been to
put Annie before Thad and about meeting with Annie and giving
her the necklace that she felt unworthy to wear. She described Abe's
cruelty and some, but not all, of Annie's past. When she came to
the end of her story, Magda had tears in her eyes.

"Bertha, we have to do something. We have to help her."

She scooted close and kissed Magda's cheek. "I knew you'd feel
that way. Will you help me find her?"

Magda wiped her eyes and picked up the reins. "Where do we
start?"

"Brooks House. Let's go see if she came back last night."

Magda nodded and circled the wagon out of the wooded
confessional. The two chatted easily on the way into town, laughing
and teasing like they always had. It felt nice, and Bertha breathed
easier.

They pulled up to the hotel just as Jennie Simpson reached the
front walk. She flashed her chubby-cheeked smile their way and
waved. "Looky who's here again. And you brung Miss Magda with
you. How ya'll doing this mornin', little misses?"

"Morning, Jennie. Goodness, but you're bright and chipper
today."

Jennie wagged her head. "Oh yes'm, I am indeed." She looked
over her shoulder then moved closer and dropped her voice to a
loud whisper. "Got me some energy tonic." She straightened. "Best
thing I ever found for the droops." Then she winked. "A sip or two
even warms a body on a blustery day like this."

Bertha laughed. "Sounds like something I need."

She clutched the pocket of her dress. "Ordinarily I'd offer up a taste." Her worried look turned to a pout. "But after ol' Doc done found out I had it, I ain't hardly got a drop left."

Bertha reached for the post to climb down, but Jennie raised a hand to stop her. "I reckon I know why you're here, and you just be wasting time coming off there." She flashed a grin. "You come to see if Miss Bessie come back, but she ain't. She ain't even coming back to the hotel on account of Mr. Abe say she gon' meet him at the station this morning, and they gon' catch a train to Cincinnata. Mercy, don't I wish I could'a told that sweet chile good-bye."

Bertha reached behind her and gripped Magda's hand. "So they've gone?"

"Don't know if the train come yet, but Mr. Abe done checked out and lef' awhile ago."

Magda squeezed Bertha's fingers. "Let's go. Maybe we can get there in time for you to say good-bye."

"I doubt I'll be able to get that close, but at least I'll get to see for myself she's all right."

Jennie beamed. "All right? Sure she all right. God gon' take care of a good-hearted soul like Miss Bessie."

Bertha called her thanks as Magda maneuvered the wagon into the crowded street. The ride up Vale to Alley Street north of town took forever at the busy morning hour. Bertha thought for sure they'd arrive too late. When they finally drew close to the bustling station, Magda pulled onto a side road and set the brake.

"What are you doing?"

She secured the reins and scrambled down. "It'll be quicker to walk from here. Come on."

Bertha caught up to her, and together they hustled the rest of the way to the station. Bertha saw Abe Monroe right away and tugged on the back of Magda's skirt. "Stay in front of me. There he is."

"Where?"

Bertha pointed. "Right there. Seated behind the driver of that hired two-seater." She scanned the area near the hack. "Where's Annie?"

The frightening man didn't sit as tall as he did the day Bertha saw him leaving the station with his arm around the bluebird. He sat hunched over, both arms resting on his knees, studying something at his feet. Despite the weather, he didn't look cold, but one knee rose and jiggled every so often, as if he couldn't hold it still.

Bertha hid behind a shivering Magda and studied him. It was the closest look she'd ever had.

He parted his thick, curly hair a touch off center, and his eyes were too small—or just looked that way centered over the wide bridge of his nose. He was far from balding, but a high forehead made it look as if his curls had receded. He had big, pouting lips and smallish ears set too high on his head.

She had to admit that somehow this odd assortment fit together in a pleasing manner but felt it must be due to his youth. As he matured, he wouldn't be the least bit attractive. The coldness of his hollow eyes caused her to wonder what Annie ever saw in him in the first place.

Though Abe kept his attention focused on his feet, Bertha still hung back, scanning the milling crowd for Annie. "Where is she?"

Magda sighed. "Nowhere."

"Are you sure?"

"Bertha, someone like Annie is hard to hide."

Bertha shaded her eyes and stared at a glint of steel in the distance. "Well, she'd better hurry. Here comes the train."

Abe became jumpier as the big engine approached. When the whistle sounded, he stood up in the wagon and squinted, taking long draws on a cigarette and blowing billows of smoke from a puckered bottom lip. When he wasn't staring down the track, he patted his breast pockets, looked at his ticket, or glanced back at his luggage. He continued his anxious dance until the Texas & Pacific belched into the station. Then he pressed a bill into the driver's hand, gathered his bags, and ran for the open car.

Her gaze locked on Abe, Magda tilted her face toward Bertha.

"What's he doing? Isn't he going to wait for her?"

"He must plan to wait inside."

Magda nodded. "Maybe."

Bertha looked up and down the platform, behind them on the street, at the ticket window, then back to the train, until the big engine roared to life and started pulling away. She watched with an open mouth as the car Abe Monroe had boarded passed out of sight. Without Annie.

Magda jabbed her in the side. "He left her."

She felt weak in the knees. "Yes, he did." She turned a bewildered look on Magda. "But he didn't leave her luggage."

Magda stared after the caboose. "He had her luggage? Are you sure?"

"Completely."

"Why would he take it?"

Bertha pinched her bottom lip together with two fingers and stared at the ground. "I can't imagine. Unless she's planning to meet him later." Her heart surged at the thought of Annie still in town without Abe watching her every move.

She pushed the thought away. "He'd never allow it. The only time she escaped his grasp is when he drank so much he passed out. Then she took chances she shouldn't."

"Out of desperation. I'd do the same in her shoes." Magda tapped both temples with her fists. "What am I saying? I'd never be in her shoes, because I'd never allow a man to treat me like that." She swiveled toward Bertha. "Would you?"

Bertha gritted her teeth until her jaw popped. "Never."

"Why do you reckon she puts up with it?"

Bertha pulled her wrap tighter and stared across the treetops in the direction of the bluff. "Annie said her beauty makes men feel the need to possess and control her. For some reason she thinks that includes all men." She shrugged. "Maybe she feels that's all she deserves."

Magda made a tsk-tsk sound. "Such a pity."

"I know." Standing on tiptoes, Bertha did one more thorough

search. Beside her, Magda squeezed her hand.

"Give it up, sugar. She's not here."

Bertha released an uneven breath. "I know that, too."

They waited a few more minutes, until the chill wind forced them to hustle back to the surrey. As they rode through town, Bertha found herself watching the crowded boardwalk for a bright yellow dress or a crop of high black curls. The surrey reached Magda's yard with hardly more than three words passed between them.

When Bertha slid to the ground by the barn, Magda called her name. Bertha paused and looked up. "Yes?"

"I'm sorry I didn't understand about Annie."

Bertha smiled. "Just be sorry for thinking we won't always be best friends."

Magda smiled back. "I'm the most sorry for that. I'll try not to forget it again."

"See that you don't." She winked and turned to go.

"Bertha?"

She spun, laughing. "What now?"

"Don't worry about Annie. She'll turn up somewhere. I'll be praying hard in the meantime."

"Thank you for that. Oh, and for taking me to the station, too."

Magda waved a dismissive hand. "Anytime. You know I'll always be—" Her eyes widened. "Great-Grandpa's knees! I forgot my errands."

Bertha covered her mouth. "Looks like I'm the one who's sorry this time. Oh, Magda. Do you want to go back? I'll go with you."

"Heavens, no. I'd rather go in and take my medicine. It's getting too cold to be out." She pulled back the rim of her bonnet and peered at the sky. "Look at that. You don't think it's going to snow, do you?"

Bertha followed her gaze. "Wouldn't that be fun?"

Not much snow fell on the piney woods of Texas, but Bertha had to admit the clouds looked different. Mama spoke often of her memories of the onset of a "snow sky" in the town in Maine where she grew up. Bertha wondered if the odd gathering of clouds overhead was what she meant.

She led her horse from the barn and held the door while Magda pulled inside. They hugged; then Bertha mounted and started up the lane.

"Be careful, and be safe," Magda called. "Don't get caught in a blizzard."

Bertha laughed and took off at a trot. She hadn't gone far when the laughter died, replaced by thoughts of Thad. She wondered where he was at that very second, who might be with him, what he might be doing. She wondered what he ate, where he slept, if the weather in Bryan was cold. Most of all, she wondered if he wondered about her.

She reached their road and saw Papa riding in from the opposite direction. She reined up and waited. He waved when he saw her and took off at a gallop. When he reached her, he tipped his derby and smiled. "What's a lovely lass like you doing on these perilous roads without an escort?"

Bertha bowed from the waist. "Waiting for my Prince Charming, and lo, he has arrived."

He wagged a finger. "No fair turning a fellow's own blarney back on him. You've been spending far too much time with me, I see. Besides that, me poor farsighted princess, it's a frog you've stumbled upon, not a prince."

He sidled up beside her and they turned down the lane. "No sign of Annie, I suppose."

She wrinkled her brow. "Abe Monroe left town this morning. . . without her. He boarded an eastbound train with her luggage. I saw him."

"You don't say, now?" He watched her, chewing on his mustache. "What do you suppose it means?"

"I've tried to figure it out. I just don't know."

Papa reached for her reins and pulled both horses to a stop. He cleared his throat and met her eyes, his expression grave.

"What is it, Papa? What's wrong?"

He shifted his weight. "Darlin', I did some checking myself

today. Asked a few questions, talked to some folks."

"And?"

He squinted at something over her shoulder, the corners of his eyes worried crinkles. "I learned some things. Frank Malloy saw Annie and Abe at Kate Woods's place on Sunday. It wasn't even the noon hour, but Abe was plying her with drinks. Frank said she seemed pretty well into her cups by the time they left. He seen them head down Austin Street to Gill's Corner then turn and cross over the Polk Street Bridge. Said they both carried bottles of beer."

"Was he sure it was Annie?"

"Said she was real pretty and wearing two big diamond rings."

Bertha nodded.

"Two or three hours later, Frank saw Abe come back alone."

Bertha thought for a minute. "So he did leave her across the bridge. I wouldn't have believed it. It's so unlike him, from all Annie said."

"You think she spoke the truth?"

Bertha's head reeled. "I don't know what I think anymore."

Papa lifted his gaze. His leather saddle creaked as he leaned to peer closely at her eyes. "Bertha, I think this is over now. Abe's gone. Annie's gone. You did the best you could for her. It's time to lay it down."

Bertha caught a glimpse of the sun between a break in the low-lying clouds. One thing was certain. That same sun looked down on Annie—somewhere. Bertha had never been asked to carry a heavier burden for another soul. Papa was right. She didn't share his notion that she'd done the best she could, but it was over.

She brought her attention back to his anxious face. "I know it's time to let it go, Papa. And I promise I'm going to try."

CHAPTER 26

Sarah stepped out of the barn and brushed her hands together to clean them from the dust of the feed bin. Her back ached, her head throbbed, but when hadn't they during the last two dreadful weeks?

Fourteen days had passed since Henry's trouble in town, and he hadn't snapped back as fast as she'd expected—from his injuries or his mood. Not being able to do his work made him even meaner. Thomas and some of the other neighbors pitched in where they could, with the plowing in particular. Sarah shouldered the rest of her husband's chores on top of her own.

She prayed daily for grace to live with Henry. He had taken on most of Dandy's more trying traits, but Henry bested the mule in cantankerousness. And despite the fact she ministered to him every spare minute, he had adopted the mule's same distaste for her.

To make matters worse, the weather turned from bad to horrid since the day of his injuries. Heavy snow had fallen in Jefferson—by far the most bitter pill for Sarah, since Henry had dangled warm winters to entice her to come south. Not much she hated more than being cold, and working outside in the snow the last few days had chilled her to the bone.

She took a lingering look at the house and groaned. She longed to go inside by the fire, take off her boots, and prop her bruised and swollen feet on a kitchen chair. But one glance at the wood box this morning told her she'd be gathering firewood today. The cookstove and fireplace had gobbled every stick she could find over the two-week cold spell. Best to get the box filled now and get back in time to start supper. Henry's appetite had made a full recovery.

She glanced toward the stand of trees. Gathering firewood wasn't her favorite chore. When she first took the job from Henry, she'd found a treasure of small, easy-to-carry branches and sticks, those that Henry would pass right over. Now all the suitable pieces she could bundle up in her apron were gone from the nearby places. This forced her to wander farther each time, which meant a longer walk back with her burden.

The days had grown a little warmer since the snow fell, but white patches still lingered in areas shaded from the sun. She decided to walk as far out as she intended then gather as she made her way back. That way she could pretend she just decided to go for a walk.

May as well find some pleasure in the task.

She stepped back inside the barn and lifted her coat from the hook. The dog lay on his side, his body stretched to full length, in a hay pile near the door. She paused beside him. "I'll be right back, Dickens. Thought I'd let you know I was going, since you're the only living soul on the place who cares."

Sound asleep, he moaned and rolled to his back with his hind legs straddled and his front legs folded to his chest. She sighed. "No, I don't need any help. But thank you kindly for asking."

She slipped into her coat, tied on her scarf, and struck out. No need carrying a hoe or a snake stick into the woods today. Too cold. Which meant snakes had more sense than people.

At the edge of the yard, she ducked under the fence and slipped into the coolness of the surrounding forest. Despite being bone-tired, despite the way her man was acting, Sarah found herself enjoying her walk in the woods. On the trail worn there by Henry's feet, she saw a few gathering birds and chasing squirrels, but the rabbits and deer were in hiding. She loved the wildlife in Jefferson—except the coons. They were funny to look at, yet true to their markings, they were bandits, every one. The rascals spent all their time stealing food from her garden, the feeding troughs, or Dickens's dish.

The sun had dared to peek through the clouds a couple of times during the past two weeks, its warmth a welcome relief. It seemed inclined to shine a bit today, but the overcast sky put up a stiff fight. A pity, since now the wind had picked up.

Sarah walked until she came to a small clearing. The last storm had littered the area with fallen limbs. There were ample good-sized pieces for her to collect and fold into her apron, with plenty left for the next time. She'd have to try to remember the spot.

She stood up to get her bearings. Unless she was mistaken, the Marshall Road lay to her right with Polk Street Bridge just a little ways up, which meant she was south of the Big Cypress Ferry. That put town straight ahead.

She pulled up her collar and fastened the top button of her coat. The sun finally quit on her altogether, and the cloudy sky pitched the thickly wooded grove into near darkness. A chill crept up her spine that had little to do with the weather. The chattering squirrels had disappeared. The birds, too, if the silence meant anything. She found herself glancing up, willing the light to come back, because when the sun left, the joy went out of the walk. Sarah reckoned she'd best stop fooling around and finish gathering so she could get on back home.

She spotted a perfect-sized limb near the ridge of a slight hill and bent to retrieve it. Then another she could reach without straightening. And one more just ahead.

Still stooping close to the ground, Sarah's hand closed around the crumbling stick as her eyes scanned the grassy mound ahead. Her body stopped so fast she jerked; then she fell back on her hands and crab-scrambled away.

Dear God in heaven, don't let it be!

She felt helpless, defenseless down on her behind, so she fought to her feet, ripping the hem of her coat as she stood.

Jesus, close my eyes! I don't want to see this!

If not for the wood bugs crawling on its eyes and from its nose, Sarah might've sworn the body was sleeping. Dressed like a lady, it rested on its back with one arm folded across its stomach. That was all Sarah took time to see.

She longed to break and run but knew she mustn't. Whoever did it might be watching. She forced herself to turn and walk away as if she hadn't seen. Certain at any second the killer would lunge from behind, she pulled her chest forward until her shoulder blades popped. It seemed as if she could see, hear, smell a thousand times better as her darting gaze searched the woods.

Just a little farther and she'd reach the Marshall Road. Just a few more steps to safety. She went a little faster. Three steps. Faster. Two more steps. Run!

She burst onto the road with legs so weak she tripped and fell. A horse and rider came at her from the corner of her eye as she went down, and dread slammed into her chest. All the strength left her body just when she needed it. Limp, she tried to crawl, desperate hands clutching at woody stobs and tall tufts of grass to pull herself along. With the last ounce of might she could muster, she thrust her body from the ground and staggered away from the road in a panic.

"Sarah!"

She didn't know the voice.

"Sarah King!"

He knew her name.

She froze, swiping tears from her eyes with dirty palms to see. If she didn't know his face, if he came for her, she'd outrun him if it meant sailing off into the bayou.

"Sarah, come here, girl. Are you all right?"

William Sims. The colonel's son. Lived in a big house on Friou Street in town.

She didn't realize she held her breath until white spots swirled past her eyes and blackness loomed. She lifted her chest and gulped. Air flooded her lungs. Giddy, she went down hard on her bottom. "No, sir," she gasped. "I ain't all right a'tall. I need help."

He got off his horse and hurried to her side. "Are you hurt?"

She motioned toward the woods with a trembling hand. "Mr. Sims, there's a lady laid up in those woods. She's dead."

His head jerked toward the grove. "Dead?"

"Yes, sir."

"You sure?"

She nodded.

He stood up and started for his horse. "Just sit right there. I'll go for help."

She reached a grasping hand toward him. "No, sir. Please don't leave me here alone."

He pointed his finger. "You do like I say. Stay here so we can find you. You'll have to show them where it is."

Sarah ran up on the road and stared after the galloping horse. "Oh, please don't leave me here," she whispered. She whirled in a circle, searching the ditches, the bushes, the trees. When her eyes lit on the woods at the place where she'd burst through, she retreated to the opposite side of the Marshall Road, her eyes still fixed on the spot. Pulling her gaze away, she turned and ran a few feet, pressed her body against a tree, and slid to the ground. How would she ever go back in there?

Well, I can't! I won't.

She could leave. Run on home to Henry. Cook his food. Do his chores. Put this nightmare right out of her mind.

But Mr. Sims knew who she was. And Mr. Sims told her to stay put.

It seemed three lifetimes before clamoring hooves hit the Polk Street Bridge. Three men appeared on the road in front of her, Mr. Sims and two others.

"Well, where is she?" one of them growled.

Mr. Sims pushed back his hat. "I told her to stay here."

Sarah knew she'd better show her face. She stood. "I'm over here."

The big man scowled at her from across the way then motioned with his hand. "Well, come over here, then."

She pushed the brush aside and hustled over the road on shaky legs. The official-looking man looked straight at her but spoke to Mr. Sims. "What'd you say her name was?"

"Sarah," he said. "Sarah King."

The man tipped his hat. "Sarah, I'm Justice of the Peace C. C. Bickford, also the ex-officio coroner for Marion County. You can call me Judge Bickford."

She didn't know what all the words meant, but the way he said them made her feel more and less afraid at the same time. Unable to speak, she stared up at him.

He pointed at the man riding the other horse. "This here's my constable, Mr. A. J. Stambaugh."

Sarah nodded at the constable.

Judge Bickford cleared his throat. "I understand you ran across something amongst those trees."

She nodded again.

"Speak up, now. If you think you found something, say so."

"I did find something. A dead woman."

He narrowed his eyes. "And you're certain of that? It couldn't have been an animal? A deer or wild hog? A bundle of trash, maybe?"

"I'm right sure of what I saw."

Looking none too happy, he pointed at the tree line. "Sure enough to have us traipsing all over those woods?"

Anger easing her fear, Sarah shook her head. "I can walk you straight to her."

The man chewed the inside of his lip, studying her hard, and then sighed. "All right. Let's go."

Leading a parade of white men on horseback into the woods had to be the most peculiar thing Sarah had ever done. Though less afraid in the company of the officers, she still checked over her shoulder every few steps to make sure they were still with her.

Glad she'd taken the time to get her bearings before she found the body, Sarah retraced her steps. She stopped within a few yards of the place where the woman lay and pointed ahead of them and to the left. "She's over on that mound yonder. Do I have to go any farther?"

They didn't answer, just got down off their mounts and walked in the direction she'd pointed. When they stopped and leaned over the woman's body, Sarah moved closer to the horses. She found comfort in the animals' warmth and size, knowing they'd be the first to sense trouble.

After the men looked around a bit, they hurried back. Mr. Sims looked sick to his stomach. The judge took off his hat, spat on the ground, and wiped his mouth with his sleeve. "How close did you come to the body?"

"Not close." Her voice faltered. "From here to that tree."

"Did you touch anything?"

She shuddered. "No, sir."

"What's the first thing you did after you found her?"

"I didn't stay there at all. I left in a walk."

The constable laughed. "Likely the fastest walk ever performed in Jefferson."

The judge gave him a stern look, and he turned away, still smiling.

Sarah couldn't stop shaking. She clasped her hands together to keep them still then pressed them to her chin. "Can I go now?"

The judge shook his head. "Not yet. I have to summon a jury and hold an inquest."

More words she didn't know. "What's an inquest?"

"An inquiry of sorts. We'll have to carry out an official investigation."

Her heartbeat quickened. "When?"

"Right now."

"Where?"

He lifted his head to motion behind him. "Right over there."

Panic clawed at her throat. "And I have to stay?"

"I need to ask you more questions. With the jury present."

"But, Judge, my husband needs me at home. He's ailing. I didn't even tell him I left." She hadn't remembered any of these details until she spoke them aloud. "Please, sir, can't I go? This trouble ain't got nothing to do with me."

"It does now. You're an official witness. When we find out who did this, there's going to be a trial. You'll be called on to testify."

The overhead trees swirled. Sarah's stomach took a sickening dive. White spots danced before her eyes again, and bitterness rose in her throat. The judge noticed, because he offered his arm and helped her sit on the ground. "I'm real sorry, Miss. . .now what was your name again?"

She swallowed bile. "Sarah."

"Sarah. That's right. Just settle yourself there and try to get comfortable, Sarah. This will all be over soon, and you can go see to your husband."

It wasn't over soon. Judge Bickford found men to serve as his jury, but it took them forever to arrive. The judge, constable, and some other men searched the clearing, collecting things from the ground and writing them all in a book. Dr. Eason came, and she wanted him to tell the judge about Henry, but he barely took time to nod in her direction before he hurried over to kneel by the body.

By the time the judge got around to questioning Sarah in front of the jury, she was faint from so many hours without food and water. He asked the same questions he had before, going round and round until her head whirled.

Night approached, making it so murky in the grove that they stumbled over each other in the dark. Judge Bickford made the decision to bring in a hack to move the body to his office, where he would take up with his inquest the next day.

At long last, Sarah was free to go—and she couldn't get away fast enough. She took the road instead of the woods, but after going just a little ways, she realized she was alone in the dark.

And the killer began to play games. He crept alongside her for a few steps, hiding in the trees to her right, his feet rustling grass and snapping twigs. He bobbed through the brush on the other side with a rattle of bare limbs and crunch of dry leaves. When he darted across the road in front of her, hunched over close to the ground, Sarah froze.

Common sense whispered that the sounds were the critters she loved, startled from their wallows by her shuffling feet, and the darting figure was nothing more than a wild boar. But her shattered nerves and wounded spirit wouldn't accept it.

She turned to run back to the comforting voices and circles of lantern light bobbing through the forest but realized they were coming out of the woods behind her, heading in the opposite direction. The tears came then, flooding her eyes and causing her nose to pour. She didn't dare cry aloud for fear the killer would hear and come after her. Pulling up her skirt, she started to run, the wind rushing past her ears, her long legs pumping in time with her heart. Sarah ran as fast as she could, sobbing the whole way, until she staggered onto the back porch.

Henry opened the screen door with a crash and folded her into his arms. He squeezed her so tightly against his chest she feared he'd hurt his ribs. Or hers. "Where were you? Girl, I been out of my mind."

"Henry!" she wailed. "I tried to come back. They wouldn't let me." She reached for his face and found it wet.

"Who? Who wouldn't let you?"

"Judge Bickford and his men."

Henry held her in the light streaming from the kitchen and studied her face. "Tell me where you went, Sarah."

"To fetch firewood." She buried her face against his chest to block out the memory of crawling wood bugs. "There was a body. In the woods. I found it."

He lifted her into his arms and carried her inside the house, though it must have caused him terrible pain. She let the tears come as loudly as they wished now. She was safe.

CHAPTER 27

Tuesday, February 6

Bertha marked another X on Mama's big wall calendar then stepped back to count the number of days since she'd last seen Thad. Sixteen. The age she'd been when she first set eyes on Thaddeus Bloom—a brash, giggly sixteen-year-old to his quiet and confident eighteen. Tomorrow she'd scratch off the seventeenth day. The age she was when he left town. The day after that, when she stepped up to the wall with her thick pencil, it would be eighteen days since Thad rode away without saying good-bye. Eighteen. The age she turned today.

"Happy birthday, sprite!"

Bertha leaped right out of her musings and almost out of her bloomers when Papa roared behind her.

Laughing, he danced up and kissed the back of her head then hooked his finger around the tasseled shade and pulled it out for a peek. " 'Tis a fine day for it, too. Will ye look at that? The sun's out."

Mama bustled into the kitchen and grabbed her apron from a hook. "Well, it wasn't shining eighteen years ago. We were shoveling snow that year, if memory serves."

"And they've been shoveling since, Emeline. It's forever snowing in Maine."

Mama gathered Bertha for a tight hug and answered Papa across the top of her head. "I'll ignore your derision for now and just say I'm glad we came south." She took Bertha by the shoulders and gazed at her face. "Happy birthday, dear daughter. And many happy returns of the day."

"Thank you." Bertha smiled and sent up a silent prayer of thanksgiving. She loved her mama before, but liked her much better now. It amazed Bertha the difference love could make in a woman's heart if she allowed it to come in.

Mama glanced at the newly crossed square on the calendar page, and a tiny frown perched on her brow. "Did you sleep well?"

"Yes, ma'am. I believe I did."

Her face softened and she nodded. "Francis, go gather eggs. I need three of the freshest you can find."

He winked at Bertha. "And they say slavery's been abolished."

She laughed as he slipped on his coat and went out. Mama gathered measuring cups and spoons, flour, sugar, butter, and milk and arranged them around a big bowl on the counter. Then she stood with her finger pressed to her lips. "Where is my saleratus of baking soda?" She turned to Bertha. "Though I regret asking you to do extra on your special day, would you mind rolling out biscuits for breakfast? I've gotten a little ahead of myself, I think. But I wanted to get this done."

Bertha pretended not to know what she meant. "Get what done?"

"Your cake, silly. For today's celebration." Her eyes danced with excitement. "We're going to have a high time. "I've invited Magda's family, of course. And the minister, along with our friends from church, our nearest neighbors, and your young friends from school. Oh yes, Moses and Rhodie Pharr. Can you think of who might be missing?"

"Only one."

Mama paused from sifting sugar into her bowl. "Oh, Bertha. I considered the possibility Thad might turn up but thought it best not to mention it. I want only your happiness today."

"I know you do." She lifted one shoulder. "I'm sure he wouldn't be able to leave school this soon anyway. Only wouldn't it be nice if he could be here?"

"It would at that." Mama tilted her head and gave her a pleading look. "Try to put Thad out of your mind, just for today, and have a good time."

Bertha bit her bottom lip and nodded. "Yes, ma'am. I'll try."

Mama reached for her mixing spoon. "While you're at it, make an effort to act pleased with Papa's gift. He tries so hard every year, and he means well."

At the look on Mama's face, Bertha's hands stilled on the rolling pin. "It's even worse than usual, isn't it?"

Mama hunched her shoulders and tittered. "Infinitely."

"Tell me."

"Words fail me, dear." She leaned to check on Papa's whereabouts then motioned for Bertha to wait while she crept down the hall. She returned with the latest copy of *Harper's Weekly* and spread it open on the kitchen table. After another glance out the window, she started flipping pages.

"*Harper's Weekly?*" Bertha laid aside the biscuit cutter and wiped her hands. "There are lovely gifts in there." She hurried around to peer over Mama's shoulder. "Books of poems. Leather cases for gloves and handkerchiefs. And look! Fur-lined collars from New York!"

Mama turned right past all the ads Bertha mentioned, as well as the ones for Tiffany & Co. and Decker Brothers' pianos. Riffling back a few pages, she stopped and placed her finger under a tiny drawing of a white skeleton.

Bertha frowned and leaned close to read the text aloud. " 'The Performing Skeleton. Fourteen inches in height. It will dance in perfect time to any tune.' " She skipped ahead a bit. " 'Seemingly endowed with life.' "

Mama took up where Bertha left off. " 'Never fails to delight, astonish, and produce a decided sensation.' "

They stood up together. Mama pressed both hands over her mouth in a useless attempt to stifle her laughter. Bertha pointed at the ad. "The astonish part is working already."

Mama gave up her fight for composure. "Oh, Bertha," she howled.

"For pity's sake, I'm eighteen. I can't receive a dancing skeleton at my eighteenth birthday party, witnessed by all of my friends."

A rattling noise from outside straightened Mama's face and sent them both scrambling—Mama to her room with the magazine and Bertha back to her biscuits. Mama came out sober and empty-handed and scurried to her mixing bowl. "What was that?"

Bertha shrugged and glanced toward the window. "I think someone's here."

Papa called a greeting, and Bertha nodded across the room at Mama, who smiled back. Neither stopped what they were doing to receive a guest. Bertha knew her mama assumed, as she did, that Papa's friend from the house behind their place had come to visit. The old man always came calling through the backyard and never ventured inside.

A high-pitched keening, like the cry of a wounded panther, ripped holes in the comforting silence, exposing every nerve in Bertha's body. She jumped back, and the sheet of biscuits slid to the floor.

Mama dropped her spoon then snatched it up, brandishing it like a weapon. Her frightened gaze left the widow and fixed on Bertha's face. "Oh my soul. Bertha, go find the source of that appalling sound."

What on earth?

Sarah rolled over in bed to find bright light streaming through her bedroom window. She raised one arm to shield her eyes and squinted at the curious sight. Each day since her first one in Jefferson, her feet had hit the floor and plodded to the kitchen long before daylight dawned. She threw back the covers and tossed her body off the opposite side of the bed, feeling around with her toes to find her shoes.

"Henry!"

No answer. Something was wrong. She just knew it. Why else would she still be in bed at this hour? Some vague memory tugged at the fog in her mind, something dark and dank with fear. She could get no better grip on her recall than her toes could get on her slippers. "Henry, where are you?"

Sarah gave up trying to reach under the bed with her feet. Padding barefoot, she crossed the room and snatched her raggedy robe from the back of a chair. Tying the belt around her waist, she reached for the bedroom door. It opened before her fingers touched the knob.

"Did you decide to join the rest of the world?"

She scowled at his grinning face. "Where were you? What were you thinking to let me sleep all day?"

He chuckled. "Seven thirty ain't exactly all day. The sun ain't been up ten minutes. Besides, you needed to rest."

"Rest?" She lifted the pitcher from the dressing table so she could fetch hot water for the basin. "I'll rest in heaven. Did you forget I have your chores, too?" Opening the door, she stared back at him. "I know you meant well, but you've put me so far behind I'll be working past midnight."

"Sarah, wait."

Sarah, wait? Sarah, sleep? She didn't have time for either. She hustled down the hall mumbling under her breath. When the passage opened onto the kitchen, she scarcely believed her eyes.

Arabella, Thomas's shy, pretty wife, stood at the sink washing dishes. Their newest baby sat up on the table while her eight-year-old sister spoon-fed scrambled eggs into her wide-open mouth. Between bites for the baby, the young girl picked through a pile of dried beans scattered across the tabletop. The oldest girl swished a broom near the door. They all gave Sarah timid smiles then went back to their work. Her work.

She looked over her shoulder at Henry's grinning face. "What's going on here?"

He took her arm and led her toward the table. "Thomas brought 'em by first thing this morning. They heard in town what happened, so they come to help. The boys are outside now, feeding the chickens and tending the mule."

The fog swirled away in a whoosh, and the thing she'd shoved aside slipped out of the darkness and faced her down. She shuddered in its presence then peered at Henry's face. Still so much she didn't understand.

He winked down at her. "Ain't it shore enough nice of them to come? They good people, Sarah."

She nodded and shared another smile with Thomas's wife.

"You hungry, ma'am?"

She nodded. "I believe I am."

Arabella took a wrapped plate from the counter and set it on the table. Then she plopped the baby on one hip and took her to the sink to wipe her mouth. "It's still warm," she said, nodding back at the plate.

Sarah sat down in front of the breakfast. She couldn't remember the last food she ate that she didn't cook. "Thank you kindly, Arabella. It looks real good." Digging into the plate of pan sausage, cream gravy, moist scrambled eggs, and biscuits, she found it *was* good. Better than hers, though she hated to admit it.

"Where's Thomas?" she asked with her mouth full.

Henry cleared his throat and took too long to answer. "He'll be back directly. He left to haul Jennie Simpson over to the Biddie house."

Sarah took another bite of her biscuit. "What for?"

Surprise lifted Henry's brows. "Well, you know." He pointed out back. "The body. In the woods."

She knew. Why would he go on about it in front of the children? She raised her brows back at him then tilted her head at the baby. "We ain't gon' discuss it right now. Besides, what does any of it have to do with Jennie Simpson?"

He shot her a worried frown. "She jus' wanted to be the one to tell Miss Bertha on account of she knew how worried little Bertha's been."

Sarah felt as vacant as a plowed field, yet every person in the room stood staring at her. "Tell Miss Bertha what? Stop talking in circles, Henry."

Henry cast a desperate glance at Arabella. She lowered her gaze, so he turned and met Sarah's eyes. "Are you saying you don't know?"

Her middle did a flip. "Know what?" She stood up so fast her chair tipped, scaring the baby and making her cry. "Stop it, Henry. I don't know nothing."

He came over and gripped her shoulders. "Sarah, that poor woman you found. . ." He stopped and swallowed hard. "The body in the woods. . .it's Miss Annie."

Thomas's boys hit the porch like twin bulls, their thundering feet shattering the hush that fell alongside Henry's news. "Mr. King!" one of them cried. "A lawman's pulling into your yard."

∽∾∾

Wiping her fingers on a towel, Bertha hurried to peer out the window.

Thomas Jolly sat in the driver's seat of a wagon parked out back. Jennie Simpson sat beside him with her face clutched in her hands. The unearthly sound came from her.

Papa stood waving his arms at Jennie to shush her while his panic-stricken eyes stared toward the house.

Bertha took off her apron and willed her feet to move. She opened the door and stepped out with Mama right behind.

As they approached, Jennie dabbed at her eyes with her palms as if blotting out a scene she couldn't stand to see, her mouth twisted in grief. "Oh, Mista' Francis, it's jus' so awful." She moved her hands, and when her eyes opened, she jumped. "Why, hello, Miz Biddie." She jerked her gaze to Bertha. "And there you is, you pitiful little thing." The sight of Bertha set her off again. She clutched her face and wailed.

"What's going on out here, Francis?"

Papa raised his brows at Mama and licked his lips. A bad sign. He walked straight to Bertha and picked up her hands. "There's dire news, me girl."

Bertha's trembling knees tried to buckle. She steeled herself and searched for truth in his eyes. "Thad?"

He looked startled. "Heavens, no, darlin'. Nothing about your Thad."

Behind them Jennie cried louder. Thomas reached to pat her shoulder, but she wouldn't be comforted. "Po' Miss Bessie," she cried, rocking back and forth. "Po' dear, sweet chile."

Bertha shifted her gaze from Jennie's outburst back to Papa. "Something happened to Annie?"

He squeezed her hands until her fingers ached. "They found her, Bertha. She's been murdered."

Mama moved behind Bertha and held on to her shoulders. "Where?"

"In the woods. Somewhere off the Marshall Road."

Bertha fought to understand. "They found her here? In Jefferson? That's impossible. She's been gone for weeks."

Jennie's full lips trembled. "It's the Lawd's honest truth, Miss Bertha. You know Sarah King? Live in the woods down off Polk? She found her body while she out fetching firewood."

"How do they know it's Annie? It could be anyone."

Papa shook his head. "It's her, darlin'."

She pulled free of his hands and backed away. "It's not true. It can't be."

"It's her, Miss Bertha," Jennie sobbed. "It's really her. I done seen with my own two eyes. She's laying over at the coroner's office. Looked jus' natural, like she's sleeping. It's Miss Bessie, all right. Your Annie, I mean. Still pretty as a picture, but jus' as dead as she can be."

Bertha turned to run for the house. She made it three steps before the blackness that chased her brought her down.

CHAPTER 28

Sarah let go of Henry and clung to the edge of the table while he stepped out onto the porch. After talking to the lawman in a low, respectful voice, he opened the screen and motioned for her. Sarah's broken heart lurched. Now what?

She picked up the half-eaten biscuit from the table and put it back on her plate, lifted the overturned chair and pushed it in, then crossed the room and ducked out the screen door to stand beside her husband.

Constable Stambaugh sat tall and self-important on a buckboard. "Sarah King?"

She started to tremble, and it showed up in her voice. "Yes, sir?"

"Judge Bickford sent me to fetch you. You need to come with me into town."

"What for?"

"Girl, you know what for. He told you last night his inquest would commence again today." His face lit up in a broad smile. "And you're our star witness."

Sarah couldn't decide if he meant to be nice or make fun. "Do I have to?"

He gave her a piercing look. "Oh yes. You have to."

She felt Henry step close to her back. "Can I bring her?"

The constable grunted. "I'm taking her with me when I leave." His eyes shifted to Sarah. "Hurry and get dressed."

She looked down at herself, amazed that she'd walked outside in her robe. She hurried past Henry and the boys on the porch, past Arabella and the girls in the kitchen, and into her room. She barely got the door closed before Henry opened it again.

"I'm going with you."

"Will he let you?"

His jaw tightened. "He ain't stopping me." He caught her whizzing past in her rush to dress and whirled her around to face him. "You all right?"

She peered into his worried brown eyes. "I'm not sure I can do this, now that I know who—"

"You can do it. I'll be there with you. Arabella said she and the girls can stay all day if need be."

Sarah pulled her best frock down from a hook. "You think it'll take all day?"

He shrugged. "Never been to nothing like it before. I guess we'll find out."

She touched gentle fingertips to his side. "Don't you need to stay here and rest?"

He placed his hand over hers and squeezed. "Knowing you're all right is the only rest I need. Hurry up, now. Let's get this over and done."

When he released her hand and started for the door, she caught his fingers again. "Why didn't you come for me?" She blinked back tears. "Yesterday, I mean?"

Henry looked startled at first then tilted his head and closed his eyes.

Her bottom lip trembled, but she managed to finish her question. "I stewed on it all night, when I wasn't wrestling with my memory, but I never did come to a sensible excuse for you." He lowered his face, and she met his gaze. "Henry, even if I was mad, even if I didn't love you no more, I'd still search for you if you went missing." Her eyes brimmed until tears slipped over the edges and streamed down her face. "Don't you know if you'd been there, I wouldn't have been so scared?"

He closed the distance between them and gathered her into his arms. "You silly woman. You ain't got the sense God give a goose."

Sarah's temper flared. She pushed on his chest, but he held her fast and stroked her hair.

"When you left the house after making my dinner to go out and do my work, I watched you head for the barn looking like the whole world rested across your back. I got so mad at my sorry self, I felt sick. The only way I could stand myself was to go to sleep. So I did."

She relaxed against him, his words a salve to her pain. She thought he hadn't noticed how hard she'd worked.

"I woke up and saw it was dark outside, and still laid up like a big old pouting boy. I waited for you to call me to supper, only you never did. When I went in that kitchen and saw no lights and no fire in the stove, I got so scared. I thought Dandy kicked you and left you laying out there hurt. . .or worse. I hauled tail to the barn, but you weren't there. Or anywhere."

His intense gaze bored into her heart. "I figured you got your fill of me and left. I didn't know if Miss Jennie took you in or maybe you found a way to book passage to St. Louis. I jus' knew I had to find you before I lost you for good. So I saddled Dandy and led him out, and that's when I seen lights flickerin' in the woods. Right out in the middle, where they don't belong." He drew a shaky breath. "Sarah, I thought. . ." He clenched his eyes shut and turned away.

Sarah pressed her face to his back. "What, Henry? What did you think?"

He shuddered. "I thought those hateful men got out of jail and come for me. I figured they seen you outside and took you instead, jus' for spite. I jus' knew they had you out there in those woods and. . ."

Sarah spun him around and pulled him close. "Hush, now.

Hush. I'm all right, Henry. None of that happened."

"I ran back to the house to fetch my shotgun, and that's when I heard you on the porch. The whole time I tended you, until you fell asleep in my arms, Dandy stood outside in the yard, saddled and ready to go. After I saw you were down for the night, I went out and put him up. Out there in the barn, I dropped to my knees and thanked the good Lord for taking care of you again, when I couldn't."

He gave her a wobbly smile. "Good thing He's there to watch over you, since I keep making such a mess of it."

She pressed his face between her palms. "Stop that. Nobody could've known what waited for me in that grove. Somebody had to find poor Miss Annie, and I guess that somebody was me."

"Henry? Miss Sarah?"

Arabella's voice behind the door gave Sarah a start. Henry pulled it open, and she stood looking ready to run away again. "That man out there's getting mighty edgy. Says you best put a move on."

Henry nodded. "We coming." He glanced at Sarah over his shoulder. "Hurry, now. I'll go stall him as long as I can."

When he closed the door behind him, Sarah shimmied out of her robe and into her best blouse and a skirt, smiling despite everything that swirled around her when the skirt's button barely fastened.

A curious notion crept into her head, and in an instant Sarah made up her mind. Kneeling, she took the unfinished white dress, full of pins and basting stitches, from the middle drawer of the chest and wrapped it in her good shawl. Then she tucked the bundle inside her coat, slid on her shoes, and joined Henry in the kitchen.

"Ready, now?" Henry grinned and jerked his thumb toward the porch. "Those boys doing they best to distract that lawman, but they running short on tricks."

Sarah gave a shaky smile and tried to still her trembling legs. "We best rescue him, then." She glanced toward the open door. "Let's go, while I still have the courage."

Henry wrapped his arm around her shoulders and tucked her close. "Long as I'm by your side, that's all the courage you need."

Thanking God to have her husband back, she gazed up at him. "Then whatever you do, Henry King, stay close by my side."

❧

Bertha steeled herself as the hinges of the bedroom door squealed behind her. Why couldn't they do like she asked and just leave her be? She understood good intentions, even their need to comfort, but she had no use for empty words of solace or promises the pain would pass. These were poor substitutes for absolution.

"I brought you some tea, dear. Chamomile. Your favorite. And look who's come to see you."

When she didn't turn, Mama plowed ahead. "Look, Bertha. Magda's here."

A tray slid onto the table beside her. Liquid trickled into a cup, and a spoon clinked on china. "Sit up, dear. I have your tea."

She squeezed her eyes tighter and willed them away. After a long pause, the cup and saucer settled onto the tray with a rattle, and Mama sighed.

"She's been like this since this morning," Mama said, as if Bertha weren't right there in the room. "Hasn't said a word to anyone."

"I'll talk to her, Mrs. Biddie."

The door opened. "I'll leave you with her, then. Oh, and there's a sandwich and slice of cake for each of you under the cup towel. I went ahead and finished her cake. Hated to see the ingredients go to waste, and besides, I needed some way to busy my hands. Try to get her to eat something, won't you?"

Magda's skirts rustled as she settled in a chair by the bed. "Yes, ma'am. I'll try."

The door closed. Bertha gritted her teeth, waiting for Magda to beg her to get up, to snap out of it, to eat something, to come to her senses and go on with her birthday celebration. Instead, Magda abruptly stood up, moved to sit down on the bed beside her, and began smoothing her brow. "This isn't just about losing a friend, is it, sugar?"

Sudden tears seared Bertha's eyes. She tried her voice but managed only a squeaky whisper. "I failed her, didn't I?"

"Oh, Bertha, you didn't."

She clenched her fists, the words coming easier now that the dam had burst. "I was Annie's last hope. I let her down. I let God down."

"How can you say such a thing? You sacrificed everything to help her. You gave your all."

"Did I? I had so many chances to say the right thing, yet it seems I never did. Even that last night I let myself get distracted, allowed my heart to be divided. All I could think about was getting back to Thad." She sobbed into her pillow. "If only I'd known it was her last night on earth. . ."

Magda leaned closer. "Her last? How do you know that?"

"It's the only thing that makes sense. Abe killed her the very next day. That's why he came back to Brooks House without her." She twisted to look back at Magda. "He must've caught her sneaking back to their room on Saturday night, and it was the last straw." She buried her face in her hands and cried bitter tears. "Oh, Magda, don't you see? While trying to help Annie, I got her killed instead."

~∞~

Judge Bickford's inquest would haunt Sarah's dreams for the rest of her days. Living through finding Miss Annie's body in the grove was hard enough. Reliving it time and again while twelve stern-faced men looked on proved taxing to her very soul. Several times during the questions, Sarah felt close to losing her few bites of Arabella's eggs and biscuit, so she found herself grateful that Henry's news about Miss Annie had cut her breakfast short.

Henry stayed as close as the officials would allow and kept a watchful eye on her the whole time. She had only to seek his eyes to find the strength to carry on. So it seemed odd, now that the inquest was over, that she would need to find a way to slip away from him a bit.

Outside the coroner's office, she reached to touch his arm. "Henry, I need to go back inside. I left my coat."

He glanced at the door. "Wait here. I'll fetch it."

She wrapped her fingers around his wrist. "No, don't." At his surprised look, she loosened her grip and managed a smile. "I mean, you'll never find it, and I know right where it is." Both true statements, since she'd folded the shawl-wrapped bundle into the coat and stashed it under a desk the first chance she got.

Henry frowned down at her then back at the building. "You sure?"

She patted his hand. "Just go get Dandy and pull him around. I'll be right back."

He gave her a curt nod and set off down the boardwalk. They had to park the rig a good ways down because the coroner's office had turned into a spectacle that rivaled the county fair. Judge Bickford had left the body exposed for public viewing, and hundreds of curious citizens had come for a chance to see.

Her heart so far up her throat she could taste it, Sarah opened the door and slipped into the building. Knowing she had little time, she hurried down the hall to the office where she'd left the coat. Though her own things lay beneath, she felt like a thief skulking beside the desk, waiting for a chance to take them.

Her gaze darted around the room. None of the clustered groups of men took any notice, as if—after all their questions—they'd forgotten she existed. After a deep breath, she ducked down and back up fast with her prize in her hands.

Sarah found the room that held Miss Annie's body by walking the corridor alongside the parade of people that stretched from outside to an unmarked door. She unwrapped the white dress, laid her coat and shawl across a nearby chair, and marched up to the door carrying the folded garment in front of her. Breathing a sigh of relief when she saw a colored woman posted outside, she sashayed over and peered down her nose at her. "Open up. I need to take this in."

The woman looked her over then knocked with one knuckle.

A young girl peered out and scowled at them. "Can't come in. We's undressing her."

Pushing down her fear, Sarah nodded at the frock in her hands. "I know. That's why I'm here."

The girl glanced at the soft, shimmering cloth, stepped aside, and reached to touch it as Sarah passed. "Ain't that purty?"

The door closed behind them, and Sarah's horror knew no bounds. Too scared of what she might see if she didn't, she kept her eyes on the floor.

"Well, well. If it ain't the very person who found our pretty customer."

There'd be no mistaking the sultry voice of Isabella Gouldy. Sarah remembered the last time she'd seen her, ducked in an alley clinging to a man. She only hoped Belle had been too far into her cups to remember the disgusted look on Sarah's face.

"Come for another little peek, Sarah?"

Before she could answer, Belle cut her off. "If you come for a job, you're too late. They're paying me and Mollie here, and these four girls."

Mollie Turk and three other women stood beside the young one who opened the door. Sarah lifted her eyes to Belle Gouldy's face. "Paying you?"

She nodded. "To strip off her things and list the items we remove for the trial. Me and Mollie get paid extra for making her burial clothes."

Sarah resisted the urge to scurry out of the room and let them get on with it. She held up the dress. "I have the grave clothes right here."

Belle cursed. "Those no-'count dogs promised the job to us."

Sarah held up her hand. "You still get paid the same, because this one isn't finished. It's only basted together and still needs a hem."

Belle stared at first then gave a bawdy laugh. "Well, that makes our job easy, don't it, Mollie? Don't expect the old girl will need more than basting stitches. She won't be putting much strain on her seams." She smoothed her hand over the bodice and whistled. "Sure is a fine cut of cloth to throw down a hole on a corpse."

Sarah stiffened. "You just see that it gets on her. I'm sure to find out if you don't, and I'll tell Judge Bickford." The tone of her voice surprised Sarah. Belle and the rest, too, by the looks on their faces. But her bluff worked. No one needed to know Judge Bickford had no knowledge of Sarah's mission.

Belle drew back her hands. "All right, all right. Seems a pitiful waste, though."

Sarah handed her offering to Mollie Turk, who took it to a small bench where her sewing basket waited. Sarah's eyes went to the bolt of rough material laid out on the table and shuddered. She tried to imagine the lovely, kindhearted Miss Annie in heavy black moleskin, but the picture wouldn't come. Peace settled around her heart as she left the room. She'd done the right thing.

CHAPTER 29

Wednesday, February 7

The wind skimmed across the surface of the murky bayou at Sarah's feet. The last traces of drifted snow, bright white against the dark sludge, looked more like icy lace where the water had lapped patterns at the surface. She pressed her hands to her swollen middle, raised her face to the warmth of the sun, and thanked God she wasn't in St. Louis.

Today, Jefferson would lay Miss Annie to rest. The townsfolk had donated one hundred fifty dollars to pay for her burial in Jefferson's Oakwood Cemetery. Perhaps now the kindhearted beauty with haunted eyes would find peace.

Footfalls came over the rise behind her and paused. Sarah smiled without looking around. "Back already?"

The familiar stride continued down the hill, not stopping until it reached her; then arms circled her from behind. "Naw, I ain't made it back yet."

"Is that a fact? So a handsome stranger holds me in his arms?"

He chuckled, his barrel chest rumbling against the back of her head. "How you know I'm handsome? You ain't looked yet."

284

She giggled and squeezed his wrists. "I know handsome when I feel it, and you feel mighty handsome to me."

Henry leaned to nibble her neck. She gave him a playful slap on the arm. "I wouldn't go getting fresh. My husband's a big man with a mean jealous streak. You wouldn't want him finding out."

He held her without answering for a spell then bent close to her ear. "While we're on the subject of husbands finding things out, I got a question for you."

She swayed back and forth, pulling him along with her. "Go ahead and ask. I might even answer."

He held her still and took a deep breath. "Did you ever get around to making yourself a dress with that pretty white cloth I bought you?"

She tensed in his arms. No matter what, she wouldn't lie. "Yes and no."

"Girl, that ain't no kind of answer. You either made a dress or you didn't."

She swallowed the knot in her throat. "I made one, just not for me."

Catching her hair in the stubble on his chin, he nodded against her head. "What if I told you there's a story around town about a fancy white dress showing up yesterday on Miss Annie's body?"

She cringed. It hadn't crossed her mind that she'd owe Henry an explanation. "Well, I. . ."

He turned her around and placed a gentle hand over her mouth. "Before you strain that little noggin, let me finish. As the rumor goes, a certain Sarah King hauled that dress straight into the coroner's office, as if sent there by Judge Bickford himself, and insisted Isabella Gouldy use it for Miss Annie's grave clothes—which means today when they lay her to rest, your white frock is going down with her." He peered closer. "All that sound about right?"

She cut her eyes to the ground. "Are you mad?"

He tilted his head to the side and cupped her chin in his palm. "Not mad. Curious. Why would you do such a thing, after hankering so long for that cloth? You hardly knew Miss Annie."

Uneasy, she toyed with the button loop on the front of his shirt. "I'm not sure I can explain it."

He caressed her hand. "Jus' do your best."

"Something about that woman touched my heart. Made me count my blessings."

"How so?"

"Since that day in my kitchen, when Jennie told me how mean Annie's man treated her, I couldn't stop thinking about how different our lives were. For all her fine clothes and big diamonds, Miss Annie cried more tears in a day than I have in a year. Yet with all that pain, she took the time to show genuine love for folks."

"She did at that, God rest her soul."

"Henry, I felt pressed to give the dress, as if the Lord Himself wanted her to have it." She waved her hand. "Oh, I know that don't make no sense, considering how Miss Annie lived her life, but it's how I felt. And I don't regret giving it."

"Reckon it was for your own benefit? Like laying down a sacrifice?"

She rested against his chest while she mulled over his words. "That could be. He's been dealing with my heart on several matters lately."

"That may be the answer to the other thing I've wondered about."

She leaned back to look in his eyes. "Which thing?"

"You mind telling me why you're so different lately?"

She smiled. "Me different? How so?"

A splash on the surface of the water pulled his gaze away from her face. He held her, staring at something over her head. "You seem quiet inside. Like a body who's made her peace."

She twisted around to face the water. Mindful of his ribs, she leaned her head gently against his chest. "I guess I have made peace. With life here in Jefferson. With God. With myself. I'm just done struggling."

He tightened his arms around her. "How'd you come to that place so fast?"

"Like I said, Miss Annie showed me a better way than hate. I think she crossed my path for that reason. And the day hate almost got you hanged, I decided not to give it one more second of my time."

He tensed. "I wish I felt that way."

She patted his hands. "There's nothing right about the way things are in Jefferson, and I won't say it don't grieve my heart. But I learned something that terrible day. Most of these folks care about us deep down, but the old ways cloud their minds, the things they learned from their folks. The others, like those horrible men, don't deserve the time it wastes to hate them."

Henry sighed. "Life can't go on like this forever. Something has to change."

"I hope it will someday. But please don't let it change you, Henry. Peaceful, loving folks like you and Miss Annie are Jefferson's hope. We've already lost her to senseless cruelty. Don't let three black-hearted strangers take you, too."

Henry stood still for a long time, until a tear fell from overhead and landed on Sarah's chest. As he relaxed against her, she sensed he'd finally let go of his pain.

After a time, he wiped his eyes on his sleeve. "Ain't you going to Miss Annie's funeral?"

She shook her head. "I don't need to. I've already said good-bye."

He sniffed then chuckled. "So Sarah's dress will be there, but she won't?"

She grinned. It was time to tell him. Until now she'd kept her secret suspicions to herself. She needed to be sure before she broke the news.

Heart pounding, she took his big, calloused hand in her own and slid it down over the front of her skirt. "Before long that little dress wouldn't have fit me nohow. Even after I deliver, I don't expect that tiny waist would ever go all the way around again." He tensed, and she flushed with pleasure. "They claim a woman's body changes after birthing a baby."

Henry let go and moved around to stare at her with furrowed

brows. He opened his mouth to speak then closed it again, reminding Sarah of the poor befuddled fish that once took a swim with his overalls. She pressed his hand tighter against her waist. "Speak up, Papa. How do you expect to teach my daughter to talk if you can't?"

He found his voice. "You mean it, Sarah?"

Smiling so hard her face hurt, she nodded.

He took off up the hill whooping so loudly he flushed a mess of wood thrushes from the nearby brush. After he tromped up and down a few times, shouting and bashing everything in sight with his hat, he ran back to her so fast she dodged for fear he'd run her down. He caught her before she got away and swung her off the ground. "Henry King gon' be a papa! You hear me, world? Henry gon' have a son!"

As if remembering her delicate condition, he stopped short and set her down gently. She took his cheeks in both hands and gave him a fierce look. "Now we have good reason to make things better in Jefferson. This baby is part of us, and she'll be part of this town."

Henry's eyes blazed. "My son gon' walk these streets with his head up, Sarah. I won't allow nobody to treat him how they done me. Or steal his self-respect like they done yours."

She shook her head. "You want change, Henry? Well, Jefferson may never change, but we can. If we raise our daughter to always look to God, her head will always be lifted, now, won't it? I refuse to pass on a legacy of hate."

They glared at each other for a spell before they both started to laugh. He nestled her under his arm and walked her up the hill. "You jus' forget that daughter stuff right now. It's a boy, and that's all there is to it."

"Hush up, Henry King. I need me a little girl to make white dresses for."

At the top of the rise, he hauled her around to face him. "I tell you what. . .if you give me a son this time, next time you can have a girl. But after that, all boys. We need brothers for Henry Jr."

She nudged him and started for the house. "Humph! Sisters, you mean. For my little Annie."

◦◦◦

Papa followed the horse-drawn hearse along the winding, tree-lined paths of Oakwood Cemetery.

The warmth of the day had long since given way to a chilly afternoon breeze, so Bertha raised her collar higher and bundled into the wool blanket Papa kept for her under the seat.

"You holding up all right, wee girl?"

She lifted her trembling chin in his direction and nodded.

Mama begged Bertha not to attend Annie's funeral, but she had insisted.

Papa stood up for her, saying, "The obligation of a friend doesn't end until the last clod hits the casket." The way Bertha had it figured, she'd not get off so easy. She fully expected the debt she owed would follow her to her own grave.

Since Annie's death, the yoke had altered but not lessened a whit. The burden of hope had become a load of guilt; one so heavy Bertha stumbled beneath its weight. And though she tried, Magda hadn't said a word to make her feel better. Before she left, she asked Bertha to pray, but she couldn't. God wasn't interested in a word she had to say.

As for Thad, she had given up on him, too. After all, she didn't deserve happiness, and Thad didn't seem to care, so why should God intervene in the details of their lives?

The hearse came to a stop in front of them, and Papa helped her down. When her feet touched the ground, she swayed a bit, so he wrapped his arm around her shoulders. "I haven't called it wrong, have I, sprite? Will this be too much for you?"

She straightened her spine. "It would be too much for me to miss it. I have to do this, Papa."

He squeezed her tight. "That's me girl."

The men hired to bear the casket were walking away from the hearse toward the open grave. Except for Mr. Stilley, Dr. Turner,

Dr. Eason, Sheriff Bagby, and a few other townsfolk, curious strangers made up most of the hushed gathering. A small band of colored residents stood off to the side, including most of the staff from Brooks House—Jennie Simpson, Thomas and his wife, and the one they called Cook.

Papa nudged her forward. "Let's go, Bertha. I'll be right here holding you, and I promise not to let go as long as you need me."

She gripped his steady arm. "I hope you mean that, because I need you."

The six men who carried Annie's casket gently lowered it into the ground with ropes. The assembled mourners crowded closer, and the minister opened the service with a prayer. Bertha struggled to focus, but her mind swirled with thoughts of Annie and the times they'd shared—their long talks about crushes and corsets and candy—and every other childish wasted word that kept her from saying the only thing that mattered. The words of faith Bertha had managed to spout seemed weak and trite. Not nearly enough to save her friend.

Bertha lowered her face to her hands just as Papa's arm lifted from her shoulders. She felt him step away, and it shook her back to the present. She felt cold and alone without the comforting weight around her neck and more than a little cross. Hadn't he promised not to leave her as long as she needed him? Yet he'd left her the second she needed him most.

She turned to see where he'd gone. He stood behind her, his features alight with a sappy smile. Confused and hurt, she faced the front again just as another comforting arm, another warm body, took Papa's place from the opposite side. Startled by the surprising familiarity, her gaze jerked to her consoler's face.

Thad!

His expression remained solemn except for the barest of smiles and a tiny wink. She glanced over her shoulder again. Papa beamed and raised his thumb.

The rest of the service became a blur of questions and scattered feelings. The poor minister might've yodeled the rest of the message for all she heard. That is, until his booming voice read the closing passage of scripture. " 'What man is he that liveth, and shall not see death? Shall he deliver his soul from the hand of the grave?' " His burning gaze swept the circle of mourners. "That's why, dear children, it becomes imperative that we who have been enlightened with the truth persist so diligently to obey the admonishment in James 5:20." He held the book aloft and began to read. " 'He which converteth the sinner from the error of his way shall save a soul from death, and shall hide a multitude of sins.' "

Bertha spun away from Thad, brushed past Papa, lifted her skirts, and ran. She ran through the idle curious, providing more than their money's worth of morbid entertainment, and past the grieving staff of Brooks House, who stared with sympathetic eyes. She passed up the wagon and didn't stop until she'd barreled through the front gate, thundered a good ways up the road, and crashed into a heavy thicket standing between her and a winding trail.

The branches clutched at her sleeves and tore long scratches in her ankles. Cruel briars crisscrossed in front, and in back her skirt caught around the thorns of a tall devil's walking stick growing up through the brush. If she attempted one more step, she'd fall facedown on the briars or be pulled back on the spiny stick. Trapped, she couldn't move an inch. Her dilemma reminded her of her life. Thad's return stirred hope in her heart, but guilt over failing Annie left her at a standstill.

Too distraught to cry, she looked around to weigh her options. If she could possibly sit down without ripping the flesh from her palms, she might manage to free her skirt from the cruel spike. She leaned to lower her body onto one arm when a hand shot out and latched onto her waist. "Don't move, Bertha. That's stinging nettle beneath you."

"Oh, Thad," she wailed. "I'm stuck."

"I can see that. Let's get you unstuck." He held her up with one hand and carefully freed her skirt with the other. When the last piece of cloth inched free, he lifted her from the thicket and set her down on the road. "Are you all right, sugar?"

With trembling fingers, she smoothed her tattered skirt. "I guess so."

"Good. Now tell me what just happened. Why did you run off like that?"

Bertha averted her gaze. "I believe I need to sit down."

Thad scanned their surroundings then took her by the wrist. "Can you walk?"

"Yes, I think so." She wasn't pretending feminine frailty. Her legs trembled so much she feared they might fail her.

Thad led her to a clearing where a big tree lay, felled by the wind in a recent storm. He took off his overcoat and spread it over the bark then helped her to sit. Settling beside her, he inched a bit closer. "I missed you, Bertha."

Surprised, she raised her head. His simple declaration brought a sweet smile to her lips. She'd expected more questions or a demand for an explanation. "I missed you, too. I'm so glad you're here. How did you hear about Annie?"

He studied his twiddling thumbs. "I didn't. Not until I got into town today."

She frowned, considering his words. "Then why did you leave school?"

"I didn't." He raised his head, and something flickered in his eyes. "I never made it to school."

Bertha couldn't trust her ears. Of all the bewildering events of the past few days, this confused her the most. "What are you saying? You've been gone for two weeks. If you weren't at school, where have you been?" She bit back the important question. If he hadn't gone to school, why had he left her?

"I spent some time down in Houston."

"Houston?"

"I got on the train in Longview with every intention of going to Bryan. When it pulled into the station, I couldn't make myself get off. I stayed on and rode it clear to Houston."

She stared up into dark brown eyes with long blond lashes and a sprinkling of tiny freckles at the corners and tried to sort out what he was telling her.

"I was plenty scared at first, but the trip gave me time to think. By the time the train hit Houston, I'd made up my mind. I won't be going back to Bryan. I'm never going to college, Bertha."

Her heart raised its head. "Does your papa know?"

He answered with a somber nod.

"What did he say?"

"It's not what he said this time; it's what I said. I told him I appreciated his intentions, but they were misplaced, that Cyrus should be going to school, not me. I told him to apply the money he'd saved for my education on sending Cy to Texas AMC." He shrugged. "The old man bucked a little at first. When he saw I meant business"—Thad snapped his fingers—"just like that, he set his dream on Cy, where it always belonged."

By now they were both smiling.

"How does Cyrus feel about that?"

Thad shook his head, remembering. "You never saw a happier boy in your life."

Bertha touched his arm. "What took you to Houston?"

He caught her hand and squeezed it. "Just north of there, in a little town they call Humble, is where our future lies. I can't explain it now, but as soon as we can be married, I'll take you there and show you."

A shock surged through her. She cringed and slid her hand away as surprise replaced the confident joy in Thad's eyes.

"What's wrong, sugar?"

"I don't know. I'm confused."

He swallowed. "About me?"

When she didn't answer, he pushed off the log and paced in front of her. "I don't know what there is to be confused about. Two weeks ago you said you loved me. How could that change in such a short time?" He stopped to glare, but his eyes glistened with unshed tears. "If I'd known you don't really care for me, I would've stayed down in Humble and saved myself a trip."

She sprang up and stood with him. "I never said I don't care for you."

Bewilderment replaced the pain. "What, then? This frog-hopping has to stop. You need to pick a toadstool and light, Bertha." Then his mouth opened. The look in his eyes said he thought he'd figured it out. "Wait a minute—I know what's wrong. You want a proper marriage proposal, and you deserve one."

He plowed ahead before she could deny it. "A proper proposal suits me fine, Bertha Maye Biddie." He dropped down on one knee. "I've already proved I'll wallow in the dirt for you."

"Wait! Please don't kneel, Thad. That's not it."

He howled and gripped his head. "Girl, you're driving me mad. If you care for me, what's there to be confused about? You'll either marry me or you won't."

"It's not a matter of will or won't," she shouted. "I can't."

Thad tugged her down in front of him and laced his long fingers through her hair, his grip too tight around her head. "That's crazy. I won't hear it. You already said you love me."

"I do love you."

His voice trembled. "All right, then. You said loving each other should be what matters most." He pulled her closer as his darting gaze roamed her face for answers. "What happened to that?"

Bertha lowered her gaze and gave in to threatening tears. Thad let go of her hair and rocked her, murmuring comfort in her ear. A few yards south, a train rumbled past on the way to the station on Alley Street. The whistle blew as the engine approached the Line Street crossing, and the woeful sound filled Bertha's chest, mourning with her and echoing her grief.

When she quieted, he patted the top of her head the way he had the last time she saw him. It hurt to remember that day, the day he said he loved her but had to leave. Now she understood how he must have felt.

He pushed her back to look at her. "I think I know what's ailing you, sugar. You don't want to marry while losing Annie is so fresh. That's all right. I can wait. For as long as it takes to grieve your friend, I promise I'll wait for you."

She shifted her eyes to his. "I don't deserve such a promise. Or hope for such happiness."

"What?" He stood to his feet, pulling her up with him. "Bertha, what's going on? Why would you say something so foolish?"

She straightened her spine and looked him in the eye. "Because I caused Annie's death."

Thad gripped her shoulders and gave her a shake. "Don't you say it again. You had no part in her death. That madman killed her for spite and greed. How could you think anything different?"

"No, it's true. Abe got mad because Annie snuck out the night before. I asked her to slip away and meet me. If I'd left her alone, she'd still be alive."

Thad stared at her so long she squirmed. With a groan, he crushed her to his chest. "Poor, sweet girl. How long have these tiny shoulders borne such weight? You need to lay it down, Bertha."

The same words Papa had said to her.

"I have no right to lay it down." She tried to pull away, but he held her.

"You had no right to pick it up. I saw how Abe treated Annie. He was bound to kill her eventually. Honey, if Annie wouldn't get away from him, there was nothing you could do to stop it."

She remembered Annie's tortured face the night they met in the alley.

"He hurt me. He always hurts me."

She saw Annie's twisted arm, the tattered gown, the fear in her eyes at just the mention of Abe's name. She ducked her head. "But I—"

Thad raised her chin with his finger. "It is not your fault."

"You really think so?"

"I know so. The only person who could've saved Annie from Abe was Annie."

His words were a balm, each one a drop of warm, soothing ointment bringing the pardon she needed. Her heart opened a crack and light poured in—except in one dark, haunted corner.

"That explains why the Lord sent me on a mission to save her.

I brought about just the opposite. I failed Him miserably."

"Now you've failed God, too?"

She tensed. Was he making fun? "Yes, Thad. I let my feelings for you distract me. Because of me, Annie died without God's forgiveness."

"How do you know that?"

She reached for the hankie she'd folded into her sash, but it wasn't there. "I just know."

He took her hand and led her back to the log, easing her down on his knee. "All right. What exactly do you think God told you to do?"

"He told me to tell Annie about His grace." She felt for the hankie again. Had she lost it in the briars?

"And you had no chance to tell her?"

"I tried."

"When?"

"The night before she died."

"Did she listen?"

Bertha swiped the back of her hand under her nose. Unattractive, but necessary. "I don't know. Maybe."

"Did she run away from you or stick her fingers in her ears?"

"Of course not."

"Then she heard you, Bertha. After that, the burden fell on Annie."

"But it's obvious I didn't say enough."

"What else might you have said?"

"That's just it. I couldn't say anything more."

He scrunched his brow. "Why's that?"

"Because. . ." The truth dawned, and Bertha raised her head. "Because she wouldn't allow it." For the first time since Annie's death, she remembered. Annie had backed away, refused to hear.

Thad drew her next to his chest. "Don't you see, goose? You did exactly what the Lord asked of you. Suppose God sent you to say those things to Annie knowing it was her last chance to hear? In that case, did you fail Him?"

His compassion broke her heart anew. Tears rolled down her cheeks. "No," she whispered.

"And did you fail Annie?"

"When you put it like that, I guess not."

He shook out a red bandanna and wiped her eyes then put it in her hands so she could blow her nose. "Sounds like you've been too hard on yourself on all counts."

The train whistle blew again in the distance, one short moan followed by a long, heartrending wail. This time it mourned for Annie. "Thad, it breaks my heart to think that after her miserable life, Annie missed heaven."

"Sweetheart, you may never know how God used your words in Annie's heart. All we can do is obey and trust Him with the rest."

"Can you trust God with the details?"

Papa had asked that question concerning her future with Thad. And look at the wonderful way God had worked out the details of their relationship.

Releasing the weight of guilt from her chest, Bertha drew in a deep breath and felt her heart surrender the last shadowed crevice to the light. She wrapped her arms around Thad's neck and urged him close. His hands tangled in her hair, and his cheek slid along hers until their lips met.

"I love you, Bertha," he said in a husky voice.

"I love you, too."

"Will you marry me?"

"Yes, I will."

"And live with me in Humble?"

"Whenever you say."

He withdrew to look at her. "You mean it?"

When she nodded, he got up and stood her to her feet. "It's rough country, sugar, and that's all I can promise you. You won't have the comfort and convenience you're accustomed to. We'll be scratching out a life from nothing." He studied her eyes. "It'll be hard work, and you'll be leaving behind everything you know. It might change you."

She cocked her head at him. "Do I have to wear fancy shoes all the time?"

"You don't have to wear shoes at all, unless you want to. There's no one around to care."

She raised her hands. "Hallelujah! Humble won't change me. It'll set me free."

His expression turned grave. "Now the important question. What would you say to a yard full of bloodhounds?"

She giggled. "Woof, woof?"

Laughing, he picked her up and hugged her until her sides hurt. Then he set her on her feet and kissed her cheek. "We'd best go. I told your papa I'd find you and bring you home. If we don't show up soon, he'll send a posse." He grinned. "I don't want to get on the bad side of Francis Biddie. Especially tonight."

She grinned, too. "What's so special about tonight?"

"If you must know, we men have a lot to talk about. I plan to ask your father's permission to marry his lovely daughter." He winked and offered his arm. "I think I'll wait until he says yes before I tell him about Humble."

Bertha slid her arm through his and winked back. "Considering who we're dealing with, you'd best wait until after the wedding."

CHAPTER 30

Saturday, March 10

Bertha gazed around her bedroom one last time. The dressing table, cluttered since her youth with sundry items necessary for her toilette, looked oddly bare with everything packed away. It reminded her of the front window last Christmas after Papa took down the tree.

Remembering her cameo brush set still in the bedside table drawer, she lifted it out as she'd done a thousand times before, only this time she'd never put it back. It would soon be on its way to a place called Humble, Texas, in the company of Mrs. Thaddeus Bloom.

Shoving the brush and comb deep inside her velvet drawstring bag, Bertha set it near the rest of her luggage then smiled at the container of tooth powder, the one thing left behind on purpose. She caught sight of her image in the looking glass and backed away from the dressing table to see more. Preening a bit in her dress of white dimity with matching wedding bonnet, she jumped when Magda cleared her throat.

Bertha looked back and grinned. "Fiddlesticks. You caught me."

"It's all right to admire yourself today, sugar. You're a lovely bride." She pointed toward the hullabaloo in the dining room. "Everyone out there agrees."

Bertha gave a playful laugh. "It's unanimous, then." She held her dress out to her sides and twirled. "It's because I'm so happy, don't you think?"

When Magda didn't answer, Bertha glanced up. Her friend sagged against the door frame, both hands hiding her face.

Bertha hurried over and gripped her shoulders. "Don't you dare. It's bound to be bad luck for the maid of honor to cry at the wedding party."

"I'm not crying," Magda protested from behind her hands. "There's something in my eye."

She swiped her thumbs across Magda's cheeks then held them up for her to see. "Which one? They're both leaking."

Laughing, they fell against each other and stumbled over to fall down on the bed. Magda rose up with red, watery eyes. "I can't believe you're going, that's all. I've had you all to myself, and just like that, you'll be gone. I've tried to be happy for you, but I'm going to miss you too much. How will I cope?"

Bertha kicked off her shoes and sat cross-legged on the bed. "I know a remedy for that. Come with me."

"Come with you? Where?"

Bertha grabbed her hands. "To live with me in Humble."

"Don't be daft. I couldn't."

"Why not? You wouldn't have to come right away. You can wait a few months until we settle in a house."

Magda shifted on the bed. "Papa would never allow it."

"Oh, I think he would if Thad promised to look out for you." She squeezed her fingers. "So you're considering it?"

Magda flinched. "I didn't say that."

"You didn't have to. If you've gotten to what your papa might say, you're entertaining the thought."

Magda shook free of her grasp. "Forget about it. It's a scandalous notion. I wouldn't think of intruding on you newlyweds."

Bertha leaned close and widened her eyes. "Don't be so hasty, dear. There's a lot going on in Humble. A world of opportunity for a single girl."

Magda tilted her head like a befuddled hound.

Bertha leaned hers back and laughed. "Men, sugar. Thad claims there are scores of unattached men. Mostly well-heeled gentlemen and businessmen looking for a place to settle. A few rough-and-tumble frontiersmen, too." She winked. "And very few women to balance things out."

Magda leaped to her feet and stood at attention. "You'll find me on the next train."

Bertha clapped her hands together. "Well, I should say so! After all, your piece of wedding cake had a ring inside. That means marriage within a year, so you'd best get busy."

"Oh, pooh. It's a silly tradition. Pretty little Rhodie got the thimble. There's no way she'll wind up a spinster. I think our pieces got switched." She held up one finger. "Although when that rascal Charles Gouldy bit into the coin, it gave me hope. He's sure to be prosperous someday, if it means he has to steal it."

They heard a knock and turned. Mama stood smiling in the open doorway. "Such boisterous laughter coming from this room! What am I interrupting?"

Bertha waved her in. "Nothing that won't keep. Come in."

"I don't need to come in, dear. You need to come out. Your new husband has scoured the grounds for you, perhaps remembering the last time you vanished." She pointed toward the front of the house. "I left him straining his neck at the parlor window. Come put him out of his misery, won't you?"

Bertha scooted off the bed and rushed to hug her. "Oh, Mama! I'm so happy."

Mama beamed down at her. "It becomes you. I've never seen you more lovely." She wiped her eyes with a lace hankie and kissed Bertha's cheek. "Your guests are waiting for you to present your gifts, and you have such beautiful things." She clasped her hands together. "There's the most stunning appliquéd Rose of Sharon quilt from Thad's mother. I understand she made it herself. Do hurry, love. I want you to see it."

Unexpected tears stung Bertha's eyes. Though Papa called her "love" quite often, it was the first time Mama ever had. She linked arms with her. "Let's go, then. Shall we?"

Bertha offered her other arm to Magda, and the three of them filed down the hall to the parlor.

Thad stood across the room, staring into the fireplace. In his dark suit, with flickering light on his face, he looked more handsome than she'd ever seen him. He glanced up, and Bertha sent him a little wave. A thrill tickled her spine when it seemed his breath caught at the sight of her. He waved back and moved toward her, stopping along the way for a quick word or a handshake with a guest. He finally reached her side, and Bertha's own breath caught when his hand slid down her back.

"Where've you been, Mrs. Bloom?" he whispered. "I've missed you."

"I'm sorry. I've missed you, too."

She took his hand and made her way to the center table piled high with wedding presents. The men feigned interest at first then settled in the corner discussing the weather. The women circled the table, complimenting Mama's embroidered pillow slips and sighing over Mrs. Bloom's quilt.

A commotion in the corner caught her eye. Papa had spotted her and stormed her way. "So here's the bonniest bride on two continents. Come along, daughter. It's time to pronounce me blessing on this fine union."

He took the newlyweds, one on each side, then stuck his fingers in his mouth and blew a sharp blast. All activity ceased, and the company crowded around them in a circle. Papa placed one hand on Bertha's head. To the delight of his audience, he reached the other hand toward Thad's, shrugged, then called for a chair. Satisfied, he began to speak. "Great God, one true God, I bring these precious souls before You, entrusting them into Your care."

His fingers tightened on her head. "Bertha Maye Biddie Bloom, may your life be filled with plenty and your womb suffer no lack. May the love of your husband warm your heart and brighten your days. May the peace of the Lord Jesus Christ follow you all the days of your life." He patted her head.

"Thaddeus Abel Bloom, may the wife of your youth bring you joy. May your pockets be blessed and your quiver full. May God shine His face on your journeys and prosper the work of your hands." He motioned for Thad to stand. "Friends and family, I give you Thaddeus Bloom and his wee wife, Bertha."

A riotous outcry and boisterous clapping ensued. The guests surged toward them, shouting congratulations and pounding Thad on the back. After Julius Ney and his wife wished them well, Rhodie Pharr stepped up and took their place.

Bertha smiled, happy to see the beaming girl. "Hey, Rhodie."

"Hey, Bertha. You sure make a lovely bride."

"Why, thank you."

Rhodie held up her thimble. "Guess I'll never be one."

Bertha took it from her hand. "Rubbish. A clear case of mistaken identity. You must've cut in front of someone."

She grinned and glanced at her brother. "I did, actually. I jumped ahead of Mose."

Mose blushed and lowered his head. Bertha always suspected the boy was sweet on her, but likely no more than on every other girl he met.

"Hey, Bertha, whatever happened to that pretty necklace my brother gave you?" Rhodie blurted. "You know, the one that looked like woven metal straws?"

Mose blushed from the roots of his hair to his turned-down collar. He leaned to yank Rhodie's long red braid. "Dumb girl. I said not to mention it today."

Bertha's own face grew warm. Rhodie meant the filigreed cross. Since Mose found it and gave it to her, Bertha didn't know how he'd react to hearing that she'd given it to Annie. "I haven't seen it for quite some time." She asked God to forgive her if the vague answer was a lie by omission. She just couldn't bear to hurt Mose's feelings.

Bertha wanted the necklace back in the worst way. Not because Mose gave it to her, but as a remembrance of Annie. Thad helped her search for it after the funeral. It never showed up at Brooks House, and the coroner's office assured her it wasn't with Annie's body when they found her, a fact that broke Bertha's heart.

She had prayed every day that it would somehow turn up. Finally, she'd had to agree with Thad's opinion that Abe Monroe, who was in fact Abraham Rothschild, son of a wealthy Ohio jeweler, took the cross when he took Annie's diamonds.

Rhodie twisted around to gloat at Mose. "See, I told you. I knew it was Bertha's. I'd know that thing anywhere."

Bertha squeezed Thad's hand. "Rhodie, what are you talking about?"

Too busy winning her argument to heed Bertha's question, Rhodie put both hands on her hips and thrust out her chest. "You owe me a nickel, Moses Pharr."

Thad, who towered over Mose, took his arm and hauled him around. "What's your sister talking about?"

The boy looked up with frightened eyes then scowled at Rhodie. "Aw, she thinks she saw that worthless trinket I gave Bertha."

Thad gave him a little shake. "I got that part. When did she see it?"

Rhodie squeezed between Thad and Mose. "Yesterday," she provided. "I saw it yesterday."

Bertha's heart pounded so hard she heard it inside her ears. "Where, Rhodie?"

Mose eased free of Thad's grip. "She claims T-Bone Taylor's sister wore it to school on Friday."

Bertha met Thad's knowing glance. Beau and T-Bone Taylor. The little scoundrels who ran thieving raids along the banks of the Big Cypress. "Theresa Taylor has my cross?"

Rhodie snorted. "Sure does. She pranced around the classroom bragging to anybody who'd listen. Said her brothers found it." She cocked her head at Bertha. "You must've dropped it somewhere, huh? That's too bad. I guess it's finders keepers, just like when Mose gave it to you, right, Bertha? Because I'll tell you this: Theresa Taylor will never give that necklace back."

Bertha clutched Thad's arm. "We have to go find it."

He nodded. "Don't worry; we will."

"No, I mean now."

He blinked and glanced around at the guests. "We can't go just yet, sugar. We have to wait until the party's over."

She shook her head. "Theresa won't give us the necklace, but her brothers can get it. We have to find them, and it may take all afternoon to track those two down." She cast a desperate look around the room. "We have to do something, Thad. I won't rest until I know if it's mine."

"Don't forget, sugar, our train leaves Jefferson in about three hours."

She tried to put her feelings into the determined look she gave him. "I won't get on it until I find out."

He sighed his surrender and kissed the top of her head. "Wait here. I'll go fix it with your folks."

Thad crossed the room and took Papa aside. They huddled a few minutes before Papa motioned for Mama to join them. He spoke quietly to her; then they hurried over while Thad turned to his parents and Cyrus.

Bertha met Mama with a tearful hug. "Are you angry with me?"

"Of course not, dear."

"Papa?"

"Go do what you must, sprite. Just try to spare time for a proper good-bye before you leave."

"I will. I promise. Please pray our efforts pay off."

Magda linked arms with Bertha. "I'm coming along to help you find them."

Rhodie squealed. "Can we come, too?"

Bertha nodded. "I'd like you and Mose both to come, if you will. We need all the eyes we can get."

After she made her apologies and accepted another round of hearty congratulations, Bertha found herself seated next to Thad in her new father-in-law's phaeton buggy amid a shouting circle of well-wishers. Mose, Rhodie, and Magda sat behind them in Mose's wagon waiting for them to pull out.

Charles Gouldy shoved his way through and crowded close to the rig. "Hey, Thad! Wait up. Are you leaving so soon?"

Thad leaned to take his offered hand. "What are your plans for the next hour or so?"

Charlie shrugged. "You tell me."

Thad hooked his thumb. "Climb in back of Mose's rig. They'll fill you in."

On the way to the Taylors' tumbledown shack, Thad looked over his shoulder and frowned. "We would be there already on horseback."

"True, but I could hardly ride the back of your mare in this dress. And those four won't fit in the saddlebag."

He snorted. "I thought you wanted to find the Taylor boys. When we roll up there in a wagon train, they're sure to bolt."

She unpinned her wedding bonnet and folded it on the seat between them. "We'll find them. You can bet on that."

"I don't know, sugar. Those rascals are slippery as greased otters."

She peered up at him. "Maybe so, but I prayed."

Thad laughed. "They don't stand a chance, then. God knows where they are."

The wagons turned down the rutted road leading to the faded cypress hovel that housed Gladys Taylor and her three unruly offspring. Hardly more than an overgrown trail, the lane ran alongside the bayou all the way up to the property. Bertha scanned the water and spotted the boys' blue dinghy gliding up to the dilapidated pier in back. She nudged Thad and pointed just as they moored the boat and crawled ashore.

Even from a distance, their gangly arms and legs looked as brown as beans, probably from time spent near the water where the hot sun reflected off the surface, baking them twice. Dodging and sparring, they ran straight up the bank and into the barn without a glance toward the approaching wagons. Behind them, the little boat bobbed low on the surface of the water, likely filled to the brim with pilfered loot.

Giddy with excitement, Bertha clutched Thad's arm. "Park right here. We'll slip around and catch them in the barn."

Thad shook his head. "We'll knock at the front door, thank you. Slipping around anywhere on this place will get you a buckshot shower." He applied the tip of his whip to the horse's rear end, and the buggy sped toward the house with Mose hot on their tail. Thad rolled to a stop and bailed out, ran around to help Bertha, then ushered her up the crumbling walkway. The others got down off the wagon but waited at the foot of the path.

The door opened before they reached it. A disheveled Gladys Taylor met them on the porch with her shotgun, staring dumbly at Bertha in her wedding dress. "What madness is this?"

Thad positioned his body between the wild-eyed woman and Bertha.

She stayed put but peered around him to see.

He took off his hat. "Morning, ma'am. We don't mean to bother you. Just came by to see your boys for a minute."

Suspicion sparked in her faded blue eyes. "My boys?" Her voice came out cracked and shrill, sounding too old for her age. "What fer?"

Thad held up his hands. "Just to talk. We're hunting information about a necklace Theresa wore to school on Friday."

When her eyebrows drew together, Bertha nudged him in the ribs.

He glanced at her and changed his tactic. "We intend to offer a generous reward."

Gladys lowered the gun onto her hip. "A reward?" She seemed to chew on the word. "For the necklace or the information?"

Bertha brushed past Thad. "Mrs. Taylor, I understand the boys found a cross on a silver chain?" She cleared her throat. "I really need to see it. If it's the piece of jewelry we're looking for, it's not worth very much, except in sentimental value."

Thad put a protective arm around her shoulders. "Ma'am, I'll pay good money for a short talk with the boys. Or Theresa, for that matter."

Gladys seemed to mull it over then shook her head. "They ain't here. Ain't none of 'em here."

Bertha opened her mouth to protest, but Thad tugged on her sleeve. "How about you, ma'am? Do you know anything about a silver cross? Maybe you'd be interested in trading some information for a few dollars."

She raised her chin. "I don't get in my children's business or rifle through their personal things. We stay friends thata way."

Frustrated, Bertha bristled. "With all due respect, Mrs. Taylor, you'd do well to keep up with their things. Because most everything in their possession doesn't belong to them."

Thad hauled her back. "Bertha. . ."

A thundercloud formed on the woman's face. She opened her mouth ready to spew, but before she let fly her venomous rant, T-Bone and Beau rounded the house, still shoving each other and laughing. They saw Thad and Bertha at the same time and froze like startled deer. Then they spun, clinging to each other for balance, and shot out of sight.

"Get 'em, Mose!" Rhodie screamed.

Springing past them so fast his image blurred, Mose vaulted into motion. When he disappeared around the house, Thad took off after him, with Charlie and Gladys Taylor close behind. Bertha, Magda, and Rhodie followed as fast as their skirts would allow.

"No!" Gladys Taylor's bloodcurdling howl rocked the secluded cove. "Don't you hurt my boys!" Seconds ticked past, bogged in molasses, as she raised her shotgun at Thad's back.

Bertha, Magda, and Rhodie screamed and scuttled forward. Bertha lunged for the gun and shoved the exploding barrel to the sky. Rhodie and Magda piled on Gladys and wrestled the weapon from her hands. She sank to the ground, rolling and screaming like a banshee.

The two boys had reached the boat and were paddling furiously down the bayou. Mose shot alongside them on the bank, running full out, with Thad and Charlie on his heels.

"Please, God, don't let them get away," Bertha prayed aloud. "We'll never find them in those woods."

Rhodie, so excited her freckles stood out, gave her head a vigorous shake. "My brother won't lose them. Mose can track a gnat in a whirlwind."

Just as the skiff disappeared around a crook in the bayou, Mose dove, but Bertha didn't see if he landed in the boat or the water. With a burst of speed to the end of the bank and a gangly soar, Charlie followed him in. Thad, his long legs hurdling fallen logs and briar patches, tore around the bend on dry land.

"Let's go," Rhodie shouted. "They'll catch them at the low crossing."

Bertha glanced at the boys' hysterical mama and decided to return her shotgun later. She hurried after Magda and Rhodie, stashing the gun in the buggy's boot before she climbed aboard Mose's wagon.

Rhodie snapped the reins, and they took off faster than Bertha believed the tired old horse could run. They rumbled past a good stretch of piney woods before Rhodie cut over on a logging road toward the bayou. At the end of it, she reined in the horse, and the three of them jumped down without regard to modesty or decorum.

Rhodie pointed ahead of her as she ran. "Through here."

Bertha and Magda followed, though branches and prickly bushes tore at their clothes. Bertha wished she'd heeded wisdom instead of vanity when she decided to stay in her dress.

They broke onto a sandy clearing at the water's edge. Just as Rhodie predicted, the rascals were caught. Thad, still in his suit, sat on the ground holding little Beau in his lap. It took Mose and Charlie, both soaking wet, to pin T-Bone to the ground. The whelps howled like wounded hounds, kicking and beating at their captors with flailing hands and feet.

"Be still, now," Thad shouted. "We don't plan to hurt you none."

Bertha kneeled on the ground next to the oldest boy and touched his arm. "T-Bone, listen to me. We just want to ask you some questions. You have my word we won't harm you or your brother." She tried to soften her eyes to a plea.

He stilled and stared back at her, his frantic gaze roaming her upswept hair and fancy dress.

Thad nodded at Mose and Charlie. "Let him go."

They pulled away from T-Bone and he sat up, scooting to rest his back against a sapling. His tongue flicked nervously over his lips as he glanced at his brother. Thad let go of Beau, who scurried on his backside like a crab to press against his brother.

Bertha crawled closer to the two frightened boys. "Rhodie saw a cross necklace that you found and gave to your sister. Do you know the one I mean?"

The question stirred visible fear to the surface. T-Bone shot Beau a warning look then stared at the ground. "We ain't gave Theresa no necklace."

"Did, too," Rhodie cried.

Bertha held up her hand to silence her. "Boys, listen to me. It's very important that you tell me where you found it."

T-Bone shook his head. "Sorry, ma'am. Don't know what you're yapping about."

Thad stooped down beside Bertha. "I'm real sorry you boys don't trust us. We could've kept you out of a heap of trouble, what with Sheriff Bagby so interested in talking to you two about that missing gold jewelry."

Beau squirmed around to look at Thad. "Gold jewelry? That's a crock. We just had one necklace, and ours was silver."

His brother whirled on him. "Pipe down, you stupid little toad." Unable to contain his fury, he took him by the throat and wrestled him to the ground.

Charlie grinned. "Nice work, Thad."

Thad lifted T-Bone by the back of his drawers and set him down hard. "I'm done playing with you, son. Start talking."

Little Beau sat up crying, his nose red and running. "We didn't kill that lady. We just wanted to have a look. Ain't never seen no dead body before. Anyway, *she* was in *our* secret hideout." An angry look came over his face. "She didn't have no business there in the first place."

Bertha pressed her hands over her mouth to stifle a sob.

T-Bone scowled but didn't go after his brother again.

Thad rested his hand on T-Bone's shoulder and spoke in a gentle voice. "We know you didn't kill her. Shoot, everybody in Jefferson knows who did. So why don't you just tell us what happened."

T-Bone's tough demeanor crumbled, and he became a scared little boy. "We didn't mean no harm. We saw her laying in the woods and ran over to help. I bent down to shake her, thinking to wake her up. That's when I saw blood on her head." He ducked his head and ground his fists in his eyes.

Thad squeezed his shoulder. "Just take your time, son."

The boy lifted his trembling chin. "I wanted to leave." He gave his little brother a careful glance. "But Beau remembered seeing that same woman in town. He said folks called her Diamond Bessie on account of all the diamonds she wore."

Beau glared at T-Bone, his eyes like a feral cat's, but T-Bone kept talking. "Beau started searching all over her fingers and ears."

Beau stood up. "Did not!"

T-Bone pushed him down and crawled over him with balled-up fists. "Yes, you did." He faced Thad again. "I swear I never touched her after that first time." He shuddered. "I couldn't."

Thad seemed to weigh T-Bone's words for several seconds before he leaned over his brother's head. "I want the truth, Beau. Lying is a useless talent. When the truth comes out, and it always does, folks tend never to trust you again." He touched the little boy's arm. "A man's word is his most valuable possession, Beau. Didn't your daddy teach you that?"

Bertha elbowed Thad, but it was too late.

T-Bone spoke up behind them. "We ain't got no daddy. Never have."

Thad mouthed an apology to Bertha. Scooting closer to Beau, he set him up. "What do you say, partner? You ready to tell us the truth now?"

Beau gulped hard. The shadows under his hollow, darting eyes made him seem eighty instead of eight. "T-Bone's right. I done it. I figured since she was dead, her diamonds would do us more good than her. Only there weren't no diamonds. I looked all over. Just when I gave up looking, I seen that silver chain. I pulled on it and that purty cross fell out." He got up on his knees in front of Thad. "I never would've took it, but I looked down and the clasp was right in my hands. So I undid the hook and it slid right off her neck."

Bertha shoved past Thad and yanked Beau toward her. "Did you say off her neck? Not from her pocket? Or out of her hand?"

Her intensity scared the boy, and he screwed up his face. "No, ma'am. It was around her neck."

She shook him. "You're sure?"

He started to wail. "I swear it!"

The minister's words from the funeral were emblazoned in her mind. " '*He which converteth the sinner from the error of his way shall save a soul from death, and shall hide a multitude of sins.*' "

Bertha crushed him to her and kissed the top of his tousled head. "Beau, you wonderful little boy. Thank you!" She lifted her face. "Dear Lord, thank You." When she released him, Beau scuttled back to his brother, staring at Bertha like she'd lost her senses.

Magda rushed over and fell beside her. They toppled in a heap, laughing and crying at the same time. Charlie, Mose, and Rhodie stood gaping at them on one side; Thad, Beau, and T-Bone on the other.

Bertha struggled to her feet and ran to Thad, burrowing into his chest. "I'll explain later. Right now I need to get my hands on that silver cross."

Thad twisted around so both of them faced the boys. "I give

you my word of honor no one here today will ever mention what we know. But that necklace belongs to my wife, and I want it back."

T-Bone's Adam's apple rose and fell. "We'll go fetch it."

"I'll go with them," Mose offered. "Make sure there ain't no funny business."

Thad pulled Beau in front of him and patted him on the chest. "I don't expect any more funny business out of these fine lads, but go ahead and ride with them if you like. We'll meet you in front of their house."

Mose motioned to Charlie. He shook his head. "What about that shotgun?"

Bertha grinned. "Don't worry—I took care of the gun. We can send it to her later, after she calms down."

Mose and Charlie herded the boys toward the boat. On the way, Charlie slipped his arm around T-Bone's scrawny shoulders. "Say, I'm in the market for a new fishing partner. You boys like to fish?"

T-Bone shrugged. Little Beau peered up at him from the other side. "Shucks, yeah. You know any good spots?"

Charlie rested his other arm around Beau's neck. "Good spots? Why, I know the best honey holes in East Texas."

Charlie's offer to teach them the words to "Old Dan Tucker" was the last thing Bertha heard before they piled in the boat and pushed off toward Gladys Taylor's place.

Bertha, Thad, and the rest climbed aboard Mose's wagon with Thad at the reins. On the way, Bertha explained the significance of Annie wearing the necklace.

Rhodie, her mouth ajar, leaned between them, listening. When Bertha finished, Rhodie gazed up at her. "You're right, Bertha. If Annie felt unworthy to wear the cross, something happened to change that or she wouldn't dare put it on."

Thad smiled over at Bertha. "Only one thing can make that kind of change. So you know what that means."

Bertha thrilled at the confirming words. "It means Annie heard me. She died at peace with God."

Magda scooted beside Rhodie and looked up at Bertha. "I do have one question. You told me Annie was drunk that last morning in Kate Woods's restaurant."

"Yes," Bertha said. "I thought about that, too. Only Frank Malloy told Papa that Abe plied Annie with drink. Perhaps she didn't want it but was too scared to refuse. I mean, how could she explain what happened to her to someone like Abe?"

Magda inhaled sharply. "That makes sense. D. P. McMullen saw them, too, on Austin Street headed for the bridge. He said Annie handed her bottle to Abe, made him take it from her. I don't think she wanted it."

Up ahead, Mose, Charlie, and the Taylor boys stood on the road in front of the house. Thad pulled up beside them and set the brake.

Mose approached the wagon and held up a flash of silver. "Here it is, Bertha. I think it's the same one I gave you."

Thad took the chain out of Mose's hand and offered it to Bertha. When she cupped the delicate cross in her palm, she remembered the words she'd shared with Annie.

"The gift this cross represents is more powerful than any laundry list of sins you may be guilty of, no matter how heinous. The cross covered them all. You just have to accept it for yourself in order to be free."

Sometime after the last time Bertha saw her, Annie Moore came to believe those words. The woman who rode into their lives a misguided sinner left the world a beloved saint. Bertha had trusted God with the details—of her life and of Annie's—and just like Papa said, God had proved Himself worthy.

Thad wrapped her in his arms and pulled her close. "We have a train to catch, Mrs. Bloom."

She smiled at him through happy tears. "And adventures to chase, if I know you."

Grinning, he leaned to whisper in a breathy voice, "And a honeymoon to get started. . .if that's all right."

On a mission to mop the confident grin from Thad's face and light a fire in his dark eyes, Bertha had set out to learn the secret of

Annie's sway over men. Gazing into his face, aglow with love for her, she realized she'd had the power within her from the start.

She tilted her chin and gave her husband a saucy wink. "Me darlin', I thought you'd never ask."

Dear Reader:

This story is woven around the actual murder of Annie Stone, aka Bessie Monroe, aka Diamond Bessie, on January 21, 1877, in Jefferson, Texas. The ill-fated Diamond Bessie left a mark so deep during her brief visit that she's still a household name in Jefferson today. I chose to call her Annie in the book, because I believe if not for one early, impetuous mistake, she'd never have needed these aliases or the others I didn't mention.

I researched for months to learn why Annie made such an indelible impression on the town. From the considerable distance of 130-plus years, I found it impossible to get an accurate look at her. Even the opinions and attitudes of her day were conflicting. Some judged her a disease-ridden prostitute without morals or conscience. Others considered her an unfortunate young girl who lost her way. Jilted and abandoned by an older man at fifteen, possibly disinherited by her family and left to her own devices, (emphasis on vices) then abused and victimized by Abraham Rothschild, she unquestionably had a rocky start.

As I stood over her humble grave in Oakwood Cemetery, I found myself in the same dilemma as Bertha Maye Biddie, the heroine of this book, who asks, "Devil or angel? I couldn't tell." I feel certain of one thing, however. From Annie's vantage point, whether resting with angels or contending with devils, she would heartily approve of using her life to share my witness.

In my cast of characters, many—too numerous to list here—were actual denizens of 1877 Jefferson and key players in the drama that unfolded before, during, and after the murder of Annie Stone. Their names are still bandied about the streets of Jefferson, especially during the annual play, *The Diamond Bessie Murder Trial*, a reenactment.

Despite the notoriety Sarah King gained from finding Annie's body, I found no further information on her, even after searching the library and the courthouse records and speaking with local historians. With apologies to her descendants, I've used creative license in writing her story.

On December 30, 1880, after three indictments and two trials, Abraham Rothschild was pronounced not guilty. He boarded the train out of Jefferson, some say for the last time. Others believe he returned at least once. According to the caretaker of Oakwood Cemetery, a handsome elderly gentleman came asking the whereabouts of Annie's grave in the 1890s. He laid a wreath of roses near her headstone then knelt and said a prayer.

In his book *The Abe Rothschild Story*, historian Fred McKenzie includes a marriage license he uncovered in Vermillion County, Illinois, showing that twenty-four-year-old Abe Rothschild married twenty-two-year-old Bertha Moore on January 10, 1877, a few days before Abe and Annie began their journey from Cincinnati to Jefferson. According to Mr. McKenzie's research, Abe went on to become a "con man, flim flam artist, and snake oil salesman" as well as "a diamond thief of the first water."

Blessings,
Marcia Gruver

If you enjoyed

DIAMOND DUO

then be sure to read

CHASING CHARITY

Texas Fortunes   *Book 2*

Coming Spring 2009